MIRANDA
AT
HEART

BOOK FIVE
THE ELLSWORTH ASSORTMENT

CHRISTINA DUDLEY

WILLIAM ELLSWORTH = (1) HENRIETTA BALDRIC   CHARLES ELLSWORTH = JEANNE MARTINEAU
= (2) CATHERINE CATCHWAY
= (3) ANNE FIELDING
= (4) MIRANDA GREGORY

BENJAMIN   AUSTIN

(1) FLORENCE = ROBERT FAIRCHILD

(1) LILY = SIMON KENNER

(2) TYRONE = AGATHA WEEKS

(2) ARAMINTA = NICHOLAS CARLISLE

(3) BEATRICE

(4) WILLIAM

THE

Ellsworth Assortment

PROLOGUE

JULY 1811

Who can find a virtuous woman?
for her price is far above rubies.
—Proverbs 31:10, *The Authorized Version* (1611)

William Ellsworth died in the happiest way possible. One afternoon in July, the entire family was gathered for his birthday: his (fourth) wife, his six children and their four spouses, his eight grandchildren. After the meal, they removed to the drawing room and rolled up the carpet for dancing and general running about by the younger ones while their patriarch looked on fondly.

It was only when six-year-old Katharine grew tired and hot from chasing her cousins and went to lean against her grandfather's knees that anyone noticed anything amiss.

"Grandpapa," the little girl said impatiently, "are you sleeping?"

He did appear to be, with his eyes shut and a beatific smile on his face.

"Let him nap, darling," said Katy's grandmother. Letting a step-daughter replace her at the pianoforte, Miranda joined her husband, intending to protect him from further disturbance so that he might doze more comfortably. But when Araminta played through four songs without rousing him to his usual applause and praise, Miranda lay her hand over his. Presently, her face pale and voice small, she called, "Mr. Carlisle?"

Araminta's doctor husband too soon confirmed Miranda's fear. Mr. William Ellsworth was no more.

For a fortnight, his death was the talk of Winchester, almost but not quite eclipsing the excitement of the yearly race season. How could it not? From a modest beginning as the grandson of a local clergyman, William Ellsworth had by his handsomeness and charm alone managed to capture the heart of the greatest local heiress, Miss Baldric of Hollowgate, who bore him two daughters and made him a very, very rich man. Thereafter he had no further need for wealthy brides, which was fortunate because his hair and looks were fading by the time he married his second wife, gone altogether when he wooed his third, and hardly even a memory when he took Miranda Gregory for his fourth. Eventually the ancient Baldric estate would pass to the oldest Ellsworth child, Mrs. Robert Fairchild, but in the meantime the surviving fourth Mrs. Ellsworth was well, well provided for.

"You know I never wanted Papa to marry a fourth time," Mrs. Robert Fairchild told her husband as he put the Hollowgate papers in order. He was the family lawyer, besides having been the deceased's son-in-law.

"I know it, my love, and am glad of that reluctance, or we might not be married now."

"Well, for that reason and a hundred others, I have been of a different mind for years and years now," said Florence, setting down her embroidery hoop and running a finger over the stitches. "Because of all my stepmothers, she has been the best. Kind and patient with Papa. Good to all my siblings—why, she practically raised Beatrice, since Bea was so young when my second stepmother died. An excellent mother to little William and grandmother to the rest."

"Mrs. Ellsworth is indeed admirable."

"Neither do I regret that Papa left her such a large bequest and the life interest in Hollowgate," Florence added, "for she has indeed proven more precious than rubies."

His eyes twinkled at her. "But won't you be sorry not to play lady of the manor at last? You were just telling me that you would give a kingdom for another closet."

"So I would, Robert, but for *two* kingdoms I wouldn't see Beatrice and William removed from the only home they've known. Besides, when our Peter goes to Winchester College next September, how empty our cozy house will seem then!"

"When Peter goes, so will go your little brother William," Fairchild pointed out. "Imagine how Mrs. Ellsworth and Beatrice would rattle around in so large a place as Hollowgate, if the Tyrone Ellsworths were ever to leave."

"I hope they never do. Tyrone suggested it, you know, when Mr. Carlisle's stepfather died and Beaumond passed to Aggie's father, and again when Aggie learned she was in the family way, but Mama prevailed on them to stay."

"In addition to her persuasion, it's far easier for him to manage Hollowgate whilst residing there," observed her husband. "If and when the estate passes to you, Flossie, I imagine we will beg your brother to stay as well, for I have no desire to play farmer."

Florence shook her head, as if to ward something off. "Let us speak no more of it. I am in no hurry to inherit Hollowgate. We have room enough and money enough, Robert, and I wish Mama may live forever. I would not see little William motherless, especially now that he is made fatherless."

"Of course we wish Mrs. Ellsworth a long, happy life," Fairchild reassured her, "but I will remind you, it would not be her death alone which would end her interest in Hollowgate. The life estate is dependent on her not remarrying, and I'm afraid, with the wealth left to her, she will be tempted by many suitors to change her state."

His wife viewed him with wide eyes. "Oh, dear me. I did not think of that! I expect you're right. Do you suppose she would welcome them? I know she is—was—so much younger than Papa—"

"She is seven and thirty, my dear. She told me when I talked with her before the will was read."

"Seven and thirty," murmured Florence. "Why, that's only a few years older than I am."

Fairchild rose from the desk to sit beside her, winding an arm about her waist and pressing a kiss to her hair. "Exactly. Only a few years older than you. Which means, I think you will acknowledge, she is by no means too old for love."

"Oh," breathed Florence again. "No indeed. Not too old at all. But—surely—seven and thirty is old enough to have one's wits about one?"

"One hopes." He shrugged lightly. "But love can be unpredictable. That is, Mrs. Ellsworth seems wise enough by any standard, but I suspect—her dutiful affection for your father notwithstanding—she has never before been in love."

CHAPTER ONE

AUGUST 1812

**I'm none of your Romantick Fools, that fight
Gyants and Monsters for nothing.**
— G. Farquhar, *The Beaux Stratagem: a comedy* (1707)

The man was still following her.

It was a hot August day, the streets quieter now the Stockbridge races had begun and the crowds fled thitherward. A handful of militia men idled about, but this man wore no uniform. With her mind full, Miranda would not have noticed him, except that he emerged from the George Inn just as she passed and had been but a few steps behind her ever since. He was a big man, moreover—burly about the shoulders—the sort whom others naturally made room for, even if the fit and fineness of his clothing did not also mark him as a person to be reckoned with.

Whatever errand he was on, it could have nothing to do with her, she told herself sternly. It was just that she was in a nettle already. Legal doings always reminded her of the distressful time following her husband's death the previous year, and this was her first outing unmarked even by the greys and lilacs of half-mourning. Miranda's sister-in-law Jeanne Ellsworth had insisted the occasion be observed with a new wardrobe from the modiste Madame Blanchet; therefore the white-with-blue print gown Miranda wore today was both beautifully cut and threaded at neckline and hem with blue ribbon. She had let Jeanne suggest curls as well because it was easier than arguing with her, with the result that Miranda hardly knew herself in the mirror. (*"Et voilà!"* declared Jeanne. "Now you are ten years younger and your bloom restored.") Not that Miranda imagined the man stalking her did so because he found her attractive. But whatever the reason he nipped at her heels, she need not suffer it, and when she turned into Parchment Street, she paused to inspect the wares in a window, that he might either pass by or declare his purpose.

He passed by. Without a glance at her.

See? Don't be a ninny, Miranda Ellsworth. Without further waste of time, she resumed her journey, expecting the man to distance her rapidly or disappear into one of the shopfronts, but instead he halted abruptly before her own intended destination: the brick-faced office of West & Fairchild. From his pocket he ferreted out a folded slip of newspaper, perusing it with a frown.

A rueful chuckle escaped her. So much for evasion. She could hardly pretend now that she was going elsewhere—not when Mr. Fairchild was expecting her.

Well, if she was doomed to be eaten by this ogre, better to have done with it at once. Miranda stopped a step from him and folded her parasol.

Without moving his head, the man raised his eyes from the paper in his gloved hand. They were alarming eyes of an uncanny pale grey, hardly darker then the silver hair streaking his temples. Miranda wondered if it was their unusual lightness or the contrasting tawniness of his suntanned skin which made his gaze so unsettling. Whatever it was, she suppressed a shiver. "Ogre" had been the wrong word for him. With those silvery eyes, he was more of an ice giant, such as her stepson Tyrone described from Scandinavian mythology.

"Yes?" he asked, his voice cool and impatient.

In spite of herself, amusement flickered again. Surely ice giants struck first and asked questions later.

Miranda gestured with her own gloved hand toward the door he blocked. "If you would pardon me..."

She expected him to leap aside with apologies, but he looked more distrustful than discomfited. "You're here to see Mr. West? I had better tell you you're too late, you know."

"Too late?" she asked, startled. "What can you mean?" If something had befallen Mr. West, surely Mr. Fairchild or Flossie would have mentioned it at once.

"I mean, if you come to inquire about Beaumond, it is too late."

"Thank you," she replied, smothering the dozen questions which sprang to mind at this pronouncement. "But that is not my purpose in being here." She gestured once more at the door, and this time he did step aside, with a bow unexpectedly graceful for his size. It was not the bow which struck her, however, so much as the mocking tip of his lips which accompanied it, but when he opened the green-painted door for her there was no more time for consideration.

Mr. Hents, the long, bony clerk of West & Fairchild unfolded clumsily from his stool to greet her, his flame-red hair the brightest thing in the dim space.

"Mrs. Ellsworth, good afternoon. I hope you are well. Mr. Fairchild awaits you in his office." Hents looked doubtfully at her accidental companion. "I did not know you would be accompanied, but I will set another chair."

"That won't be necessary," she told him. "This gentleman and I are not together."

"Oh!" cried Hents. "Oh. Sir, then you are—"

"Wolfe," said the giant. "Colin Wolfe to see Mr. West. I wrote last week."

"Ah, yes." Hents tugged at his ink-stained cuffs. "Er—why don't you take that chair, sir. Mr. West is out but will return any moment. You will be quite comfortable and confidential here." Despite a thriving practice, the office of West & Fairchild was a two-room affair, and Mrs. Ellsworth with her long-standing relationship and prior appointment must of course be seen in the inner office.

Without another look at the man, she swept inside to meet her son-in-law. She had put the matter off for months until Mr. Fairchild finally mentioned it in his gentle way. "You will want to specify who will care for Willie and what will belong to him, should he be so unlucky as to lose you as well. You may be sure all his family will care for him, but it helps to be specific with your wishes."

This afternoon she was specific. "Mr. Fairchild, as Hollowgate has always been Willie's home, and as the estate passes to Florence when I die, and as your Peter is his closest friend, I ask if you and Florence would be so good as to—take him in—if something happens to me. To be his guardians until he is of age. He will, of course, go to Winchester College with Peter next month, so I hope he would not be too much trouble—"

She had practiced this speech so that she could say it without tears, but Mr. Fairchild's pen was already scratching away. "Of course, Mrs. Ellsworth. Flossie and I hoped it would be so. We only—feared—perhaps, that you might prefer your brother Mr. Gregory, if only because he and his wife have no children of their own..."

With a shudder Miranda thought of lively, happy Willie shut up in her brother Clifford's narrow house in town, where his wife Jane was forever wincing and fidgeting if Willie spoke too loudly or knocked into the furniture or upset the salt cellar.

"No," she managed. "Please—Mr. Fairchild—*Robert*. If you and Florence are willing—"

"We are willing."

They smiled at each other.

The money was easily settled. Every other Ellsworth was well provided for, and her brother had money of his own; therefore all she had might go to her son to establish him in life.

When Miranda rose again, it was with a weight lifted from her. She was healthy and not so very old, and she had no intention of dying and leaving Willie to face the world without her, but it was reassuring all the same to know he would be neither alone nor penniless. And she had her late husband to thank for that. Whatever William Ellsworth might have lacked in youth or handsomeness or cleverness, and however much of duty had been mixed with her own fondness for him, he had loved his family and shared them with her, so that she and Willie were as much a part of the clan as the rest.

Mr. Fairchild led her past the shelves and boxes and blue bags of documents to open the door, where the first thing to meet her eyes was the tall stranger, seated at a table with Mr. West, the two of them bent over a contract.

"Mrs. Ellsworth," the older lawyer greeted her, as both men rose. The difference in the men's relative sizes put her in mind of the lion and the mouse from the fable, though she supposed Mr. West was more like Aesop's grasshopper, the way he rubbed his long hands together.

"May I introduce you to a new neighbor?" West offered in his characteristic hiss. "This is Mr. Colin Wolfe, the new tenant of Beaumond. Mr. Wolfe, may I present Mrs. Ellsworth of Hollowgate, just a hop, step and jump from you down the Weeke footpath. Mrs. Ellsworth has a young son just your son's age, and he too will start as a junior at Winchester in September."

Mr. Wolfe made her his second bow of the day, this one so graceful she could have taken an oath he was smothering amusement again. Why?

"A pleasure, Mrs. Ellsworth. As 'manners maketh man,' I am glad to have this second opportunity to address you, for I was unpardonably rude earlier."

She curtseyed, smiling faintly. He now meant to be charming—he *was* charming, if she were willing to be charmed.

When she said nothing, a grin came and went across his features. "Ah. You have seen through my ruse. By calling myself 'unpardonably rude,' I confess I hoped you would contradict me, Mrs. Ellsworth. That you would insist on pardoning me. But it seems you will not even ask me why I was so discourteous to you."

"Perhaps because your eagerness in securing a beautiful, well-situated home such as Beaumond requires no explanation," she murmured.

"How cutting a tiny word like 'perhaps' can be! In any event, Mrs. Ellsworth, despite your refusal to be offended, I will defend myself, as we are to be neighbors. As Mr. West said, my son Edmund will attend the College in a few short weeks, and as he is quite all the family I have in Hampshire, I wish to live near at hand, in order to see him on those various saints' days and 'remedies' the school allows, besides the longer vacations."

"Yes," Miranda softened. "I do understand that. I have that same wish with William—my son. When his older brother Tyrone was at school there, he visited at every holiday, which made the rest of the family very happy." A gentle smile lit her features. "Beaumond will serve you well for that purpose, Mr. Wolfe, and I congratulate you on gaining possession of it. Good day to you."

When she was gone the men resumed their seats and paperwork, Wolfe scratching signatures wherever West pointed, but the former's thoughts were elsewhere. In truth, he was thinking of Mrs. Ellsworth, mother to a son of equal age to Edmund. With her curling hair and mild blue eyes and modish dress, the woman appeared much younger than she could possibly be. And her voice—warm and low and attractive—

"If it would not breach any confidences, Mr. West, tell me: how does Mrs. Ellsworth come to have another son old enough to have already left Winchester?"

"She doesn't," answered the lawyer simply, blotting and sanding the page before him. "The Mr. Tyrone Ellsworth referred to is her stepson. It's plain you're new to town, if you don't know the story of the William Ellsworths. The Mrs. Ellsworth you just met is the fourth of that name. Her boy William is the youngest of the six children and the only one of whom she is the mother." Leaning forward, West added in a hissing whisper, "And my partner Fairchild in there is married to the oldest of them. You will do well to be on good terms with the family, for they're quite prominent in these parts. Wealthy and prominent. Nearly as wealthy and prominent as your landlord Mr. Weeks, whose youngest daughter is married to that same Tyrone Ellsworth of whom we spoke."

The new tenant gave an appreciative whistle. "Looks like I've landed in the thick of it, then."

"So you have, sir, but they're good folk."

"If I might ask, how did this Ellsworth come to have four wives?"

Mr. West blinked. "Oh, pardon me. I should say—Ellsworth is no more. He managed to outlive the first three, but he himself died over a year ago. This last Mrs. Ellsworth is a widow, living at Hollowgate with her boy and youngest stepdaughter and the Tyrone Ellsworth family."

"A widow!" He was quick to add conventionally, "I am sorry to hear of the family's loss."

"Yes, sir. As a widower yourself you understand." The lawyer cleared his throat. "In any event, friendly folk, the Ellsworths. If your boy Edmund happens to befriend young William, he'll be in clover, because that family does stick together."

To Mr. West's surprise, Wolfe's lips thinned. "I see. Well, in my experience, a little family can go a long, long way."

If Mr. West hoped the new tenant would expand on this interesting topic, he was disappointed, and at the conclusion of their business, Mr. Colin Wolfe took his leave.

"Make a copy of this, Hents," the lawyer ordered, "and I'll take it with me when I call on Weeks." He dropped the lease upon the clerk's desk and returned to the inner office.

"Wherever did you find that fellow?" his partner Fairchild asked.

"Did you see him, then?"

"I glimpsed him when Mrs. Ellsworth left. At his size he'd be a difficult man to miss."

"Hails from Kent, he says, and was himself a product of the King's School. After his wife died last year he 'wanted to make a change' or some sort, which is why his son will be enrolled at Winchester. Apparently he knew Weeks' son-in-law Mr. Linus Chester at university, and Chester vouched for him."

"And he can afford the exorbitant rent Weeks set?"

"Easily. There is some estate back in Kent. He put down the first three months' worth all in one go."

"If there's no wife, will some aged aunt or unmarried sister keep house for him?"

"He didn't mention one," West shrugged. "But you saw him. If he's rich as all that and looks like that, I don't suppose he'll stay wifeless for long. How old would you guess he is? Forty? Five and forty?"

"Split the difference, perhaps," said Fairchild, "and put it at two and forty."

"That's right. Older, but not old enough to scare anyone off. I daresay he will have his choice of any lady in Winchester, young or old."

Fairchild grinned. "I don't know about *any* lady. My wife's youngest sister is eighteen, and I would hazard a guess that two and forty in her eyes sounds old as the pyramids."

But his partner had seen too much of the world to concede the point. "Miss Ellsworth may not be tempted to set her cap at a Mr. Wolfe in her first year of balls and assemblies, but I assure you any girl who's seen more than a few seasons will not disdain him."

"Mm." Fairchild straightened the papers before him and restored them to the Ellsworth box. "Well, time will tell. And knowing Winchester, an abundance of information will soon be abroad about the man, with odds given and bets placed, and we all will have to sort the fact from the conjecture."

Chapter Two

[He]…had all along regarded this Alliance rather as a Marriage of Convenience than of Love.
—Addison, *The Spectator,* No.164 (1711)

For a century or more, the Perrys of Canterbury, Kent, had been a modest family of clergymen and schoolmasters with neither ambition nor opportunity to rise above their middling condition, but all that changed when Miss Maria Perry succeeded in capturing the fancy of the local squire Hieronymus Wolfe. The resulting match was as little unhappy as other ones built upon foundations of physical love alone, and it yielded five children, of whom only Doria, Miss Wolfe, survived into adulthood. In the meantime, shortly after her own dazzling marriage, the former Miss Perry had the chagrin of seeing her younger brother disgrace his new Wolfe connections by marrying a shopkeeper's daughter. Adding insult to injury, over the years his humble union yielded five children of its own, all gifted with rosy healthfulness, if not fortune.

The Perrys and the Wolfes of both generations were not especially close, therefore, but it was the heiress Miss Wolfe who first suggested the two families be joined anew.

Her father had taken a fall from his hunter and lay aching and cross in the weeks afterward on the sofa in the front parlor, watching his wife sew while poor plain Doria read dull things to him or plodded with heavy fingers through tunes intended to be sprightly.

"If I die of this, Maria," complained Mr. Wolfe to his wife, "I suppose you and Doria will run Cantergreen into the ground before all's said and done. An estate never thrives under a woman, and you'll probably marry some blackguard of a fortune hunter before I'm cold."

"I'm sure I've never given you cause to complain of my conduct, Mr. Wolfe," his wife said resentfully. "And I've sense enough to keep your steward on if we lose you."

"As if that would do any good. Craven will cheat you, if you don't keep a sharp eye," he rejoined. "I think Doria had better marry someone with a head on his shoulders. Hear that, girl? Stop playing that dirge and come and give an account of yourself. How is it that I've paid for nigh on a decade of fancywork and fripperies, and you've yet to bring a man to the point?"

"It has hardly been for lack of trying!" protested Doria's mother, knowing the sad, puddinglike girl would be unable to repel this attack. "We thought Sir Patrick would speak after his wife Lady

Cogswell died, but it was his nasty daughter who undermined the match, I suspect."

"Miss Cogswell only said it would be uncomfortable to have a stepmother her own age," Doria spoke up in her flat voice. She had not been bothered when the possibility of marriage to Sir Patrick Cogswell failed—any more than she had been bothered by the possibility of it succeeding. In truth Doria preferred her finch and lapdog to any gentlemen she had yet met.

"You're rich enough to catch someone better than that old codger," her father persisted. He beat at the sofa cushion. "How has it come to this? There have been Wolfes at Cantergreen for two hundred years, and I have done my best, and now it will all go to pieces." He did not wait for his wife to gather breath to defend herself from his unspoken charges, but dealt the cushion another blow. "You must have a husband, Doria, and he must become a Wolfe!"

"Become a Wolfe!" mother and daughter echoed.

"And why not? If I am to hand over my money and my patrimony, the least the worthless recipient can do is take my name. You should be glad of the condition. It means whoever this creature is, he need not boast any name of his own. He need have neither fortune nor fame but only something between his ears, do you hear me?"

Doria merely frowned, chirping for her finch to light on her finger, but her mother swelled with indignation. "Why waste another instant, then? If we are so undiscriminating, let us send for the nearest Tom, Dick, and Harry and set them an examination! I tell you, we will not have it, Mr. Wolfe! I never thought to see the day when such things would be said in my hearing—"

"Colin is clever," said Doria. With a handkerchief she wiped up her bird's depredations.

"Colin?" her mother breathed. "Can you mean your cousin, my brother's son?"

"He is the only Colin I know. He's younger than I am and doesn't think of me any more than I think of him, but the Perrys do have four daughters to marry off, and I'm sure my uncle and aunt haven't got money to spare them."

Mrs. Wolfe dropped to the settee. "But Colin is—"

"*Too* low?" wondered Doria. "*Too* poor?"

"Too proud," grimaced Mr. Wolfe. "Oh, those Perry relations of yours are certainly nameless enough and penniless enough, but from the way that boy of theirs carries himself, you would never guess he felt it."

"I don't think he does," Mrs. Wolfe concurred, the parents finding themselves in rare agreement. "He may be clever, Doria, but he is also handsomer than he ought to be. Too handsome for his own good."

Doria shrugged. She coaxed her finch to her finger again, that she might return it to its cage. "It was merely a suggestion. I think it would be more pleasant to be married to Cousin Colin than to old Sir Patrick."

"Well, put it from your mind," commanded her mother. "I do not see why my brother should be rewarded for marrying so beneath his connections."

"And that's *your* pride speaking, Mrs. Wolfe," her husband jeered. "Haven't you any imagination, woman? Why, the Perrys would be twice as mortified for their destitute son to marry Doria, when they heard our conditions! The apple of their eye to be no longer a Perry!" For the first time since his accident, Mr. Wolfe laughed, though probably only he derived enjoyment from the sound. "But a son without a profession—unless he can secure some pitiful curacy—and four unmarried daughters—ah, our offer will tempt them sorely, or I'm not Hieronymus Wolfe."

He was in fact, it turned out, Hieronymus Wolfe.

Mr. and Mrs. Perry were sifted first, the lofty Mrs. Wolfe calling upon them in their narrow, shabby, noisy dwelling. Visits to the Perrys always gave her a headache, though this day she was spared the usual tattoo of the family running up and down the stairs because all four girls had crammed on the sofa to gape at her, their aunt Wolfe's visits being rare and therefore eventful.

Some women would have been daunted by seven pairs of eyes fixed on them, but Mrs. Wolfe accepted it as her due.

"Brother, what does my nephew Colin have planned, when he returns from university?" she asked, after having sipped the weak tea and set her cup down.

"Nothing as yet, sister," admitted James Perry. The days when he might have spoken to Mrs. Wolfe with insouciance were long gone, poverty and care having done their work. "We thought perhaps he might...be placed under articles of clerkship..." The truth was, not only had he and Mrs. Perry thought of it, but they had discussed whether the Wolfes themselves might be persuaded to suggest it to their lawyer. Even now, Mrs. Perry nodded at her husband to introduce the matter, much as Macbeth's lady encouraged him to screw his courage to the sticking place.

"You want him to be a lawyer?" Mrs. Wolfe marveled.

"That or a clergyman," piped up Miss Pippa, drawing a frown from her mother. "But no one can imagine Colin reading and writing all day or giving sermons or sitting at bedsides. He is so very large."

Mrs. Wolfe thought her nephew's size the least of his disqualifications for those professions, but she listened to her younger brother hem and haw for a few minutes on why entering into articles would be the making of his son, and didn't the Wolfes think their man Mr. Witherby quite the capable and discreet and respectable—

"James," Mrs. Wolfe interrupted, "Mr. Wolfe and I have been thinking."

"Yes?" breathed both Perrys, their pulses quickening. Mrs. Perry's foot stole over to press her husband's.

"Your Colin has always been an active, quick-thinking sort of person."

"Yes," nodded Mr. Perry, though he did not see what "active" had to do with becoming a lawyer.

"Colin is exactly that, Mrs. Wolfe," Mrs. Perry put in eagerly. "Active and quick-thinking."

"Just so." Mrs. Wolfe took a deep breath. However strenuously her husband insisted their plan put the Wolfes in the position of grantor, it was nevertheless an awkward thing to propose marriage. She shifted in her lumpy seat, but it was the very discomfort of the finest chair in the house coupled with the sight of her nieces' worn dresses which straightened her spine.

"James," she said again, "Mr. Wolfe and I have a proposal to make."

A few days later, Colin Wolfe—then Colin Perry—received the letter which would change his life.

Blackfriars Street
Canterbury

4 June 1794

My dear son,
How your family and I look forward to your imminent return. I know you have enjoyed your years of freedom and the wider view of the world made available to you whilst at university. Your diligence at King's got you that scholarship, and I trust that trait in your character will continue to stand you in good stead.

It is natural that you will feel some reluctance to return to the confines and limitations of home. Moreover, I know you were willing, but not eager, to be placed under articles of clerkship if your mother and I could find someone to take you. Therefore I hope the news I impart here will appear in the light of a welcome alternative.

Your aunt and uncle Wolfe have a proposal to make, Colin, and it would be the making of not only you, but your sisters as well. You know the Wolfes have had the misfortune to lose all their children save your cousin Doria, and if she were to marry, Cantergreen would no longer be the Wolfe estate as such. In short, they offer to make you their heir, on two conditions: first, you take the name of Wolfe; and second, you marry your cousin.

Of course you will want to reflect on this. You would be a wealthy, landed gentleman, for which your education has suited you, if not your family circumstances. I realize Doria might not be the bride of your choosing, but you are both sensible creatures who would be able to rub along as well as most couples, if you determined to do so. Indeed I now admit more of domestic happiness depends on the possession of sufficient money than I would ever have thought possible as a young man.

There is more. If you accept the Wolfes' proposal, your uncle has generously offered to provide substantial portions to your sisters, that they might make marriages "more in keeping" with the dignity their Wolfe connections demand. It is my great regret that I have been unable to give all of my children more of what their hearts have desired and their goodness deserved.

*My dear son, the choice is yours. Neither your parents'
desires nor those of your sisters should outweigh what
you feel in your heart, and if you refuse this offer, you
still might have the law or the church to fall back on,
or possibly a schoolmaster position. All of those would
likely require your uncle's influence, which he may balk
at giving if we disappoint him, but that is neither here
nor there.*

*There is no need to write to us. Only let us know your
decision when we see you again.*

Your loving father,
Thomas Perry

Colin's instinctive response was to recoil. Marry *Doria?* He had
never, never considered his cousin in that light. Not only because
she was his cousin (and not a particularly popular one, the Perrys
much preferring the jolly, unpretentious cousins on their mother's
side). Doria was older by at least five years. Doria was plain. Plain as
porridge—in both appearance and disposition. Doria was dull. One
might spend hours in her company without her making any distinct
impression.

When he received that fateful letter he was a young man at the
height of his self-conceit and powers. He had long been "Peerless
Perry," carrying the day wherever he went: from playing field to
assembly room to the Senate House at Cambridge. And it had often
struck him as regrettable that he had neither title nor fortune, for

then he surely would have ended as the prime minister, with at least a countess for his wife.

What his life was to be after his Pembroke days ended and he returned to Canterbury—that was merely a blank which he seldom thought on. Something would turn up. He was certain of it. Whatever that something might be—and it was never the three professions his father cited in the letter—Colin did not doubt he would excel at it as he had everything else.

Therefore, how could his father even *suggest* such a fate for him? How had his father not laughed his uncle Wolfe from the room for the bare idea of it? Money could not buy a Perry!

It was with this conviction that he arrived home again in Blackfriars Street. The house was smaller and dingier than he remembered. As the lone and adored son he had his own bedchamber, while his four sisters squeezed into the other, but even this space granted to him now seemed inadequate to hold either Colin or his possessions, and certainly not both at once.

His family asked nothing of his decision for the first day, though he saw their impatience and curiosity restrained with difficulty. He saw as well that the oldest of his sisters was pale and quiet, and when he asked his youngest sister Pippa about it, she whispered, "It's because Betsy is in love with the curate Mr. Popple, but they cannot afford to marry." And when he saw with what relish they ate the dinner roast that evening, Pippa likewise explained, "We haven't had meat for a little while. Mama was feeling poorly last month, and there were doctor's bills."

"Why did no one write to me about how embarrassed our circumstances were?" he demanded of her, while his second sister Jenny played his old favorites on the spinet. Two keys were broken, which left funny little gaps in the tunes.

"What do you mean?" asked Pippa, surprised. "Everything is the same as it ever was. Papa and Mama always pinch pennies. I suppose they had to pinch a little harder to provide you with an allowance when you were gone, and now that Betsy, Jenny, Katie, and I are so big, I heard Mama say everything costs more. But if you won't marry Doria—and I can't say I blame you—I plan to save the family by marrying a rich man." She declared this with fourteen-year-old confidence, as if rich men could be plucked like berries from a bush.

Colin slept little that night.

He had been vaguely aware of his parents' sacrifices while he was away. His scholarship had paid his tuition, room, and board, but there had been countless incidentals which accrued: his gowns and clothing; his instruments of sport; tips for the bedder and the porter; the little meals and drinks and outings every undergraduate must subsidize from time to time in order to hold up his head; not to mention the expenses of travel back and forth every vacation. But with the self-absorption of youth Colin had assumed there was always money to be had from somewhere and dismissed further analysis from his mind.

This and more came to him as he tossed in his narrow bed. He had to sleep diagonally to fit between head- and footboard, and still his feet hung over the side of the mattress.

He was a grown man now. One who should no longer drain the family coffers but rather fill them. For pity's sake, even little Pippa recognized her duty and accepted it! How much more should he, the oldest and the son?

But marriage to Doria?

Impossible.

Suppose he were to go to his uncle Wolfe and offer to work for him? It took no more than an instant to dismiss the thought. If his uncle wanted a worker, such would have been his proposition. No, Wolfe wanted his family name carried on. He wanted his unpromising daughter married. And offering instead to work for him would only strike the man as what it was: a rejection of both the Wolfe name and the Wolfe daughter.

Even if Colin were placed under articles to someone—anyone—his uncle would resent it. Would see it, again, as a rejection. The Perrys would neither be able to ask Wolfe to use his influence nor to supply any of the costs.

I am in a box.

But if he married Doria—another restless toss at the thought, the coverlet sliding to the floor—then what? That colorless creature at his board, in his bed. The decades stretching before them. Could they come to care for each other? He must make the effort to care for her or die, because he did not think he could live a life without love. But if he tried and failed?

When Colin Perry rose the next morning, his broad shoulders were squared under the heavy, heavy mantle of adulthood. He set his features as well, that his family—anxious already to assume the best—might not suspect what his decision cost him. While he could not be cheerful, they did not expect cheer, and were satisfied with his measured acceptance.

Mr. and Mrs. Perry cried; Betsy cried, flying to tell her curate of their miraculous windfall; Jenny jumped and clapped her hands and suggested they purchase a pianoforte. Katie both cried and laughed. Only Pippa was solemn. She took his hand later, when she found him pale and drawn, the first visit having been made to Cantergreen.

"If you can do it, Colin, so can I," she vowed.

"Do what, Pip?"

"Try to *see* Doria for the first time," she answered. "Distinctly. Because, if one can truly see a person, there must always be something in that person one can love. Don't you think?"

His voice was hoarse. "I don't know. I hope so. Time will tell."

Chapter Three

A prudent Mind will be always preparing, till prepared.
— Samuel Richardson, *Pamela* (1741)

Go along, you two," Miranda prodded her son William and step-grandson Peter. "We have measured you, and now you will only be in the way."

The two eleven-year-old boys needed no further urging on the warm and dry late August day, and they were gone at once, across the terrace and onto the lawn, Willie's golden head paired with Peter's dark one, the dogs Scamp and Pickles racing after them.

She turned from the morning room window with a sigh. Willie looked more and more like Miranda's childhood memory of his father, the golden, roguish, charming William Ellsworth who had courted Miss Baldric. Not only did young William inherit his late father's coloring, but he shared his sunny disposition. *It's better this way*, Miranda told herself. *If he had been pale and shy like me, the other boys at Winchester would eat him for supper.*

Taking up her work again she gave her stepdaughters Florence and Beatrice an apologetic smile. "They are both still so small. It's hard to believe the day has already come for them to go away to school."

"I know just how you feel, Mama," said Florence. "I was happy to come here today because Robert calls me a sad fidget of late. But some of those jests and tricks played on the new boys! They might be school traditions, but I persist in thinking them no better than bullying."

Beatrice glanced up from the surplice she was stitching. "You're no help at all, Floss. Can't you see you're infecting Mama with your fears? Willie and Peter will have each other, which Tyrone says is a deal more than he had when he was a junior."

"You need not blame Florence," Miranda returned with a chuckle, her needle flashing as she hemmed Willie's shirt. "It happens I am perfectly capable of working myself into a state without your sister's assistance. Men do seem to think such treatment of the new boys is a matter of course, but I wish either Peter or Willie were big as an ox. Then the older boys would think twice before troubling them."

Before Florence could reply, the door opened to admit the footman Bobbins. "Mrs. Fellowes."

With a prominent clergyman for a brother, Miranda had known the dean's wife for decades, and the marriage between Miranda's second stepdaughter Lily and Mrs. Fellowes' grandson Simon Kenner cemented the connection. Nevertheless, as the Dean and Mrs. Fellowes were now in their eighties, Mrs. Fellowes was more often found in her own parlor than in others', and her call came as a surprise.

"Mrs. Fellowes, what a pleasure to see you today," Miranda said, when curtseys and greetings had been exchanged. "You find us working to prepare Willie and Peter for school."

"Do carry on," said the old woman graciously. "It has been a long time, sadly, since any of my grandchildren were so small, but I know there is plenty to be done."

"I hope you and the dean are in good health?"

"Oh, yes. Mr. Fellowes has passed many of his duties on to younger men, and there are the expected trials of growing old, but I daresay we will be around some while yet."

The usual things were said, diocesan matters discussed, and so on, but Miranda's suspicion that Mrs. Fellowes would not have troubled herself unless she had some a purpose in mind eventually proved well-founded. It was when Beatrice made some excuse to slip from the room that the dean's wife came to the point.

"Ah, Miss Ellsworth, before you go. I had something to say which might interest you."

Bea sat back down, her smile somewhat fixed. "Yes, madam?"

"Indeed. It concerns my granddaughter Amelia. You all remember the Wrights, of course." (They did, Lily having once been engaged to Gilbert Wright, before preferring his cousin Simon Kenner. An uncomfortable subject which Mrs. Fellowes, too, was eager to skip over.) "Amelia is the youngest child of my younger daughter and just newly turned eighteen. Like you, Miss Ellsworth."

Beatrice tried to look bright and interested here.

"Emmy has been much indulged, I confess," her grandmother continued, "and now she has got the notion she would like to spend the autumn and winter in Winchester with her grandparents."

"How lovely," said Miranda. "I know how fond you are of all your grandchildren."

"Oh, spending time *en famille* is not Emmy's primary aim, I daresay. We are merely a means to an end. You see, she complains of mouldering away at Meadowsweep and dreams of being in a busy town, where she may amuse herself at balls and assemblies and plays and such—as if the dean and I were up to such frolics!"

"Have you refused her, then?"

"Not precisely." Mrs. Fellowes pursed her lips and for the first time looked uncertain. "Miranda, my dear, I will be frank. Now that you are out of mourning and will be chaperoning Miss Ellsworth to various activities—I wondered if you might be willing to look out for Emmy as well. Only on occasions when you yourselves already planned on attending, of course. I know it is an imposition, and we would be certain to have a servant accompany her to wherever you were going, so that you need neither fetch her nor see her home, but—"

"Mrs. Fellowes, say no more," Miranda interrupted, reaching to squeeze the old woman's arm. "It will be no imposition at all. Every girl welcomes a friend in such situations, wouldn't you agree, Bea? And keeping an eye on two girls is no more difficult than keeping an eye on one."

"Oh, thank you, dear, dear Miranda! Such a weight off my mind, and Emmy will be delighted beyond words. Let us just hope, Miss

Ellsworth, that you don't both fall in love with the same young man, pretty girls that you are. If that can be avoided, all will be well."

"Thank you, madam, but Miss Wright may have him, whoever he might be," spoke up Beatrice, "for I am not in the least hurry to marry."

"I won't let her, you see," Miranda interposed, seeing Mrs. Fellowes' bosom swell at the girl's forthright words. "Having lost Mr. Ellsworth, and with Willie going to Winchester, I would be bereft if Bea were to leave me so soon. I might just keep her until she is thirty, if I can."

Mrs. Fellowes raised thin eyebrows. "If you will pardon me for saying so, Miranda, I would not be surprised if *you* remarried before Miss Ellsworth was thirty. You are looking remarkably well."

"What nonsense," returned Miranda, blushing. "Even if I wished to remarry, I know any man who makes up to a widow of eight and thirty with a young son is not drawn by her appearance."

"And yet Mrs. Fellowes is right about your looks," put in Florence, happy to hear this evidence of her stepmother's caution. "My aunt Jeanne was boasting of the '*métamorphose complète*' she had effected with your wardrobe and new coiffure, and I do not think she exaggerated, Mama."

"Enough!" cried Miranda, turning even deeper scarlet. "Let us change the subject, or I will turn you all out of the house."

"Speaking of being turned out of the house, where is Mrs. Weeks this morning? I had hoped to see her sweet little twins."

"Aggie's sister Mrs. Chester and family are visiting from London again, so she and the babies have gone to spend the week at The Acres."

"What a shame. Another time, perhaps. Is Mr. Weeks pleased with his new tenant? If he is not, he may take this chance to tell his son-in-law Mr. Chester what he thinks of his friends."

"I've no idea," answered Miranda, and she was glad her color had not receded entirely, for she was aware of her face heating again. She had thought more than once of the man with the disconcerting eyes.

"Has Mr. Tyrone Ellsworth not called upon the man?"

"Not yet, I'm afraid. The harvest..."

"Mr. Fairchild called at Beaumond in the way of business," offered Florence. "Because Mr. West couldn't go. He said Mr. Wolfe seemed like a sensible man and that he liked Beaumond very well so far."

"Did Mr. Fairchild see the boy?"

"Only in passing—the boy was riding, and very capably, too, Robert thought, for one his age. Robert said if he had not known better, he would have guessed the lad to be thirteen or thereabouts, because of his size. But because his father Mr. Wolfe is quite a—tall and large man—he supposed it was no great wonder."

Florence and Miranda exchanged an understanding look. Yes, this Edmund Wolfe had the good fortune to be "big as an ox," unlike poor Willie and Peter.

"Did this Mr. Wolfe have a housekeeper?" Mrs. Fellowes asked next.

"Robert said he brought back the late Mr. Taplin's housekeeper. She had married in the meantime, so Mr. Wolfe hired her husband as well."

"Hm," grunted the dean's wife. "Obliging of him. But no man likes to be alone. I expect Mr. Wolfe will make merry while his son is at school and soon bring a wife home to Beaumond."

"That's just what Mr. West said to my husband," agreed Florence. She turned teasing eyes on Miranda. "You must be our eyes and ears, Mama, since you will be at the balls and such."

"I? Why not Beatrice?"

"Because Beatrice will be *dancing*, of course. So you must be our spy. Mind you pay attention because Mrs. Fellowes and I will want reports."

"Pooh," said Miranda. "I can't be expected to watch two young ladies *and* Mr. Wolfe. You and Mrs. Fellowes will simply have to find another source."

While their female relations plied needles and tongues, William and Peter ran and raced, threw sticks for the dogs, and had a talk of their own.

"Do you suppose we'll be thrashed by the bigger boys?" William said when both dogs and boys were worn out and lying on the bank of Hollowgate's creek boundary. The creek was dry, save for a muddy puddle here and there, which they had explored with sticks, looking for bugs.

"I expect so," said Peter. "My Mama has been in a tremble lately."

"Mine too."

"But my father says, though there may be a bully or two, and the junior boys are made to work hard for the prefects, generally it's great fun."

"That's what my brother Tyrone says too," agreed William, rolling onto his stomach and smoothing Scamp's ears flat. "That for every unpleasant task the prefects make the inferiors do, they also keep order and do ten useful or kind things for the younger boys, like keep the bullies from having their way."

The boys were silent a moment, and then Peter ventured, "Some of the boys will be quite big and old, I suppose."

"I suppose."

"And a prefect is no protection from a bully if a prefect *is* a bully."

"Not a bit of it."

Truth be told, it was not only William and Peter's mothers who were in a tremble of late, and their conversation having veered too close to their fears, the boys took refuge in activity again, springing up to whoop and holler and wrestle with the dogs. In their rumpus, they neither saw nor heard the approach of a stranger, and he might have ridden right over them, had Scamp and Pickles not broken off in their play to bark at the interloper.

It was a boy on horseback, both boy and horse sharing the same red-brown coloring and fine trappings. The rider looked older than they and a great deal bigger, but this was Hollowgate land the trespasser stood on.

"Who are you?" demanded William, with Peter at his shoulder.

"Edmund Wolfe. Of Cantergreen in Kent." He did not have a deep voice, but nor did he pipe shrilly like a young chorister. His voice was, however, strangely flat.

"How do you come to be in Hampshire, then?" asked Peter. "Did you ride all that way?"

"No. I rode from Beaumond. My father and I are the new tenants there."

While William and Peter had surely heard their elders discussing new tenants, they had paid no attention, so they were more interested in the boy than his circumstances.

"If you come from Kent, why are you living at Beaumond?" frowned William.

"Because I'm going to Winchester at the end of the week."

"Going *back* to Winchester?" Peter questioned.

"No. Going for the first time."

"Why, so are we," said William. "But we're eleven."

"So am I."

Now both boys frowned at the newcomer, trying to determine if he was telling them a thumper, but while they did so, he dismounted and came closer, leading his horse. Besides being all-around thicker, Edmund Wolfe was an entire head taller than Peter, who was an important inch taller than William, and if it had not been for the harmlessness of the big boy's expression, William and Peter might have been tempted to take an ignominious step backward.

"I don't know anyone in Hampshire," said Edmund in that same flat voice.

"I don't suppose there's anyone in particular to know," returned William easily, feeling himself on stronger ground here, with his large and well-connected family.

"I'm Peter Fairchild," blurted Peter. "And this is my uncle William Ellsworth."

It was Edmund's turn to frown. "Don't you mean your brother or your cousin?"

"No. Uncle. Long story. His oldest sister is my mother."

"And my mother is his step-grandmother," added William.

"All right," said the big boy. He dismissed the puzzle with a shrug. "Do you want to ride my horse?"

This show of unexpected generosity did the trick. So much so that Peter did not mind admitting he had never been on a horse. They had a thousand questions for Edmund: what was the horse's name? How old was it? Had he brought Pilgrim from Kent with him, or was Pilgrim a Hampshire native?

Edmund answered everything patiently enough. He laced his fingers to assist Peter into the saddle, assuring him that Pilgrim was old and plodding, which was why Edmund himself was trusted with him. The new threesome made a little tour of the Hollowgate park, Scamp and Pickles circling and trotting in vast circles about them, until at last William's protesting stomach could no longer be ignored.

"Want to come to dinner?" he asked Edmund. "Our cook Wilcomb is first rate."

"All right," said Edmund. "If there's a groom to take Pilgrim."

Which is how Miranda came to be surprised when the boys at last reappeared. Edmund Wolfe needed no introduction, she thought, bemused, as William blundered through it nonetheless. For the lad was the picture of his father—or what his father must have looked like decades earlier. Edmund's eyes were brown, rather than ice grey, but the chestnut hair was the same (without the silver, which would surely come), as well as the build. In personality, however, there would be no confusing father and son. Where the father had been quick, first surly and then mischievous, the son was stolid and quiet. He spoke when addressed but not otherwise, though Edmund was, Miranda reminded herself, only eleven.

"Does your father know where you are, Edmund?" she asked.

"No, Mrs. Ellsworth."

"You are certainly welcome to join us for dinner, but perhaps it would be wise to send a note to Beaumond, so that he does not wonder what has become of you."

"All right." Then he joined the boys at the pianoforte, where William played a comic song while Peter chinked one of the upper keys in rhythmic punctuation.

Smiling to herself, Miranda went to the desk and drew out a sheet of notepaper.

Some twenty minutes later, Quill discovered Mr. Wolfe by the stables, interrogating the groom. "What do you mean, Tolbert lost sight of him?"

"He has a good seat, that lad," the head groom replied. "Master Edmund took a hedge Tolbert knew his own mount would balk at, and by the time he rode over to the gap, the boy was gone."

"Pardon me, sir," interrupted Quill. "Message for you from Hollowgate."

"From *Hollowgate*?" Colin plucked it from the footman's fingers and stalked some distance away. A minute later he strode past, saying, "Never mind, Downing. Master Edmund is found. Tell Mrs. Ackerman I will take dinner in my study."

When he was alone, he carried the note to the window and unfolded it again.

In a flowing, legible hand he read:

Hollowgate

1 September 1812

Dear Mr. Wolfe,

I hope this note finds you well. It seems your son Edmund came upon my own son and grandson during his ride, and the boys have formed an acquaintance. My William invited Edmund to dine with us, and we are happy to host him. As we dine rather early, I estimate you may expect him home by four o'clock.

Your obedient servant,
Miranda Ellsworth

Colin's response to this missive took him aback. He did not mind his son making friends in this new place, of course, especially friends among future schoolmates. And they must be easy and agreeable sorts, to welcome Edmund so quickly, for had the situation been reversed, it would never have occurred to Edmund to ask anyone to his home.

No—his brow furrowed. The feeling which he could not at first identify and then could not explain, was...envy.

Chapter Four

I think a woman of sense may entertain some degree
of affection for a brute...But, alas! The best things may
be abused, and the kind intentions of providence per-
verted! Thus we may sometimes see a fine lady, act as
if she thought the dog, which happens to be under her
precious care, was incomparably of more value, in her
eyes, than a human creature.
— Jonas Hanway, "Remarks on Lapdogs" (1757)

Was there ever a father and son more unlike? Colin wondered. It was a question he had asked himself at least once
a day since Edmund was old enough to speak. Or not to speak, as it
happened.

Having been raised with four sisters, speech for Colin had been a necessity for survival. A necessity which became habit and a habit which grew into a pleasure.

And then he married Doria. Within a week of marriage Colin learned that, having neither fur nor feathers, he held little interest for his wife. To her finch and her lapdog Doria was fluent, affectionate, even effusive. She petted; she coaxed; she cooed. But if Colin asked to sit beside her, Mopsey must be displaced, which Doria would submit to with a look of pain and many apologies to the dog. And when feathered Hoppy would answer the call of nature on Colin's shoulder or head, Doria would only giggle, "Naughty finchy."

At first Colin saw her fondness for her pets as a hopeful sign. Such warmth promised equal or even greater warmth for a husband, did it not?

It did not.

It wasn't that she disliked him. If asked, she would have said she was perfectly content with her husband, but Colin imagined she would have said as much of any spouse who neither beat her nor forbade her to keep pets. To her husband she was ever even-tempered and taciturn. After their wedding breakfast, when he made a little speech about how he hoped they would make the best of their match and grow to love each other, she answered, "I don't see why not." And later that night, when they had done their duty and lay side by side in the darkness, Colin said, "I wonder if there will be many children," to which Doria replied equably, "Papa certainly hopes so."

He did not know it then, but those early hours exemplified the entirety of their married life. He would try to reach out, to form a deeper understanding, a deeper bond between them, and she would respond with impenetrable tranquility, feeling she was meeting him halfway. As the months and years passed, the barrier between them blunted something inside him, until he came to picture their union as one vast, smothering, heavy blanket, from which no more than a toe could be thrust out from time to time. When Hoppy hopped the twig was one of those times. Optimistic Colin imagined he might thereafter claim more of his wife's regard, but when her grief passed, she simply got another finch. By the time Mopsey too went the way of all the earth, Colin had learned his lesson and did not make the same miscalculation.

If Edmund had not been so long in coming into the world, Colin likely would have given up sooner, but the child took his time. In fact, Doria's father did not even live to see the desired Wolfe heir to Cantergreen, and it might have been despair over his foiled scheme which hastened him to his reward. Nevertheless, the wait served one purpose: after so many years of regular attendance in the marriage bed, and in hopes of producing a sibling for Edmund, the couple kept up their weekly intimacy, much as Colin took care to wind the drawing room clock every Sunday evening.

But these efforts, however faithfully undertaken, never yielded another child, and Colin thought things might have gone on in this manner, world without end, had Doria's own dear pets not proven her literal downfall.

The chief villain was a daughter of the original Mopsey, called Ding-Ding, and it must be admitted that Colin loathed Ding-Ding. For one thing, Ding-Ding took her lapdog responsibilities very seriously and was to be found snoring upon her mistress whenever Doria happened to sit down. For another, Ding-Ding was wildly possessive, raising her bullet head with its bulging eyes to growl at Colin any time he entered the room. And for a third, Ding-Ding was an inveterate slug, never moving quickly unless doing so might trip someone.

It was this third characteristic which proved fatal for Doria Wolfe. For one afternoon, according to the maid scrubbing the hall floor below, as Doria pursued her finch hither and yon to return it to its cage, Ding-Ding saw her chance. Protuberant eyes jealously trained on the feathered rival for her mistress' affections, the lapdog streaked across the landing directly into Doria's path. Eyes and hand raised toward her finch, poor Doria never saw her doom approach. As she fell, she screamed in unison with the scrubbing maid, both helpless to prevent catastrophe.

Thus was Colin Wolfe, after nearly twenty years of marriage, set at liberty.

He found himself lord of the manor—a manor he almost hated for the cost it had exacted—and father of a young son who...didn't talk.

No, that wasn't it. Edmund spoke when spoken to, as his mother had, but he did not share spontaneous confidences. He did not bounce around like other boys his age, demanding his father look at this and acknowledge that. He would follow Colin when practicable, to be sure, but he did so quietly, impassively, as if he were a footman. And the few times he spoke up unbidden only struck his father with dismay, for it was, once, to ask for a dog, and the second time to ask for a pony.

Suppose Edmund turned out to be but a boy version of his mother Doria? Suppose the smothering blanket of Colin's marriage was thrown off, only to be replaced with a cobweb coverlet which provided no warmth and soon drifted away from lack of substance?

It was these fears, combined with Colin's dislike of Cantergreen, which determined him to make a change. Edmund might have been born to inherit the estate, but by heaven he would do so as Colin's son!

They would leave Kent. Strike out anew. Edmund need not attend the school his father and grandfathers had. In Winchester both father and son could climb from the channels dug for them and have a look about. Edmund could become whatever he pleased—the money for which Colin had sacrificed so much made that possible. And Colin—well, he might marry again. He might take the portion of life left to him and wring from it drops of the joy he had so long been missing.

These thoughts passed anew through Colin's head when he read the message from Hollowgate. He ought to be pleased his inexpressive son had somehow fallen in with these more active boys, but without having made any progress toward his own goals, Colin was apt to feel abandoned.

Giving himself an inward shake, he threw himself in an armchair in the study, staring into the fire. The opportunity to become his own person would come to Edmund through his father's engineering and the mere fact of being at school, but if Colin were to make anything new of his life, he must take steps.

"Your dinner, sir," announced Quill. The footman set the tray on a nearby table, but it was plain to see the master was preoccupied, and odds were the cook might have dished up surplus kitchen scraps without it being noticed.

Indeed, as Colin absently served himself, his mind turned instead on his autumn plans. The Wolfes would be seven years or longer in Winchester—until Edmund left for university—and if Colin were not to die of loneliness in the meantime, he had better set about making new acquaintances and finding himself a wife. Both tasks would be awkward enough at first, and it would have been easier to begin work during the summer when Winchester buzzed with races and balls, but that could not be helped. At least his eligibility would make him of interest to neighboring families, and so the jobs would be undertaken hand in hand, each speeding the other.

He might begin with calling at Hollowgate, now that Edmund paved the way, though there was nothing to be gained there and indeed something to be avoided. While doubtless his new Wintonian neighbors would delight in pairing a widow and a widower, Colin had a different sort of bride in mind.

When he pondered remarriage, the woman who stood beside him took no more distinct form than to be Doria's utter opposite. Young, where Doria was older. Pretty, where Doria was plain. Vivacious, where Doria was lumpish. Beyond these traits he did not think, having no need for more money and no interest in rising in rank.

From his encounter with the Widow Ellsworth at the office of West & Fairchild, it had been obvious that, apart from being rather attractive for an older woman, Mrs. Ellsworth was no anti-Doria. And in one respect she was very Doria-like: she was quiet, a quality he dreaded now. But, as West had informed him, the family was established and well-connected and worth knowing for those reasons alone.

"I will call after getting Edmund off to school," Colin told the empty room. "Next week will be soon enough. Mustn't be giving the widow any ideas."

Still, when Edmund returned in the early evening and father and son sat in their usual silence, Colin reading and Edmund on the floor rolling a ball back and forth between his hands (there was no dog to play with at Beaumond—the murderous Ding-Ding having been left behind in Kent), the boy surprised him by volunteering a remark.

"Willie's womenfolk were sewing him clothes."

Colin's head flew up. He had already asked a few questions, of course, and received minimal answers, so this extraordinary tidbit had the effect of revelation. It reminded him of coming upon a doe and fawn in the woods—one had to hold perfectly still lest they take fright and leap away. After a moment, he merely raised an eyebrow, but it sufficed.

"And Peter's. Because they're all the same family."

Colin swallowed, not even daring to shut his book. What did Edmund mean by it? That he did not like the clothes which had been professionally sewn for him? That he liked the coziness of having family to prepare one for school? Did he miss his Perry cousins? He had never given any indication that he would miss that side of the family if they left Kent.

Despite Colin's careful measures, the housekeeper Mrs. Ackerman chose that very moment to rattle in with the tea things. Setting the tray down, she briskly set about brewing the beverage and preparing their saucers while asking Colin a question about the next day's menu. Though she was efficient with her work, by the time she finished and handed them their cups, Edmund was blank again and the moment gone as if it had never been.

That Saturday Colin called for the chaise. Edmund's trunk was strapped to the back, and the head groom Downing mounted the near horse for the short drive to the College of St. Mary in Winchester. Colin tried unobtrusively to gauge his son's mood, but Edmund was impassive as ever, neither pale nor flushed, and certainly not chatty with nerves.

In fact, the little journey might have passed without one word spoken beyond those of Downing to the horses, except that, when they turned into Canon Street from Southgate, Edmund blurted, "There are the Ellsworths!"

There were enough of them, certainly. Colin saw two young boys accompanied by several adults, but the Wolfes could hardly stop in the street, and Edmund had to content himself with hallooing (Edmund *hallooing?*) and waving his hat as they drove past.

"We'll see them shortly," Colin said, and Edmund might have nodded but he *said* nothing.

All was confusion when they drew up at the Outer Gate. Porters came to unstrap Edmund's trunk, and the Wolfes passed through to the Outer Court while Downing drove on. Winchester College being a self-sufficient community, Colin noted the brewery taking up one side of the court, with stables on another, and the warden's quarters and offices making up the rest. The warden George Huntingford himself was about that day to oversee the entrance of the new pupils and to show the families courtesy, but Edmund had no interest in the man and merely watched the Outer Gate until the Ellsworths appeared.

Of the group Colin recognized the lawyer Mr. Fairchild and Mrs. Ellsworth, but it was the latter on whom his eye lingered. It had not been altogether fair to lump her in his mind with Doria. Dressed in blue spotted muslin with matching bonnet and holding the arm of a younger gentleman, she was no nubile maid, but neither was she as old as his late wife, nor even, Colin suspected, as old as he himself. In his distraction he did not notice Edmund bending his steps toward them until he was halfway there, and Colin quickly excused himself to follow.

Fairchild took it upon himself to perform introductions before the boys elbowed each other and darted away, and when he said, "Of course you've already met my mother-in-law Mrs. Ellsworth," his wife Mrs. Fairchild cried, "Has he? Mama, you never mentioned it. Even when Edmund joined us for dinner."

"Didn't I?" Mrs. Ellsworth fluttered, going rather pink.

"In all the preparations leading to this day, you have had much on your mind," Colin supplied graciously. "Including feeding Edmund, for which I thank you."

She looked down at the stones of the courtyard, and with the difference in their heights he could only see the crown of her bonnet. He discovered this rather annoyed him, and he heard himself add, "Mrs. Ellsworth, in your brief acquaintance with him, you may have realized my son is not a talkative boy, but when he returned home, he mentioned, in what I can only suppose must have been a spirit of envy, that your William's clothes were being made by your hands."

It worked. She raised her head, her gentle blue eyes trying to read him. What she concluded from her scrutiny Colin couldn't guess because he hardly understood himself. What had made him say the clothes were made by her hands? Those were not Edmund's actual words verbatim.

"Poor boy," she said, her lovely voice quiet. "Grief has a way of catching one unawares."

It was Colin's turn to color. Had that been it? Had Edmund been trying to express that he missed his mother?

Thankfully his discomfiture went unnoticed by the others in the hubbub. Mr. Fairchild and the Tyrone Ellsworth person were chaffing William and Peter about tricks played on new boys, while Edmund looked on, a half-smile curving his lips. Mrs. Fairchild was dabbing her eyes and biting back loving admonitions, and young Miss Ellsworth was laughingly trying to seize her little brother and nephew in an embrace.

It was Miss Ellsworth who looped one arm through her step-mother's and the other through her brother's after they bid the boys farewell, saying, "Shall we go to LaCroix's for our coffee and biscuits?"

"La Croix's?" echoed Tyrone Ellsworth. "What would you know of the place?"

"Silly—it became our tradition every year after we had seen you off. The rest of the family would go to La Croix's. The first year we did it, we met Robert and his sister there, did we not, and Robert cast sheep's eyes at Flossie."

"You," growled Mrs. Fairchild with a mock frown, pinching her. But her sister's teasing succeeded in distracting her from the loss of Peter. "He did no such thing."

"Well, if I didn't on that occasion," rejoined Mr. Fairchild, "I certainly won't miss the chance now. What do you say, Wolfe? Care to join us for a refreshment?"

Colin had originally thought he might wander College Street, looking into the booksellers' shops, followed perhaps by a visit to Mundy's, to see the statues and paintings, before walking back to Beaumond, but these plans failed to tempt him now, and he agreed to the proposal at once.

Frederick La Croix, confectioner, was found near the end of College Street, past John Burdon's bookshop, and indeed College

Street seemed, unsurprisingly, altogether comprised of bookshops, fruiterers, and confectioners.

The party succeeded in securing two tables, and the Fairchilds naturally sitting beside each other, and Miss Ellsworth taking the chair between her brother and her stepmother, that left the seat on Mrs. Ellsworth's other side open.

It was exactly what he had dreaded the other day—the idea taking people that an older widower and widow would make a fine match. But there was no other chair. And judging from the way Mrs. Ellsworth turned her back to him to address Mrs. Fairchild, Colin suspected she too would like to quash the supposition before it could take hold. While that ought to have reassured him, annoyance flickered for a second time that day. *Have no fear, dear lady, I have no intention of making up to you.*

With nonchalance he dropped into the chair, but the effect was spoiled when his large person knocked into the flimsy table. Colin smothered an oath, his hand flying out to steady it, only to close hard over another—a bare one, for the widow had been in the process of removing her gloves.

She gave a little gasp, though he released her as instantly as if she had been a glowing-hot stove. Or was he the stove? For his face heated as it had not since he had been a gangling youth.

"Pardon me," he muttered.

Her reply was equally muted, but he saw her cover her crushed hand with the other in her lap. He ran his own along his leg, to rid it of the memory of her delicate fingers.

Sensitive Mrs. Fairchild started in with discussing what should be ordered and what had been tried in the past, with her brother and sister soon adding their own suggestions, and the awkwardness passed. Or the others passed over it.

But Colin was aware of Mrs. Ellsworth's chair turned the slightest angle away from him. And though the skirts of her blue-spotted muslin brushed against his trousers and her slender arm was not four inches from his own, he sensed she had withdrawn from him in her mind.

He could not account for it.

Instead of impressing the woman with his unconcern for her, he had blundered about, trespassing and blushing and behaving for all the world as if he felt entirely otherwise.

No. He could not account for it at all.

CHAPTER FIVE

Come, fellow, follow us for thy reward.
— Shakespeare, *Henry VI, Part II,* II.iii.1148 (c.1591)

With little William gone to school, Miranda turned her attention to the chaperone duties she would take on for Beatrice and Miss Wright. Beatrice had of course attended the Domum Ball with the rest of her classmates from Mrs. Turcotte's Seminary for Young Ladies, but she had declined attending the summer Race Balls.

"All my sisters are busy with their families, and you have just finished with mourning, Mama, and have Willie to get ready for school. There will be time enough for such things in the autumn."

Miranda submitted, but Beatrice's decision niggled. Shouldn't young ladies her age be frivolous butterflies, eager to flit here and there in their finery? Not that Miranda herself had ever been such a creature, but it troubled her that Beatrice preferred by far to stay home, enjoying the company of her family over that of her school friends.

"You know we will be expected to appear at everything social this autumn and winter," Miranda warned her, "now that I have agreed to chaperone Miss Wright. If we do not go, Miss Wright cannot."

"I know," sighed Bea. "Although I don't see why Lily can't do some of the duties. Lily is, after all, wife to Miss Wright's cousin and Mrs. Fellowes' granddaughter by marriage."

"You know very well why Mrs. Fellowes does not ask her and Lily does not offer," scolded Miranda. "After Lily broke her engagement to Miss Wright's brother, she will hardly be wanted there."

"I don't see why not," persisted Beatrice. "That was all years and years and years ago. I hardly remember it."

"Because you were—what—six or seven at the time? Trust me, darling. The older people remember it."

Mrs. Fellowes wrote to invite Miranda and Miss Ellsworth to a gathering at the deanery, "out of doors, if the weather permits," at which would be present Miranda's new charge, as well as "sundry clerical guests."

"Oh, Mama," protested Bea. "*Must* I? 'Sundry clerical guests'? I will be the only person there under the age of sixty."

"You forget, poor Miss Wright will also be under the age of sixty," Miranda laughed. "Why don't you pop in with me, and you and she might condole with each other or escape to look in shop windows on the High Street."

Familiar with Mrs. Fellowes from childhood, perhaps Miranda ought to have known better. That is, perhaps she should have guessed that such an efficient woman would have more than one motive in inviting her to the deanery. *Had* she guessed, Miranda doubtless would have been as eager to cry off as her stepdaughter.

The day of Mrs. Fellowes' gathering was clear and dry, and voices from the deanery garden carried to them as they approached.

"Look, Mama—there's a face."

There was indeed a face, a young, pretty, pouty one, peering from the window as they came around the building. It disappeared as soon as they noticed it, but the next instant its owner flew from under the pointed arches of the deanery porch to accost them.

"Mrs. Ellsworth? You *are* Mrs. Ellsworth, Grandmama's friend?"

"Yes, and this is my daughter Beatrice, Miss Ellsworth. You must be Miss Wright."

"How do you do. Won't you call me Emmy?" Miss Wright's curtsey was more like the spring of a jack-in-the-box. "Grandmama said to wait, and she would introduce us, but I couldn't bear to be in the garden another moment. It's full of fusty old men in their fusty, rusty black frocks, like a flock of crows. It made me think staying with my grandparents was not my best scheme, but how else am I to be near the fun?"

Before Miranda or Beatrice could answer, Miss Wright took both of Beatrice's hands in her own and spread them wide. "Let me see your dress. It's pretty. Did Madame Blanchet make it? Papa has given me an allowance, and I plan to spend it with her, but I will have to wear something I already have to Thursday's assembly. We *will* go to Thursday's assembly in Upper Brook Street, will we not, Mrs. Ellsworth?"

Miranda gave her assurances. "Now shall we proceed to the party in the garden?"

"Only if Miss Ellsworth and I—may I please call you Beatrice?—can run away afterward! Oh, Beatrice, we will be the best of friends. I know it. I have a *feeling*. I'm glad you're pretty. When Grandmama told me she had found me both a chaperone and a 'little friend,' I confess I had doubts, even though I knew you were Simon's Lily's sister. Lily is so very pretty, isn't she, though I daresay she's over thirty now."

Beatrice caught her stepmother's eye, but Miranda kept her face blank. Yes, they would have their hands full with Miss Wright, apparently. But perhaps she only spoke this much because she was nervous to make their acquaintance. She was indeed a pretty girl, her honey-brown hair a shade lighter than Beatrice's and her figure rounder, but the two girls were of a height and might have passed for cousins.

Just as Emmy described, clergymen crowded the deanery garden, but Mrs. Fellowes emerged to greet them. "Ah, Miranda, I see Emmy has already found you. Yes, yes, dear. You and Miss Ellsworth may run along. I suspect some of our younger, unmarried clergymen will be disappointed not to have the opportunity to chat with you, but they will simply have to wait for the assembly on Thursday. Go on."

Before her grandmother finished her sentence Emmy Wright was fluttering away, pulling Beatrice after her, and Mrs. Fellowes released a long breath. "Oh, Miranda. How grateful I am you will help keep an eye on that girl. I am far too old now to chase after her, and chasing is exactly what it will take, I admit to you now. She has a good heart but a flighty spirit. Or perhaps eighteen feels flighty to two and eighty!"

Despite her misgivings, a lifetime of deference to the dean's wife assisted Miranda in making the expected demurrals. But that same lifetime of knowing each other allowed Mrs. Fellowes to see through Miranda's polite words.

"I know. It is a great favor I ask of you," she said heavily. "But I do not mind telling you I have a reward for your labors in mind."

Miranda regarded her with amusement. "Indeed, ma'am? What would that be?"

"Come with me."

With no appearance of hurry or having a destination in mind, Mrs. Fellowes leisurely guided Miranda through pockets of the "flock of crows," most of whom Miranda had known for years, if not her entire life. They included her brother Clifford, holding forth to a clutch of patient listeners; Mr. Hemple, curate of her own parish of St. Eadburh's; and prebendary of the cathedral Mr. Kenner, Lily's husband and Miranda's son-in-law. But when these were greeted, Mrs. Fellowes led her across the grass to where the old dean was seated, leaning on his cane, a few strangers standing in a loose semicircle about him.

"Ah, Miranda," smiled the dean, "what a pleasure to see you today. You see we have some newcomers to our diocese. Allow me to introduce Mr. Lyfford, the new chaplain at the county hospital, Mr. Dodge, who replaces Mr. Kindly at the Quiristers' School, and

Mr. Bracewell, the new curate of St. Martin Winnall. Gentleman, this is Mrs. Ellsworth of Hollowgate."

The three men turned, beaming upon her, just as the dean and his wife were beaming upon her, and Miranda understood at once.

So this is how it is going to be.

Her "reward" for guiding Miss Wright through the perilous thickets of young-ladyhood was to have an acceptable second husband chosen for her? Because what else could a wealthy widow not in her first youth desire, when her year of mourning was done, except someone to spend the second half of her life with?

Indignant color flared in her cheeks, but *not* being in her first youth, Miranda was able to check the words which rose to her lips.

Steady, girl.

After all, Dean and Mrs. Fellowes loved her. They meant well, even if she deemed their interference impertinent. They recognized, as all the world must, that the wealth her late husband bequeathed her would make her a target for fortune hunters, just as Miranda believed protecting Beatrice's generous portion required caution, and the Felloweses must be congratulating themselves that they could steer worthier gentleman Miranda's way.

Mr. Lyfford was the oldest of the chosen bachelors, a man long as a pole and nearly as lean. Miranda guessed he must be Mr. Wolfe's height, but two of Mr. Lyfford could fit inside one Mr. Wolfe. The chaplain had agreeable features behind little wire spectacles, and what remained of his hair consisted of a ring of silver-white encircling his head, offset by a flourishing tuft in front.

The second candidate Mr. Dodge *looked* like the head of a quiristers' school. That is, he was younger than Mr. Lyfford, but the job of herding and managing sixteen restless young boys already left him with a harried air and lined countenance. Miranda imagined if she married him, the first thing he would do would be to retire and live off her money.

As for the third gentleman, she wondered if the Felloweses had meant to present him at all, or if he had just happened to be standing with the others. For the curate Mr. Bracewell was neither older nor unhandsome. While not as large nor imposing as, say, a Mr. Wolfe—why was she comparing everyone to Mr. Wolfe?—nor was he as sinister. No—that wasn't right! Mr. Wolfe was not *sinister*, so much as mischievous. Dangerous. Bold. Miranda pinched herself. *For pity's sake—let us have no more of Mr. Wolfe.*

Mr. Bracewell could be forgiven for thinking himself the cause of the widow's sudden blushes. Certainly Mr. Lyfford and Mr. Dodge thought so, for they frowned at him, thinking it was just like a woman to prefer the poorest man, simply because he was good-looking.

"What an honor, madam," declared Mr. Lyfford loudly, bending toward her like a toppling obelisk. "A signal honor. I know the Ellsworth family has long been a generous benefactor to the hospital."

"Mm," said Miranda, thinking she must ask Tyrone later if this were true. She could not recall her late husband ever mentioning it.

"An honor indeed," echoed the harried Mr. Dodge, not to be outdone. "So many Ellsworths have passed through College."

"But sadly none were quiristers," replied Miranda. "My stepson Mr. Tyrone Ellsworth plays the fiddle but does not often sing, and my young William can hardly be made to sit still for ten minutes together."

Having said something to the first two, she thought it only fair to address Mr. Bracewell, whether the Felloweses intended to put him forth or not, so she asked, "How do you like the congregation at St. Martin Winnall, sir? Is it your first curacy? I confess I have never been inside that church, being a member of St. Eadburh's on the other side of Winchester."

"It is a small church and still smaller congregation," answered Mr. Bracewell. "My uncle by marriage is the rector, but his age and health no longer permit him to carry out his duties, so Dean Fellowes here has called upon me."

"It's a start," said the dean. "The church building will tumble down soon enough, and the rectory might go tomorrow, but it's a start."

"I will have to see the church before that happens, then," Miranda smiled. "Is there a choir? You sound like you might be a singer, Mr. Bracewell."

"How kind of you to say, Mrs. Ellsworth," he replied (as Lyfford and Dodge glowered). "I'm afraid I have no ear for music, but I do love to dance, and if you will be at Thursday's assembly, it would be my honor to partner you."

Off her guard, Miranda sputtered an instant before bowing her head and thanking him. Not to be outdone, Messieurs Lyfford and Dodge were quick in turn to secure their own dances, and she could only marvel inwardly that she, who had thought only of her duties as chaperone at the assembly, was now certain of standing up at least three times.

The dean's wife must have decided enough had been accomplished that day, for after a few minutes she made excuses for them both and led Miranda away.

"My dear Mrs. Fellowes," hissed Miranda, when they were out of earshot, "what can you be about?"

"Now, now, Miranda, how long have I known you?"

"Forever," she replied shortly, "but are you or are you not attempting to matchmake for me? I am now eight and thirty years old! That's nearly forty! And I do not recall you interfering before I married Mr. Ellsworth, when I suspect everyone despaired of me as a hopeless spinster."

Mrs. Fellowes stroked her hand soothingly. "You had your brother to watch out for you then, and while you had a respectable portion, you are now wealthy. Whether you like it or not, Miranda, you will be pursued. I know you're no foolish young miss whose head will be turned by any passing rogue, but it never hurts to put some worthy gentlemen before you."

Exactly as she had thought, and Miranda made another effort to smother her temper.

"Can you honestly say you have no wish to marry again?" pressed the dean's wife.

"I-I don't know. I haven't given it a great deal of thought yet. I've only got done mourning, you know."

"You mean *wearing* mourning," observed Mrs. Fellowes. "For while I trust you respected Mr. Ellsworth and were fond of him, I do not think his death broke your heart."

Miranda made no response to this, but she kicked at a tuft of grass. They had reached the deanery porch again, and Mrs. Fellowes leaned against one of the arches with a sigh.

"I do not say I expect you to fall in love with poor Mr. Lyfford or Mr. Dodge," she went on. "And if you do not choose to rescue Mr. Bracewell from his obscure curacy, some other woman will gladly undertake it. I only say you have the freedom to choose again and to choose according to your heart. But I hope you will not therefore choose unwisely."

For whatever inexplicable reason, Mr. Wolfe reappeared in Miranda's mind's eye, and her reply emerged more peevish than she would have liked. "Thank you, Mrs. Fellowes, for your concern. You have always been a friend to me, and therefore I think I will walk in the cathedral yard to meditate on what you have said, until the girls return."

She should have given Bea and Miss Wright—*Emmy*—specific instructions to return after a half-hour, Miranda scolded herself. The High Street was not long, but a girl fresh from the country like Emmy might want to inspect not only the wares in the windows but also every item within. And if that were the case, would Beatrice be able to coax her back to the deanery before nightfall?

Rescue came from an unexpected quarter.

For Miranda was on only her third circuit of the cathedral close, lingering beneath the cloisters, when she heard Emmy's high, excited laugh and Beatrice's more subdued chuckle. Rushing to the end of Curle's Passage to meet them, she collided with something very large and solid which knocked the breath from her. Something which turned out to be Mr. Colin Wolfe.

"Gracious me!" he exclaimed, hastening to untangle himself from the girls' hands, which were looped through either arm. "Is that you, Mrs. Ellsworth? What do you mean by dashing into me like that?" He seized her by the shoulders to steady her, giving her a gentle shake of reproof.

"You—you may release me," she gulped. "I am fine. I do apologize, though I believe I got the worse end of the staff."

"Better let me be the judge of that," he replied. "That bonnet brim of yours nearly sliced my throat." But his lips twitched as he released her, hands dropping back to his sides.

"I see you've met Miss Wright," said Miranda primly.

"He has," Emmy plumed herself. "He saw us looking in the window of the millinery in the Square and popped his head between ours and made me scream in surprise! But Beatrice knew him and performed the introduction. Mr. Wolfe is *so* gallant. He begged to partner each of us on Thursday, and when Beatrice said we must be going because you would be waiting for us, he insisted on accompanying us back to the deanery."

Mr. Wolfe begging to partner the girls? Aware of a sudden, burning little knot of unhappiness in her breast, Miranda said, "Thank you, sir. I will take Miss Wright home from here."

His odd silver eyes narrowed at her averted gaze, but after a pause he submitted to the dismissal. With his swift, graceful bow, he turned on his heel and went.

Emmy's pretty brow furrowed. "Oh, Mrs. Ellsworth, why were you so stern with him? We were having such fun."

"Your grandmother is expecting you home," was Miranda's evasive answer. "I don't know how pleased she will be with you granting dances to strangers you meet in the street." Even as she said it, she accused herself of hypocrisy, for had she not just granted *three* dances to virtual strangers?

"But he wasn't a stranger!" argued Emmy. "He knew Beatrice. And *I* think he's not only gallant, but terribly, dreadfully handsome!"

Bea shivered. "Emmy—he must be old enough to be our father because he has an eleven-year-old son."

But Emmy shrugged. "Well, *I'm* not eleven, so he clearly isn't. Old enough. But pooh! If you don't like him, I don't mind because then he may be one of my beaux."

Miranda said nothing, merely leading the girls back toward the deanery. But she could not help thinking the "reward" Mrs. Fellowes granted her for taking on Emmy Wright might not begin to repay the possible cost.

CHAPTER SIX

Their purpose is to parle, to court and dance;
And every one his love-feat will advance
Unto his several mistress.
— Shakespeare, *Love's Labour's Lost,* V.ii.2004 (c.1595)

It had been years since Miranda attended an assembly or ball. Not since she had chaperoned her stepdaughter Araminta some eight years before, she realized, and even then it might only have been once, since Minta was usually accompanied by an older sister. Miranda's husband William Ellsworth had not been much for balls or dancing, though he and his children adored the activity at home. Therefore, as in all things, Miranda had submitted to remain quietly at Hollowgate with him.

She sent the maid Monk to fuss over Beatrice, but soon enough both Monk and Beatrice were in Miranda's dressing room.

"I'll do, won't I, Mama?" asked her youngest stepdaughter, giving a twirl.

"You will indeed," replied Miranda with an approving smile. Beatrice was her usual neat self, only— "Didn't you want Monk to curl your hair?"

Beatrice heaved a sigh. "Oh, Mama. When Miss Wright—*Emmy*—and I went and looked in the shop windows, she told me in great detail how she would dress tonight, including the circlet wound with flowers that would crown her *curled* hair. And it made me think I wouldn't curl my hair at all; nor would I wear a single flower, or she would think I was imitating her or trying to compete with her."

"But of course she wouldn't think that, darling. No one would think that. Why, most all of the women there will have curled hair, including me, and we are not trying to—compete with Emmy." Even as she spoke Miranda felt her face warm. But it was true—she was not trying to compete with the girl. The very idea of someone of her age and experience doing so was ridiculous and humiliating. Because of course the blooming Miss Wright would win every time. Blooming, unspoiled Miss Wright.

Still, she understood Beatrice's reluctance and would let her alone. Giving her a kiss on the cheek she added, "Do whatever you like, dear. Your hair is so shining and pretty it needs no adornment."

They were silent a few minutes, Beatrice fiddling with her turquoise bracelet while she watched Monk winding Miranda's hair on the iron. Then Bea said, "Suppose no one asks me to dance. What do I do, then?"

Miranda couldn't imagine that would be the case, Emmy Wright or no Emmy Wright. Besides being lovely, Beatrice had a healthy portion and connections to the best families, clerical and otherwise. But she gave her a reassuring smile. "Sometimes there aren't nearly enough gentlemen, and even the most popular girls find themselves without a partner. If that happens, you simply come and stand beside me."

"But suppose you are dancing yourself?"

"But I'm not there to dance!" laughed Miranda. "You mustn't suppose—" she began, before breaking off. "That is—I don't mean to dance *much*. I could not avoid agreeing to do so with three of the—older—gentlemen Mrs. Fellowes introduced me to at her gathering. But the rest of the time I will be anchored in place, keeping an eagle eye on you and Emmy, so let there be no unseemly goings-on." Her teasing tone drew a smile from solemn Beatrice.

"You might have to dance with at least one more person, however, Mama."

"Might I? Who would that be?"

"Mr. Wolfe," answered Bea. "Because when we ran into him, it wasn't only Emmy and me he said he wanted to dance with." She paused to heighten the effect of her speech, but her stepmother was pulling on her gloves and said nothing.

"He said he had as yet so few acquaintances in Hampshire that he was determined to dance with every last one—or the female ones, at least," she explained. "And who does he know apart from you and Flossie, who won't be there?"

"Ah, well," said Miranda, "after tonight he will, I trust, have more female acquaintances than he knows what to do with."

Drawing the chaise to a halt before the assembly room in Upper Brook Street, Greaves assisted the Ellsworths to alight, and no sooner did Miranda's slipper touch the pavement than Emmy Wright scurried forward, exclaiming, one of the deanery maids on her heels.

"Here they are, Davidson, so you can run along now," Emmy said, shooing the maid with her hand.

Davidson ignored her, asking Miranda in afflicted tones, "What time should I return for her, Mrs. Ellsworth?"

"You needn't, thank you," Miranda replied. "Please tell Mrs. Fellowes we will drive Miss Wright back to the deanery afterward, and likely that will always be the arrangement."

"Oh, goody goody!" cried Emmy. "It's so much more fun to ride than to walk when one is dressed up." The girl was arrayed exactly as she had described to Beatrice, and Miranda had to admit the effect was breathtaking. Had Mrs. Fellowes' maid managed those curls?

She led the girls up the steps and helped them pass off their cloaks. In the racing season the Winchester balls were crowded affairs, but autumn brought diminished numbers, and Miranda was relieved to note the respectable number of gentlemen. Unless too many of them retired to play cards or otherwise chose to shirk their duties, Beatrice should not lack for partners.

A swift, involuntary glance showed her Mr. Wolfe had not yet arrived, and she was not the only one seeking him. Emmy bounced on her toes. "Where can he be? I hope he comes soon." Not even an introduction to the fine-looking curate Mr. Bracewell served to distract her long, though Miranda saw Bea blush and murmur a barely intelligible response to the clergyman's greeting.

"As I have reached you first, Mrs. Ellsworth," Mr. Bracewell said, "I hope you might grant me the first dance."

Her eyes widened. "Oh! I have not forgotten my promise to dance, sir, but you had better choose another partner for the first because I could not possibly stand up without making sure Miss Ellsworth and Miss Wright are taken care of."

She thought he would understand her hint and ask one of the girls, but he merely took up a post beside her as if he belonged there. Nor was he dislodged when Messieurs Lyfford and Dodge appeared, and those two gentlemen were obliged to admit defeat, accordingly falling back and claiming dances from Beatrice and Emmy.

"Just so," said Mr. Bracewell with satisfaction when the other two bowed and drifted away. "If you will excuse me, I will return shortly."

No sooner was he gone than Emmy began to complain, stamping her slippered foot. "What awful luck! What a way to begin an evening! Was ever a girl more unfortunate?"

"Good heavens," came a low, amused voice. "What calamity has befallen you, Miss Wright? Have you lost a blossom from your hair?"

With a shriek she whirled around—all three turned—to see Mr. Wolfe behind them. "Mr. Wolfe! There you are! I thought you would never come." For a second Miranda thought Emmy would throw herself at him after this artless confession, but the girl managed to refrain, instead prancing and giggling and tossing her head. "No indeed, I have all my flowers. Do you like them?"

"Very nice," he said mildly. "But what was the disaster? Did one of your beaux defect to Mrs. Ellsworth here?" His gaze slid to Miranda, and she managed to sustain it.

"No—worse," returned Emmy, "for one of Mrs. Ellsworth's beaux defected to *me*!"

"Don't be silly," Miranda said shortly. "To speak of beaux is absurd at my age, even if I had not just met the man the other day."

"Well, I don't know what else he would be called," retorted Emmy, speaking to Miranda but making sheep's eyes at Mr. Wolfe. "For he said you had promised him a dance, and when he found you were taken he had to ask me!" She lowered her voice conspiratorially. "I don't mind telling you, Mr. Wolfe, but this 'Mr. Lytford' I am saddled with is a hundred, if he is a day, and it isn't very kind of Mrs. Ellsworth to dance with the dashing younger man and leave the relics to Beatrice and me. She is supposed to be our chaperone, after all."

"How remiss of her," he responded, matching Emmy's confidential whisper. "You had better have your revenge by passing off one of your beaux on *her*, and one perhaps equally ancient." With that he addressed Miranda. "What would you say, madam? Have I come too late, or have you a dance to spare me?"

"Absurd," said Miranda again, unable to prevent her blush this time. Believing him in jest she made no reply, instead busying herself with retying a ribbon on Beatrice's sleeve.

Emmy filled the gap. "It's all very well to talk of avenging me, Mr. Wolfe, but don't forget you promised to dance with me as well. My first few are taken, but there is the one right before the tea...Mr. Wolfe—are you listening? Why do you not answer me?"

"Pardon me," he said, affecting a start. "I'm afraid I'm not at liberty to answer until Mrs. Ellsworth answers *me*. Suppose I were to ask you for the dance right before the tea, and then Mrs. Ellsworth said she had thought long and hard about it, and the only dance she could offer me was the one right before the tea! Imagine my blushes."

Miranda raised unwilling eyes to his mocking ones, but he only smiled benignly. It seemed that, for whatever reason, he was going to pester her until she answered.

"The fourth dance," she muttered. "I am free for the fourth dance or thereafter."

"Not till the fourth!" he marveled. "What a belle. Alas. That is what comes of my arriving five minutes late. The fourth it is, then, Mrs. Ellsworth." He turned to her charges, arranging his dances with them as the musicians finished their tuning and began playing through the first piece to refresh the dancers' memories. Everywhere in the assembly room gentlemen went in search of their partners while girls rehearsed the steps once more in their heads. Miranda was thankful that Mr. Wolfe made them another bow and wandered away before Mr. Bracewell came for her, lest she have to endure further comments and knowing looks from the man.

For all his noble brow, waving dark hair, and strong jaw, Mr. Bracewell disturbed Miranda's equanimity not a jot, and she could bear his nearness and his conversation—nay, even taking hands or linking arms with him—without undue distress. Perhaps it was because she suspected he was a good ten years younger than she, if not more. And while he attracted admiring glances from the other ladies in the set, these he politely ignored, and Miranda did not know whether to be flattered or amused by his steady regard. Even Bea peeped at him often, and Miranda briefly considered directing Mr. Bracewell's attention thitherward. But Beatrice was so young!

The thought brought her up short. After all, the age difference between Mr. Ellsworth and Miranda had been twice as much, and no one had thought anything amiss. By that same measure, Mr. Bracewell would be entirely suitable for eighteen-year-old Beatrice.

"What is it, Mrs. Ellsworth?" her partner asked solicitously. "You frown."

"It is nothing. I was thinking of my duties to my charges," she lied. But to lend her words credence she peered down the line, past Beatrice and Mr. Dodge to Emmy and Mr. Lyfford. Mr. Lyfford's tuft waved extravagantly as he took hands in his foursome to go in circle, but neither Emmy nor the second lady in the group spared it a glance. Because both girls were occupied in glowing up at Mr. Wolfe. Mr. Wolfe, who was saying something which Miranda could not hear, but it must have been delightful because they all laughed, save Mr. Lyfford.

Mr. Bracewell followed her gaze. "Ah, Miss Wright seems a lively sort, and I know the other young lady dancing next to her is as well."

"You know her?"

"Miss Paulson. A member of my flock." There was a note in his voice that made Miranda glance at him. Had he, too, felt a disagreeable twinge at the sight of Miss Paulson's open admiration?

Whether he had or not, they both fell silent, and Mr. Bracewell only roused himself as the dance ended. "This has been a treat, Mrs. Ellsworth."

Miranda managed not to blurt, "Has it?" But it was a near thing, and she could not help dimpling. But then Mr. Dodge appeared to claim his dance. Poor Mr. Dodge! Even without a herd of quiristers to look after he was harried, his forehead lined and neckcloth awry. A lock of lank hair drooped across his forehead.

"What a marvelous job you have done with your daughter Miss Ellsworth," he began as they crossed. "An amiable young lady. Quite a credit to you."

Whether Mr. Dodge was making up to her or to Beatrice with his compliments was hardly worth determining, for Miranda was certain he would not succeed with either. But she said the proper things and tried not to watch Mr. Wolfe partnering an elegant black-haired lady of upright figure.

You are here to watch Beatrice and Emmy, she chided herself. There was nothing to see with Bea, in any event, who danced dutifully with the spindly Mr. Lyfford. And Emmy flirting with the handsome Mr. Bracewell only alarmed Miranda because, after every giggle or lavish smile bestowed on the curate, Emmy would then glance at Mr. Wolfe, to see how he took it.

Which brought Miranda right back to trying not to stare at Mr. Wolfe.

Her dance with Mr. Lyfford followed, the next and last step in the rotation. Mr. Lyfford and his tuft of hair swayed and waved above her, and after he paid Miranda some flowery compliments, they spoke of the county hospital with diligence. Emmy flirted with Mr. Dodge (who appeared thunderstruck), while Beatrice glided beside Mr. Bracewell. Poor Bea hardly knew where to look, and Miranda ached to see the girl's blushes. Dear me! Was Beatrice going to suffer her first *tendre*?

Well, better an affection for Mr. Bracewell than one for Mr. Wolfe.

Miranda shut her eyes momentarily after this uninvited thought streaked through her mind. What was wrong with her? Was she herself conceiving a *tendre* for that man? Was this what it felt like, this mixture of awareness and discomfiture and—and *longing*?

Heaven and earth.

How utterly, utterly mortifying. Was she for the first time, at the advanced age of eight and thirty, going to make a fool of herself? And over someone she scarcely knew? Going to surrender even a fragment of her heart to someone who neither asked for it nor even thought of it? Just look at him there—dancing every dance with a pretty partner. All of them younger, all attractive, all admiring. When men aged as Colin Wolfe had, women found it piquant, even challenging. But when women aged—they simply became invisible.

Miranda did not deceive herself. Had she not a penny, she doubted any Mr. Lyffords or Mr. Dodges or Mr. Bracewells would be clamoring for her company. Without her money, she would have been, at her age, as much a part of the background as every other older woman present. She would have receded into the featureless line of chaperones, never to be seen again.

Fortunately for Miranda, Mr. Lyfford was not as observant as Mr. Bracewell had been, and he demanded no explanations for her troubled expression. Indeed, when she murmured, "Do tell me some of the greater challenges facing the hospital," his gratification knew no bounds and his tongue ran on wheels, requiring only an occasional, "My, my" or a click of the tongue to keep him going.

And in the meantime, Miranda made herself promises.

No one would ever, ever know her weakness. And the most important No One among all the other no ones was Mr. Wolfe himself. There would be no seeking him out, no vying for his attention, no special efforts made to please. She would not try to bring up his name in conversation or suggest anything which might bring him in her orbit. She must even give over the evening's temptation always to be peeking at him. Why she stole glances in the first place she could not justify, since the sight of his lovely partners gave her more pain than pleasure.

She would expunge the man ruthlessly from the soil of her heart before he put down roots. Or deeper roots, she should say, for how was it that the mere making of these vows caused the knot of unhappiness in her breast to tighten? It could not take terribly long, this process of ripping out shallow roots. Every gardener knew weeds grew stronger and harder to pull up with each passing day.

There would be just the one hurdle to be faced: her dance with him. But that would last twenty or thirty minutes, and then it would be over. He would probably be looking over her shoulder the whole time anyway, planning his attack on the next young beauty. Or maybe he would forget altogether that he had asked her.

He did not forget.

Miranda had just risen from her curtsey to Mr. Lyfford when she found Mr. Wolfe beside her. How had he possibly got from one end of the room to the other so quickly?

"Fourth dance," he said.

Miranda ignored him as much as it was possible to ignore so large a person. Holding out her hand to Mr. Lyfford, she thanked him.

"Such a delight! A glimpse of paradise. I hope we might repeat the pleasure another time, Mrs. Ellsworth."

Mr. Lyfford's effusive tendency annoyed her, but she was on the point of making the expected response when she remembered she must lay the groundwork for future avoidance of Mr. Wolfe. Therefore, flustered, she replied, "Oh, perhaps, though Mrs. Fellowes would not thank me to be always dancing when she has asked me to watch Miss Wright."

Lyfford gave an uncertain chuckle. "Ah, well. Perhaps I should ask you to dance this next with me, then, before the good dean's wife puts a stop to it."

"Can't," said Mr. Wolfe amiably, waiting through all this as if he were watching a diverting interlude.

"What, sir?" sputtered Mr. Lyfford, straightening his elongated frame until he stood an inch taller than the other. "What do you mean, 'can't'?"

"Nothing offensive, my good man, so there'll be no call to knock me down. I mean only that, unless Mrs. Ellsworth has forgotten or intends to cut me, I believe it's my turn."

CHAPTER SEVEN

**Hear me before your rashness
makes it quite too late to hear.
— Joseph Harris, *The mistakes, or,
The false report: a comedy* (1691)**

Colin was conscious of a singing, electric tension within himself as he led Mrs. Ellsworth to the set. In fact, he had been conscious of it the entire evening, as one would be aware of a hot wire threaded through one's center.

He was enjoying himself.

He was *alive*.

It was everything he had hoped: the sudden expansion of a world which had narrowed to the width of a coffin. Here were new surroundings. Light. Music. Dancing. New acquaintances. Flattering attention from every direction and every age. Young women like butterflies, hovering about him in their finery, hanging on his words and laughing at his merest pleasantries. Every last one of them an anti-Doria! How had he denied himself so long?

If momentary doubt assailed him at the commencement, a fear he might be classed with Lyfford as a codger or a trial to be endured, that anxiety soon vanished. For it happened that, whenever he requested the honor of a young lady's hand, she leaped at it. Miss Wright had, Miss Paulson had, Miss Terwilliger had. Everyone seemed to think him a first-rater. A diamond.

Granted, in Colin's eyes the young ladies seemed *very* young. Almost children, reciting lessons in charm and flirtation. It was plain Miss Wright would quickly grow into a proficient, while Miss Terwilliger would need much practice, but Colin thought he preferred Miss Paulson's style of straightforward admiration above either because it involved fewer giggles. But no matter his partner, he treated them all with identical avuncular good cheer, no more no less. For it was one thing to enjoy admiration and quite another to encourage any hopes.

Nor did his enjoyment prevent his gaze from wandering up the room from time to time toward Mrs. Ellsworth and her own three partners. What was she about? She seemed like a rational creature, and yet here she was—despite being entrusted with other duties—entertaining these danglers as if she had no idea what mischief men could invent! Surrounded by the county's freshest young misses, what could Lyfford, Dodge, and Bracewell want with an older woman such as her, if not her fortune?

But even as he called her old, some part of him noted her grace and lightness, the clearness of her gaze. Mrs. Ellsworth played no games, coined no smiles. When Dodge took her hand to cast outward, it seemed to Colin he too could feel her delicate fingers, the ones he had accidentally smashed at La Croix's.

She should be warned, he decided. With no husband to protect her and no chaperone to the chaperone, someone must warn her about fortune hunters. He hardly knew her, of course, but hearing advice from someone wholly uninvolved would gild the pill. After all, if any family member took it upon himself to caution her, might she not suspect an ulterior motive?

No, he would be the best messenger. But before he possibly angered her, he would indulge himself. Relax his guard. Brush the cobwebs from his own skills in flirtation and see if he could get those mild blue eyes of hers to flash and sparkle. It might even prove the best preamble to the thorny topic...

Mrs. Ellsworth was serene, even stern, as she faced him across the floor, her lashes lowered. Rather long lashes, he observed, surprised again. Thick and darker than her light-brown hair.

He wanted her to look at him. He did not expect chatter from her, but he thought she might at least look at him, as she had looked at Bracewell and Dodge and Lyfford. The hot wire running through him sparked, and he pretended to stumble.

That did it. Her eyes flew wide and her tender mouth parted in surprise.

"Oho," he said, "your wits haven't entirely gone wandering, then."

"How could they?" she replied. "For if you were to trip and fall upon me, it might cost me my life."

He grinned. "I will remind you, Mrs. Ellsworth, that it was *you* who dashed into *me* outside the cathedral."

"So I did, though had I dashed against the cathedral itself, it could not have struck me any harder."

Just when he congratulated himself that he got her talking, and in a fashion that bordered on flirtatious, she went quiet again, her gaze seeking out her charges.

"You will have your hands full with Miss Wright, I daresay."

"You would know about that," she muttered.

"What was that, Mrs. Ellsworth?"

She blinked at him innocently. "I said, how do you like your first Winchester assembly, sir?"

Her lie didn't even have the correct number of syllables, but he let it pass, merely raising a wry eyebrow.

"I have met many lovely people already," he answered, "and am inclined to believe I—*we*—will be quite happy in Hampshire."

After a pause she said, "And does Edmund agree with you? How does he like College?"

"I—don't know. They haven't had a holiday yet, of course."

"No, not till the feast of St. Matthew, but—" she went a faint pink "—I thought he might have said in a letter."

Colin felt his own face warm. Oh—then Mrs. Ellsworth's son William had written to her? It hardly need be said that Edmund's reserve encompassed his pen as well as his tongue.

She understood at once, and then she did look at him willingly, her eyes sympathetic. "You need not imagine Willsie wrote two pages, crossed. It was a note barely worth the name, and one of the scant two sentences was a request for our cook Wilcomb to send some of her shortbread!"

"But he said something about how he was faring?" he persisted.

"Ye-e-es...that he and Peter were put in the same chamber and that their prefects were strict but fair."

"Did he—mention Edmund?"

"He...did not. But, as I said, it was a very brief note. And I would be glad to ask after him when I write next, if you like." When they took hands again, she pressed his gently. With any other partner that evening, it would have been rank coquetry, but with Mrs. Ellsworth it was—it made his throat tighten. What was her strange power, that she could cut so easily through the humbug and lightness of polite conversation, to expose what he would keep hidden, sometimes even from himself?

Nor was she finished with her slicing, it seemed, for even her attempt to change the subject unsettled. "Tell me about Kent, Mr. Wolfe. I have never been. In fact, I have never been farther east than London. What is it like? Do you still have family there?"

"It's lovely. And yes," he said, more curtly than he intended. Which naturally made his reticence all the more obvious and awkward, but beyond giving him a puzzled frown, she let it alone.

Perhaps it was the dread of discussing family and antecedents which made him forge ahead clumsily.

"Did your husband never take you traveling?" he blurted. "To the coast or Bath or what not?"

Her look was wary. "We rarely traveled. To Oxford once or twice, to visit Tyrone when he was there. To town *very* occasionally. But all our family are here, and William preferred to be at home. Beatrice takes after him in that respect."

"But what of you? Would *you* have liked to travel?"

Mrs. Ellsworth's chin rose, and Colin supposed his tone had been oddly belligerent. "I don't know," she answered at last. "The question never presented itself to me. Would your Mrs. Wolfe have enjoyed this removal to Kent?"

Tit for tat.

He could not prevent a grimace. "So long as her pets came, I don't think Doria would have cared if we transplanted ourselves on the moon."

At his tone Mrs. Ellsworth stared and was late in beginning the figure-eight, forcing him to wait as well, in order not to cross in front of her. By the time they returned to face each other again, her lips were pressed in a line.

Here it comes—the matronly reprimand. And I daresay I deserve it for that jab at Doria.

But he was wrong.

Mrs. Ellsworth pressed her lips together even harder, causing them to disappear altogether, but then—a most unexpected sound.

She laughed. A warm, girlish laugh that she tried at once to stifle, only to have it burst out again. "Forgive me," she murmured. "It's just—dear me—do tell me how long one must be widowed before such opinions are allowed."

His own mouth twitched in answer. "I would venture it depends on the person. And probably they are never allowed in most cases. Mrs. Ellsworth, I hope it is true when I say I would never have said such a thing about my wife if you yourself were not a widow. That is, if you yourself did not understand that the deceased was not always a perfect saint."

"Speak for yourself," she retorted, before yielding to another wave of merriment. "Heavens." She fanned herself with her gloved hand. "You must pardon me, Mr. Wolfe. I have not been...in society in recent years, and I am sadly out of practice. It might be more fitting for Beatrice to chaperone *me*, than contrariwise."

That was when he spoiled everything, he thought later, when he revolved the scene in his mind. For everything had been jogging along. There they were, quite enjoying themselves, and there he was, thinking he had never considered the possibility of friendship with a woman, but if he ever had one, Mrs. Ellsworth would serve admirably—and then he dashed it all to pieces.

Because he replied with, "Perhaps you indeed ought to consult Miss Ellsworth. She seems a sensible girl who might prevent any rash, foolish acts."

"Do you mean foolish acts like laughing at your jokes, Mr. Wolfe?" she asked teasingly.

"I mean ones like remarrying in haste."

The mirth drained from her face, to be replaced by puzzlement. "What? I beg your pardon but what *can* you mean?"

"I mean, of course, that you're a fair target because of your—circumstances—Mrs. Ellsworth, as you can see from the attentions paid you this evening, and I would caution you."

"My 'circumstances'?" she repeated, her voice rising in pitch. "You mean my fortune, I suppose. And your implication is most unchivalrous."

"What implication?"

"That the gentlemen would seek me out for no other reason than for my money," she rejoined swiftly.

"Mrs. Ellsworth, this is kindly meant—"

"Oh? Then I will thank you to keep your kindness to yourself!"

"I did not say Lyfford and Dodge and their ilk danced with you only for your money—"

"No, indeed. You meant to say, I suspect, that the money came second to my youth and ravishing beauty."

"Mrs. Ellsworth!" he cried again, dismayed to find 'the best laid schemes o' Mice an' Men, Gang aft agley.' The dancers nearest them glanced over, and Colin struggled to rein in his temper.

"I did not intend to insult you," he said through gritted teeth. "After all, *I* asked you to dance, and I don't want your money."

"No. You asked me to dance in order to hector me." Her jaw worked as if she were fighting tears, and Colin felt like a villain. An angry villain, but a villain all the same.

"You realize, don't you, that I might issue you the same warning, Mr. Wolfe," she resumed. "Only—wealthy widowers are expected to marry again. It's almost their duty! But wealthy widows—if wealthy widows remarry, they must be fools. They must be 'taken in.'"

He threw up his hands. "I, for one, have no intention of remarrying in haste."

"And you suppose I *do?*" she hissed.

"You needn't fire up so—"

"No, no," she interrupted, "I am behaving badly, I know. And your own conduct is no excuse for mine. But if you did indeed dance with me so that you might tell me some home truths, I beg you would allow me to return the favor."

What else could he do? He bowed his head in permission, not that Mrs. Ellsworth seemed inclined to wait for it.

"*You* may have no intention of 'remarrying in haste,' but your mere presence at this assembly will raise hopes of that nature in many a young lady's mind."

"How can I help that? I did not come into Hampshire to become the Hermit of Beaumond. If I hope to make a home here, of course I must enlarge my acquaintance, of course I must be seen. And if I attend an assembly, of course I must either ask women to dance or hide in the card room, and I'll warrant the good folk of Winchester would find more to criticize if I hid in the card room!"

Mrs. Ellsworth was nothing if not reasonable and fair-minded. Even in her temper he saw his words were not without effect. She shut her eyes a moment, taking a long, settling breath.

"You are right," she said simply. "It is not you who are unjust, I admit. It is the world. You cannot help every girl and her mother scheming to marry you simply because you are there. I only ask that you will grant me the same latitude. That you will see that *I* cannot help everyone expecting me to be a lonely old fool, ready to leap upon the first man who asks, simply because I am a widow."

"Fair," he said. "Fair enough."

The dance was drawing to a close, but instead of feeling relief, Colin wished it might go on a little longer. Long enough for them to recover some of their earlier easiness. For though they had wrung these concessions from each other, the truce they came to felt altogether...insufficient. Were they friends? He doubted she would apply such a term to him, but he was all too conscious that he would very much like to apply the term to her.

"Who do you dance with next, Mrs. Ellsworth? Is there a fifth partner?"

"There is none," she replied. "Now I will be the dutiful chaperone and fade into the woodwork with the other older ladies."

"You could never," he said, meaning heaven only knew what. But classing her with the assemblage of staid matrons struck him as incongruous. Even if she was the same age as some of them, had any of those women Miranda Ellsworth's hidden fire?

"Of course I could," she replied, making her curtsey. "It is by virtue of having quarreled with you that I have gained distinction in your mind. If you were to offer the rest of them similar provocation, you would soon be able to tell them apart."

That was all she knew, Colin told himself grimly as he escorted her to precisely the station against the wall she indicated. Not all women could be provoked. He had been married to Doria for over fifteen years and had never once succeeded in riling her.

Mrs. Ellsworth had managed to do one thing: the hot wire within him lost its charge. Though he danced every remaining dance, including the dance before the tea with an Honourable Miss So-and-So, and though he continued to charm and amuse, the rest of the evening felt comparatively flat. If his partners noticed they gave no sign. They chatted and smiled and flirted and teased; they threw him arch looks and rapped him with fans; they hinted for second dances and frowned upon rivals.

It must be because his row with her cast a pall, he decided. Her warning that all the young ladies were setting their caps for him robbed him of his delight because it made him leery.

But that wasn't it, because even before his interchange with the widow he had already demonstrated a healthy leeriness.

It must be because he was unused to being at odds with a woman. It had been impossible to sustain an argument with Doria or even to start one, so it should be no surprise that clashing with Mrs. Ellsworth upset him. And no surprise that, whenever his gaze slid in that lady's direction, he felt his pulse speed.

Very well.

He would call at Hollowgate and ensure the matter was laid to rest. He would apologize once more for his interference, she would assure him of the sincerity of her pardon, and he would go in peace.

CHAPTER EIGHT

**He hath cast me into the mire,
and I am become like dust and ashes.**
— Job 30:19, *The Authorized Version* (1611)

Miranda was determined not to be at home the following day. Not only did she dread calls from Mr. Lyfford, Mr. Dodge, and Mr. Bracewell, but she wanted desperately to be left in peace for a few hours. Or, better yet, to be too busy to think.

By the time the Ellsworths took home Emmy Wright, yawning and triumphant, and returned to Hollowgate, it was well past one. Miranda tumbled into bed, mercifully too exhausted to be heartsore. When was the last time she had been up so late?

But the heartsoreness returned with a vengeance when she opened her eyes in the late morning.

He thought her a fool.

A fool who would mistake gentlemen's attentions for true affection.

No—he thought her worse than a fool. Because he held it necessary to remind her she held no charms beyond her money.

She groaned, rolling onto her stomach and burying her face in the pillow. What would it matter if doing so might make a crease in her skin? As Mr. Wolfe hastened to inform her, no one was interested in elderly Miranda Ellsworth's appearance. He, least of all.

Apparently one was never too old to learn something new, Miranda scolded herself. For this day's lesson was obvious: eight and thirty was not too old for vanity.

Rolling onto her back again, she bore out this conclusion by rubbing fiercely at her cheeks to eradicate any possible damage.

Worse, the lesson came with a corollary: eight and thirty was not too old to have one's vanity *mortified*. Because what had Mr. Wolfe told her, apart from what she had already told herself? That if anyone chose to pursue a widow of eight and thirty, who was mother to one son and stepmother to five others, when he might marry a blooming girl and begin with the equivalent of a tabula rasa, that man could only be motivated by a desire for wealth.

That, in so many words, had been Mr. Wolfe's message, and it should not torture her since she agreed with him.

But it did torture her.

"Get up," she said aloud. "Get up, Miranda, and go to it."

She threw off the coverlet as if she could throw off self-pity in the same manner. Eight and thirty might not be too old for vanity, and it might not be too old to have that vanity mortified, but it was certainly too old for moping.

She must obliterate Mr. Wolfe from her heart? Well, so much the better that he held such an opinion of her! It was but one short step from vanity to pride, and Miranda would take that step. For no one knew her secret—her ridiculous attraction to Mr. Wolfe—and no one need ever know. She would bury it in oblivion. For the sake of her own pride she would prove to herself, if no one else, that she was no fool.

"In fact, we will see who is the bigger fool," she muttered, unbraiding her hair and brushing it with unusual violence. "Mr. Wolfe may say he is in no hurry to remarry, but I doubt he's clever enough not to get caught! And it would serve him right if it's Emmy who does the catching."

Apart from Beatrice, the family was well into its day by the time she emerged, but Miranda found her daughter-in-law Aggie in the kitchen, consulting with Wilcomb and the nurse over the twins' porridge.

"Let me have one," Miranda commanded, taking one of the plump little baby girls in her arms and nuzzling her. "Mmm...Joan, I see. And let me give a kiss to little Margaret. Did they make a good breakfast?"

Some discussion of the infants' diet followed, but Aggie was soon plying Miranda with questions about the assembly.

"Yes, the number of gentlemen was more than adequate, and Bea and Emmy Wright danced every dance."

"Every dance! Heavens. No wonder Bea sleeps and sleeps. But she had better get up soon because some of her partners will likely come calling."

"Yes," agreed Miranda, "and won't you be so obliging, Aggie, as to sit with her if they do?"

"I would be happy to, Mrs. Ellsworth, only where will you be?"

"I have neglected some of our neighbors too long," she replied lightly. "Therefore I thought I would bring a basket to the Jeromes and one to poor Miss Hambly."

Aggie could not repress her shudder at the mention of the Jeromes, which was precisely what Miranda predicted. She hoped charity which was simultaneously self-serving still counted at least a little as charity, for she had chosen her objects knowing no one among the Ellsworths would willingly accompany her.

Miss Hambly was harmless enough, a lone, aged spinster living along the Weeke footpath. The death of her ancient aunt Mrs. Hambly some years earlier had scarcely eased Miss Hambly's situation in terms of money, but nor had it dampened her cheer, and she greeted Miranda with the usual effusions.

"Ah, Mrs. Ellsworth, like an angel you always are. Thank you, thank you for the basket. You are too, too, too kind. Won't you sit down? Ah, Hollowgate apples and—bless you!—a partridge. Has Mr. Tyrone Ellsworth been shooting, then?"

"I'm afraid he has never been one for shooting, Miss Hambly. Indeed, I blush to tell you this one was shot by Mrs. Nicholas Carlisle—by Araminta, that is. She claimed her little son George wanted very much to go shooting, but none of my sons-in-law do much of that, with the possible exception of Mr. Kenner, so she took it upon herself to demonstrate."

"My!" breathed Miss Hambly. But she had known the Ellsworths too long to wonder at Mrs. Carlisle's antics. "Did she bag many?"

"Two, to be precise. Mrs. Tyrone Ellsworth was with her at the time, and Aggie declared Minta shot more trees and clouds than anything else, but it was just as well because we haven't any hunting dogs, so they had to retrieve the birds themselves."

"And you've given me one of the two! Ah. So generous!"

"But I see I have not been your only visitor," said Miranda, to stem Miss Hambly's thankfulness. She gestured at the silver vase full of hydrangeas. "Did Mrs. Hemple bring you those?"

To her amazement, Miss Hambly's faded cheeks washed with pink. "Oh, dear me, no. Those are not from our good curate's wife, though Mrs. Hemple kindly sent me soup this week. Those are—those are from Beaumond."

"From *Beaumond*?" echoed Miranda, flabbergasted.

"Yes, indeed. From the new tenant there. Have you met him? A Mr. Wolfe. He was so kind as to call and introduce himself. He said he was meeting all the neighbors."

"But you live nowhere near Beaumond!"

Miss Hambly looked a little hurt by Miranda's incredulity, and she explained humbly, "My cottage is on the footpath from Weeke, so I am no near neighbor, to be sure, but I suppose he was out riding or walking and saw it."

"Of course," amended Miranda hastily. "And you keep your place so trim and inviting. Well. They are lovely flowers indeed."

"Aren't they?" Miss Hambly fluttered. "I'm afraid I was too open in my delight, however, for Mr. Wolfe then said, 'You like them, do you? I will ransack my gardens and hothouse and make sure you have a new bouquet every week.' Wasn't that too, too kind of him?"

"It was—is, rather—marvelous."

When she bid Miss Hambly farewell some while later, Miranda could not help but dart wary glances up and down the Weeke footpath. Whatever Mr. Wolfe's bizarre social habits, however, he was at present nowhere in sight.

Miranda debated. If these were his propensities, did she dare visit the Jeromes? They lived farther from the footpath but undeniably nearer Beaumond as the crow flew.

Shame at her own misgivings ultimately prevailed. Was she really considering neglecting her duty (not to mention returning to Hollowgate with Wilcomb's basket undelivered) because she was afraid to see the man? The *charitable* man?

Setting her shoulders, she picked up the basket and continued on her way to the Jeromes'.

Compared to poor Miss Hambly, the Jeromes were better off. Old Mrs. Jerome had an able-bodied son who sometimes worked, his fondness for gambling and carousal generally limited to racing season and the darker winter months. Moreover, Mrs. Jerome's daughter-in-law spun as much wool as she could manage and served the old woman with a patience Miranda could not fathom.

"So you've finally come again, have you?" grumbled old Mrs. Jerome, scowling at Miranda.

Miranda smiled in return, but more because she spied neither Mr. Wolfe nor any telltale hydrangeas. "I have. Good morning to you both."

"It used to be the great families knew their duties," sniffed Mrs. Jerome. "Mrs. Baldric that was came nearly every fortnight."

As the occasions referred to, whether real or not, occurred a good half-century earlier, Mrs. Jerome could not be gainsaid—not that Miranda or the younger Mrs. Jerome made the attempt. The younger woman merely unpacked the basket with soft, grateful glances at their visitor, while Miranda sat and listened to the familiar catalogue of grutching and fault-finding and nostalgia for the days of Mrs. Jerome's youth, when the world was a paradise second only to Eden.

"Look, Mother," said the younger Mrs. Jerome. "Wilcomb's shortbread and her quince jam. Shall I serve you some?"

"If you must, you must, though I would think that cook of yours would remember, Mrs. Ellsworth, that my teeth are not what they used to be."

"There's milk, too," said Miranda, taking a tumbling child on her lap. "You might soften the shortbread in it."

Mrs. Jerome grumbled, unable to think of an objection to this suggestion and, besides, wanting the shortbread very much. Quickly a dish was made up and set before her, the child looking on longingly, just as a knock came at the door.

Faced with the unprecedented challenge of hosting two separate visitors at once, the younger Mrs. Jerome froze with spindle in hand and stared at Miranda.

"Shall I get that, then?" Miranda offered.

The woman nodded, and Miranda set the child down, slipping him a fragment of biscuit from his grandmother's plate. Then she marched to the door and threw it open.

"Why, Mr. Wolfe!"

"Mrs. Ellsworth." Removing his hat, he ducked his head to peer around her. "And the ladies of the house. What good fortune to discover you here, Mrs. Ellsworth, for you may perform the introductions."

Dazed, she retreated a step to allow his considerable bulk entrance. "Whatever are you doing here?"

"I am being neighborly." From behind his back he produced a bouquet, this time of chrysanthemums, and strode across the room to present them to old Mrs. Jerome. "Madam."

The old woman gaped up at him, a crumb of shortbread clinging to her chin.

"Mrs. Jerome, this is Mr. Wolfe, the new tenant of Beaumond. Mr. Wolfe, the two Mrs. Jeromes."

"I'll put those in some water," breathed the younger Mrs. Jerome, springing up to receive the flowers. "Would you like some shortbread and milk, sir? Mrs. Ellsworth was so kind as to bring some."

Noting how old Mrs. Jerome clutched her goods closer at these words, he said, "Thank you, no. And who is this little chap?"

The little chap, whose own father was built on more modest terms, sucked his fingers and hid behind Miranda.

"Say how-do-you-do to Mr. Wolfe, Samuel," she instructed, but that only made the boy's eyes well, so Miranda resumed her seat and pulled him again onto her lap.

The younger Mrs. Jerome, having found a bucket for the chrysanthemums, started to drag the settle over, but Mr. Wolfe leaped to assist her. "How hospitable of you, Mrs. Jerome. How did you know a person of my size finds some chairs difficult to squeeze into?" Before she could answer, he fairly knocked the back of her knees with the only other chair in the room, and she obediently sank onto it.

"There," said Mr. Wolfe, perching delicately on the settle, which gave an ominous creak. "Now we are all comfortable."

"Thank you, sir," said the younger Mrs. Jerome, as if he were the host and they the guests.

Indeed, thought Miranda, the man had a way of dominating a space, especially one as confined as the Jeromes' cottage.

A little silence fell, broken only by the mumblings and chewing of old Mrs. Jerome.

"Beautiful country, this," Mr. Wolfe began loudly. "Beaumond is everything I could have hoped, and now that I have met you—" with a half-bow toward the Jeromes "—I will have made the acquaintance of all my neighbors."

The Jeromes made no audible response. The older plunked another wedge of shortbread in her cup of milk, and the younger spun furiously, her eyes entreating Miranda to take charge of speaking to the grand gentleman.

But Miranda was as addled by his sudden appearance as the other two. She cast about for something to say, something which would both ease the awkwardness as well as demonstrate that she viewed him with utter indifference.

She cleared her throat.

"I hope you are not overly fatigued from the assembly," said Mr. Wolfe. He nodded at the Jeromes. "I had the good fortune to meet Mrs. Ellsworth at the assembly last night."

"Thank you," Miranda answered, her voice happily steady and cool. "Despite my age, I was not crippled by fatigue."

One of his eyebrows lifted at this response. "No more than I, then, at *my* age, I trust."

Miranda said nothing. Was that meant to be a half-apology for calling her *old* the night before? Now as a concession, he courteously lumped himself with her?

Unknown to her, Colin felt equally at a loss. He turned his hat in his hands and then set it beside him on the settle. He had risen that morning at his usual hour, but the leaden weight on his spirit was not merely lack of sleep. It was the burden he had laid upon himself to apologize to Mrs. Ellsworth. Of course he could not ride over to Hollowgate for some hours, but he did so as soon as he thought it decent, only to find all of Winchester there before him.

He exaggerated, of course, but not much. Colin had taken one look at the number of horses tied up before the house and decided to leave his floral offering on the steps where Titus couldn't eat it. Then he followed the footman to the drawing room, calculating how he might draw Mrs. Ellsworth apart for long enough to have his say out.

He need not have bothered, for she was not there. Miss Ellsworth was, as was her sister-in-law Mrs. Tyrone Ellsworth. As were blasted Lyfford, Dodge, and Bracewell, along with a handful of other gentlemen calling on Miss Ellsworth.

The gentlemen talked of the Battle of Smolensk, which had taken place some weeks earlier but which was only now in the London papers. Lyfford held forth on battlefield medical care, which the ladies listened to with polite attention, while the other gentlemen fidgeted, impatient to introduce their own opinions. And Colin, though ordinarily as willing as any other Englishman to lambaste Napoleon and say what must be done to defeat him, could not be bothered with the man today. He edged his way around the room until he stood casually near Miss Ellsworth. Then he bent to pat the dog (Scamp growled) and murmured, "Is Mrs. Ellsworth not feeling quite the thing?"

She turned startled eyes on him. "Dear me. I should have said at once, Mr. Wolfe, only we had been talking about it before you came. Mama is quite well, thank you, but she is out. Gone calling."

"Oh?" Idly he stroked Scamp's ears, and the dog got up and moved away, well able to discern when the affection given him was a blind. "Calling at the deanery, I suppose?"

"Not calls like that," she answered. "She was taking baskets to two of our less fortunate neighbors, Miss Hambly and the Jeromes."

"Is that so? Miss Hambly I have had the pleasure of meeting, but not the Jeromes."

"That's because the Jeromes aren't a pleasure to meet," put in Mrs. Tyrone Ellsworth, causing Miss Ellsworth to giggle. "Or at least old Mrs. Jerome is not."

"Pleasure or not, I have made it a goal to meet all my neighbors as soon as possible," he resumed blandly. "Which way do they live?"

And now here he sat, with old Mrs. Jerome devouring her snack on one side and young Mrs. Jerome on the other spinning wool into thread as if her life depended on it, and Mrs. Ellsworth doing nothing at all. But he too could do nothing at all for as long as she chose to.

After some minutes he ventured pleasantly to old Mrs. Jerome, "That shortbread must be delicious."

"A-are you certain you aren't wanting some, sir?" young Mrs. Jerome squeaked.

Colin was tempted to accept the fearful offer, just to watch old Mrs. Jerome squirm, but Mrs. Ellsworth widened her eyes significantly at him and gave the barest shake of her head.

Then he *really* wanted to accept. The corner of his mouth curled.

Resignedly, young Mrs. Jerome laid aside her work, even as her mother-in-law growled something about, "Them that weren't asked to come," but before the long-suffering younger woman could march to the scaffold, as it were, Miranda spoke up.

"Please, don't bother getting him any. For it happens Wilcomb made a double batch. Wilcomb is our cook, you remember," she threw at him. "We will send some to Beaumond as soon as I return home. Which had better be now, I'm afraid."

So glad was old Mrs. Jerome not to share her goodies with the giant man that Miranda was spared the usual parting remarks about how, in the good old days, Mrs. Baldric's calls had not only been more frequent, but had lasted longer.

Soon enough the two guests were standing outside the cottage, Colin unwinding Titus' reins from the pump and Miranda tying the ribbons of her cloak with quick, exasperated fingers.

"Mr. Wolfe," she began, "I know you are new here, but I wish you would not tease old Mrs. Jerome. It is tempting, I realize, for she's so cross and impossible, but doing so only puts her in a temper, and poor young Mrs. Jerome is the only one on whom she may relieve her feelings."

"I suspect a woman like old Mrs. Jerome is perfectly able to put herself in a temper," he returned, "without help from anyone else."

But this would get him nowhere. He had sought her to make an apology, after all, not to vex her anew. Therefore he hastily added, "Henceforth I will take your word to heart, however, for indeed poor young Mrs. Jerome has her hands full with that one."

When he saw her shoulders lower in relief and her expression soften he made advantage of it. "Mrs. Ellsworth, I have a confession to make."

Instantly her guard was raised again. "Oh?"

"Yes. It was not by chance nor from an eagerness to share the delights of old Mrs. Jerome's company that I came here. In fact, I called at Hollowgate this morning (where you are much missed, to judge by the gentlemen I discovered in the drawing room), and, when asked, your daughter Miss Ellsworth revealed your whereabouts."

Miranda steadied herself, ruthlessly stamping down any hope which dared lift its head. Then she said without a tremble, "Well? And here I am."

"Yes." He cleared his throat. "The matter is this: I—er—wanted to beg your pardon for my...discourtesy last night. Er—people of our age and position, both male and female, must often be in danger of having their...finer qualities overlooked, or, rather, overshadowed, when money is involved. I did not—I did not mean to imply that you were...devoid of these finer qualities."

Her chin came up. She was blushing like a girl, and her normally mild blue eyes sparked at him.

There it was again, he thought. That secret fire of hers. Unbidden, it flashed through his mind: *Wonder what her marriage with old Ellsworth was like.*

"Thank you, Mr. Wolfe," she said coolly. "I appreciate your desire to make yourself clear. I hope you will also pardon me for any show of temper."

He grinned, making her heart do a little bounce. "You're no Mrs. Jerome, but perhaps with a few more decades of practice..."

Fleeing the effects of his charm, Miranda raised a hand and hurried away, calling over her shoulder, "Good day to you. I will send the shortbread along."

Colin swung himself up on Titus and watched her go.

"Interesting little creature, that one," he muttered. "Wouldn't you say?"

Titus, however, maintained his usual reserve. And when Mrs. Ellsworth was gone from view, with a click of his tongue and a squeeze of his thighs, Colin set the horse toward Beaumond.

CHAPTER NINE

O ALMIGHTY God, who by thy blessed Son didst call Matthew from the receipt of custom to be an Apostle and Evangelist: Grant us grace to forsake all covetous desires and inordinate love of riches, and to follow the same thy Son Jesus Christ, who liveth and reigneth with thee and the Holy Ghost, one God, world without end. Amen.
— Collect for the Feast of St. Matthew,
***Book of Common Prayer* (1662)**

There being no assembly the following week, Miranda thought it possible to avoid meeting Mr. Wolfe again, but she had not counted on Emmy Wright. Notes arrived daily at Hollowgate: did the Ellsworths care to visit the market? Would Miss Ellsworth like to walk up and down the High Street to shop? Did Beatrice and Mrs. Ellsworth plan on attending the Winchester music meeting?

Dutiful chaperone that she was (and determined as she was not to hide from Mr. Wolfe), Miranda consulted Beatrice on each of these occasions, and on each of these occasions, they went.

"It's not fair," complained Emmy as they perused the food offerings in the Market House. "The gentlemen all called on Beatrice after the assembly, but not a one of them called upon me!"

"I suspect it is more intimidating to call at the deanery," offered Miranda, inspecting the cones of loaf sugar. "Your grandparents are so respected in Winchester."

"You mean to say they are so *old*," sighed Emmy. "So old and living in the shadow of the cathedral, and the house is positively *infested* with clergymen coming and going. In fact, the only one of my partners who came was Mr. Bart, and even he begged my pardon when he was shown into the parlor and asked if Grandpapa would return home soon, for he had some diocesan business to discuss with him!"

"Half the gentlemen who called at Hollowgate were there for Mama," Beatrice laughed, "so you needn't envy me."

"I don't care, really," Emmy contradicted herself. "But I did think Mr. Wolfe would come. *He* shouldn't have been afraid of anyone, being older himself."

"He didn't, then?" asked Miranda lightly.

"No, and I waited and waited at home all day Friday and all this morning until you came—oh! There he goes!" She pointed eagerly at a passing phaeton, just as they emerged into the street. It was unmistakably Mr. Wolfe holding the ribbons, his broad shoulders appropriating the majority of the space in the dashing vehicle, but leaving just enough room for a fair passenger who laughed and clutched her bonnet. "Who was that with him?" Emmy demanded. "Did you get a look, Beatrice?"

"I think it was Miss Paulson, but I can't be certain."

Whoever it had been, however, it had not been Emmy Wright, and she grew sullen afterward, so that the Ellsworths were glad to deposit her back at the deanery. Sunday was church, but on Monday the girl coaxed them out again, this time to investigate netting supplies at the haberdasher's in the Square. Here Emmy was twice unlucky, for they arrived just as Mr. Wolfe was leaving, in laughing conversation on this occasion with Miss Terwilliger.

"Mr. Wolfe! Miss Terwilliger!" cried Emmy. "Good afternoon."

Mr. Wolfe made his elegant bow and nodded at each of them in turn. "Good afternoon. I hope your shopping will be as successful as my own has been." He lifted the brown-paper wrapped parcel in his hand.

"Did *you* not meet with success, Miss Terwilliger?" Emmy asked boldly, seeing that she grasped only her stocking purse but no parcels.

"I—have put off this particular errand," replied Miss Terwilliger with a blush. "Because Mr. Wolfe put me in mind of a book I promised Papa I would fetch for him from the circulating library. We are going there now."

Miranda was not the only one who suspected the girl had no thoughts of fetching any books until she learned Mr. Wolfe was headed in that direction, but she took a cautioning hold of Emmy's elbow.

Emmy shook it off. "My goodness, there was a book I have been meaning to get as well! Mrs. Ellsworth, why do we not accompany Mr. Wolfe and Miss Terwilliger?"

"I'm afraid the book will have to wait," Miranda said firmly. "There is time for only one errand today, and as we are already here..." With a quick curtsey she moved farther into the shop, leaving Emmy and Beatrice no alternative but to follow her, but Miranda was suitably punished for her obstruction the rest of the outing by having every comment of hers answered with a toss of the head and every suggestion of ribbon or trim sniffed at.

Miss Wright fared slightly better at the Winchester music meeting, for Mr. Wolfe sat across the aisle, several pews forward, where she could watch him to her heart's content. At the interval, seizing Beatrice's hand, Emmy and several other young ladies swarmed him, and he entertained his admirers with spirit and flow.

Or, at least, that was how it appeared to Miranda. She herself was beset by her three suitors, Mr. Lyfford, Mr. Dodge, and Mr. Bracewell, and thus obliged to give them polite attention and make appropriate responses. When Emmy returned to her seat, Miranda was therefore surprised to find a now-familiar furrow marking the girl's brow.

"What's the matter?" she murmured, unable to resist asking. "Did you not succeed in speaking with Mr. Wolfe?"

Emmy shrugged, but Miranda saw her twist her fan in her lap. It was not till she and Beatrice were alone in the chaise, rain pattering on the roof, that Miranda learned more. Patting a yawn from her mouth, Beatrice leaned against her arm.

"Do you know, Mama, if not for Emmy's preoccupation with Mr. Wolfe, I would say I was beginning to like her. She is lively and full of ideas, and because she talks a lot, I don't have to."

"She is indeed lively," was Miranda's measured response.

"But whenever Mr. Wolfe is around or *might* be around, it ruins everything." Bea straightened, pulling back the curtain to see the drops running down the pane. "Tonight, for instance, we all had to go and stand around him, as if he were the sun and we the planets. And he's a very pleasant man and had interesting things to say about the music and really *listened* to what others said to him, but—"

"But...?"

"But it was as if he were a schoolmaster hearing lessons. He gave no girl any more attention than another and was equally agreeable to all, which should have made Emmy happy, but instead it vexed her."

"I suppose she would have preferred to be singled from the rest," Miranda suggested. "For better or worse, she has conceived a *tendre*, but if he does not reciprocate her feelings, maybe with time she will cease to think of him."

"I hope so," agreed Beatrice solemnly. "But I wish he wouldn't make Emmy angry with *me*."

Miranda drew away from her to see her more clearly. "What on earth do you mean, dearest?"

"I mean there I was, hovering at the edge of the circle, when Mr. Wolfe raises his voice and says, 'How are you and Mrs. Ellsworth enjoying the concert, Miss Ellsworth?' and then everyone looks my way, as if I had been hopping up and down, begging him to notice me."

"And how did you answer?"

"I said 'I like it very well, thank you,' just so everyone would stop looking, but then he said, 'And Mrs. Ellsworth? I can see Lyfford, Dodge and Bracewell have driven her into a corner, so even if you young ladies cleared a path, I wouldn't be able to put the question to her.' So then I had to say more! I told him you thought the Canzonettas charming. Because you did, didn't you, Mama? I hope you don't mind."

"I don't mind," said Miranda.

"I thought you wouldn't. But Emmy positively hissed at me afterward about how unseemly it was to put myself forward, and I was so outraged I said she would know all about that, wouldn't she, so now I suspect we will have to smooth it over next time."

Chuckling ruefully, Miranda let her head fall back against the cushion.

She and Mr. Wolfe might never hold another conversation of any length or importance, but it seemed they were still communicating in a fashion. Via Beatrice she understood he had told her the truth: he had no wish to remarry at present and was being very careful not to mislead any of his numerous admirers. Nor had he neglected the opportunity to remind her what he thought of her three swains.

Later, Miranda blamed Mr. Lyfford for her inattention to circumstances on the Feast of St. Matthew.

As soon as the curate Mr. Hemple dismissed the congregation, she left her family to linger and converse, while she hurried home to confer with Wilcomb.

"Master Willsie's first holiday," beamed the cook. "Never fear. It's all in hand. All his favorites, and plenty of it."

"Well, let me help," Miranda urged, tying on an apron. "I will cut the seeds out of the raisins for the whitepot." As Wilcomb's recipe required an entire cup of them, besides a cup of dates which must be pitted, Miranda was still working when the maid Boots appeared.

"There you are, madam! Bobbins and I have been looking everywhere."

"Has William come already?" she asked eagerly, beginning to wipe her hands clean as the kitchen maid Clement untied her apron.

"No, madam. It's a Mr. Lyfford calling."

Miranda narrowly avoided groaning in dismay, but Boots guessed at it because she added, "Bobbins put him in the small parlor because the others fled when he told them who had come."

Cowardly custards! Not that she blamed them. Beatrice and Aggie had borne the heat of the day on Mr. Lyfford's prior visit, after all.

Marching after Boots, Miranda braced herself.

The wind must have gained in strength since the church service because Mr. Lyfford's tuft of white hair was quite wild. He was engaged in trying to bring order to it when she entered the room.

"Mrs. Ellsworth, how fortunate to find you at home this time." He gave his toppling bow, causing the tuft to spring loose again.

"Yes, here I am. I would not be anywhere else today because this is my son William's first holiday from Winchester. Mr. Tyrone Ellsworth says Willie will have morning services and likely be assigned cricket duties thereafter, but when that is done he should be at liberty, so we expect him at any time." It was, she admitted to herself, a fairly heavy hint that Mr. Lyfford's call should be short, but the hospital chaplain did not appear embarrassed by it.

"I hope, then, Mrs. Ellsworth, that my gift will encompass him," he beamed.

"Your—gift?"

The smallest parlor did not hold her workbasket, so Miranda extracted some tangled netting she found thrust between the cushions, which was either Aggie's pitiful handiwork or something chewed by the dogs.

"Yes," declared Mr. Lyfford. "My gift." Springing forward, he presented her with a flat parcel. "I meant to present it sooner, but there was a sudden demand after the music meeting."

Bemused, Miranda slid her finger under a corner of the brown paper, opening it to reveal two of the Haydn Canzonettas they had heard, "The Mermaid's Song" and "A Pastoral Song." Despite them coming from him, she could not hide her pleasure.

"Why, how delightful! Thank you, Mr. Lyfford. This will indeed be a gift for the whole family. How very thoughtful of you."

The genuine smile which lit her face encouraged him very much, and he hastened to pick up his chair and set it nearer hers. "How pleased I am you will enjoy them. I hope you will invite me to hear your family perform. To judge from your speaking voice, your singing must recall the angelic host."

"Thank you," she almost grimaced, stiffening in sudden awareness and setting the sheet music down beside her. How she wished he would leave off with the ridiculous compliments! "I don't know that I do much singing before strangers, but I am sure, when my family have had time and practice, you would be welcome to listen."

As a hospital chaplain, Mr. Elias Lyfford was by no means blind to signals given by a person's words and attitudes, and he quickly saw he had overstepped. He had alarmed the widow and set her on her guard. Therefore he now retreated, both in person, shifting his chair away a few feet, and in address.

"Take all the time you require," he said grandly. "But I hope, in practicing, you will remember the pleasures of that evening. How excellent is music, for expressing the ineffable! Are we joyful? It helps us to dance. Are we sad? It gives our mourning voice. Do we dare not speak? It speaks for us."

The wonder of music was safer ground, and Miranda unbent partially. When he proceeded to soliloquize on Examples of the Efficacy of Music on Hospital Patients, she relaxed further, listening with as much patience as she could while she untangled the netting. Perhaps he was leading up to a request for a donation. Miranda had spoken with Tyrone and learned that, yes, her late husband had given a gift or two to the hospital, and she was willing enough to continue the practice, especially if doing so would send Mr. Lyfford on his way.

Here the chaplain found himself in a predicament. He could see he was making progress, but toward what? All his talk had been of the hospital. If he were to get down on one knee now and offer for her, would she not be surprised at the turnabout? Or would goodwill toward the hospital extend toward its chaplain? And he must be quick about it, whatever he decided, if this son of hers threatened to appear at any moment. But if it were too soon to propose, should he not salvage what he could and secure a donation for the hospital?

He must test the water. See if movement toward personal matters met with kindness or reproof.

Drawing himself up, he smoothed his tuft. "Mrs. Ellsworth, I cannot tell you what joy it brings me to have a sympathetic listener."

"Oh. Thank you." Miranda held up the netting and picked at a remaining knot.

"I grew up without siblings, you see, and lost my parents when I was at university."

"I am sorry for it, sir."

"But perhaps it is my lonely life which has enabled me to connect with the hospital patients—to form ties of sympathy and understanding."

"That makes sense. They are fortunate to have you."

Perhaps it was the softness of her voice. Its native warmth lulled him.

With another dab at his tuft, Mr. Elias Lyfford committed himself. He would make the fatal plunge.

"Mrs. Ellsworth!" He jumped up to dash across the small parlor and lower himself to one knee, but the edge of his shoe unluckily caught the corner of the carpet, pleating it up before him so that one foot slipped over the well-polished floor as a skater over ice, while the rest of him was left behind. Not being a naturally flexible man, the stretch his legs were put to resulted in a roar of fear and pain, followed by a noisy collapse at her feet, his head landing squarely in her lap.

The door opened.

"Mercy!" breathed Aggie, peering over Boots' shoulder. "Is—everything all right?"

Mr. Lyfford was attempting to scramble up, but his leg muscles refused to cooperate, so it was a clumsy affair. Miranda assisted with a panicked shove, her face aflame.

"It is nothing. Mr. Lyfford fell down. Am I needed, dear? Or would you like to join us?"

"No, thank you, Mrs. Ellsworth. That'll do, Boots. You may go," added Aggie, though Miranda thought dismissing the maid at this point was like shutting the stable door when the horse was already in the next county. Boots, for her part, vanished at once, eager to spread the shocking news of the hospital chaplain sprawled in the mistress's lap.

"I just wanted to say that I sent a note to the Fairchilds," Aggie explained, "in case they would like to join us for dinner. They might prefer Peter all to themselves, but I wanted them to know they would be welcome."

"That was so thoughtful, Aggie. Thank you. Willie hasn't come yet, then?"

"Not yet. Well. I'll leave you now. Good day to you, Mr. Lyfford."

Still breathless, the hospital chaplain managed no more than a wave and a nod, but he succeeded in hauling himself into his chair as the door shut again. "Mrs.—Ellsworth. I b-beg your pardon. I cannot begin to express my chagrin at my lamentable clumsi—"

"Please, Mr. Lyfford, say nothing of it. These accidents do happen." Miranda thoughtlessly stuffed the netting she had worked so diligently to untangle back between the sofa cushions and rose, only to wring her hands when she remembered Mr. Lyfford would then be compelled to struggle to his feet. "Please—do not trouble yourself, sir. But you see I should probably return to the kitchen now. I was helping our cook with the dinner. I do thank you for calling and for the music."

But Mr. Lyfford was not to be denied now. Not when he had already paid a price in pain and embarrassment. "Mrs. Ellsworth," he panted. "I beg you—hold one minute. There is something I would say."

Miranda fidgeted like a schoolgirl at her first dance lesson. *Please, please, please let it be a petition for money.*

But no.

With another groan, he lowered himself to one knee. Lord only knew how he would ever get up again.

"Mrs. Ellsworth, you may have guessed from my attentions at the deanery and the assembly and the music meeting and again today, that I have been—*enraptured*—by your charms."

"Please don't, Mr. Lyfford."

"Simply *enraptured.*"

"Mr. Lyfford, I beg you will excuse me—"

"Stay, Mrs. Ellsworth!" he commanded. "I must tell you that, from the moment we met, I was utterly convinced you were the woman I had waited for all my life. So lovely, so charming, so amiable, so wise, so kind, so—so—"

"So rich?" she supplied, vexation spurring her.

"What?"

"Come, Mr. Lyfford. Let us be frank. If I were not so very wealthy, would my manifold charms so soon have thus overpowered you?"

Her candor rendered him speechless for a minute, but he rallied. (He also tried to rise from his knee, but a twinge in his thigh making him think better of it, he remained in his supplicatory position.)

"Mrs. Ellsworth, your honesty—your straightforwardness—is as refreshing as it is rare, and only adds to your virtues. I utterly deny, however, that your fortune contributes to my feelings for you, except in that it makes possible my confession of them. In all truth, I am not a rich man, and had you not had some moneys of your own, I would have been forced to nurse my ardor in secret, unable ever to act upon it. Unable to hope it might ever be spoken."

"Well, now it has been spoken," returned Miranda, with commendable self-control, considering that what she would like to do most in the world would be to box the man's ears. "And I thank you for your *professions*." She gave the word more emphasis than she meant to, but he had touched upon a sore spot. If he had not pretended to discover quite so many charms, he would have pleased her better. "But I'm afraid I have no intention of remarrying at present. Please accept this as my final answer, and I hope my refusal will not prevent us from remaining—friendly—in future. Thank you, Mr. Lyfford. If you don't mind, I will let you see yourself out."

Such an encounter was not easily recovered from, and Miranda in her weakness retreated to her bedchamber to avoid questions and whispers. Some tears were shed, more in anger and vexation than anything else. How mortifying to have Mr. Wolfe be right! For him to say Miranda's suitors only wanted her fortune. The speed with which Mr. Lyfford fell at her feet only validated this conclusion, and the chaplain's enumeration of her supposed other allures added insult to injury.

She might not be as lovely as Mr. Lyfford insisted, but the day's emotions did not mend matters, so then she had to repair the redness and puffiness of her eyes, and altogether it was more than an hour before she descended to the ground floor again to find the table being set for dinner and Tyrone gone to call the boys in.

"The boys?" asked Miranda. "If Peter came, where are the Fairchilds?"

"Peter didn't come," answered Beatrice. "It's the other one who's here. The big one. Edmund Wolfe."

Chapter Ten

When he was yet a great way off, his father saw him, and had compassion, and ran, and fell on his neck, and kissed him.
— Luke 15:20, *The Authorized Version* (1611)

By one o'clock Colin decided Edmund wasn't coming.

He had spent the morning refusing to anticipate his son. On the contrary, Colin walked into Winchester to read the newspapers at the coffee house, leisurely and thoroughly. He walked back, only glancing behind him on the Weeke Road twice or thrice and telling himself Edmund might have preferred the footpath.

At half-past one he still lingered in the drawing room because the windows looked out on the drive. It was one thing to tell himself Edmund had decided not to come and another altogether to believe it. His first holiday, and the boy didn't bother to come home?

He had written—one short paragraph—that Colin suspected Mrs. Ellsworth bribed from him with the gift of shortbread, but the paragraph told his father nothing. *I am in Fifth. There are eight of us. I am the second Junior in Chamber. Because of my size I am always chosen as the fire-screen.*

Colin told himself he would ply the taciturn boy with questions when he saw him in person, and now he did not come!

But—lo—someone else approached. Someone on horseback. A liveried servant. The man slid off, tapped the horse on the muzzle and, without bothering to tie the beast up, climbed the Beaumond steps, slipping out of view. Was it some urgent letter? Perhaps Edmund had taken ill. But would the headmaster send a liveried servant to tell him?

Taking a seat and opening a book, Colin waited. He heard Quill answer the door, followed by muffled conversation, voices rising and falling, even a chuckle. Edmund could not be ill, then. Just when Colin thought he would burst with impatience, he heard the footman approaching.

"Note for you, sir, from Hollowgate."

Without even a lift of his eyebrows, Colin reached for it.

Hollowgate

21 September 1812

Dear Mr. Wolfe,

I am writing to invite you to dinner this very afternoon. In fact, as soon as you receive this, if you choose to join us. Please send your response with Gotch and let us know if we should wait for you.

It seems your son Edmund came home with my son William, which is perfectly agreeable with us—the more being the merrier, as it were—but I thought you might have planned on seeing him.

Yours respectfully,
Miranda Ellsworth

Colin crumpled the note in his hand. Edmund gone home with William Ellsworth! Without even a word to his own father?

The footman cleared his throat. "Your answer, sir?"

Colin turned fiercely on him. Unjustly, truth be told. "Was this what you and that fellow were chuckling about?" he demanded. "Master Edmund not coming to Beaumond?"

"What? No, sir!" The unexpectedness of this charge startled the footman from his usual impassivity.

"What, then?"

"Sir, nothing at all to do with Master Edmund. Or Beaumond, even. It was—just a trifle of servant's gossip Gotch shared." In his eagerness to deflect Wolfe's temper, he unwisely added, "Some nonsense. It seems a Hollowgate maid discovered Mrs. Ellsworth with a gentleman caller *flung across her.*"

Quill realized his mistake as soon as Wolfe sprang up, his face darkened. "I'll thank you not to repeat such things about a respected and respectable neighbor."

"Yes, sir," gulped Quill. He retreated a step. "Er—what message for Gotch, then? The undergroom from Hollowgate, I mean."

"You may pass that identical message to Gotch," Colin bit out.

"Yes, sir. To be sure. But—uh—in answer to the note?"

"I'll go. Tell Tolbert to saddle Titus."

"Good afternoon, sir," the Hollowgate footman greeted him. "Please, follow me."

The undergroom Gotch had had the good sense to stay out of Colin's sight, but Colin could not help viewing every servant with suspicion now. Had *this* one too just come from spreading rumors and lies about Mrs. Ellsworth? His wrath was not entirely justified, he realized. For while half of him resented their chatter, the other half wanted to ask who, exactly had been closeted with the woman.

But he put this vexing question aside for the present as he was ushered into the drawing room, where sat Edmund, taking up more than half of a chaise longue. His son rose with signs of neither haste nor embarrassment. "Good afternoon, Father."

"Welcome, Mr. Wolfe," said Mrs. Ellsworth, hurrying toward him after she rose from her curtsey. "How pleased I am you could join us at such short notice. We have just been hearing all about my William's first fortnight at school, but we deferred asking Edmund any questions, that you might hear his answers as well."

He saw that she either had a cold or had been weeping, for her eyes and face were pink, and he promised himself he would get to the bottom of the matter before he left. For the present, he held out a parcel. "Thank you for your kind invitation. This is a little something for the family, but you needn't open it now because I suspect I have held up dinner long enough."

They were seven at table, with Mrs. Ellsworth at the head and Tyrone Ellsworth at the foot. Because of the size of Colin and his son Edmund, they were given the entire side of the table to Mrs. Ellsworth's right, with the other Ellsworths ranged across from them.

Later Colin would think it was both one of the most pleasant and most painful meals he ever had. Pleasant, in that Edmund spoke more words in the space of two hours than Colin could ever recall, and painful, in that Edmund spoke more words in the space of two hours than Colin could ever recall.

Which was not to say Edmund spoke a great deal. But somehow, in the noise and flow of the Ellsworth table, he jumped in or was coaxed in more than once.

"The prefects aren't a bad bunch," little William informed the table, "at least compared to other years, some of the older Juniors say. Except for Grimes. He hates any boy who is bigger than he is."

"And he's a gnat," said Edmund to the chunk of bread in his hand.

"So he is, Wolfe!" cried Willie, thumping an enthusiastic fist on the table. "Grimes is a gnat! A shrimp!"

"A peppercorn," said Edmund.

"A pygmy!"

"A hop-o'-my-thumb."

Both boys gave way to laughter, Willie's a shout while Edmund's was silent, his shoulders shaking. His father stared at him.

Miranda interposed. "Is this poor Grimes as small as all that?"

"You wouldn't call him 'poor Grimes' if you saw how he was," insisted William. "But, no," he admitted. "Honestly, he's about my size, though he's four years older. It's just that everyone seems small to Edmund here. And Grimes is small in character because he uses his position to bully all the Juniors."

"Is the dastardly Grimes a prefect in your chamber?" asked Tyrone Ellsworth.

Willie's gaze slid to Edmund across the table, but Edmund had resumed drinking his soup. "No-o-o...Grimes is in Fifth."

"Fifth?" spoke up Colin, he too glancing at his son. "Isn't Fifth your chamber, Edmund?"

"Fifth, yes."

"Then does he bully you?"

Edmund only hunched nearer the table, reminding Miranda of when the dog Pickles chewed something he should not have. On such occasions, Pickles would hide his head behind the window-curtains until his dishonor passed. As for Colin, he regretted the question the instant it left his lips because he could see he had shamed his son.

It was Tyrone who rescued them. "Of course he does, I imagine. Or tries to. There's always at least one of those sorts about, sadly. But if your chamber's other prefect is worth the name, he will prevent such things if he can."

"Forster's all right," muttered Edmund.

"But do you *like* school, boys?" Miranda pressed, trying to keep motherly anxiety from her voice. "Or think you will grow to like it?"

"It'll turn up trumps," Tyrone encouraged them. He added with a teasing grin, "And you'd better grow to like it, Willie my boy, because I have no intention of tutoring you until you're ready for university." But William needed none of this.

"It already has turned up trumps!" he insisted. "There isn't much schoolwork to do, and Seniors do get high-handed from time to time, but there's great fun to be had. Peter and Mundo and I like it very well, generally, don't we, Mundo?"

"Mundo" regarded William in his stolid fashion, but the corners of his mouth tipped up at last. "We do."

Relief flooded Colin, and he could hardly determine what comforted him most: Willie's obvious liking for Edmund, Edmund's hint of a smile, or the mere fact that his son had been given a nickname. To the father's discomfiture, he felt his throat constrict. Because it would all come right in the end, bullying prefect or no bullying prefect, if Edmund liked Winchester and had made friends.

His gaze met Mrs. Ellsworth's, and it was so obvious that they were experiencing similar feelings, they could not help but smile at each other. Yes. It would be all right.

Through the conversation around the table, Colin was able to interpret the bare lines of his son's earlier note. Edmund being the "second Junior in chamber" meant he was the boy responsible for the chamber's crockery and was further required to produce a pint-cup of any beverage at any time of day when requested by his superiors.

"But Peter has it worse," declared William, "because he's a prefect's valet and has to fetch Rushworth's water in the morning and carry his washing things and his books all through the school to chapel in the morning and back in the evening."

"I begin to see why Florence and her Robert argue about these things from time to time," Miranda sighed. "You see, Mr. Wolfe, my oldest stepdaughter has always thought the school too demanding on its youngsters, and her husband Mr. Fairchild has always replied that, not only do manners makyth man, but the process is also helped along by a good dose of manual labor."

"Not to mention mischief, revilement, and martyrdom," quipped Tyrone, at which they all laughed, and his wife Aggie flicked him with her fingers.

"Edmund, you wrote to me that you are always chosen as the fire-screen," Colin addressed him, hoping the boy in this setting would answer in more than a monosyllable. "Did you mean that in a literal sense?"

The ladies gasped in incredulity, but Edmund only nodded, and it was left to William to exclaim, "Well, that only makes sense because Mundo is just the right size. If *you* were a prefect, Mama, and the fire got too hot, you would be glad of him to shield you from the blaze."

"Indeed, I remember fire-screen duty," Tyrone chuckled. "That falls under 'martyrdom' because one needs to rotate continuously to prevent scorching."

Again the ladies protested this abuse, but Colin saw once more that little curve to his son's lips and understood it took much of the sting from the practice to know a grown man like Tyrone Ellsworth, too, had once been a living fire-screen.

When the lingering meal was finished and Wilcomb's whitepot devoured, the boys reluctantly agreed they should return to school, Tyrone offering to drive them in the barouche. In the flurry of embraces, Colin decided once more to push his luck. He took hold of Edmund's shoulders, which Edmund tolerated admirably.

"My boy, this has been delightful, but I hope you will come to Beaumond at Michaelmas."

Edmund made no reply, but his brow knit.

"And perhaps write to me in the meantime, if only a line or two," Colin pursued. "Is there anything you wish me to send? Any food or other item?"

"No, sir. I don't know." The boy's large shoulders slumped. Then he pulled himself loose to bend down and play with the dogs. Colin watched him, a matching frown marring his own brow, and it was only when Edmund shook his hand at the last that he gave his father a glimpse into his opaque thoughts.

"Beaumond is quiet," he said.

And then he was gone.

Miranda fully expected Mr. Wolfe to excuse himself once Tyrone and the boys departed. Aggie had, in order to trip upstairs and see how her babies Joan and Margaret fared, and Beatrice retreated to the pianoforte, turning over the new music Mr. Lyfford had presented.

But no. Mr. Wolfe stared absently into the drawing room fire, which must mean he intended on staying for tea.

She wondered if he resented her interference. He had seemed to appreciate the meal with his son, but perhaps he resented her *knowing* he appreciated it. Perhaps he resented the obligation of it. A small sigh escaped her. Was it not already hard enough to raise a child alone? Shouldn't all help be welcome, even if it was uncomfortable to admit needing help?

As Beatrice played, Boots entered with the tea things, so with a last glance at Mr. Wolfe, Miranda settled herself to prepare it.

"May I?" Taking a seat, he accepted the cup from her, refusing the offer of sugar and milk.

"You look dreadfully solemn," said Miranda. "Did you not think the boys were looking well?"

"Yes. *Yes.* As well as could be expected. That is, yes."

Miranda's eyebrows rose, but she let him gather his thoughts, and soon enough he favored her with a severe look.

"He said—Edmund said—Beaumond was 'quiet.'"

"Well, I imagine it is, compared to school, where there are eight boys in his chamber alone."

"I don't think that's what he meant."

"Oh! Then you think he meant compared to Hollowgate? I suppose it is. There is always so much activity here. So many of us, not to mention the dogs—"

His mouth twisted. "You think if I got Edmund a dog it would mend matters...?"

"He does seem to like Scamp and Pickles," Miranda replied deprecatingly. "And getting a dog is much more manageable and quicker than getting him a family."

That forced a short laugh from him. He ran fingers through one of the silver streaks at his temple. "So it is."

"Mr. Wolfe—if you would pardon my asking..." Miranda's heart beat faster. He had not to this point been very forthcoming about his family in Kent. People only knew that he *was* from Kent, an estate in Kent. She set down her own teacup. "I know you don't want to marry anytime soon, as we have discussed, so perhaps it would be worthwhile to ask...other family members to join you. Have you not got that favorite stand-by? A poor relation, or an unmarried sister, or perhaps even a widowed one with children? For years I was my brother Clifford's companion at the rectory."

"I don't think Edmund longs for an elderly woman or maiden aunt at Beaumond," answered Colin dryly.

Which did not answer her question. Miranda was tempted to drop the matter, but her next words emerged almost without her consent. "Such a person might make it—easier—for you as well. She would provide some companionship."

He too set his cup down and leaned back in his chair, one elbow on the arm of it and his hand rubbing his chin. "How thoughtful of you, Mrs. Ellsworth." His pale eyes glinted. "But what makes you suppose I long for companionship? It was Edmund we were speaking of."

"So it was." There was something challenging and almost flirtatious in his look, but she forced herself to shrug. "Far be it from me to disturb your hermitical tendencies, if you are content to live alone with only paid servants for company. I could never do it. After Tyrone and Aggie married, they spoke of building a lodge on the property and removing there, but neither my husband nor I wanted them to go. And when William died, I was so very glad to have the house full." Her mild blue eyes turned on him, candid and clear. "I know you've made Miss Hambly's acquaintance—I saw your hydrangeas there. So you will understand when I confess—I dread ever becoming a Miss Hambly, old and alone."

His expression softened. "Poor Miss Hambly. Her circumstances are indeed unenviable. But I would argue that the situation is altogether different for a single man."

"Of course it is. Especially if that single man has money. I need no persuasion to see the obvious. The situation would be different in large degree for me, too. Because of my money."

To her surprise, he sighed. "That's right. The glories and wonders of money. It can buy comfort, companionship, even a spouse."

He was thinking of Doria again, which was fortunate because Miranda thought of Mr. Lyfford and went quite crimson.

To hide her discomfiture, she hurried onward. "The introduction of family members at Beaumond would yield additional benefits, I believe."

His grin returned. "You mean, besides noise for Edmund and undesired companionship for me?"

"Yes." She ignored his joke. "They would provide chaperonage, if some of the young ladies called upon you. I find the presence of my relations at Hollowgate makes it easier to go about my life."

"I see..." his voice lowered to a rumble, and he sat forward, his large frame suddenly looming close. "At last you make sense. Note how the presence of Miss Ellsworth throws a cloak of propriety over my visit. Not only my visit, but over my sitting so near to you."

Miranda couldn't help it. She edged an inch away, as if, like Edmund in Fifth Chamber, she were the fire-screen in danger of scorching. Nor was her movement lost on him, and the corner of his mouth quirked as imperceptibly as his son's ever did.

"And her practice on the pianoforte quite drowns whatever indecorous speeches I might be making to you, my dear Mrs. Ellsworth."

"I am not your dear Mrs. Ells—"

"Good heavens," he interrupted, in his usual voice. He straightened. "I *thought* the piece sounded familiar. But it took a few minutes of Miss Ellsworth's practice before she played them at the expected tempo. Is that not one of Haydn's Canzonettas we heard at the music meeting?"

Miranda thought of Mr. Lyfford's gift and blushed again. "Er—yes."

But Mr. Wolfe was on his feet, striding to the instrument. "Brava, Miss Ellsworth! You must have enjoyed the performance indeed, to rush out and purchase the music."

"But I didn't," answered Beatrice, her fingers still poised above the keys. "That is, I enjoyed it, but this music was given to us today by Mr. Lyfford."

To the young lady's surprise, Mr. Wolfe's eyes narrowed with a dangerous glitter, and she drew back, alarmed. But she must have imagined it, for it vanished the next instant, and he was saying, "Delightful. Do, please, keep playing. Your mother and I are enjoying it vastly."

After a hesitation, Beatrice obediently applied herself again, but she was not sorry when Mr. Wolfe recrossed the room to resume his seat.

Miranda had made use of the short reprieve to calm herself and master her expression. It would never do for Mr. Wolfe to suspect how easily he discomposed her. But she need not have bothered, for he made mincemeat of her efforts with his next speech.

"Forgive me, Mrs. Ellsworth. You were saying something about the presence of relatives providing chaperonage and perhaps making themselves useful in the prevention of gossip? Yes. Curious you should say so, for I heard a choice tidbit myself this afternoon. Lyfford's music reminded me of it."

"O-oh? Well. I'm sure it need not be repeated here," Miranda replied. "The only defense against gossip is never to repeat it."

"But I thought you considered the presence of relatives a more effective defense against gossip."

Miranda waved a vague hand and began to gather the tea things. "Yes. Of course. And so they are."

"And yet your own relatives seem to have left you all unguarded today, if rumor is to be believed," he persisted. "For a little bird told me that Lyfford called here and—how shall I put it?—made rather *free* with the privilege."

She considered denying it but knew it was already plain to him from her discomfiture that the gossip was true. Therefore, with what dignity she could muster, she lifted her chin and said frostily, "He may have. He *did*. What I mean to say is, as you predicted he might, Mr. Lyfford proposed to me and was refused."

"Then what," he mused, affecting the same detachment, "was he doing lying in your lap, madam?"

It was Miranda's turn to blaze up, and blaze up she did.

"He *fell*, Mr. Wolfe," she hissed. "He was crossing the room, and he *fell*. You know how tall and pole-like he is! I could have been sitting in the next county, and he would still have landed on me. So you can just go back and tell all your gossiping friends what really happened. But never, never mention it to me again."

Miranda was not impulsive by nature, nor harsh, and she was already thinking she would lie awake half the night dwelling uncomfortably on this loss of self-control and what Mr. Wolfe would think of it, when he put a hand to his eyes and began to cough.

"Mr. Wolfe!" she cried. "Are you all right?"

Her alarm made Beatrice break off from her playing mid-chord, so that the choking sound he made was audible to them both.

Had he swallowed his tongue? "Shall I get you another cup of tea?"

He waved these attentions away, his fit now causing his shoulders to shake while the women stared. It was only when he removed his hand from his eyes that Miranda saw tears in the corner of them, one now slipping down his cheek, just as his great big bellow of a laugh burst out.

"Oh," she said helplessly. "You're not dying. You're laughing."

"My apology," he managed, still chuckling. "I didn't mean to distress you or Miss Ellsworth. It's just that it's been a very long time since I received such a set-down, and I quite enjoyed it. But now I will be going. Not only have I overstayed the time, but it is past time now for me to indulge my—what did you call them?—my 'hermitical tendencies'. Good evening to you both."

And on that unaccountable note, he took his leave.

It was only some time later, after Tyrone had returned and Aggie rejoined them, that Beatrice fell upon the parcel Mr. Wolfe had brought and unwrapped it.

"Why, look, Mama," she urged, bringing it to her. "He had the same thought as Mr. Lyfford. Or nearly. I'm glad he chose a different one."

For lying in Miranda's lap was the music for yet another Haydn Canzonetta. This one being "She Never Told Her Love."

CHAPTER ELEVEN

**All and each that passed that way
Did join in the pursuit.
— William Cowper, *The diverting history
of John Gilpin* (1782)**

Emmy Wright's next plan to thrust herself under Mr. Colin Wolfe's nose was inspired by reading *Sense and Sensibility*. The popular novel had been hard to come by, but at last she secured a copy from the circulating library beside the White Hart, and the very next day shot a message to Hollowgate.

"Emmy wants to walk the downs," Beatrice announced at breakfast.

"It will have to wait for another day," her stepmother answered. "Only see how dark the sky is. It will surely rain again."

"She wants to walk the downs *near Beaumond*," Beatrice clarified. "And she has already secured her grandmama's consent."

"Oh, bother," muttered Miranda, not at all eager to plod through grass and mud so that Emmy might glimpse her *beau ideal*.

"I suppose Miss Wright schemes to fall down a slope in sight of Wolfe and be carried by him back to the deanery," said Tyrone as he munched his toast. He, of course, had read the novel months earlier and then read it to the family. "Let us hope she's the only one who tumbles, however, or Wolfe will be at his wit's end. He's a big fellow, but carrying three of you might be a bit much."

"Perhaps he could convey us in shifts," suggested Beatrice.

"Or tie you all together end to end and drag you," Aggie proposed.

"Very funny," said Miranda. "But I suspect Mr. Wolfe is too sensible a man to be out in the first place, and more likely all Emmy will catch is a cold."

In this Miranda proved prophetic, for not only did Emmy catch a wretched cold after the outing, but she and Beatrice did as well, resulting in them all missing the second assembly of the month. Emmy might have considered the bargain worthwhile if their soggy walk on the downs had indeed led to an encounter with Mr. Wolfe, but it had not (he being as sensible as Miranda supposed). The three women had glimpsed the house from a distance, Emmy squinting through the drops in every direction so she would not miss him, and the girl had even genuinely slipped and fallen headlong—all to no avail. No Mr. Wolfe appeared, and it had been Miranda and Beatrice who were obligated to haul her up.

There was something luxurious about a cold, however, Miranda had to admit as she lay in bed on the Thursday of the assembly. Her head might ache and her nose run, but at least she earned a reprieve from dancing with men she didn't want to dance with, and from watching (or trying not to watch) Mr. Wolfe dancing with everyone under the sun.

Colin scanned the gathering again. No, the Ellsworths were most definitely not in attendance, and the dancing had begun a half-hour earlier. Promenading beside Miss Simpkins, he didn't even notice the downward pressure she applied to his hand, that he might have to apply upward pressure to hers, and their handclasp broke apart.

"Dear me," he said, catching hers up again, "how slippery silk gloves can be, though yours are a lovely pink."

But Miss Simpkins was not to be fobbed off by an easy compliment. She had found Mr. Wolfe an absent partner and nowhere near as charming and attentive as he had been at the last assembly. Well, what did she care? The first time her mama praised the man's eligibility, Miss Simpkins dismissed him as "too old by far," only to change her mind after dancing with him. But now her opinion swung back. See? He *was* too old, and this fatal absence of mind might be a forerunner of senility. (It probably should be mentioned that Miss Simpkins was but sixteen.)

Colin gave himself a shake. Why should it matter to him, if Mrs. Ellsworth failed to appear? But it did. He admitted to himself that he had looked forward to further conversation with her. With Mrs. Ellsworth one managed to get beyond the superficialities of ballroom and drawing room. One managed to discuss real things. Perhaps it was because he had been clear with her from the start that he had no intention of shackling himself again soon, and the whole matter was taken off the table, as it were. He smothered a grin. If he were suddenly to stand at the top of the room and announce the same to all present, would it have the same magical effect of enriching and deepening his conversation with *every* woman?

Returning Miss Simpkins to her mother, he proceeded to bow over the hand of Miss Paulson, unwittingly outmaneuvering Mr. Bracewell, who had wandered thither with the same intent.

Miss Paulson purred with satisfaction and laid her hand in his, sailing away without a backward glance at the beaten curate, who was then forced to apply to Miss Simpkins.

Miss Paulson is a pleasant creature, Colin told himself. If re-marriage were a horse race, she would likely be a favorite. She had brown hair and blue eyes like Mrs. Ellsworth, and she was not given to giggling, but there the resemblance appeared to end. But did it? If Miss Paulson did not share Mrs. Ellsworth's gift for cutting to the heart of matters, perhaps it was because she had been given no opportunity to demonstrate fellow-feeling.

They took their place in the set, Mr. Bracewell and Miss Simpkins lining up below them. Miss Paulson tingled with awareness at their nearness and hoped Mr. Wolfe would notice as well, but Colin failed to.

"How have you occupied yourself these rainy days, Miss Paulson?" he asked.

"It's been so dull, Mr. Wolfe! I sat within doors and helped Mama and thought I should go mad. All Mama cares about are tedious things like housekeeping and my younger sisters and brothers. You have no idea how fortunate you are to live alone, Mr. Wolfe. It must be like a dream! Sometimes I imagine I will steal away to live in a cave at the top of a mountain, with only wind and snow for companions."

"'Hermitical tendencies,' some call them," he mused. "You must be a remarkable young lady, if you could be happily thrown on your own resources in such an isolated setting for any length of time."

Miss Paulson looked confused by this, she really having only meant to impress him with the idea that they were similar in nature. To get over the difficulty, she asked, "What did *you* do, Mr. Wolfe? I am certain it was far more exciting. Men's lives are by nature more exciting."

"I do not know if even your willingness can find anything to envy in my last few days. I did estate business, wrote letters, read books. But I did see my son Edmund on St. Matthew's Day."

"How delightful for you!" she said, clasping her hands before her breast appealingly. "And for him. Because I suppose he idolizes you."

Colin's mouth twisted ruefully. But then he remembered this could be the moment for his experiment.

"In truth," he said therefore, "I'm ashamed to say I don't think Edmund does anything of the kind."

"Ha ha!" cried Miss Paulson, jabbing him with her folded fan. "What a naughty fib! But you mustn't fish for compliments from me, sir. I am scrupulously honest and beg that others be so in return."

He bowed, as much as one could bow, when one was dancing and it wasn't required by the figures. "Indeed, I was being honest. I sometimes fear I might vanish to a mountain cave of my own without the boy even noticing."

"Hm." Her smile stiffened with uncertainty. "Well—la. It's a peculiar age. He'll sing another song when he's older."

"Would you say your father and younger brothers are close?"

"Oh, I—suppose so."

"What do they like to talk about together?"

Poor Miss Paulson's brow creased, as she tried to recall a single silly thing her papa and John or Powell said to each other. Why was Mr. Wolfe being such a bore tonight? Unless...unless he meant to discover how she would feel about being a stepmother!

"Perhaps...things like, if Powell may go with Papa and John to shoot pheasants this year, and how soon before fox-hunting may begin," she answered. "But—it's Mama my brothers would be lost without. If anyone needs two parents, it's my brothers. Boys, you understand. Very attached to her."

The arrow struck home, for a shadow fell across Mr. Wolfe's face. Miss Paulson trembled. Was it so easy? She had thought for years that Mr. Bracewell admired her and would offer for her, poor though he was, but he never had. Should she have planted the idea with him, as she just had with Mr. Wolfe?

She ventured a peep at Mr. Bracewell as they performed a cross. His countenance was as stern as her partner's. But what had he to take offense at? He had had his chance. To be sure, Mr. Bracewell was younger and therefore handsomer than Mr. Wolfe, but he was so very poor! Poor and dilatory. So poor that he was chasing that old widow Mrs. Ellsworth, who must be ten years older than he, if she was a day. And so dilatory that the woman might turn eighty before he managed to speak.

Pique swelled her bosom. She would teach the pitiful curate a lesson for toying with her so long. But first she must get Mr. Wolfe to stop moping.

Favoring him with a glow, she said, "How is it that you speak of wanting to meet everyone in Winchester, sir, and yet you invite nobody to Beaumond?"

"Because I haven't a hostess—yet. I'm an old widower, you know."

"Oh, pooh! 'Old'!" Miss Paulson fluttered her fingers at such nonsense. "If you were to give a ball, Mr. Wolfe, I could suggest ten matrons who would be delighted to serve as your hostess. You don't know what rarities private balls are."

"Must my hostess be a matron?"

"Of course she must," she replied demurely. "Only imagine what everyone would say, if she were a single young lady!"

The music wound to a close, and he made her a deeper bow before taking her hand to lead her from the floor.

"But will you consider it, Mr. Wolfe?" Miss Paulson pressed. "A ball at Beaumond would be the highlight of the autumn."

"I will *consider* considering it." To soften his refusal he gave her a little smile, but it vanished when he turned to face a veritable wall of young ladies before him, all casting him hopeful glances, while behind them stood a second wall, this one of mothers observing him beadily.

It was another hour before he could escape to the card room. An hour spent trotting Misses Terwilliger, Banks, and Browning about the floor. Only Miss Browning the rector's daughter was at all inclined to discuss serious matters, but Miss Browning was herself so dour and unsmiling that Colin thought she had the opposite problem—she would never be able to share a joke. *Doria, all over again.* But no—that wasn't fair to Doria, who was not dour so much as utterly indifferent.

The whist and quadrille tables having already been formed, Colin had to join the loo table with its collection of elderly men and women, and his sitting down there caused quite a stir. One man applied his quizzing glass to conduct a full inspection; one woman shouted to the one beside her that, "It's that dashing Mr. Wolfe," at which the one shouted at gave him a hard squint before replying, "'Tisn't."

Before Colin could pronounce that, yes, he was indeed that dashing Mr. Wolfe, another man dropped into the open chair next to him, and he glanced over to see the curate Mr. Bracewell.

"Oh, Mr. Bracewell," quavered Tisn't, "what an honor. Have you come to play with us?"

"For a bit. Would you allow me to perform the introductions?" Between Shouter's deafness and Quizzer's blindness and Tisn't's skepticism, this task was more challenging than usual, but at last it was accomplished and cards dealt to the newcomers.

"Surprising to see you hiding in here, Wolfe," said the curate.

Colin considered his hand and discarded it for miss. Not that the spare hand improved matters. "Why so?" he answered. "You're here as well. Were you finding the company a little thin?"

Mr. Bracewell frowned, but perhaps that was because he was obligated to waste a trump under Quizzer's higher card. "What do you mean by that?"

Colin shrugged. "Only that you as well as I danced with the Ellsworths, mother and daughter, as well as Miss Wright, and none of them are here tonight. But perhaps you didn't notice."

"I did not expect them here," the curate replied. He managed to secure the last trick, leaving Colin looed and required to add more fish to the pool. "For I called at Hollowgate this morning and learned the Ellsworths are sadly unwell."

"Are they?" Colin was unable to disguise his dismay. "Nothing serious, I trust."

"Bad colds. But Mrs. Tyrone Ellsworth assured me the patients had both been seen by Mr. Carlisle the doctor, and he saw no cause for anxiety. I regretted, however, having brought no better gift on the occasion of my call than some sheet music. A Haydn Canzonetta, to remind them of the pleasant music meeting." (Here the clergyman preened himself on the thoughtfulness of his offering, while Colin inwardly rolled his eyes. No wonder it had taken some days to lay hold of copies, if every one of Mrs. Ellsworth's suitors chose to present her with one! *Not* that he was one of Mrs. Ellsworth's suitors.)

The curate regarded him with an unreadable expression as Shouter dealt out the next hand. "As a wealthy stranger to these parts, Mr. Wolfe, you've drawn your fair share of attention among the ladies."

Even had he not been annoyed by Bracewell's superior knowledge of circumstances at Hollowgate, Colin would have had no response to this either. He would send fruit from Beaumond's hothouse, he decided. Whatever the gardener could gather.

"Don't you feel it would be sportsmanly, therefore," continued Bracewell, "to let the other fellows in the field know which quarry you fly at?"

"Why should I?" he returned evenly. "If I did happen to 'fly at' the woman someone else has chosen, how would that affect his odds?"

Bracewell scooped up his second trick, drawing a groan from 'Tisn't. "It would materially reduce them, as you are probably aware," he said in a low voice. "I will be frank with you, Mr. Wolfe. I have made up my mind to try my luck with the widow Mrs. Ellsworth. I am not the only one in pursuit, but I hear Lyfford has already spoken rashly and been refused, so there's that. And while you don't know me from Adam, I daresay, I would consider it a favor if you too would withdraw your attentions from her."

"I was not aware I was paying the widow attentions," Colin replied through clenched jaw.

"Of course you have. You have been calling there, I hear."

"At Mrs. Ellsworth's invitation. Our sons are in school together." His brow darkened. "And how, may I ask, do you know of Lyfford's unsuccessful proposal and of my visit to Hollowgate?"

"Your visits," corrected Bracewell. "In the plural. How else would I know? Servants talk. When I call there I keep my eyes and ears open. Do you mean to tell me, then, that you do *not* have any intentions toward her?"

Colin thought the curate ignorant of human nature if he thought hanging this flag of defiance would drive another man away. On the contrary—it made Colin want to confound him out of sheer spite.

"I haven't decided yet," he told him blithely. "For any man with thoughts of marriage, Mrs. Ellsworth must certainly be considered. So wealthy and well-connected, you know."

"But *older*," scowled the curate. "Her age is decidedly not in her favor."

"I understand your concern. She is most certainly older than you, Bracewell."

The parson drew a sharp breath. "I meant older in general. Her age tells on her, with so many fresh young blossoms floating about."

Colin turned his unsettling eyes on the young man to great effect, for he saw Bracewell's Adam's apple bob in a gulp. "If Mrs. Ellsworth is so disadvantaged by her relative antiquity," Colin mused, "I wonder that you do not settle on a fresher, younger blossom yourself."

Here the deal passed to the curate, and he postponed answering while he shuffled the cards and offered them to Colin to cut.

"As you are a rich man," Bracewell said finally, his voice stiff with offended dignity, "you can have little notion how a man in my position must consult other factors. Make certain compromises. I cannot choose altogether according to my taste because, without some amelioration of my financial state, I could neither hope to support my own family, much less continue to contribute to the needs of several siblings as I currently do."

"Ah. There you are wrong, Bracewell, for I do know all about that, as a matter of fact. All about sacrificing oneself on the altar of family duty. For how do you think I came by all my wealth?"

Bracewell could not tell how in earnest his companion was, but he thought it wiser not to ask questions. "Oh, indeed? Yes, well. Ahem. You understand, then, why I am in no position to indulge myself and must make what effort I can to...win the widow, despite her age or condition or...or lack of vivacity."

Colin slapped his cards down. "You would be lucky to get someone like Mrs. Ellsworth. Her 'condition,' my eye! Do you mean her wealth, which you have your covetous eye upon? Or the fact that she has a school-age son already? Take heart, then, for he won't encumber you with his presence more than a few months a year. And as for her lack of vivacity, perhaps you bore her, sir, for that is the last description I would apply to her."

The astounded curate sputtered in disbelief, his handsome face aflame. "You're mighty critical, Wolfe, considering you just admitted to having married for practical reasons yourself!"

But before Bracewell had finished speaking Colin was already calling himself an idiot for such a show of temper and bad manners.

Nor was Bracewell wrong in accusing him of hypocrisy. What was it about Mrs. Ellsworth which made him behave so badly?

"I beg your pardon," he said abruptly. And then repeated it to each of the other card players, whether they could hear him or not, see him or not. "Inexcusable, my conduct. It is a long time since I played cards so badly."

"Bad luck," shouted Shouter.

Tallying up his losses, Colin scribbled out IOUs to Quizzer and Bracewell before excusing himself and returning to the ballroom.

Let the women hound him again. It was better than hearing Mrs. Ellsworth abused by so unworthy a fortune hunter.

CHAPTER TWELVE

**I presently thought of a Stratagem
to fetch them back again.
— Defoe, *The life and strange surprizing adventures
of Robinson Crusoe* (1719)**

Dear Mrs. Ellsworth," her daughter-in-law Aggie greeted Miranda the first morning she was well enough to come down for breakfast, "how glad I am for your recovery. Tyrone and I are in danger of being suffocated by the floral offerings you have received."

"But we *have* enjoyed the oranges and grapes," said Tyrone.

"Oranges and grapes!" echoed Miranda. "Which of my poor swains could have afforded them?"

"It was Wolfe," he answered, "who, I think, can safely be called neither poor nor a swain."

"I was just thinking of the Wolfes," she rejoined quickly. "Because Michaelmas will be upon us, and Willie will come home again. Suppose he brings Edmund with him this time. Do you think we should send Mr. Wolfe an invitation to dinner, just in case?"

"You mean, should we send an invitation sooner than before we are actually sitting down to eat?" asked Tyrone dryly. "I vote Aye. It does strike one as more welcoming than, 'You may as well come, since your son is already here, and we will do our best to stretch the food.'"

But the Ellsworths were anticipated.

For when Bobbins brought in the post, Miranda found in her little stack a letter from Mr. Wolfe himself.

Beaumond

26 September 1812

My dear madam,

I was most sorry to be informed of your and Miss Ellsworth's recent illness. Mr. Bracewell assured me at Thursday's assembly that you both suffered from nothing more severe than a cold, therefore I hope you will be sufficiently recovered by Michaelmas to dine at Beaumond. Shall we say at four o'clock?

You are too perceptive a person not to see through my ruse, so I make no secret of it. Of course I plan to write

*to Edmund and tell him of the invitation. If he thinks
any and all Ellsworths will be at Beaumond for dinner, he will either (1) come directly home for his holiday, or, (2) accompany you hither from Hollowgate. I
suspect the latter because, as you pointed out, there are
no dogs at Beaumond.*

*Please do let me know if you approve. I would be glad to
extend this invitation to the Robert Fairchilds, if their
son Peter would enjoy being included.*

Your obedient servant,
Colin Wolfe

Aggie clapped her hands. "Oh, do let us go, Mrs. Ellsworth! I would like to see what he has done with Beaumond and report to Papa, of course."

"I don't really see how it can be refused." Miranda made a rueful face. How could she be expected to keep her vow of avoiding Mr. Wolfe and quashing her feelings for him, if they were repeatedly to be thrown together? "Suppose Willie's friendship continues with Edmund! This can hardly be something we do every saint's day!"

"Perhaps after this one we could simply issue a perpetual invitation," suggested Tyrone, "that—to paraphrase Wolfe himself—any and all *Wolfes* will always be received at Hollowgate, the presence of one being enough to indicate a more general welcome."

Midmorning found Miranda at her escritoire, dispatching their acceptance to Mr. Wolfe, as well as notes to the deanery to ask after Emmy's health, and lines of thanks to Messieurs Dodge and Bracewell for the flowers sent. Half fearful the latter two gentlemen might pay their respects in person, she could not help cringing when the footman Bobbin appeared, but to her relief it was Mrs. Fellowes and Emmy.

"What? Is Beatrice still abed?" cried Emmy, bouncing in. "I feel a hundred times better. A *thousand* times better!"

"I believe it was the girl's chagrin at missing the assembly which proved the most effective cure," her grandmother observed wryly.

"Beatrice said she would come down tomorrow, perhaps," said Miranda, leaving her desk to join the dean's wife. The two of them exchanged an amused glance at Emmy's restlessness as she skipped about the room teasing the dogs and inspecting the ornaments.

"Grapes!" she squealed. "May I? Fruit and flowers! I received a nosegay from Papa and Mama, and Lily sent over some broth, but not a single gentleman sent so much as a carnation!"

Miranda was not about to mention the giver of the fruit in front of Emmy, but Mrs. Fellowes put fire to flax by saying, "You are a popular woman, indeed, Miranda. Who presented all these?"

"I can't be certain," she prevaricated, opening her workbasket. "Aggie received them for me because I was in bed."

"Nonsense," said the practical woman. "I suppose Mr. Dodge and Mr. Bracewell were two of the givers, but don't tell me Mr. Lyfford still hopes against hope."

"No...he has given up, I believe."

"Well, too bad for him," Mrs. Fellowes shrugged. "I could have advised him not to leap at you like that. I'm glad Mr. Dodge and Mr. Bracewell have more sense."

"I can't credit them with any," Miranda said, "for I am no more tempted by them than by Mr. Lyfford."

The dean's wife chuckled. "They have not improved upon further acquaintance, then?"

Miranda made a helpless gesture. "They are both—all—respectable gentlemen enough, if one overlooks them chasing after an old widow simply because she is rich—"

"You are not *old*, Miranda," interrupted Mrs. Fellowes. "When you are my age I will allow you to call yourself such, but certainly not yet."

"Then am I allowed to say I am a widow 'past my first youth'?" Miranda returned, her tone a little impatient. She selected a new thread of embroidery silk. "Women are not like men, I'm afraid, Mrs. Fellowes. The world views a *man* my age and in my situation as eminently eligible, but if *I* were to remarry, the same world would say, with the apostle Paul, that it would have been better for me to remain single, but I must have lacked self-control."

"The apostle Paul!" Mrs. Fellowes waved the venerable authority away in a manner which would have alarmed the dean her husband. "The apostle Paul thought the Lord would reappear any moment, so of course he didn't want everyone running around like Emmy here, with their heads full of nonsense. But the world has gone on, and we must go on too. Listen to me, dear: you needn't marry Dodge or Bracewell, of course, but you must not close your heart unreasonably. Just because a man sees the value in your fortune does not mean he would not come to see *your* value. It is true that men have it easier, but it does not follow therefore that you must have it *hard*."

"My head isn't full of nonsense, Grandmama," Emmy said stoutly.

"Of course it is. It's to be expected at your age. If I were to open the top of your head and turn you upside down, nothing would fall out but a bit of fluff."

"And I don't blame Mrs. Ellsworth one bit for not wanting to marry Mr. Lyfford or Mr. Dodge or Mr. Bracewell," the girl went on, ignoring her grandmother's affectionate reproof. "I wouldn't marry them either, though Mr. Bracewell is terribly handsome. The man I marry must be older and wiser—but still dashing and fun."

They were within half a word of Mr. Wolfe, and Miranda would have steered them away, but Emmy was too unsubtle to hide her feelings. Twirling a bare grape stem between her fingers she heaved a sigh. "How I hated to miss the assembly. I suppose all the other girls mobbed him and likely have the start of me now—as if they didn't already, what with Miss Paulson driving with him and Miss Terwilliger accompanying him to the circulating library."

"If you're speaking of Mr. Wolfe, I'm not certain he is any more fond of one than the other," Miranda heard herself say.

Emmy pounced on her. "Why do you think that? Has he talked of them with you?"

"Emmy, how could he have?" Miranda lied again—was spouting untruths becoming a habit? "I was not at Thursday's assembly either." Her conscience catching up to her mouth, however, she soon added, "Though I will confess that he did come to Hollowgate for dinner on the feast of St. Matthew because my son William invited Mr. Wolfe's son Edmund. Oh—and we are to go to Beaumond at Michaelmas so the boys might be together again. But there wasn't any talk of young ladies on the first occasion and likely will be none on the second."

"What?" gasped Emmy. "It's not fair! Everyone gets to see Mr. Wolfe but me! Why did you not invite *me* to dinner that day, Mrs. Ellsworth? I am your *especial charge!* If you had, surely Mr. Wolfe would have invited me for Michaelmas as well. He would have thought me as much a part of the group as Beatrice. How could you be so thoughtless? Is it that you want him for yourself?"

"Emmy!" gasped Mrs. Fellowes and Miranda in unison, though their common horror had disparate causes.

"Where are your manners, child?" her grandmother scolded. "Your fondness for that man makes you forget how you should speak to your elders. Besides, have you not been attending? Mrs. Ellsworth is unfortunately the last woman in the world to think of keeping a man to herself. Though, tell me, Miranda—should I be concerned about this Mr. Wolfe person? Having never met him I am trusting entirely to your judgment. Is he the sort of person Emmy should set her fancy on? It is disturbing to have his name connected with so many."

Miranda carefully completed her stitch and held out her hoop as if to study her progress. Gradually her pulse slowed, though her face still felt hot. "Mr. Wolfe is a respectable gentleman, but—not one in a hurry to remarry, I don't suspect. Mrs. Fellowes, he seems uniformly...friendly to all the young ladies, but I do not think he means them to read it as—as interest."

Another wail rose from Emmy, and she hurled herself down on the piano bench, striking a jangling chord and sending the sheet music fluttering.

"*Emmy*," her grandmother protested again, "do behave like a lady."

The girl ignored this as well, bending to retrieve the fallen music. "'She never spoke her love,'" she read. "Oh! I loved this song. I loved that whole evening. Mrs. Ellsworth, may I take it and copy it?"

"Of course."

"And you have other Canzonettas, too. But perhaps I won't take them all at once because you or Beatrice will want to play them too." With another sigh she pressed the music to her bosom. "At the meeting Mr. Wolfe said this one was his favorite. I'll surprise him! I'll learn to play it and sing it, and then—oh, Grandmama! May we invite him to the deanery to hear me?"

"Foolish girl! One doesn't just invite single gentleman by themselves. They'll know it at once for an ambush."

Emmy pouted. "I'm at such a disadvantage! I suppose I would have to invite others of his acquaintance. Would you and Beatrice come, Mrs. Ellsworth, as decoys? And would you promise not to flirt with him? I certainly won't ask Misses Paulson or Terwilliger!"

All in all, it was a relief when the visitors from the deanery left, though Emmy threw Miranda a final reproachful glance as she went, asking, "If there were some natural way to include me in the Michaelmas dinner, you would do it, wouldn't you, Mrs. Ellsworth?" Somehow Emmy's suspicions made Miranda feel vaguely sneaking, as if she really were trying to keep Mr. Wolfe to herself. Worse yet, self-defense was impossible. If Miranda were to confess all, if she were to say, "I would avoid Mr. Wolfe if I could, for the protection of my own heart," instead of relieving Emmy it would only increase her mistrust.

And who could blame the girl?

When it came to Mr. Wolfe, Miranda could not honestly even say she trusted herself.

Michaelmas dawned clear and mild, but given Beaumond's distance from town, Mr. Wolfe thoughtfully sent his coach for the boys and the Robert Fairchilds, leaving the Hollowgate denizens to debate their own mode of transportation. Aggie was for walking and Miranda for having Greaves prepare the coach. Tyrone voted for the barouche, saying, "Soon it will have to be put up for the winter, so why not enjoy it while we can?"

"I vote with Tyrone," said Beatrice. "The barouche, for then we may be certain Emmy Wright can't climb on the roof or in the basket and stow away with us."

Miranda had never been to Beaumond, the Taplin family which used to own it having belonged to a different parish, and the two sons of the household being younger than herself. Aggie had described it as neither so grand as Hollowgate nor so modern as her childhood home The Acres, and when they turned in the drive Miranda saw a square and unexceptionable house set in a pleasant park.

"Goodness, if I were Mr. Wolfe I would hire an army of servants," Beatrice declared, "or it would be too lonely for me."

"Maybe his estate in Kent was twice as large," suggested her brother, "and Beaumond feels cozy."

"Even if his estate in Kent was larger, he would have had the late Mrs. Wolfe, as well as his son Edmund, for company, and two is better than one."

"'And a threefold cord is not quickly broken,'" finished Tyrone. "Though truly, Edmond speaks so little I'm not sure he would count as an entire fold in the cord."

This made them laugh, and Beatrice conceded, "Well, Edmund may not speak much—or at all—but his *body* would be there in any case, a good, substantial one. And perhaps the late Mrs. Wolfe was a chatterbox."

"Mr. Wolfe has set up games on the lawn," Aggie observed as they drew nearer, her voice rising with excitement, for she loved all sports and games. "Pall mall, an archery target, shuttlecock!"

"Mercy," groaned her husband. "We'd better strike our colors at once, Mama, for whatever little amusement we offer Willie and company at the next holiday will certainly fall short of this mark."

"What warlike language, Tyrone," Aggie laughed. "The games might well be for us, for I do believe Willie and Edmund only played in the brook and threw sticks for the dogs at Hollowgate."

Miranda said nothing, too aware of the thump of her heart when she saw Mr. Wolfe emerge to stand at the entrance, like the sphinx at the gate of Thebes. No one as yet suspected her feelings for the master of Beaumond—even Emmy Wright's accusation was no more than a fear-inspired guess—and that was how it must remain.

As they drew up, the boys came dashing from the house, splitting to either side of Mr. Wolfe like a stream around a boulder, the Fairchilds following more decorously behind. He opened the door of the barouche before Greaves could get to it (Gotch had begged off, being reluctant to face the ireful Mr. Wolfe again, in case he was still ireful), and extended a hand to Aggie, who bounded out with a hurried, "Good afternoon, Mr. Wolfe—wait for me, boys! I'll play."

"Mrs. Ellsworth, Miss Ellsworth, I am so glad to see you in health again." He grasped her hand—no, he took it more lightly than that—but Miranda wanted to snatch hers back, and she thanked him while avoiding his gaze.

"The fruit you sent was a treat," Beatrice told him, not being hampered by embarrassment. "Everyone got some. Even Scamp and Pickles before Bobbins caught them at it."

"Ah. Perhaps my note should have read, 'For the ailing,' rather than the more general 'For the Ellsworths.'"

"It wouldn't have helped," said Tyrone, "because our pets are sadly unlettered."

This was what Mrs. Ellsworth meant by a full house, Colin thought later, as his gaze circled the table. He could not remember a time seeing his son so animated. Not that Edmund talked more than usual, but he grinned and chuckled and nodded. When asked a question by the adults or appealed to by William or Peter, he answered in phrases, rather than single syllables.

It was Mrs. Ellsworth who posed the question Colin was dying to ask, and she cunningly addressed it to her own son, rather than Edmund. "What tricks has Grimes the prefect been up to, Willsie?"

"He's gone Continent," answered William around a mouthful of pudding.

"He's traveling?" she puzzled.

"Sick-house," Tyrone and Fairchild corrected her in unison, while William nodded.

"He tripped over a stack of cricket bats when we were in Meads and broke his ankle and his head," explained Peter, not at all regretfully. "It's his own fault because Puncher was longstop and missed a ball, so Grimes went whistling over to roar at him and likely give a clow—a box of his ears—but Puncher took to his heels—"

"Grimes—transported with rage—" put in Edmund, laughing silently.

"—Chased him," Willie took up the thread again, "and clungle-bungle-dungle *smash!* He gets tangled up and down he goes!"

"Cried like a baby," said Edmond.

"Oh, dear," said kind-hearted Mrs. Fairchild, but even she looked like she was trying not to laugh.

"I suppose we ought to pity him," Miranda sighed, "but you boys have painted such an unsympathetic character."

"Poetic justice," pronounced Tyrone, thumping a fist on the table, to which his brother-in-law and Mr. Wolfe contributed heartfelt hear-hims.

"Did no one help the wretched boy up?" Mrs. Fairchild persisted.

"That's just it, Mama," said her son Peter. "No one was in any hurry because I suspect even the other prefects think Grimes a toad-eater to the masters, so it was Edmund who picked him up first, though Willie and I went to help when we saw him do it."

"We weren't a lot of help, since we're shorter, so Edmund just ended up slinging Grimes' arm about his shoulders and dragging him away," said William.

"Mm," put in Edmund.

"And now Grimes calls Edmund 'the only Inferior worth a tinker's curse' and will probably follow him like a puppy dog once he comes abroad," concluded Peter.

"I feel Peter and I should at least be worth *half* a tinker's curse, since we did try to help," added William.

"Goodness! What a perfect example of virtue being its own reward," Beatrice marveled. "I applaud you, Edmund."

Colin thought nine out of ten other boys might blush to be addressed thus by a pretty young lady, but Edmund accepted it stolidly. Not that Colin cared. It was too satisfying to know the prefect could no longer harass and abuse the child, and more satisfying still to observe these new clues to his character. He threw an involuntary glance toward Mrs. Ellsworth to see if she shared his gratification, but she was smiling at her son and saying something teasing. She hadn't had ten words for Colin that afternoon. Not that she snubbed him, but she never seemed to be standing nearby or looking his way. When he wandered in her direction, she somehow drifted another. And much as he liked the Ellsworths altogether, and occupied as he was in gleaning what he could from Edmund, Colin was conscious of frustration niggling him.

Frustration tied to Mrs. Ellsworth's remoteness.

Every other unmarried woman in Winchester fawns on me, he thought, not without justification. *Miss Wright, Miss Paulson, Miss Terwilliger.*

He would remember that thought later and wonder if, like the unfortunate prefect Grimes, he too was the recipient of poetic justice.

CHAPTER THIRTEEN

**...Suddenly the clouds united over their heads, and a
driving rain set full in their face.
— Austen, *Sense and Sensibility* (1811)**

They were so long at table that it was after six when they rose
to adjourn to the drawing room.

"The glass has fallen pretty sharply," observed Robert Fairchild.

"And no wonder," said his wife, coming to his side. "I thought it
was getting darker just because it was nearly sunset, but the clouds
are quite thick."

At her words, those same clouds burst, and rain began to drum
on the terrace outside the windows.

"We had better not stay longer," said Fairchild. "The boys will
need to return to College. Wolfe, may we trouble you to bring the
coach around?"

The order was given at once, but then there was the problem of the Hollowgate Ellsworths and their barouche.

"It will be no matter," Miranda assured her party. "Aggie and Beatrice may put up the hood and the cover, and they will be reasonably shielded from the rain."

"But Mrs. Ellsworth, it is *you* and Beatrice who have only lately recovered," Aggie pointed out. "Tyrone and I will be perfectly fine getting a little wet. He has a beaver hat, and I have my invariably robust constitution. Therefore you two must take the covered seat."

When Miranda began to object, Tyrone laughed. "Let's not row about it. Would it help to keep the peace if *I* were to monopolize the entire rear seat and leave the three of you to shiver in the rain?"

"As good as that suggestion is, Ellsworth," interposed Colin, "I have another. Let the coach take the boys and the Robert Fairchilds first and then return for you Hollowgaters. There is no need for anyone to sit on the rainy side in the barouche, if you are willing to be patient." This proposal was immediately approved, and within a quarter hour the first party departed.

"Come," said Colin. "Let the rest of us adjourn to the library. It will be cozier for tea, and those who don't feel sociable may take refuge in a book. Mr. Taplin amassed a rather fine collection."

Tyrone was at once absorbed in perusing the shelves, while Aggie recognized the maid as one from The Acres and had many questions for the girl, leaving Beatrice and Miranda to sit with Mr. Wolfe. Beatrice, not being in love with Mr. Wolfe as her friend Emmy was, naturally fell silent and delegated conversation to her stepmother. And Miranda—wished for her workbasket or, indeed, anything which might conveniently occupy her gaze and attention.

For his part, Colin settled back in his favorite chair, scrutinizing Mrs. Ellsworth beneath lowered lids. She was thinner, perhaps, from her illness, but her smooth countenance had fine color. Firelight burnished her light-brown hair with a golden halo, transforming her to a Fra Angelico angel. He chuckled to himself. No Fra Angelico angel had Mrs. Ellsworth's hidden fieriness, however, he would warrant.

"Miss Ellsworth," he began, "I have a question which I will put to you, for fear your stepmother would accuse me of fishing for compliments. Tell me—which fruit did you most enjoy from the basket I sent? The gardener asks my preferences for the hothouse, now that I am master here."

Beatrice glanced at Mrs. Ellsworth, who pretended interest in Aggie's preparation of the tea.

"I liked the grapes, sir."

"A good choice. What about you, Mrs. Ellsworth?"

Her lips twitched. "Oh, pardon me. Were you fishing for compliments?"

Then he did grin. "Did I catch any?"

"Since by your own admission you did not grow the fruit, Mr. Wolfe, if I praise the oranges, the compliment by rights belongs not to you but to your gardener." Accepting her cup from Aggie, she gave the tea a stir and replaced the spoon in the saucer. "Therefore, I tell—him—freely the oranges were my favorite."

"I thank you on his behalf," said Colin with a complacent bow of the head, "and gleefully snatch up the auxiliary compliment which fell my way."

"*Was* there an auxiliary compliment?"

"To be sure. For you would have no notion of my gardener's skill with oranges if not for my own thoughtfulness and generosity in sending the basket in the first place."

She hid her smile by taking a sip of tea.

"But it was a near thing," he continued, "trying to find a spot to place my offering, amidst the numerous other tributes."

Miranda's cup rattled against its saucer.

"That's what I said," laughed Aggie. "Mrs. Ellsworth and Beatrice are so popular! You cannot imagine the burden placed upon me, Mr. Wolfe, when either of them—or both—leave the receiving to me. And it happens more often than you would think."

"Aggie," Beatrice frowned, "now Mr. Wolfe will say we are the ones fishing for compliments."

He shook his head, clicking his tongue in sympathy. "That must indeed be trying, Mrs. Tyrone. Let us hope, however, that your duties never come to include receiving any proposals by proxy—that would be too much to ask, I think."

Miranda choked on her tea. To her mortification, one ladylike cough did nothing to mend the matter, and a louder, more violent series of them followed. She managed to replace her cup on its saucer, but not without slopping a generous amount of liquid in her lap.

"Mama!" cried Beatrice, and "Mrs. Ellsworth!" cried Colin and Aggie.

Miranda held up a hand as she continued to clear her throat, wishing herself miles away in solitary peace. But, no, Aggie and Beatrice must spring up in concern, and Tyrone must stride over to thump her between the shoulder blades. Even the maid, returning to poke up the fire and remove any discarded tea things, flew over to cluck over her stained dress. All the while, after first sitting forward in his chair, Mr. Wolfe relaxed again, regarding the hurly-burly with ill-disguised amusement.

"Madam, if you please," said the maid, "you and I are nearly of a size, I daresay. If you would like to change your dress, you would be much more comfortable. And I can soak this one in hot water to see if we can prevent the stain from setting."

It was useless for Miranda to protest that she was perfectly fine and didn't want to bother anyone. She was overruled by all.

"Come with me, Mrs. Ellsworth," Colin addressed her as he took up one of the candlesticks. "Let me show you to a chamber where you may change." To the maid he added, "Diggory, if you would tell Clarke to build a fire in the rose bedroom and bring the dress there..."

Resigning herself, Miranda followed him from the drawing room back to the entrance hall, where a simple but elegant staircase with iron balustrade led up to the first floor. A sconce holding five candles graced the wall halfway up the stairs, but beyond that the house was in shadow, the light of Mr. Wolfe's candlestick illuminating glimpses of painted pilasters and arabesques.

The rose bedroom lay at the end of the passage in the northwest corner of the house, and when Mr. Wolfe used his candlestick to light the sconces in the chamber, Miranda could not repress an indrawn breath at her surroundings.

"What a charming room!" It drew its name from the pale pink background of the paper covering the walls, on which trees climbed, flowers bloomed, and birds fluttered. The furniture was dark carved Chippendale from halfway through the previous century, with the bed canopy hangings and coverlet matching the rose of the paper and carpet. Rococo scrollwork decorated the overmantel, each loop containing a bracket on which a porcelain figurine stood. The warm candlelight reflected from the gilded mirror and the silver fender, grate, and fire irons. Taken in total, Miranda had a dreamy feeling she had been transported to the enchanted bedchamber of a princess.

"I believe it must have belonged to the late Mrs. Taplin," Colin said, "for a connecting door leads to a bedchamber of matching size where I sleep."

There being no appropriate response to such information, Miranda made none.

He rubbed his hands together and knelt down by the fireplace. "Rather chilly from lack of use, though, wouldn't you agree? Who knows how long it will take Diggory to find Clarke. Like most masters when they find a good and useful servant, I try to make Diggory feel important, but that means sacrificing Clarke, the maid-of-all-work. Clarke finds Diggory overbearing and thus makes herself scarce to spite her, leaving me—alas—to build fires myself from time to time." Throughout this speech he had been doing precisely that, while Miranda went to one of the casements to see if the rain lightened any.

It being dark out, she could see nothing but the room reflected behind her, but being embarrassed to find herself alone with Mr. Wolfe, Miranda took the trouble to unfasten the long window and open it.

The rain had indeed let up into a gentle shower, and such a delightful freshness rose up from the outdoors that she leaned over the sill to put her head out, glancing down to see where the lights from the lower floor spilled over the grounds. But instead of grass or shrubs or paving stones meeting her eye, Miranda saw a face.

She screamed, leaping back as if the window had burned her, to be engulfed the next instant in Mr. Wolfe's arms, though how he got from the fireplace to her side in an eyeblink was a mystery to be pondered later.

"Good heavens, Miranda! What is it?"

His voice came to her muffled, as one of her ears was crushed against his chest and the other in the crook of his elbow. She felt the slow thump of his heart against her and one of his large hands in her hair.

"A-a-a face!" she gasped. "She looked like a g-ghost. P-pale. White. Streaming."

He released her the next moment, leaving her cold and bereft and still alarmed, to take up the fireplace poker and stride to the window in two steps. Miranda braced in preparation for curses and blows, but to her astonishment Mr. Wolfe then flung the poker aside to jam both his arms and shoulders through the casement and lean outward.

Taking hold of something and bracing a knee against the pretty papered wall, he gave a grunt and a heave, tumbling back into the room with not a ghost as Miranda supposed, but a very real, very solid, very corporeal *person* landing on his chest.

Another squeal escaped her—stifled this time as quickly as she could—but Mr. Wolfe merely set the interloper aside, rose to his feet, and then held out a hand to the person.

"Miss *Paulson*?" marveled Miranda. "Can that possibly be you?"

The young lady gave a toss of her chin, sending drops of water flying from her drowned locks, and wrapped her soggy white wool cloak closer about her. "It seems I've interrupted something."

Miranda only stared. The girl was found lurking outside a gentleman's first-floor window at night, and this was her response? Mr. Wolfe pulled a linen towel from the commode in the corner and offered it to the young lady.

"It's disgraceful, if you ask me," Miss Paulson sniffled, dabbing at herself with the cloth. "Someone of your age."

"Someone of my age?" murmured Miranda, still puzzled. "You mean my age is disgraceful?"

"I mean someone of your age trying to—to—invade a gentleman's bedchamber!"

"Actually, my bedchamber is adjoining," said Mr. Wolfe amiably, pointing a thumb over his shoulder. There was a little hum in his voice, as if he were trying to subdue a laugh.

Comprehension began to dawn on Miranda, an understanding mirrored in the color washing over her cheeks. "Oh! I think I see...though it cannot possibly be so. Do you mean to say—you accuse me of—forcing my way into this place, in order to *entrap* Mr. Wolfe?"

"What else would you call it?" Miss Paulson demanded. "To be caught in a gentleman's—that is, in his neighboring bedchamber, alone with him?"

"Good thing *you* came along, Miss Paulson," agreed Mr. Wolfe. "Or who knows what might have become of me."

"Never mind what *I* am doing here," Miranda rallied, ignoring the impossible man's jokes. "I need not explain myself to you. *I* was not the one who trespassed on someone else's property and scaled a wall by some means, all to peer in somebody's bedroom window!"

"Because *you* had already schemed your way in," retorted Miss Paulson.

Before Miranda could find words for her indignation, the door opened to admit both Diggory and a scowling creature looking appropriately resentful who must be the maid-of-all-work Clarke.

"Dear me!" said Diggory, a clean, folded dress hugged to her bosom. "More of you."

"Yes, another visitor in need of succor, Diggory. Beaumond is awash in them tonight, so to speak. But as Miss Paulson is several inches taller than Mrs. Ellsworth, I can only hope there is someone in the household of suitable stature, so we may offer the same hospitality to the former as we have toward the latter."

"I'll see, sir." Diggory placed the dress on the bed and gave it a pat, glancing at Miranda, before taking herself off again.

"You built the fire already," grumbled Clarke. Being short, with a broad chest and arms thick as tree trunks, she would be no help in providing clothing for Miss Paulson.

Mr. Wolfe swiveled on his heels to regard the blazing fire, as if he had never noticed it before. "Why, so I did. But perhaps you could still be of assistance, Clarke. Would you go to the drawing room and bid Mrs. Tyrone Ellsworth to come up? Mrs. William Ellsworth will require assistance dressing, now that I sent Diggory away again on another wild goose chase."

"Mrs. Tyrone Ellsworth?" repeated Miss Paulson faintly, when the burly servant was gone. "Is she here, too?"

"Of course she is. I invited all of the Ellsworths of Hollowgate for dinner today, as well as the Robert Fairchilds, because our three boys are friends and had a holiday from school. They are all downstairs. Mrs. Ellsworth here had the misfortune to spill tea upon her dress, so I led her to this chamber where she might change her clothing."

Miss Paulson's throat worked for a minute, but to her credit she mustered her dribbling dignity and said to Miranda, "I do apologize then, Mrs. Ellsworth, for my misconstruction of the matter and my rash words."

Miranda could hardly say the same, but she bowed her head in acknowledgement.

Mr. Wolfe leaned against one of the bedposts, crossing his arms over his chest. "So there it is. I have explained her presence, and I have dispatched Diggory to see to your immediate needs, so now I have leisure to ask you, Miss Paulson, the reason for your visit."

"I can't—please don't make me tell you, in front of her." She stabbed a finger in Miranda's direction.

"Well, I'm afraid you'll have to tell me in front of someone," he replied mildly, "for if the evening has taught me anything, it's that an unmarried gentleman such as myself faces countless perils, even in the privacy of his own home. Would you prefer I call a servant to chaperone us while I hear your story, or a different Ellsworth? My own preference is for Mrs. Ellsworth. Not only is she already at hand, but she's a rational, discreet sort of person."

Given those alternatives, Miss Paulson flung caution to the wind. "I just wanted to see you!" she pleaded, taking a few squashy steps toward him across the carpet and wringing her hands. "It seemed a very long time until the next assembly, and even at the last one you disappeared into the card room halfway through. Oh, Mr. Wolfe! I rode over in the rain just for a glimpse of you. I know appearances are bad, but—but—I honestly had no further plans. I was walking the grounds, trying to work up my courage and almost decided just to go home, but then I saw the light up here and thought you might be—going to bed—so I—I—"

"You acted impulsively," he finished for her, his tone still even and not unkind. "But Miss Paulson, as someone far older than you in years, let me advise you not to take such risks in the future. I can trust Mrs. Ellsworth (and doubtless the other Ellsworths) to keep your activities this night secret, but I cannot promise the same of my servants." He gave a regretful sigh. "It really is so hard to find good help! Look at Clarke there, who can barely be asked to build a fire without leading one to fear being murdered in one's bed. If I asked for confidentiality and tact into the bargain, I would be left to run Beaumond single-handed."

"Oh, Mr. Wolfe—do not jest! Do you not think part of you would have been glad if we were—forced to marry?"

Miranda turned away at this bald confession of the girl's feelings. Both the frankness of them and the methods employed were so vastly different from anything she herself would dream of that she hardly knew where to look.

When Mr. Wolfe answered, there was no more laughter in his voice. "Miss Paulson, I have been married before. And I tell you a union without a foundation of mutual love and respect would not serve."

"But I certainly—! That is, we might—we could—"

"We *might,* as you say. But this way—the way you have chosen tonight—does not often lead there. At my age, Miss Paulson, I feel a fondness for the proprieties. They are like—like a firm back or seat or arm to a chair, giving it shape and support, to prevent one falling over or spilling out or otherwise injuring oneself. Does that make sense? Therefore, considering the friendship I feel for you, I advise you to foster an appreciation for them as well, that you may come to no harm."

The disappointed young lady was spared having to answer this by a knock on the door, followed by Aggie's entrance. That Clarke had already seen fit to share the surprising appearance of this additional guest was obvious from Aggie's lack of surprise and her murmured, "Miss Paulson."

Over her shoulder bobbed the returned Diggory, and behind Diggory loomed a liveried footman.

"Found another dress, sir," said Diggory, and "The coach has returned, sir," announced Quill.

"Excellent work, Diggory, and thank you, Quill. Now, Miss Paulson, if you would go with Diggory, and Mrs. Tyrone, if you would help Mrs. Ellsworth, I believe everyone will shortly be set to rights and sent on his way. Miss Paulson, the coach can easily accommodate you, as well as the four Ellsworths, so there will be no need for you to ride back to town in the wet. One of my grooms can easily return your horse tomorrow." Reaching the door, he turned to give them a final bow, and Miranda was certain she saw the gleam of humor returned to his pale eyes. "If you would excuse me."

Chapter Fourteen

Assure your selfe, I will you not forsake.
— Edmund Spenser, *The Faerie Queene*, i.vii.sig. G5v
(1590)

While the Hollowgate Ellsworths did not discuss Miss Paulson's scandalous appearance at Beaumond with the world at large, they most certainly discussed it among themselves.

"I can't condemn her," Aggie said the following morning, when the three women were gathered, Aggie holding one of the twins and Beatrice the other. "Heaven knows when I was Miss Paulson's age, I would have gone to Beaumond to chase after Mr. Francis Taplin if Minta hadn't stopped me. And Mr. Wolfe is a far worthier man than Mr. Taplin ever was."

Beatrice, who had also been present the night Aggie referred to, sat up from blowing bubbles on baby Joan's stomach. "But you didn't intend to go to Beaumond to compromise Mr. Taplin, Aggie! You wanted to see how he was recovering from the carriage accident, and that to me is a great difference in motives."

"I don't know," said Aggie, putting baby Margaret to her shoulder and patting her back. "Miss Paulson and I were both guided—or *mis*guided by our affections—to do what we did. That is all. It isn't as if Miss Paulson wanted to entrap Mr. Wolfe for his money, or anything of that nature. She really does like him, I think."

"I wonder that he doesn't return her affections," mused Beatrice.

"It might not be that," spoke up Miranda from her sewing. "He told her such schemes were not the proper way to build a foundation for marriage. He did not tell her it could never be. Moreover, he called her a friend."

"Emmy is prettier," Bea went on, now making faces at Joanie to make her giggle. "And she has a bigger portion, as does Miss Terwilliger. I don't think Miss Paulson has much at all."

"Lack of fortune need not be an obstacle, if he chooses Miss Paulson," Miranda said calmly. "He simply may not be in a great hurry to choose. And there I sympathize."

"Of course you do!" cried Beatrice. "Because you don't intend to marry again soon, do you?"

"Mrs. Fellowes would like to marry me off again, but I am content as I am."

"Exactly. Oh, Mama, don't listen to Mrs. Fellowes!" urged Beatrice. "She needn't put her oar in, when we are going along so well."

"Indeed, Mrs. Ellsworth, we would be bereft without you!" said Aggie.

"Mama, you remarrying would ruin *everything*," Beatrice insisted. Taking up Joan, she came to sit beside her stepmother. "Why, you would have to leave Hollowgate to live with—whomever—and Flossie and Robert would come here, and then where would I go? And Willsie, whenever he was home from school?"

"My dear girl, I am not going anywhere. Did I not just say so? But even if I did, you and William would of course be welcome wherever I was, though you at least would also be perfectly welcome to continue living with the Fairchilds."

"But—I've always lived with *you*, Mama! You know I hardly remember my mother—the third Mrs. Ellsworth. It's always been you. *You've* been my mother. How then could I not live where you live?"

"But I just said you could, darling," Miranda reassured her, marveling at this outburst. Still, Beatrice's words made a little knot form in her breast that was half joy and half pain.

"But I've also always lived at Hollowgate!"

"That won't go on forever, in any event," Aggie pointed out. "You yourself are old enough to marry now, Bea, and when you do, you too will go and live with your husband and be happy to do it."

"I don't want to marry. I want to live at Hollowgate with my family forever and ever."

"Dear Beatrice," Miranda said, "I know you don't like change, but you've lived with various changing combinations of your family your entire life, and I daresay you've survived."

"Because I've always been at Hollowgate, and I've always had *you*, Mama, no matter who got married or who went where. Besides, everyone who got married and left Hollowgate didn't go particularly far."

Miranda hardly knew whether to laugh or weep at Beatrice's fuss, so she leaned to kiss her hair. "We are wasting our breath, dear girl. For you do not have to marry now if you don't want to, and neither do I. Haven't I already refused Mr. Lyfford?"

"*Anyone* could refuse Mr. Lyfford," Beatrice retorted. "That proves nothing."

"Well, it proves I don't want to remarry just for remarriage's sake," Miranda persisted, "and, though nothing may ever come of them, I promise you as well that neither Mr. Dodge nor Mr. Bracewell offer any temptation."

Here Beatrice, instead of appearing soothed, gave her a level look. "What if Mr. Wolfe were to ask you?"

"Mr. Wolfe!"

"Of course, Mr. Wolfe. Just because you are older than the girls running after him does not mean you are therefore blind to his charms. *You* cannot say he is too old, or that it's a pity he has a son. Nor is Mr. Wolfe foolish like Mr. Lyfford or gloomy like Mr. Dodge or too young like Mr. Bracewell."

"A man's age, appropriate or not, and fellow bereavement are not reason enough to marry him," Miranda replied briskly, her needle continuing to flash in her tiny, even stitches, "even if he were inclined to ask me, which I doubt he is."

It was not an outright denial, and Miranda could only pray a clever girl like Beatrice wouldn't notice. To distract her, she hurried on. "The one you ought to issue warnings to is Mr. Wolfe himself!

At least Mr. Lyfford came to offer for me in broad daylight and in full sight of my family and the servants. But living alone as he does, who can prevent Mr. Wolfe being ensnared, the next time some reckless girl takes the chance?"

The Ellsworths were not the only ones concerned for Mr. Wolfe's reputation and liberty. After Miss Paulson's unexpected visit, Colin realized that, if steps were not taken, he might find himself bound again in a second union not of his choosing, and from this one there might be no escape.

"This is ridiculous," he growled, pacing the library when the Ellsworths were gone. "Can a man not live on his own without fear of traps being laid for him? Must I post guards at every bedchamber window?" Surely Miss Paulson would not try the same desperate ruse again, but what guarantee did Colin have that no other woman might?

It had been sheer luck which saved him this evening. If Mrs. Ellsworth had not spilled tea on her dress, the first lights in any bedchamber would have been in his own. Miss Paulson would have waited, shivering and damp, counting the minutes until she thought his valet would have departed...

Nor would she have needed even to knock on the glass. Colin always cracked the window for the fresh air, summer or winter. Miss Paulson would only have had to push it further open and climb in. There would have been no warning whatsoever. No warning and no recourse.

As it was, he thought with a shiver, he would shut and lock his windows tonight and every night, from now on.

He laughed mirthlessly. What he needed, come to think of it, was a chaperone. Some eminently respectable woman whose presence alone would shout to the world that Colin Wolfe and all his dealings bore not the slightest hint of impropriety.

A chaperone.

He had a fleeting memory of Mrs. Ellsworth in his arms. Too fleeting. Her slender form stiff with fright but then yielding, warming, softening, like clay in a sculptor's hands. But it was over almost before he could register it. Like a fool, he had released her to confront the cause of her fear, not knowing it would be the aggravating Miss Paulson. Not knowing the moment could not be recaptured.

How differently would he feel if, as he lay in his bed alone, fingers tapped at the casement, and it was Mrs. Ellsworth there, shivering and asking to be held?

Colin gave himself a shake.

Good heavens. One would think he was beginning to have feelings for the woman.

With a yawn and a stretch, he chose a volume from the shelf and took up the candlestick. The way lay clear ahead. He did not want a chaperone, but apparently he would have to have one. Which meant there was really only one choice.

He would write to her the first thing on the morrow.

The porch door of the deanery shut with a slam, and flying footsteps were heard.

"Girls, girls," admonished Mrs. Fellowes, frowning up at her granddaughter Emmy and Miss Ellsworth, both of the young ladies breathless and flushed. "What on earth?"

"Don't tell me," teased Miranda, replacing her feet on the fender, now that she saw it was not the dean or some clergyman come to call. "You saw a handsome soldier." To the dean's wife she added, "With the militia's general meeting the High Street was positively *swarming* with them."

"There were plenty of soldiers in fine uniforms to be sure," Emmy panted, "but that wasn't it, Mrs. Ellsworth. It was that Beatrice and I were walking past the George Inn just as the Flyer from London arrived—"

"And among the other passengers," Beatrice interrupted, "this fashionable lady in green climbed down—"

"And was taken in a gentleman's arms!" Emmy exclaimed. "But not just any gentleman's arms—the arms of Mr. Wolfe!"

"We knew it was him because Mr. Wolfe is so very large, you know—"

"Mr. Wolfe, publicly embracing a strange woman!" Emmy almost danced with the agony of it. "I could have fainted at the sight! As if there weren't enough young ladies after him already! And I'm afraid I did scream a little, Granny—"

"But I hustled her away, Mrs. Fellowes," Beatrice assured her, "and it was so crowded and noisy that I daresay no one noticed. But it's really too bad, because if she hadn't drawn attention to us, we might have stayed and learned more. We might perhaps even have drifted by on accident and forced him to make an introduction. And now we will never know."

"Of course we will know," Miranda returned in her most matter-of-fact manner. "There are few secrets in Winchester." Her heart pained her, and she was too aware of a plunge in her spirits. *Another woman? And this one he embraced in public?*

"It must be a visiting sister or cousin," Mrs. Fellowes said decisively. "You mark my words. I've not met the man myself, but from all reports he is gentlemanly, and unlikely to be making such a display with anyone else."

"True," Miranda and Beatrice said in unison, and even Emmy looked hopeful again for a moment. Then she sagged once more. "Gentlemen do marry their cousins, however."

The dean's wife, long removed from the heartaches of youth, gave a philosophical shrug. "Ah, well. I am certain the mystery cannot continue long. All will be revealed by Thursday's ball. Emmy, would you ring for the maid? Miranda, you must try the biscuits our cook made. A new recipe, mind you! You know how attached the dean was to his mother's ginger biscuit, but I told him, after over fifty years, I must have something new..."

As it happened, Miranda was not forced to wait until Thursday's assembly to learn the identity of Mr. Wolfe's mystery lady. The very next day, just as Mr. Dodge and Mr. Bracewell were making their bows in the morning room, the footman Bobbins appeared once more in the doorway.

"Mr. Wolfe and Lady Hufton," he announced.

She and Beatrice exchanged glances, but there was neither time nor privacy for more before their latest visitors were in the room.

Miranda had not seen Mr. Wolfe since the dinner at Beaumond and its disturbing aftermath, and it was all she could do to school her expression into something approaching calm. Fearing her color told tales, when she rose from her curtsey she quickly bent to hide it, reprimanding Scamp for growling at Mr. Wolfe and then seizing Pickles, who was trying to jump up at Lady Hufton.

With a writhing dog in her arms, she backed away, praying the callers would interpret her blush as exertion, and she turned to thrust Pickles at Bobbins.

"…The pleasure of introducing my second sister Lady Hufton," Mr. Wolfe was saying. "Jenny, this is Mrs. William Ellsworth, Mrs. Tyrone Ellsworth, Miss Ellsworth, Mr. Dodge, and Mr. Bracewell."

Mrs. Fellowes had guessed rightly, then, with her usual wisdom. Emmy would be relieved. Miranda smothered a rueful chuckle. *Who do you think you are deceiving, Miranda Ellsworth? You, too, are relieved.*

Though sharing her brother's coloring, Lady Hufton was built along more diminutive lines. She did indeed wear very smart cloth-ing, and yet Miranda could not help being reminded of a wood-land shrew. One dressed in crewel-wool embroidered muslin and beautiful striped boots, but bearing a pointed, twitching nose and squinting small eyes nonetheless.

Somehow everyone found a seat, Lady Hufton taking the one Miranda had abandoned, so that in the shuffle she ended up beside Aggie with no work to occupy her hands.

"My husband Tyrone will be sorry to have missed you," said Aggie. "He is meeting with the steward." After a pause she added, "Tyrone is Mrs. Ellsworth's stepson. Mrs. Ellsworth is mistress at Hollowgate." Everyone in Winchester knew Miranda was mistress of Hollowgate and could probably even explain the terms of the late William Ellsworth's will, but Aggie did not want a stranger to think her husband supposed himself master. Miranda's hand slipped over to grasp hers.

"Do you live in Kent as well, Lady Hufton?" Miranda asked politely.

"I don't know what you mean about 'as well,' since Colin no longer lives in Kent," Lady Hufton sniffed. The company gave a little chuckle, though the woman did not join them. "But, yes, Sir John and I live at Stourwood Park outside Canterbury."

The usual questions followed, leading to the usual subjects: the route taken, the discomfort of travel, the state of the roads, the quality of the inns, the quality of the companions, and so forth.

"Thankfully, with my children away at school and my husband so busy hunting and shooting, I need not return until December, I daresay," Lady Hufton concluded. "Colin requested the company and convenience of a hostess at Deaumond, and I was the only sister who could be spared at present."

Miranda's eyes met Mr. Wolfe's at this last statement, and his brow rose in mock alarm, almost drawing a laugh from her. She looked quickly away.

So he had taken her advice! Well, if he had been inclined to dismiss it before, it must have been Miss Paulson's escapade which persuaded him. She wondered how many sisters Mr. Wolfe had and would have been glad to ask, but it felt unfair to ask Lady Hufton a question she would have hesitated to ask Mr. Wolfe.

Mr. Bracewell, to the secret satisfaction of all the Ellsworth ladies, stepped into the breach. "How many Wolfe sisters *are* there, Lady Hufton? And are there other brothers, as well?"

Lady Hufton's beady eyes turned on Mr. Wolfe with what could only be described as surprised reproach, and she issued an uneasy titter. "Hmm...isn't it funny Colin has not—ahem. That is, Mr. Bracewell, there are no other Wolfe sisters and never were. We were all Perrys. Perry sisters, and Colin was our only Perry brother. He, of course, took the name of Wolfe with his marriage, and we four sisters all gave up the name of Perry when we ourselves were wed."

The surprise her story engendered was universal, but, apart from a tiny gasp from Beatrice, well hidden by courtesy, the questions which arose left unsatisfied.

It was Miranda who returned them to safer ground.

"Well, we welcome you to Hampshire, Lady Hufton, and do hope you will enjoy your time here."

"Jenny will have to earn her keep," said Mr. Wolfe lightly. "I warned her that I would work her hard." He tapped his fingers on the brocaded arm of the chair. "You see, apart from having you

Ellsworths and the Fairchilds to dinner on Michaelmas, I haven't done any entertaining to speak of. Therefore it was kindly suggested to me by Miss Paulson—" (He broke off in innocent surprise, when all three Ellsworth women and Mr. Bracewell the curate, inhaled in unison.) "Er—as I was saying, Miss Paulson kindly suggested some time ago how welcome it would be to the neighborhood if I were to give a ball at Beaumond. Therefore I propose to do so, with Jenny's help, in a month's time, and you are the first to know of it."

Delight met this announcement, and then there was plenty to talk about and none of it awkward. Miranda was allowed to lapse into silence—somehow Aggie's work found its way to her hands—and she picked steadily at the snarls and knots, smoothing the fabric in her lap, until the visitors began to make sounds of departing.

"Miss Ellsworth, there being still a month until the Beaumond ball, I hope you will promise me a dance at Thursday's assembly, as Mrs. Ellsworth has," said Mr. Dodge in his usual dreary fashion. Beatrice accepted with good grace, murmuring a fluttered second acceptance when Mr. Bracewell said much the same thing.

"Don't forget me, when you're handing out dances, Miss Ellsworth," Mr. Wolfe entreated her, "though I do go about things hind-end foremost and ask you before asking your stepmother."

"Will you be at the assembly, then, Mr. Wolfe?" Beatrice asked.

"Of course I'll be at the assembly! Unlike you and Mrs. Ellsworth, I have yet to miss one. Yes, indeed, Lady Hufton and I will be there. But first we must complete our round of calls today. I want absolutely all of my acquaintance to learn of my gracious sister's presence and to receive their invitation to our ball."

Then they were all on their feet, Scamp waking from his nap to complete a few figure-eights around various legs, and the next minute the callers were gone.

"Well!" said Aggie, retrieving her sewing from Miranda and chuckling over its improvement. "How do you like that?"

"Emmy will be so, so, so excited about the ball," Beatrice declared. "Do you suppose Mr. Wolfe will pay his first call at the deanery today? She will be over the moon if he does!"

Miranda didn't answer, but Aggie laughed. "The real question is, will he call at the Paulsons? Will he sit there with his new tiny dragon beside him and dare Miss Paulson to try inveigling him again?"

Chapter Fifteen

Long since we were resolved of your truth,
Your faithful service and your toil in war;
Yet never have you tasted our reward.
— Shakespeare, *Henry VI, Part One,* III.iv.1723 (1591)

The Ellsworths were not far off in their guesses. Colin and his sister did indeed call at the deanery, at the Paulsons', and at the Terwilligers', among sundry other families, introducing Lady Hufton to all his new acquaintance and extending invitations to the November ball. He had not, of course, told his sister of Miss Paulson's clandestine visit to Beaumond, so that Lady Hufton was left to think that the unfortunate young lady suffered from overmuch blushing.

At last the work was finished, leaving brother and sister alone in Colin's phaeton, making their way through streets crowded with those come for the quarter sessions.

"What do you think, Jenny? Will you like your time here?"

"I expect so. My life was so dull at home with the children gone. Sir John is so very dull, you know." As it wouldn't be polite for him to agree with her, he held his tongue, and she soon went on. "But I still cannot understand, Colin, why it was necessary for you to remove so far from Kent. Yes, I realize Edmund is at the college and you would like to see him on holidays, but what is a spare afternoon, here or there, when you must uproot your entire existence? You already had an estate, yet you lease another. You already had acquaintances as well as family, yet you choose to begin again. If you wanted to remarry, there were any number of girls in Kent, yet you replace them all with a brand-new set, interchangeable, as far as I can see."

"Now, now, Jenny," he chided. "That was just spiteful. Can you really not distinguish one young lady from another, out of all those I introduced you to today?"

Lady Hufton squinted at him. "You know what I mean, Colin. I am quite serious." She folded her arms stiffly. "It's because you're still angry with us, after all these years, isn't it? You blame us for your years of unhappiness."

He was silent for some minutes, seemingly intent on his driving, but when at last they made their way through the town's north gate and turned into Swan Lane, he said quietly, "Jenny, I *was* resentful at first. For years, I admit. Discontented and apt to blame everyone—our parents, you girls, Doria and her wretched father—everyone but myself, though none of it could have happened without my consent. But then Edmund came along, and I realized I wouldn't have had my son without all the rest of it. So resentment gave way to resignation, a resignation tinged with gratitude."

She sighed, unwinding her arms and reaching briefly to touch his knee.

"Which is why," he continued, "with Doria gone, I thought I would make the most of what all those years had given me. I would make a new life, but one that kept as close as I could to Edmond. He's not an easy boy to know, Jenny. He doesn't talk much. Sometimes I couldn't even say if he feels anything for me, but I'll stick by him until he tells me to go away."

Her thin lips curved. "Be grateful, then, that Edmund *is* a boy of few words."

Swan Lane became the Weeke Road, and buildings gave place to recently-harvested hop fields. Lady Hufton tucked the blanket closer about her lap.

"Colin," she began again, "you mustn't think we were not aware of what you sacrificed for all of us. We've talked of it so many times. Sir John would never have deigned to consider me as a wife, if not for the connection and the portion your marriage provided. And Betsy has been so happy with her Mr. Popple, whom I doubt would have been chosen for that second living if not for the older Mr. Wolfe's influence. As for Katie, she has her health problems, you know, but she is grateful she can afford the doctor's bills and that she didn't have to marry that old man who offered for her years ago. And Pippa!" Lady Hufton gave a deprecating chuckle. "Pippa might have married her baron in any case, being Pippa, but it delighted her to be richer than he was, so that the dowager Lady Arthur must swallow her grumbles."

"The glories of money," agreed Colin dryly.

Lady Hufton gave him a hard look. "Such is the way of the world, yes. But Colin—what I mean to say is, we sisters have discussed it at length, and we all agree it is your turn to be made happy."

"Gracious me! I thank you."

"I am serious, brother," she reproved. "You have earned your right to happiness."

Shaking his head, a lopsided grin twisted his mouth. "Do you think I am disagreeing with you, Jenny? No, indeed, we are all of us—we former Perrys—in perfect agreement. And now you understand why you all must leave me alone about removing to Hampshire. I consider my presence here part of my future happiness."

"All right, then. I will explain it to them all. But I want you to know, Colin, that I consider it my duty to assist you toward that future happiness while I am here, beyond playing your hostess at Beaumond."

"That sounds frightening, Jenny. What can you mean by that?"

"I mean your sisters all think you deserve to have the youngest, prettiest, most delightful second wife you can manage."

"Jenny," he said sternly, "I thank all my sisters for their goodwill, but I don't intend to have my second wife chosen for me."

"There *is* to be a second wife, then?"

He rolled his eyes. "I imagine so. Eventually."

She sat back with complacency, adjusting her gloves. "Exactly. Very well. Choose for yourself. Though I assume I have already met the leading candidates in the field...?" When he made no reply, she said, "And I hope we are both old enough that you would not summarily reject someone simply because I preferred her."

"How could you possibly have a preference, Jenny, when you called them all 'interchangeable'?"

"Don't quibble, Colin!"

With the reins in his hands, he turned his palms up in mock surrender. "I beg your pardon, then."

"Well, aren't you going to ask me who I mean?"

"I wait with bated breath, my dear."

A frown marred her brow. Had Colin always been so flippant? She supposed he was going to make a fool of himself and there was nothing she or her sisters could do to prevent it, but at least she could tell them she tried her best.

"If you ask my opinion, I would cast my vote for Miss Ellsworth of Hollowgate."

He inhaled sharply. "Miss Ellsworth? *Miss* Ellsworth?"

"Of course 'Miss'! I could hardly mean the married one."

"Well—there were two of them unmarried there. Miss Ellsworth and Mrs. William Ellsworth."

"Mrs. William Ellsworth? Oh! You mean the stepmother? The quiet older woman who looks like she wouldn't say boo to a goose? Of course I don't consider *her*, Colin."

"I suspect Mrs. Ellsworth is the same age as you or Betsy or Katie, and I cannot imagine you would like to be dismissed as a 'quiet older woman' not worthy of consideration."

"Colin—what on earth are you talking about? Let us keep to the matter at hand, if you please. Of the young ladies I met today, I would say Miss Wright was the prettiest, but Miss Ellsworth had the more placid demeanor. She spoke just the right amount. Not too seldom, like Doria, nor too much, like so many others her age. She did not seem so *hungry* for you as Miss Wright or Miss Terwilliger or Miss Browning or Miss Banks—"

"If she did not *seem* 'hungry' for me, Jenny, it is because Miss Ellsworth is *not* 'hungry' for me! The girl is just out of school and views me as an uncle or grandfather, I daresay."

"Nonsense. A man in his prime, such as you. Rich and handsome besides. You must not mistake her tranquility around you for indifference, brother."

"Nor should you mistake it for affection, sister."

"Besides being attractive," Lady Hufton continued blithely, "Miss Ellsworth is your equal in rank and has portion enough not to throw herself at you for your money. Moreover, she has a younger brother Edmund's age, which would give her a natural sympathy for your son. Altogether, if you were to choose her, I think you would do very well."

"And supposing I were to choose someone else?"

She shrugged her narrow shoulders. "Of course you must please yourself, Colin. I thought it worthwhile to speak my piece, as far as that goes. If you prefer one of the others—that silly Miss Wright who goggles at you; or Miss Paulson who cannot peek at you without turning plum purple; or Miss Terwilliger who has no distinguishing characteristics of any kind that I can make out—you would know best about that."

Colin made an indeterminate sound in his throat, which his sister interpreted as him pondering her words deeply. In fact he was reconsidering deeply his decision to invite her to Beaumond.

He had wanted Betsy or Pippa to come. Of all his sisters, they were the most compatible. But his youngest sister and husband were in town for the general election and would remain for the entire season at Lord Arthur's insistence. And devoted Betsy never left her husband's side, if she could help it, so that left Jennifer, Lady Hufton, or Katie, who always fancied herself ill. Katie made the choice for him, declaring her health would not allow her to travel at present, so it would have to be Jenny. And after a mere twenty-four hours of Jenny's presence, Colin already found himself wondering if it wouldn't have been preferable after all to be captured by the next scheme laid for him.

For better or worse, the mitigating presence of Lady Hufton opened the floodgate of return callers to Beaumond. The following two mornings Colin found himself pinned to a chair making conversation with every mother, aunt, grandmother, or other designated chaperone in the county, while the marriageable girl smiled and fluttered and blushed, clearly having been told to behave herself. Others came—his landlord Mr. Weeks, the vicar and his wife, Mr. West the solicitor.

On the third morning Colin rose early to escape both Jenny's company and the inevitable callers, choosing instead to go shooting, though he had never been much of a hunter and was in fact a rather mediocre shot. At first the embarrassed Beaumond gamekeeper pretended not to notice, but after an hour or two of only one piddling pheasant being bagged, Holder could not forbear offering a few helpful hints. The elder Mr. Taplin, former master of Beaumond, had been an excellent marksman, Holder frequently boasting that "pheasants are nowhere safe on the property, neither on the ground nor flying above," but those days were gone, clearly.

To the gamekeeper's great relief, when they waded through grasses to higher ground, Wolfe glanced back toward the house. "What would you say, Holder? Is the coast clear?"

Holder squinted, despite the morning having amply proven he possessed the sharper eyesight. "Aye, sir. Looks like most of the visitors are gone, except for one or two, and Lady Hufton may get done with them in the time it takes to walk back."

"Time to hang up the hatchet, then."

The gamekeeper made no argument, accepting the gun from him, and they turned toward the house in companionable silence.

"Thank you very much for the tea," Miranda said to Lady Hufton. "We had better be going now."

"But I wanted to show Mr. Wolfe how I learned that Canzonetta he gave you Ellsworths!" protested Emmy, taking hold of the pianoforte as if she feared Miranda might drag her off.

"Mr. Wolfe has gone shooting, child," her grandmother Mrs. Fellowes admonished. "And heaven knows he may not return for another hour or two. We cannot trespass on Lady Hufton's time so long."

"But Beatrice and I have been *practicing*," Emmy insisted. "Haven't we, Bea? Beatrice plays, and I sing."

Lady Hufton straightened in her seat. "Colin gave the Ellsworths some music? My word, he will certainly want to hear that." She glanced at the mantel clock. "Why don't you perform it for us, girls? Even if Mr. Wolfe does not return in time, I, for one, would be glad to hear it."

Miranda suppressed a sigh. She had not wanted to call in the first place, though her vow to avoid Mr. Wolfe as much as possible had thus far proven laughably unsuccessful. But when Mrs. Fellowes and Emmy drew up at Hollowgate in the deanery landau, Emmy pleading for them to come along and Mrs. Fellowes adding her more muted invitation, there was no escape.

"*Everyone* has been calling at Beaumond," Emmy declared. "It is the talk of the town, and Beatrice and I are the only ones who have not yet returned Lady Hufton's visit."

"Bother Lady Hufton," Beatrice answered, unwittingly speaking for Miranda as well. "You know it's Mr. Wolfe you want to see again. As if Thursday's assembly were not soon enough."

"You must forgive my granddaughter's eagerness, Miss Ellsworth," said Mrs. Fellowes. "And I freely confess to you, Miranda, that your presence and Miss Ellsworth's would make that eagerness less obvious. Well—perhaps not less obvious, but if you two were to join us, your company would *dilute* Emmy's sad impetuosity."

They agreed, of course, there being no alternative. And great had been Miranda's consolation to learn Mr. Wolfe had gone out—a consolation so mixed with disappointment that she was angry with herself.

Emmy hopped up from the instrument to seize Beatrice's arm. "Come on, then! Don't be shy. Lady Hufton wants to hear us."

"She Never Told Her Love" was not terribly long, even though the tempo Beatrice played at was even more "largo" than written, but before the final notes faded, the drawing room door opened and Mr. Wolfe entered.

"Oh!" yelped Emmy, flushing to her hairline. "Mr. Wolfe!"

"Please, do not let me interrupt," he said in a silky voice, making his bow.

"We finished," said Beatrice.

Lady Hufton burst into applause as she rose. "But you must favor us with an encore, Miss Ellsworth, Miss Wright, because I am certain my brother will want to hear such a charming piece. Colin, how was your hunting? You nearly missed a lovely little impromptu concert, but I hope the young ladies will give it to us again."

Beatrice glanced at her stepmother, but Miranda only gave a tiny shrug.

"Come, Colin. Sit by me," urged Lady Hufton, patting the sofa. Her seat gave the fullest view of Beatrice at the pianoforte, as well as of Miranda, opposite, and he took the place offered him willingly enough.

With a droop of resignation, Beatrice obediently put her fingers to the keys and played the opening chords. Lady Hufton listened with her eyes half closed as if she had never heard anything so heavenly. Mrs. Fellowes appeared earthbound enough to press her lips together in warning at Emmy, who, in a fit of nerves, was swinging and flapping the ends of her new swansdown boa, waiting and waiting for her cue to begin. In truth, thrills coursed through Emmy because Mr. Wolfe had never seen her new boa, so snowy white and plush. It was wound once about her neck to draw attention to her eyes and the fairness of her complexion, but the ends hung freely, and she could not resist playing with them, to give her hands something to do. Swing and flap. Flap and swing. Swing and wring and flutter.

In all this handling, the delicate boa, though carefully glued and stitched together by a London milliner, began to give off little puffs of down. Not enough to diminish the plushness of the article, by any means, but quite enough that, when the moment came and Emmy at last drew a deep, deep breath, that breath included several of the tiny feathers.

She knew disaster had struck the instant she felt the tickle at the back of her throat, but it was too late for retreat! Beatrice was playing the last chord—

"*She—*"

Emmy got no further.

Even that first word was swallowed in a monstrous *Hoch!* If this were not bad enough, the explosion was followed by an even louder and more insistent series of sounds, as if a trumpeting elephant were stamping upon a honking goose.

AAAAAaaaakabrack! Hem! Bra-a-a-ck! Huh! HOCH!

"Emmy!" cried Miranda, leaping to her side before Mrs. Fellowes could even struggle up from her chair. "Are you all right? Drink some tea, dear." Having not seen the minute, fluffy culprits which caused the convulsion, Miranda thought the poor child was having some sort of fit.

Much fuss and excitement followed, and poor Emmy was too mortified by the coughing she could not stop to enjoy Mr. Wolfe's concern. Nay, with the self-consciousness of youth she rather wished she were dead and buried, but she had to settle for sitting beside Mrs. Ellsworth and hacking periodically into her handkerchief, when she was not dabbing at her streaming eyes.

Hesitantly, Beatrice made to slip from the instrument, but Lady Hufton was not to be thus thwarted. She hadn't cared a bit about Miss Wright having an opportunity to show off in any case. "Wait, Miss Ellsworth! I suspect your friend would appreciate a reprieve from our attentions, and why should we be deprived of the pleasure of hearing you? You may play the piece *and* sing, I daresay, or at least play the piece."

"Oh! Er—I would rather not sing, thank you," said Beatrice, sinking back despondently.

"What about you, Mrs. Ellsworth?" Mr. Wolfe turned to Miranda with a face of bland innocence. "The music having been a gift to all the Ellsworths, I hope you too have had a chance to try it."

"Mm," she responded vaguely, making a deprecating motion with her hand.

"Yes, Mama, do join me," pleaded Beatrice. "You know you sang it so beautifully when Tyrone and I accompanied you, and your singing will cover any blunders of mine."

"I'm sure the music alone will do nicely," Miranda demurred, her color heightening.

"Oh, do, Miranda," Mrs. Fellowes added to the urging. "I haven't heard you sing since the rectory days."

Under this combined attack Miranda had no choice but to yield, and just in time, too, for her drawing back had vexed Lady Hufton. Why must the ordinary creature make such a to-do of her reluctance? Did she not want to put her stepdaughter forward? If there was anything Lady Hufton despised, it was a woman who could not lay aside her own vanity for the sake of another, especially when that other was one she was obligated by family ties to assist!

But even Lady Hufton's heart was then softened by Miranda's singing, and she grudgingly admitted to herself the woman had a decent voice for her age.

And Colin—he had suggested Mrs. Ellsworth sing to spare Miss Wright, as he had suggested, but also to counter his sister's machinations. But there was another reason, which he only admitted to himself hours later: Mrs. Ellsworth sat there so quietly, making herself as invisible as Jenny thought her. But Colin knew that wasn't the whole Miranda Ellsworth, that peaceful surface. He knew—he had seen—the vivid, fiery spirit she so carefully concealed. The one tamed through years of long practice. And he suspected he would glimpse that hidden side of her again if she sang. Not only he, but

Jenny would see it as well and perhaps acknowledge her as a person worthy of notice. Miranda Ellsworth deserved that much.

It worked. Because Lady Hufton would later say grudgingly, "Who knew still waters ran so deep? I would not be against hearing her again, and at greater length."

But Colin had not expected his own response to her warm, vibrant voice. It brought to mind once more that bare instant when he held her. It made him wonder what it would have felt like to hold her longer.

She never looked at him once. She faced Beatrice instead. But every note, every word passed through him, leaving its mark.

"'She never told her love,'" Miranda sang, "'But let concealment, like a worm in the bud, feed on her damask cheek...She sat, like Patience on a monument, smiling at grief.'"

CHAPTER SIXTEEN

For, as when Painters form a matchless Face,
They from each Fair one catch some diff'rent Grace;
And shining Features in one Portrait blend,
To which no single Beauty must pretend:
So Poets oft do in one Piece expose
Whole *Belles-Assemblées* of Coquets and Beaux.
— William Congreve, *The Way of the World* (1700)

The first assembly in October promised to be well-attended, coinciding as it did with the end of the quarter sessions and the general meeting of the Hampshire militia. The town was full to bursting, with seemingly every room taken in every inn and lodging house.

On such an occasion all the Ellsworth family would be in attendance, including those not living at Hollowgate: the Fairchilds, the
Kenners, the Carlisles, Tyrone and Aggie.

"I don't mind tonight at all," Beatrice announced as the Ellsworth
coach made its slow way toward St. John's Rooms. "For I can dance
with my brothers-in-law and not all those strangers."

"And don't forget your actual brother," Aggie teased, poking her
husband. "Tyrone will do his duty. I myself cannot wait to dance
and will gladly take all the strangers you don't want, Bea! It has been
too long—since before Joan and Margaret were born."

"Since before we eloped, you mean," her husband chuckled. "It
took some time to live that down."

"True enough," agreed his wife, "but we have been so utterly respectable ever since that I hope Beatrice's unwanted strangers might
not even know of our past scandal."

"And how can you call such people strangers, Beatrice?" Miranda
asked. "Mr. Dodge and Mr. Bracewell are well known to us by now.
Too well known, perhaps."

"And don't forget Mr. Wolfe," put in Aggie. "For he asked you as
well, Bea."

"Yes...even if he had not, I fear his sister Lady Hufton would have
compelled him to it, on pain of death," Beatrice grumbled.

Miranda joined with the others in teasing the girl, but inwardly
she thought Beatrice as astute as ever. It had been plain to Miranda
as well that Lady Hufton thought Beatrice a good match for her
brother and a better one than Emmy. Equally plain, but far more
painful, was the realization that, far from thinking Miranda a *poor*

match for Mr. Wolfe, Lady Hufton simply did not consider her at all.

It had been this humbling reminder of invisibility which guided her toilette that evening. When Monk came to dress her, the maid found Mrs. Ellsworth had laid out a plain grey silk with lilac ribbon at the waist and sleeves.

"Your half-mourning, madam? I thought you had chosen that nice blue one with the silver thread."

"I changed my mind."

"Oh, madam—not the cap!" The distraught maid held up the grey silk cap. "It makes you look a hundred years old."

"Monk!"

"Of course I will do whatever you like," said Monk, "but it was bad enough having to dress Mrs. Carlisle before she married because she never cared a pin what she looked like. These things reflect on a person, you know. And what is the use of my efforts, when they are not appreciated?"

"Monk, of course I appreciate your efforts. We all do," Miranda tried to placate her. "How pretty you make Beatrice look."

"Mrs. Tyrone Ellsworth's maid Banniker boasts constantly that she never saw hair take a curl so well as Mrs. Tyrone's," Monk grumbled on, "and that Mrs. Tyrone lets her try whatever she pleases—anything at all from Ackermann's or the Bell Assembly, but you know Miss Beatrice always wants her hair the same, not even curled, and now you—" Monk held the offending cap up between thumb and forefinger, shuddering. "It's one thing to look hideous when one is in mourning, madam, but another altogether to insist on it afterward like a hairy shirt."

Faced with this unexpected opposition, Miranda crumbled. "Very well, very well. There's no need to talk of hair shirts. I did not realize it would pain you, Monk. Never mind the cap. You may do the usual curls."

Monk flung it aside joyously. "Just the usual ones? Because I did see this one plate in the Bell Assembly, where we might wind some fabric—I suppose it had better be lilac to match—around your head this way..."

When they had gone, the maid had reason to do some boasting of her own below stairs, for she congratulated herself that she had completely frustrated Mrs. Ellsworth's unfathomable desire to appear at the assembly as a dowd. The dreadful half-mourning gown could not be avoided, but Monk insisted on a silver filigree chain with amethyst pendant and matching earrings, and the lilac silk fabric she contrived into a layered headband holding back a fountain of shining curls.

"If they only looked at Mrs. Ellsworth from the neck up this evening," Monk later told Aggie's Banniker, "they wouldn't be far mistaken to call her a belle."

"Pooh," said Banniker, rather put out by the success of Monk's handiwork. "No person only gets looked at from the neck up, and whoever heard of a belle Mrs. William Ellsworth's age?"

Greaves drew the coach up in the Causeway outside St. John's Rooms, and Gotch assisted them to alight.

"Only see how many people are here!" cried Emmy Wright, darting forward to greet them. "Here they are. You may go now, Davidson. How do you like my dress? I added the lace. And this is my mama's circlet. What do you think? Mr. Wolfe and Lady Hufton have already gone up. Beatrice, you will certainly admit he is handsome tonight."

Her chatter continued as they entered, were relieved of their cloaks, and climbed the stairs, all of which took more time than usual.

"They might have done better to hold this ball in the cathedral yard," Tyrone observed. "The room might allow for two lines of dancers, but anyone not dancing will have to press himself against the wall or escape to the coffee room."

He was not far off, for when they entered the main room at last, with its rose-colored walls ornamented by white plasterwork and portraits of Winchester notables, they were confronted with a sea of people. And for once, Miranda noted, the number of gentlemen appeared to outnumber the ladies! Unsurprisingly, with their general meeting happening, there were a great number of Hampshire militiamen, their red coats contrasting with the blacks and dark greens and dark blues of the other men, those drawn by their various responsibilities at the quarter sessions, in addition to Winchester's usual clergymen and ecclesiastical sorts serving the cathedral and diocese.

But even with all these gentlemen, old and new, Miranda's gaze found Mr. Wolfe at once. Well, Mr. Wolfe and Mr. Lyfford, to be precise, because both were a head taller than anyone near them and because they were speaking to each other. She supposed the feather waving beside Mr. Wolfe's shoulder must adorn the head of Lady Hufton.

"There he is!" squeaked Emmy, hopping a little until Miranda laid a firm hand on her forearm. "But we will never reach him."

Indeed, like the Israelites before the Red Sea, they faced a barrier which did not appear surmountable by mortal means. The Tyrone Ellsworths were the first to be swept away, Tyrone catching sight of their Weeks' relations and taking Aggie with him. Then a battalion of clerical acquaintances elbowed their way over, determined to trade upon their long familiarity with Miranda to secure Miss Ellsworth and Miss Wright for partners. These were followed by the master of ceremonies Mr. Rigford, who had been pressed into service by several soldiers to perform introductions, after which time Mr. Dodge and Mr. Bracewell made their way over to remind the three ladies that they were already promised dances.

To Miranda's dismay, the latter two then took up positions flanking her. Mr. Dodge had claimed her first dance and Mr. Bracewell her second, but it was as if they both recognized Mr. Lyfford had disqualified himself, and they were the only two remaining contenders in the field.

"Mrs. Ellsworth," mourned Mr. Dodge, "I do not know if your son Master William has written to you of it, but my quiristers will be giving a special concert in the College chapel next week, in honor of the Feast of St. Luke."

Miranda hid a smile. She could not think of a subject her Willsie was less likely to mention, but she answered politely, "How delightful, Mr. Dodge."

"Do you think so?" His harried features lightened. "My pupils sing in all the chapel services, to be sure, but it is rare for anyone outside the college to hear them. Therefore I have spoken to the warden about allowing this concert to be open to the public. While he was not ready to go so far, he agreed that a few family members of the current Wykehamists should be permitted to attend."

Her courteous interest blossomed into the genuine article at the thought of seeing William in his school setting, even if he were only sitting in another pew with his collegemates. "Really? Why, then, if it is permissible, Mr. Dodge, I would very much like to attend! And perhaps I might reserve a seat or two for the Fairchilds? I suspect at least my daughter Mrs. Fairchild would be eager to accompany me."

Dodge could not forbear throwing Bracewell a triumphant look, which he loftily pretended not to see, but indeed the curate was inwardly gnashing his teeth that he had no similar occasion on which to astound Mrs. Ellsworth with his abilities. He could hardly invite her to hear his sermon on a Sunday, for she had her own parish church, and there were besides some in his flock who whispered, most unjustly, that Mr. Bracewell was better to look at than to listen to.

When the Fairchilds squeezed their way through, Miranda barely heard Florence's "Mama, how lovely you look!" in her eagerness to tell them of the quirister concert. Mr. Fairchild chuckled, saying with a deprecating nod to Dodge, "I thank you for my share, but as an alumnus of the college, I have heard enough of the quiristers singing to last a lifetime." But his wife shared Miranda's opinion, thinking of how she would see her son Peter in this new setting, and she too gladly accepted Mr. Dodge's invitation.

Mr. Dodge would have been vastly contented had the matter ended there, but the draft he received from this cup of joy was not to be unalloyed with bitterness. For Mrs. Fairchild and Mrs. Ellsworth were still plying him for more details when that blasted Mr. Wolfe appeared, his enormous self suddenly crowding Dodge backward and his pale eyes impudently taking his measure.

"What's this? A concert in the Winchester College chapel? What a splendid idea, Dodge. I feel such nostalgia for the quiristers we had at King's when I was a boy."

"Thank you. Er—sadly, as you probably realize, Wolfe, space is somewhat limited in the chapel—"

"How fortunate for me, then, that Fairchild has no wish to go and that Mrs. Ellsworth and Mrs. Fairchild are such slender creatures," replied the interloper amiably. "Please accept my gratitude for this chance to see how my son Edmund fares at school. He's not much for letter-writing, I'm afraid. Isn't that so, Jenny?"

Lady Hufton's thin lips thinned further to be excluded from the concert, for which she blamed Mr. Dodge, but the man having long experience with cosseting wealthy potential school donors, he scrambled to make amends, asking her if he could have the pleasure of partnering her later in the evening.

The musicians began playing through the music of the first dance, and Mr. Rigford signaled from the top of the room that the first set was forming. With chest swelling once more, Mr. Dodge edged around Mr. Wolfe to claim Miranda, while Mr. Bracewell took Emmy.

"Then it must be my turn, Miss Ellsworth," Mr. Wolfe addressed Beatrice.

Lady Hufton gave a pleased sigh, quite audible to her brother, and it must have been Colin's contrariness which made him then turn to Mrs. Ellsworth and say, "If I count correctly, I will be honored with you as my third partner...?" At least the woman didn't misconstrue his words as interest in her, and Lady Hufton fully approved Mrs. Ellsworth's downcast eyes and murmured, "I expect so. Thank you."

As much as Mr. Dodge would have liked to lead Mrs. Ellsworth as far as possible from his rival Bracewell and the tiresome Wolfe, he manfully martyred himself, assuming she would be happier keeping an eye on her charges. In fact Miranda thought Beatrice and Emmy safe in these circumstances, with so many family members present, and when the couples took hands-four she found Beatrice and Mr. Wolfe must be in their quartet to begin. It was only for the first time through the figures—after that she and Mr. Dodge would rotate down the room while Beatrice and Mr. Wolfe progressed up—but it was long enough for a mortifying incident.

For it happened that, the first time the foursome took hands to go in circle, Mr. Dodge with great intrepidity dared to squeeze Miranda's fingers. The unwelcome sensation caused her eyes to flash and her nostrils to flare, but, with admirable self-command, Miranda resolved to ignore it. This time. But she equally resolved that, if he tried it again, she would not let it pass.

The second half of the pattern was a reverse of the first, the two couples taking hands again to turn in circle in the opposite direction. And perhaps it was this reversement which addled her, for, when she felt her hand squeezed once more, she turned instantly to the offending Mr. Dodge and hissed, "Leave off this paddling at *once*, sir. It is very disagreeable to me."

"I—er—but Mrs. Ellsworth, I—" Mr. Dodge sputtered, going scarlet as a sunrise.

Confused by his obvious befuddlement, Miranda was on the point of begging his pardon when she heard a choking sound over her shoulder. One glance showed her Mr. Wolfe's bulky form hunching—actually *hunching*—with muffled laughter as he passed up to the couple's new position.

Had he—had he been the one to squeeze her fingers the second time? His refusal to meet her accusing gaze when she stared fixedly at him, along with the ruthless pressing-together of his lips, told her all she needed to know. The wretched prankster! He must have guessed at Mr. Dodge's offense based on her own response, if he had not witnessed the offense itself. And then to do it again himself, causing her to snap at Mr. Dodge!

But eventually Miranda's sense of humor prevailed, and though regretful of her own display of temper, she could not help choking back a giggle.

"Sir, it was quite reprehensible of you to squeeze my hand when I was dancing with Mr. Dodge," Miranda addressed him at once when it was his turn to partner her. She could not help smiling to save her life because he pretended to meet her with the expression of a dog who does not know if he will be stroked or beaten.

"How could I refrain?" he replied. "No one who has discovered your hidden temper could resist setting a match to it. It's all the more satisfying because of your unassuming surface, Mrs. Ellsworth. You *seem* the irreproachable sort of person elderly dean's wives choose to chaperone their granddaughters, but I have seen the truth too many times otherwise to be deceived."

"I hope you can be trusted to keep my secret then," she replied, with a twinkle which would surely have horrified Lady Hufton, had that good lady not been far away at the bottom of the room, standing up with a beefy canon-residentiary.

"Never fear. I can keep secrets as well as you."

At the teasing note in his voice, which sent a prickle up her backbone, a belated warning bell sounded in Miranda's head. Where were all her firm resolutions to resist the man? Avoid the man? If he had uncovered her hasty temper—a temper even she was unaware of having, three months earlier—what more might he find? What more might he expose to her own gaze and the gaze of the world, if she allowed this to continue? Because the worst—the most humiliating—was still unknown to him.

For the briefest moment as she cast outward and trusted she would not be observed, Miranda screwed her eyes shut and sent up a prayer. *Oh please, God, may he never guess I care for him. May no one ever guess.*

If the man could not be avoided—and it appeared he could not—she must guard herself even more rigorously. Guard her conduct. Guard her tongue. Guard the delight in his company which threatened constantly to leak out.

As if in divine spite of these strictures Miranda had just delivered to herself, Mr. Wolfe said, "There is one thing I see you mean to publish to the world, however."

No curiosity! No coyness! No flirtation!

"Oh?" she asked, as indifferently as she could.

"You mean the world to know—or at least Greater Winchester—that loveliness is not confined to the youngest of your sex."

Colin no sooner spoke the words than he cursed himself. What was he about, saying such things? He would give Mrs. Ellsworth *ideas*, when he had been so careful with all the younger women to avoid just such entanglements.

But it's true, pointed out some inner imp not under his control. *She does look lovely. As lovely as any of the younger women here. Lovelier, because she has lived and suffered and still has that soft sweetness to her.*

"I only mean such an observation, of course, in all friendliness," he added idiotically.

Why so flustered? the imp mocked. *One might almost imagine you began to be in love with her. But no, no. You, Colin Wolfe, with the world at your feet and your choice of the young ladies in Hampshire. You must have other reasons for thinking again and again of that moment she was in your arms. Other reasons for resenting how Jenny ignores her existence.*

Because she was looking at a point to the left of his ear, Miranda failed to notice her partner's confusion, or the grimace he made after his last inanity. She failed even to register it as an inanity, distracted as she was by the literal words.

Friendliness. His compliment, which had made her foolish, unruly heart leap, was offered in "friendliness." Such as he had offered Miss Paulson, when the girl abased herself by climbing up in the rain to what she thought was his bedchamber.

Miranda sent up a second silent prayer, this one of thanksgiving. Thank God for this sobering reminder. Thank God that only she need ever know of her folly, her wistful half-hopes. There had been no witnesses and, please God, there would be none.

This prayer, for better or worse, was granted. For though during the dance more than one pair of eyes drifted from time to time toward the couple, in every instance when the figures separated them, those eyes followed Mr. Wolfe, rather than Mrs. Ellsworth. And at this precise moment, as Mr. Wolfe's imp shared its detached and disturbing reflections, only one gaze in the entire ballroom happened to be trained on the man's face.

Further down the set, a tiny gasp escaped Beatrice Ellsworth, one too quiet to draw her partner's notice.

"Oh," she whispered. "Oh, dear."

CHAPTER SEVENTEEN

**Every purpose is established by counsel:
and with good advice make war.
— Proverbs 20:18, *The Authorized Version* (1611)**

I t would ruin everything," Beatrice told herself. "*He* would ruin everything. I did not think him so unkind."

Though it was unkind, perhaps, to call him unkind. Would "thoughtless" be a better word? Because, if Mr. Wolfe were to decide he admired Mrs. Ellsworth, it would not be from unkindness. Nor would it be from stupidity. In fact, Beatrice would grudgingly think the better of him for having noticed her dear mama's thorough excellence amidst the noise and distraction of the dozen young ladies vying for him.

But if Mr. Wolfe were to love Mrs. Ellsworth, and she were to return his affections, it would be the end of Beatrice's world! They would marry. They would remove to Beaumond. Or worse—to Kent! Mrs. Ellsworth would of course say Beatrice was welcome to come with them, and that Willie must go in any event, but both possibilities were *im*possibilities! Beatrice could not bear to be exiled from Hollowgate; but nor could she bear to be separated from her mama and younger brother.

Please let her not love him back.

For the remainder of that dance, Beatrice ignored her partner Mr. Bracewell nearly to the point of rudeness, so occupied was she in scrutinizing Mrs. Ellsworth's face. Fortunately the curate had inquietudes of his own and did not venture to interrupt her. And what Beatrice found in the ensuing fifteen minutes did much to soothe her ruffled spirit. For her dear mama's countenance could not have been more serene. There was no blushing, no tilting or tossing of the head, no coquetry. Mrs. Ellsworth maintained throughout the same calm half smile. When Mr. Wolfe spoke to her, she answered, but not at length. Beatrice could not hear them, naturally, but with her eyes opened to Mr. Wolfe's secret, she could discern that Mrs. Ellsworth's demeanor did not satisfy.

But it greatly satisfied Beatrice. Because her mother's tranquility meant it was not too late. Not too late to intervene. Not too late to *prevent* the fulfillment of Beatrice's fears. If only Mr. Wolfe's heart was involved at this point, there was hope. He would be disappointed, of course, but heaven knew he had other women to choose from, and he likely would be perfectly satisfied in the long run. Therefore, Mr. Wolfe's potential sufferings could be dismissed without undue guilt.

Still, Beatrice Ellsworth was a just girl, and she sought other trusted opinions before the night was through. At an assembly with so many gentlemen, she had little leisure to speak apart with her older sisters, but she grabbed what opportunities she could.

"Would you say Mama was likely or unlikely to remarry?" she asked her sister Lily, when they happened to be seated beside each other for the tea.

"Likely," said Lily, not perturbed in the least by the question.

"Whatever makes you say that?" demanded Beatrice. "Does she not seem perfectly content to you?"

"She does," answered Lily. "Which is what makes me think she cannot be perfectly content, for who ever is?"

"But why do you think that means she would remarry? Do you think her...fond of anyone?"

Lily stared at her. "Goosey. I don't mean she's already got the next bridegroom picked out. I only meant she isn't terribly old, and you and Willsie are nearly grown. Of course she will marry again. She's too rich for the gentlemen to leave her alone for long. Eventually one will wear her down."

"But supposing I didn't want her worn down quite yet?"

"What a sad fidget you are, Bea! I think it far more likely Mama would talk herself out of it, nine times out of ten. She is too much in the habit of putting herself last, you know. She would probably deny herself the moon, if you or Willie had the least objection."

Beatrice had never found Lily much good to talk to, but on this occasion she was pleased and relieved that her second sister said nothing of Mr. Wolfe or Mrs. Ellsworth already having her feelings engaged. And her insight about Mrs. Ellsworth's self-denying nature was valuable indeed.

Later, when Beatrice saw her third sister Araminta getting the hem of her dress repaired, she hastily tore the lace on her own sleeve, that she might excuse herself to claim the same maid's services.

"Have you seen Mama dancing tonight, Minta?"

"I have. It's delightful. You know Papa would never come to any of these things, and it makes me sad because she is such a good dancer and loves it at home."

"Would you say she seems especially fond of any of her partners? Lily thought it likely Mama would remarry at some point." Beatrice tried to add this last as nonchalantly as she could.

Minta considered, whistling absently to the tune and tapping her foot until the maid begged her to hold still, please.

"She certainly is in demand."

"Lily says that's because she's rich and not so very old."

"And...pretty," decided Minta. "That's a new fashion with her hair, wouldn't you say? It hurts to say it, but Lily is probably right. But don't fret about it, Bea. She doesn't look besotted with anyone here. She looks as she always does. So I would say you are safe for the present. And besides, if you don't like whoever she marries, you may always live with one of us: Tyrone or Flossie at Hollowgate, or Nicholas and me in Canon Street."

"Safe for the present"? It was as much as she could hope, and Beatrice "kept all these things" for later pondering in her heart.

Her last and oldest sister Florence she took aside when they were outside St. John's Rooms after the ball had ended. There was little time for privacy, and Beatrice could see Flossie's husband was eager to get away, so she must come directly to the point.

"Flossie," Beatrice whispered, tucking her arm through hers. "Look at Mr. Wolfe over there, speaking to some of the others. Do you think Mama has feelings for him?"

Florence, who had been in process of patting away a yawn, inhaled sharply, her eyes widening. But she was never dismissive of her youngest sister, no matter what odd whims might take the girl, so she dutifully peered in the direction requested.

Mr. Wolfe had his back to them, but in the lamplight Florence could see a semicircle of female admirers gathered about him. Adoring Miss Banks, Miss Terwilliger, Miss Browning, Miss Wright—possibly Miss Paulson in the shadows. And then, to one side, a step behind Miss Wright, Mrs. Ellsworth. Her hands were folded neatly before her, and she did not appear to be attending, but rather to be looking out for the appearance of the Ellsworth coach. No—she had been looking for the deanery maid Davidson, for when Davidson stole up, Mrs. Ellsworth smiled and said something and touched Miss Wright's shoulder.

"I would have to watch her more closely, darling," Florence whispered back therefore to Beatrice, giving her a hug around the shoulders and guessing at what troubled the girl. "But at first glance I would say, no, Mama seems her usual self. And she is too sensible a person to like a gentleman simply because he turns other ladies' heads."

Beatrice's heart left her throat and settled back in her bosom where it belonged, so that she could be quite cheerful on the ride home. With her conscience thus made easy, she did not even lie awake for very long making her plan because the way forward seemed plain enough.

The next day was clear and sunny, and Miranda was unsuspicious when Beatrice asked if she would like to take a walk. "Perhaps across the grounds toward The Acres," she suggested. "You know Mr. Weeks never minds if we venture there, and Aggie says the landscape gardener has completed the diversion of the stream to create a pond."

Eager as always to dodge Mr. Dodge and the equally ubiquitous Mr. Bracewell, Miranda agreed, not guessing at the trap laid for her. "At least Aggie cannot complain of us abandoning her, since she and the babies go to see her sister Mrs. King today."

The skies might be blue, but strong winds whipped at their skirts and sent red and yellow leaves whirling across the Hollowgate lawns.

"Doesn't the fresh air feel wonderful?" asked Beatrice, skipping a little ahead. "There were so very many people at the assembly last night, and it grew so warm from the dancing that I was surprised no one fainted. But I suspect no girls wanted to faint, or they might miss something."

Miranda smiled. "You're at a lovely age. A flowering age."

"Mama, when you were eighteen, did you ever love anyone? I mean, before you married Papa?"

There was a pause. Miranda looked off toward the little wood, where several pigs had been turned loose to feed on tumbled acorns and beechmast.

"I lived a quiet life at the rectory," she said at last. "So I suppose the answer is no. There was one canon of the cathedral who had a beautiful singing voice...but he never married, of course, and he died young."

Beatrice caught at her stepmother's hand. "Oh! I never heard that story! How sad! Do you think, if he *hadn't* been a canon, and if he *hadn't* died young, you might ever have loved him?"

That made Miranda laugh. "You mean, if he had not been himself? How could I answer that? But come—I thought you don't like to talk of love, silly girl."

Beatrice stopped short, releasing Miranda's hand so she might clasp her own to her chest. "I don't. Not usually. But...I have been thinking."

Miranda's eyes widened. Could it be? Was Beatrice going to confess to a *tendre* for Mr. Bracewell?

"Yes?" she prompted gently, wrapping an arm around Beatrice's shoulders and setting them in motion again. She knew it was easier to share confidences when one had something else to look at. "And have you made a discovery?"

They were nearly to the brook separating Hollowgate grounds from The Acres, hardly more than a muddy bed at this time of year, and Beatrice waited until they picked their way across to reply.

Then the moment was upon her.

"I have been thinking," she began again, "of what sort of qualities in a man I admire. Not for *now*, you understand, but for the future."

Miranda felt a tug at her heart. Ah, at Beatrice's age, how soon the present could become the future! It would be so lonely, if Beatrice married. To go from being the mother of two to the mother of one, and he away at school for months of the year! Would it be much different than if she had simply been the spinster great-aunt of her step-grandchildren?

But soon enough she gave herself a firm mental shake. *This conversation—this* moment—*is not about* you, *Miranda Ellsworth.*

"Tell me," she murmured. "You are a prudent, commonsensical girl, and I have every faith in your judgment."

"Thank you, Mama. I will say then that I find I admire, first and foremost, the...wisdom which comes with age."

This was so unexpected Miranda laughed. "The wisdom which comes with age? My dear girl, when one is eighteen, *everyone* is older. Therefore you will have a wide field to choose from."

"No, Mama, I mean—significantly older," said Beatrice. "The gentlemen nearer my age seem so silly. Like...overgrown puppies."

"I see." Miranda was warier now. "When you look about you, then, which gentlemen seem...less so?"

"Well...Mr. Lyfford, of course. He is quite old," Beatrice began timidly, it seeming too sudden to run right at Mr. Wolfe. But this dodge only made things more difficult because her stepmother stopped altogether, dropping her arm to stare at her.

"But not him so much," the girl amended quickly. "In fact, not him at all. Because—he isn't as wise as he could be. I suppose I would—prefer—someone like—like—like a Mr. Wolfe."

Miranda took a step back, one arm lifting as if to ward off a blow. "Mr. Wolfe? He—is quite a bit older than you, darling."

"No older than Mr. Lyfford," returned Beatrice promptly. Her courage rose with having got the words out. "And no older than Papa was to you. He might even, I think, be closer in age to me than Papa was to you. And you and Papa were happy, were you not?"

Miranda's arm fell back to her side. She felt faint, but she took a few slow steps onward, more to hide her response from Beatrice than from any desire to see Mr. Weeks' new pond. A gust of wind picked up a handful of dead leaves and tossed them at her, like wheat at a wedding.

It was absolutely true, what Beatrice said. The disparity in age between Miranda and her husband William Ellsworth had been even greater, but—

"Your father and I did manage to find contentment in our union," Miranda answered slowly, feeling her way. "Fondness and contentment. But—we were fortunate in that, and in little William, of course. However—" she held up her palms "—I am widowed, as we know, while there is still likely a great deal of life to be lived. I wouldn't wish that on you, my dear."

"Thank you, Mama." Beatrice took her arm again and felt it trembling, but Beatrice thought it was because she had reminded her of painful things. And when Miranda gently shook her off, Beatrice hurried away from the subject of her father's death.

"It isn't only Mr. Wolfe's age and greater maturity," Beatrice explained. "I like how he cares for his son and how good-humored he is. Emmy calls him handsome and dashing, and he is certainly those things, but those qualities matter less to me, I daresay." She caught at one of the leaves and twirled it by its stem, peeping from under lowered lashes at her stepmother. Had she said enough?

"Beatrice," said Miranda, her voice low and steady and calm, "tell me plainly: if Mr. Wolfe were to offer for you, would you be tempted to accept?"

Having foreseen the question, the girl was prepared for it, and she had concluded a half-truth was better than a lie.

"I would *not* accept," she declared. "Not now. I am too young and have no inclination to marry straight away."

"But—if you refused him, he might ask another before you decided you were ready, dear."

"That is the chance I must take," said Beatrice stoutly. "It's one thing to like a person, but quite another to persuade yourself no other person will do. Suppose I leaped at his offer, only to grow a few years older and discover we weren't such a felicitous match?"

But everything Miranda knew of Beatrice told her this would not be the case. The girl disliked change, after all. And who could blame her, after having lost her mother at a young age and then recently her father? Consider, for instance, how many years it had taken to persuade Beatrice to attend Mrs. Turcotte's Seminary for Young Ladies, when she preferred to stay at Hollowgate, following around first her sister Florence and then Miranda. And when Beatrice liked or disliked someone, she was nigh unmovable. Why, she *still* loathed the very name of Francis Taplin, who had once broken Aggie's heart and pawed at Minta, and the man had been gone from the country for years and was only remembered as a family joke!

No. If stalwart Beatrice had even begun to think of Mr. Wolfe in the light of a potential partner, Miranda could not foresee anything to deflect her from the path of liking him better and better as time passed. He might never return Beatrice's feelings, but, short of him marrying someone else, Mr. Wolfe's possible indifference would have nothing to do with how Beatrice herself felt. She might even *prefer* indifference for now! It would give her time to ponder and grow used to the changes taking place in her own heart.

And she, Miranda? How did she feel about the morning's revelation?

It is a godsend.

For what more effective way to ensure both that she expelled Mr. Wolfe from her heart and that no one ever learned of his residence there to begin with? She could never, never indulge tender feelings for a man her own daughter might prefer. *Did* prefer. She absolutely could not—would not—do that. Which meant her wretched, embarrassing secret would die with her, and hopefully the more quickly for having never been told.

It will hurt a little, for a little while, Miranda told herself. They had reached a prospect of Mr. Weeks' new pond, and she put a hand to her forehead, as if to shield her eyes from the glare. With the other she took Beatrice's hand, giving it a swing.

"Very well," said Miranda, sounding almost playful. "Let nothing be done too hastily. Who knows? An even older, wiser gentleman may come along, and then where would you be, if you had accepted Mr. Wolfe? For instance, have you considered Mr. Spacks the prebendary? I do believe he's all of ninety."

Beatrice laughed at that, and glad to be done with her unpleasant task, she happily pulled her stepmother down the slope toward the water, turning the talk to anything and everything else. Perhaps she need not have said or done anything at all! Perhaps her mama didn't care a fig for Mr. Wolfe and never would have, but it didn't hurt to make sure of things.

It will only hurt a little while, Miranda recited inwardly the rest of the morning. *A little, for a little while.* She had survived many things, and she would survive this as well.

A little, for a little while.

Chapter Eighteen

Beshrew me but I love her heartily;
For she is wise, if I can judge of her,
And fair she is, if that mine eyes be true.
— Shakespeare, *The Merchant of Venice*,
II.vi.965 (c.1596)

I declare, I have not slept so late in an age! I danced holes in my slippers last night," Lady Hufton announced as she scurried into the breakfast room. "Too bad I am already married because there were so many handsome gentlemen there! Who could have imagined such a delightful time?"

Tossing aside the letter he had been reading, Colin resumed his meal. "I'm glad you enjoyed it."

After a sweeping glance to be certain no footmen lurked, she wagged a finger at him. "Is that all you have to say? I tell you I might elope and abandon Sir John, and you say you are glad I enjoyed it?"

This drew a reluctant grin. "Good heavens. I wasn't aware you were in earnest, Jenny. Poor Sir John, to be so easily forgotten."

Lady Hufton wrinkled her nose at him with alarming cheerfulness. "Never mind my dull husband, Colin. I am far more interested in talking about *you*. Tell me: which of your fair partners did you most enjoy dancing with? As a lady, I would give the palm to Mr. Kenner the prebendary. Very graceful. Not that you aren't graceful, Colin, but you are such a large person I can't help fearing for my feet."

"I have never stepped on your feet, Jenny."

"Come now. Don't avoid my question. Which of your partners did you like best? I still have it for Miss Ellsworth, but I am perfectly content to change my allegiance to whichever young lady you choose. If you will be happy, *I* will be happy for you."

Colin hesitated. But he had made up his mind the night before, and the sooner Jenny gave up her ridiculous preference for Miss Ellsworth, the better.

He took a measured breath and then—made the plunge. "Very well, Jenny. I will tell you, if you like to know. The partner I most enjoyed dancing with was Mrs. Ellsworth."

Her sharp little eyes blinked wide, and she set down her teacup "Impossible man! You mean Mrs. Tyrone Ellsworth, I suppose? She's pretty and lively, I grant you, but sadly already married."

"As is *your* choice, Mr. Kenner the prebendary."

"Oh, Colin, do be serious! Tell me which of the *unattached* ladies you preferred."

"I did," he replied with vexatious calm. "Mrs. William Ellsworth is a widow and therefore unattached. I am not teasing you, Jenny; I am entirely in earnest."

"You—prefer—" Lady Hufton's brow creased, and she squinted out the window, trying to recall the quiet widow's face. It did not come. Only a cloudy remembrance of—pah!—a grey-and-lilac half-mourning gown and some curled brown hair.

Alarmed, she looked back at her brother, but his pale eyes and set face gave nothing away.

"Do you mean, simply, that you preferred dancing with her to your other partners?" twitched Lady Hufton. "Because she is perhaps lighter on her feet or—or not so tiresomely eager?"

"Mrs. Ellsworth is indeed both of those things, but those are not the weightiest reasons for my preference."

With nervous fingers, his sister began to tear apart her toast. "Oh. Ah." The fragments shattered on the tablecloth, and she pushed her plate from her. "You know her better than I, of course."

"By which you mean you cannot understand me."

"Oh, Colin! It's that—you might have *anyone* now!" she reminded him, as if he might have forgotten. "Anyone at all. Therefore, why would you choose another Doria?"

At the flash of his pale eyes, Lady Hufton shrank back, like a shrew overshadowed by a passing owl.

"Mrs. Ellsworth is no Doria," he said icily. "I will pardon you for saying so because you have so little acquaintance with her."

Really, he was being unjust, he knew. For how could Jenny be blamed, if she did not appreciate Mrs. Ellsworth after two meetings, when Colin himself had not seen the woman clearly (nor his own heart) for two entire months? Perhaps two months was an exaggeration. Surely he had not been in love with Miranda Ellsworth for two months. Two months would date from that August day when they met outside West & Fairchild, the day he snarled at her, imagining she too wanted to lease Beaumond.

But now that his eyes had been opened, he wondered at the world's blindness. The world saw her, when it saw her, as a widow pursued for her money, as if she had not manifold other desirable qualities. Surely it was better that way, or Colin would have to keep an eye on more than Dodge and Bracewell, but with the zeal of the newly converted he could not help but want to force his views willy nilly upon his sister.

"I have been brusque with you," he began somewhat stiffly. "And ought to beg your pardon as well for speaking ill of the dead. I trust you understand what I say of Doria is only for your ears."

"Of course," agreed Lady Hufton, meek as milk.

"Doria was, I think everyone would agree, not the most vivacious of women. Not prone to chatter or effusions of emotion. She did her duty in life, but enthusiasm was perhaps reserved for her beloved pets."

His sister made no reply, for indeed every word he said was true and defense neither possible nor necessary under the circumstances.

"But Mrs. Ellsworth," he continued, "though quiet in company, is not without vivacity. Nor humor, nor agreeableness, nor wit! Indeed, she does not lack even fire, when put to the test."

"You have...put her to the test, brother?" asked Lady Hufton.

He smiled. "I have irked her more than once, let us say. But Jenny, I believe if you come to know her better, you will like her better."

"I will, Colin," Jenny vowed, not being a woman to run her head against a brick wall if it could be avoided. "If I cannot, it will not be for lack of trying." She would be sorry to tell her sisters their brother had settled for so mousy a creature, but if Colin thought she was attractive, it would suffice. It would have to.

"Think of it! I do not know who would be made happier—me or Edmund—to be joined to the Ellsworths. The boy has already taken to Mrs. Ellsworth's son and grandson, and I suppose I might marry anyone I pleased without him noticing, so long as I left him to run about with them. At least if I married Mrs. Ellsworth I would still see him on holidays and vacations without having always to inveigle the entire family to Beaumond. And Edmund says more words in the Ellsworths' presence than he ever does when alone with me. Not many words, mind you, but *more* of them. And what he does say, Mrs. Ellsworth has a natural sympathy for—a natural understanding."

As Edmund's aunt, jealousy pricked Lady Hufton—had his Perry aunts not always sympathized with the boy as well? Colin was infatuated to be sure! How could anyone say with certainty what young Edmund Wolfe thought or felt?

Not overeager to hear her brother go on at length about Mrs. Ellsworth's supposed perfections, she cleared her throat delicately. "Do you suppose she—ah—returns your feelings?"

For the first time that morning, uncertainty shadowed his countenance. "I...couldn't say yet. I think we are friends, and I think she prefers my company to any of the other gentlemen hovering about her. But that's a far cry from wanting to marry me. I take courage nonetheless, that it's a start, and I intend to ride over to Hollowgate this very afternoon to begin my siege, as it were."

"Shall I come too, Colin? I might at least occupy Miss Ellsworth and Mrs. Tyrone Ellsworth, if they are there, so you might have a word aside."

But what man wanted a witness to his courting? He frowned, and Lady Hufton was quick to add, "You must consider: if she is so contained and decorous a person, Colin, you cannot go about it roaring and thundering and speaking of 'sieges.' You must be more subtle than that."

To her surprise, he listened.

"Yes, I daresay you are right, Jenny. Lyfford—one of her rejected suitors—made that mistake and was summarily sent about his business."

"Exactly. If you do not ask prematurely, you cannot be refused prematurely."

"And she *would* refuse, If I surprised her with it," he muttered. "Refuse, and tell me it was her final word on the matter. No. You're right. I must try to sound her first. Sound, but also woo."

Lady Hufton turned her head, so that her brother would not see her roll her eyes. He would not be able to check himself for long, she suspected. It was too in his nature to take the bull by the horns, and likely timid Mrs. Ellsworth would flee away, shrieking figuratively, and matters would be quickly at an end. Well, what must be must be!

Perhaps things might still come right in the end, with her own favorite Miss Ellsworth prevailing.

"Mrs. and Miss Ellsworth have gone for a walk," Bobbins the footman told them, shouldering the front door to shut it against the wind. "Mrs. Tyrone Ellsworth is away visiting, and Mr. Tyrone Ellsworth is surveying the new plowing. I'm afraid it's just the dogs, sir, madam."

Scamp, with his usual acumen, curled a lip at the perfunctory hand Colin dangled before him.

"Do you know in which direction Mrs. and Miss Ellsworth walked?"

"Oh, Colin—it's so very windy out," protested Lady Hufton.

"Toward The Acres, sir. But not along the Romsey Road. They went over the grounds."

"You wait here, Jenny," he told her. "I'll just take a quick look, and if I don't see them, I'll come right back. I'll see myself out, Bobbins."

"You would be very comfortable in the small parlor, madam," Bobbins assured her. "And Mr. Tyrone Ellsworth has left stacks of books in there. But if you would prefer the drawing room with the pianoforte..."

Her nose twitched, and, with a sigh, Lady Hufton followed the footman, the ribbons of her bonnet fluttering forward as her brother opened the door behind her.

He did not have to venture far before he saw them. He had just come around the outside of the house and passed the walled garden, climbing the rise beyond it, when he saw the two figures in the distance. Even so far away he could distinguish Mrs. Ellsworth's fuller figure and admired the wind pressing her skirts against her legs.

The two women halted even before he raised a gloved hand in salute, and Colin wondered if—hoped—Mrs. Ellsworth's heart sped when she saw him, as his did. How had he missed it before?

Easy. Slow and steady wins the race.

He would have called to them, but he knew the wind would carry the sound away. Therefore he merely bowed and waited.

The two ladies reached for each other simultaneously and then came on.

If Colin could have put a finger to Miranda's pulse, all would have been revealed, but as it was, when they were closer and he saw the flattering pink of her cheeks, he ascribed it to the whipping wind.

"Good afternoon, Mrs. Ellsworth, Miss Ellsworth. Have you had a pleasant walk?"

Neither one of them managed to meet his gaze directly, and under other circumstances he would have been amused, for Mrs. Ellsworth looked over his right shoulder and Miss Ellsworth past his left.

"We—saw Mr. Weeks' new pond," replied Beatrice.

"What was wrong with the old one?" He held out his arms to each side. "May I? I fear you may be tired, and the wind will succeed altogether in blowing you away into Berkshire. Or, wait—" He pretended to consider. "—would that way be Wiltshire?"

With equal hesitation, each one took an arm. They might have been butterflies alighting on his sleeves, so lightly did their hands rest.

"It must be Berkshire," he continued, when neither answered. "For Beaumond lies in that direction, and Beaumond is north and west of Hollowgate."

"Did—Lady Hufton enjoy the assembly?" Miranda asked at last. She must make a show of being her usual self, for if Beatrice was only discovering her feelings for Mr. Wolfe, she would likely not manage a word.

"She did. Vastly. I suspect with her children at school and Sir John being Sir John that she will find Hampshire far more amusing than Stourwood Park."

"Is Sir John not very good company, then?"

"Let us just say, if Jenny were a fox or partridge or pheasant or deer, Sir John would never cease to pay her the closest attention."

"Ah. There are many gentlemen like that," said Miranda. She congratulated herself on the easiness of the conversation. Why, it was nothing, to pretend Mr. Wolfe was just another person with whom to discuss trivialities!

If she were a good stepmother, however, she would try to include Beatrice in the talk. Or would that be being a bad stepmother? For Miranda did not believe Mr. Wolfe at all enamored of Beatrice, and perhaps drawing her to his notice would raise fruitless hopes in the girl's heart. But, on the other hand, what if, like many gentlemen,

Mr. Wolfe only required prompting to see what was right beneath his eyes? Would a good stepmother provide that prompting, or would she do what she could to prevent the match, wishing her daughter to choose a younger man?

So involved was Miranda in her inner debate that she did not realize Mr. Wolfe had asked her a question until he said, "This dratted wind! I said, Mrs. Ellsworth, was Mr. William Ellsworth a mighty hunter before the Lord?"

"Oh! Pardon me. He—er—I cannot recall him ever going shooting, as a matter of fact. My husband rode out on estate business, of course, nearly every day in season, but when there was not work to be done, he far preferred staying at home, within doors." Miranda pressed her lips together. "Perhaps in his far younger days. I would have to ask my brother-in-law Charles Ellsworth. You understand, by the time my husband and I were married, he was...past all that."

"If you don't think it impertinent, Mrs. Ellsworth—how much older *was* Mr. William Ellsworth?"

She swallowed. How did this come to be about her? And about the doubly-delicate subject of May-December matches? She must turn the topic as soon as possible. "Many years, I suppose. I-I-I hear Beaumond has excellent shooting."

"If it does, it is wasted on me," answered Colin shortly. Then, to his companion's distress, he asked, "What of you, Mrs. Ellsworth? Are you by nature as much of a home-sitter as your late husband?"

"I have been whatever my duties require," she replied, releasing his arm on a pretense of adjusting her glove. They were nearly to the house again.

"Meaning, I suppose, you were a home-sitter when your husband was alive, and now you are a 'woman about town' because of your chaperoning responsibilities." He paused in their walk, extending his elbow once more, so that she was obliged to take it. "But I suspect the latter is truer to your nature because, it seems whenever I call at Hollowgate, you are more often out than in."

"Mm," said Miranda. She could hardly say that half the time she fled her comfortable home to avoid callers. "And—what of you? Do you like to gad about?"

"It made for a pleasant change at first, but now—" He broke off, having almost said, "But now it seems to depend on whether or not I will see *you*." *Slow and steady. Slow...and...steady.*

A great big drop of water plopped upon his sleeve, followed shortly by another and another.

Beatrice ripped her hand from Mr. Wolfe's arm and scampered to her stepmother's side to pull on her. "Rain! We had better hurry."

Miranda threw her a startled look, but she let go of Mr. Wolfe as well and submitted to her daughter's tugging, only calling over her shoulder, "We can escape it if we pass behind Florence's garden, where the trees—"

The wind and Beatrice's insistence whirled away the end of her speech, but in an instant Mr. Wolfe had unfastened the three buttons of his greatcoat and shrugged it off. "Here, Miss Ellsworth," he commanded, holding it aloft. "You hold one end and I the other, and we will all come safe to harbor."

Mr. Wolfe being a large man, his coat, too, was large. But not so large that three people could huddle under it without being thrust into close proximity. Miranda found herself nearly in the hollow of his arm as they proceeded, that same arm held just above her shoulders but brushing and bumping her throughout. A warm, manly smell rose from him, a compound of horse and exercise and pomade, which made a corresponding warmth rise to her face, though she kept it angled toward Beatrice. In her rush, however, Beatrice dragged on her end of the coat, and somehow so light a girl kept managing to pull Mr. Wolfe into Miranda, so that he murmured, "Pardon me. Ooh! Confound me for an awkward oaf," and Miranda would have taken an oath the man sounded more amused than apologetic.

He *was* amused. But the potent charm of Mrs. Ellsworth's unexpected nearness would have made short work of *slow and steady wins the race*, had they not reached the terrace steps just then. As it was, Colin wondered if he could contrive for Beatrice to re-enter the house first. If so, then he might steal a—well, steal a *word*—only a word—with Mrs. Ellsworth. Because surely he could control himself enough not to crush her to him, bringing his mouth smashing down upon hers! At least, he thought he could.

He was not put to the test, however.

There was the door opening and the maid standing there, hesitating and fussing, with an umbrella half open, and the opportunity was lost.

It was long enough, however, for Colin to decide, *Slow and steady be hanged. I will speak, or I'll eat my hat.*

Chapter Nineteen

**When the Heart is a fire,
some Sparks will fly out of the Mouth.
— Thomas Fuller, *Gnomologia: adagies and proverbs*
(1732)**

There you are!" cried Lady Hufton in the small parlor, setting down her book and rising. "And the walk has agreed with you, I can see by your fine color."

"I am sorry there was no one here to sit with you," said Miranda, but this was waved away in an outpouring of good-humored pleasantries and remarks about the previous evening's assembly and participants that left Miranda almost bewildered, still confused as she was by having huddled under Mr. Wolfe's greatcoat.

That same disturbing Mr. Wolfe stood with his back to the fireplace, his expression hooded and his eyes fixed somewhere above his sister's head, no matter how Lady Hufton straightened or bent to try to catch his gaze. She would just have to proceed on her own instinct, which she did, beginning to turn her questions to Miss Ellsworth in particular. What was Miss Ellsworth's depth of acquaintance with the gentlemen who partnered Lady Hufton? For being so new to Winchester, she was anxious to surround herself with the best company, and she could not help but notice that Miss Ellsworth also danced with Mr. So-and-So and Sir Such-and-Such and Mr. What-Was-His-Name-with-the-Blond-Hair.

Her diligent work earned its reward when Beatrice said of Mr. What-Was-His-Name-with-the-Blond-Hair, "I wanted to laugh because he looked so much like one of the Baldric portraits in our long gallery, only without the ruff *à la confusion* and the doublet decorated with black-lace stripes."

"How fascinating! Could you possibly show me the portrait, Miss Ellsworth? Colin will tell you I have a great fondness for portraits. At Stourwood Park I am positively *hemmed in* by generations of Huftons, captured in every style and age."

Beatrice hesitated. "Oh. If you like. To be sure. Mama, Mr. Wolfe, would you like to join us?"

Miranda had seen the particular portrait a thousand times, but not wanting to be left alone with Mr. Wolfe, she agreed at once, only to resume her seat when he said, "No, thank you, for my part."

Lady Hufton giggled, "Such things bore my brother, Miss Ellsworth. You must forgive him for being such a Philistine." Then she laid a light but peremptory hand on Beatrice's arm, and the girl was obliged to go, not without throwing Miranda an uneasy smile.

The door shut behind them.

Colin stepped toward her.

The door opened again, to admit Boots with a tray holding the chocolate pot and a plate of Wilcomb's ratafia cakes.

"What is this?" wondered Miranda.

"While you were out, madam, we thought you would want us to be hospitable, and we asked Lady Hufton if she would like tea or coffee or chocolate, and she said chocolate. And Wilcomb was going to serve the ratafia cakes with the evening tea, but she said it wouldn't hurt any to put some on the tray now."

"I see. So thoughtful of you all. Thank you."

With another bob, the maid whisked away, leaving Colin and Miranda alone again.

He was tempted to thrust a chair back beneath the handle of the door to prevent additional interruptions, only to dismiss the idea as too alarming. Come to think of it, every thought he had at present was alarming.

"Would you like some chocolate, Mr. Wolfe?" Miranda asked quietly.

For a man so large, he moved silently until he loomed over her. "Mrs. Ellsworth."

"Won't you sit down?"

"Mrs. Ellsworth." He did not seem to be able to get beyond that. He took the chair opposite hers.

Miranda was too apprehensive to remark Mr. Wolfe's oddness, but she must fill the silence, or he would think something wrong.

"How does Lady Hufton like Hampshire so far?" she asked, inserting the molinet in the chocolate pot and rolling it between her hands. "It sounds like the assembly was a splendid success. Too bad there won't be another one for a fortnight, and by then those gathered will be much diminished. You had better warn her of that, Mr. Wolfe. The militia meeting and the lawyers and such will have gone, and she will be thrown back on the Mr. Dodges and Mr. Bracewells of the world—"

Miranda got no further, for the next second, her bare hands around the chocolate stick were enclosed between both his own. "*Miranda.*"

She gasped at the heat of their contact, jerking her hands away and nearly tipping the chocolate pot over.

"Forgive me," he rejoined at once, straightening the pot. He balled his fists. "I did not mean to—that is, I meant no disrespect—I should not have—"

Miranda's blood was rushing so violently it almost drowned out his stammered apologies. Oh, heavens. What was happening?

He sprang up, retreating to the fire to give her time to recover, all the while kicking himself for his impetuosity. *Start with words before you grab at her, you witless ass! Words!*

Words. Yes. If it wasn't too late and if he had not already botched the delicate creation which was their friendship.

"Forgive me," he repeated in more measured tones. "There was something I wished to speak with you about."

"Then say away," she answered, rubbing her collarbone when her voice emerged scarcely audible. "Say away, Mr. Wolfe."

"Yes."

He took a deep, steadying breath and resumed his seat. "Mrs. Ellsworth, I pray I am not alone in believing that our deepening acquaintance with each other has been a—good thing. I had not known you long before I thought you a woman of uncommon understanding and sympathy. A rational and valuable—neighbor." (He had been about to say "friend" but vetoed it for "companion," which he vetoed in turn for the unsatisfactory, insipid "neighbor.")

But the word "neighbor" acted as a cool compress to Miranda's fevered head. Ah. She was a rational and valuable *neighbor*. He had something he wished to speak with her about. He sought counsel. On what, she could not imagine. His son Edmund! Yes, it must be. This was about Edmund. She had reacted too violently to his touch and nearly revealed all—might even have revealed too much. But she could throw a cloak of dissimulation over her blunder and perhaps salvage the situation.

Miranda therefore lifted her chin and forced a quick smile before returning to the chocolate pot, removing the molinet and laying it on the tray so she could pour out the pot's contents. "Thank you for your kind words and good opinion," she said. "I too have been gratified that the new tenant of Beaumond should be such an...addition to the community."

Colin narrowly escaped groaning. It was one thing not to throw himself at the woman, babbling of his passion, but quite another for her to speak to him as if they were at a blasted parish meeting.

"And I know my son William shares my—is glad as well," she went on, holding out the two-handled cup to him. "He and my grandson Peter have always been close, but the duo has become a triumvirate, it seems."

He took hold of his cup just as he had received it, as if both he and it were carved from the same block of marble, and Miranda faltered. His grey eyes, narrowed now, had never been more disconcerting.

She took a tentative sip of her own chocolate and then set the cup down before a tremble told any tales. "Was it about Edmund you wished to speak?"

"Yes. That is—no." He took a hasty sip from his own cup. "This is delicious." It might have been pond water, for all the consideration he gave it. He must get on with it. He knew Jenny, like a good lieutenant, would drag poor Miss Ellsworth up and down the whole gallery if she could manage it, but they had already been gone five minutes, possibly longer.

"What I wished to say was that, as I have come to know you better and better, my...appreciation of your kindness and—and—" *Say "beauty," whispered the imp. Women like to hear of their beauty.* "—Er—wisdom—has grown in turn."

Miranda's encouraging smile became rather fixed by this point. What woman's would not, to be given praise which, while pleasant, might apply equally whether she were thirty or a hundred and thirty?

"Has Edmund run into some difficulty?" she prompted, to spare him more of this preparatory buttering up.

"What? No. None that I know of. Not that he would tell *me*, as you probably know. I would more likely find it out at the next holiday at the dinner table in conversation with *your* family." Now thoroughly distracted and growing irritable, Colin attempted to return to his subject matter. "The only way in which Edmund impinges on what I have to say is that, of course, it would affect him as it would any member of the family, yours or mine."

Her lips parted slightly, but she said nothing, and Colin tried to take heart. She was a perceptive enough woman that she must be able to pick up the thread of his discourse from this hint, and if she did not immediately stop him, should he not have hope? Had she stopped Lyfford at this point? No—Lyfford had been allowed to continue until his ill-fated attempt to get down on one knee. Colin decided he would keep his seat and avoid that hazard.

Once more he drew his chair a few inches nearer. "*Miranda.*"

"Mr. Wolfe. I have not given you leave to call me that."

But he would not be waylaid by minutiae or technicalities. He began again. "Mrs. Ellsworth, then. This may come as a surprise to you, but I hope you will nevertheless give it mature consideration. Ahem. I have not done this for some years, but as I have been attempting to say, in my bungling way, I—it has occurred to me—er—to put it in parliamentary or, indeed, military terms, suppose we were to 'join forces'?"

"'Join forces,'" repeated Miranda. She dared not make any assumptions, but it certainly *sounded* as if he were leading up to a marriage proposal. That is, if he didn't already consider the proposal made. Her insides felt in a tangle. *Was* he proposing? And, if yes, why now, the very day when accepting him had become impossible?

"What goal or object did you have in mind, sir," she answered carefully, "which this joining of forces would bring about?"

Then Colin did groan and briefly put his head in his hands. "Mrs. Ellsworth, you must pardon me. It seems I was too hard on Lyfford's clumsiness. Well, he is welcome in return to a hearty laugh at *my* expense. I have only done this once before, you understand, and as on that occasion matters were pretty well arranged before I entered the picture, I could not vouch for speech even being necessary."

Oh, heavens, Miranda thought. Then this *was* a proposal.

Panic spiraled through her. She must stop him at once. Mr. Wolfe was too proud, too confident a man, to forgive her if she allowed him to embarrass himself. But how dearly—oh, how dearly—she would love to hear him out!

"Mr. Wolfe," she breathed. "Of course you are pardoned, but perhaps we should talk of other matters now. Other than—than poor Mr. Lyfford or his—his—his attempt—"

"You're right." He caught at her hand. "Never mind him. Miranda—Mrs. Ellsworth, rather—what would you think of—me—as a husband? No—wait—don't pull away. I'm no good at this sort of thing. That much is obvious. I would say it in verse, if I could, but I can't. Would you ever be able to consider me in the light of a husband?"

At last she succeeded in wrenching from his grasp, her face crimson. "I think we had better not talk of it," she whispered, as if Beatrice might be just outside the door. "Thank you very much, but—you—had better choose someone else."

Abruptly he sat back in his chair, dumbfounded not so much by her refusal as by the manner of it.

"Mrs. Ellsworth, let me try again. I daresay that was the worst proposal made since the world began."

"No, please," she interrupted. "Do not try again. There is no need, Mr. Wolfe. Please. Let us say no more about it."

To her consternation, instead of appearing abashed, he sat forward again, his eyes going altogether silver.

"Say no more about it? How can we say no more about it?" he demanded. "Will you not even do me the courtesy of giving a reason for this summary dismissal?"

She swallowed, aware that every tick of the clock brought Beatrice's return nearer. "I have told you: I have no present plans to remarry—"

"Then tell me you will not marry me now, but you will bear it in mind for the future. I do not ask you to name a day, only to say whether I might or might not have hope."

"No hope!" panted Miranda, waving her hands helplessly. She was too distressed to express herself with any subtlety or gentleness and added again, "You had better pick someone else."

"Your wits have gone begging, if you can speak of it in so cavalier a fashion," he returned, his voice so loud that she shrank. "I'm choosing a wife, not what to eat for breakfast!"

"Shhhhh!" She put a finger to her own lips, as if that might hush him. "Lady Hufton and Beatrice will return any second."

"Mrs. Ellsworth, we will have this discussion now, or we will resume it the first instant I can drive our dear relations back out of the room. *Why* do you say there is no hope for me? Have you decided you will never marry again, for whatever such a vow is worth, or do you object to *me* in particular? Am I a Lyfford to you? A Dodge? A Bracewell?"

"No, of course not," she conceded, seeing he would not be easily denied. "You're a...perfectly amiable man."

Oh, Lord, she groaned inwardly. Worse and worse. "Amiable" was the last word to be applied to Colin Wolfe. And it certainly seemed to offend him, for he fired up at once.

"'Amiable'? Confound 'amiable'! I will not be fobbed off with your blasted 'amiables.' Tell me frankly what you dislike. Is it my looks?"

"N-no. Your looks are—just fine."

At this second tepid reply, Miranda thought he might hurl the chocolate pot across the room. "My age, then?"

"What possible objection could I have to your age?" she wondered, surprised into a laugh.

"Who knows? Bracewell is younger than I, at any rate."

"Mr. Wolfe, it has been amply proven in the past month that *no* woman in Winchester objects to your age."

"Is it something in my character which disgusts you?" he persisted. "I am too brusque, too forthright."

She could not repress a sigh and directed her gaze at the carpet. "No. Nothing like that. Please, Mr. Wolfe. Call it a lack or a flaw in my *own* character—"

"You have no flaws in your character."

"That's just nonsense," she reproved. "Everyone has flaws in his character."

"Then tell me which of mine you disdain," he took it up swiftly, "and I will work to remedy them."

"It is a flaw not to take a lady at her word, sir," she said, with what severity she could manage.

"Then I will work to correct that immediately, once I have persuaded myself the lady is speaking the whole truth. Mrs. Ellsworth, I do not think I deceive myself to say we have become...friends. And if we are friends, and if I am 'amiable' and my looks 'just fine,' in addition to my largely-tolerable character, what reason can you give me for being unwilling *ever* to try if you might learn to like me better?"

"You are too...pushing," she accused at last. "Mr. Lyfford did not give me a fraction of the trouble."

He was silent for a spell. He nodded, his lips pressed together. Then he rose and made a circuit of the room, stopping at the mantel, where he glanced unseeingly at the clock face.

"Yes," he said finally. "That is fair. I am too pushing. Or I have been today. It is a measure of how far my heart and my passions are involved." He turned slowly, deliberately, to look at her again. "Because I love you, Miranda. I have fallen in love with you. Therefore I have pressed you and still press you. For can you tell me you feel absolutely nothing for me?"

Mercy.

Tears threatened, and she could not breathe. Oh, it was not fair! Not fair at all. Words she had never heard addressed to her in her whole existence—spoken now when they must not be listened to.

They must not.

No matter how she would rejoice to throw herself at his feet in gratitude for his affection.

How could she possibly answer? She could not tell the truth, that she had begun to love him the afternoon they took their sons to school, when they shared their tiny moment of understanding. She had begun then and gone on without pause or diminution until she now confessed to herself that she loved him with her whole heart.

Ah. It hurt.

No, the truth could not be uttered.

Doing so would betray Beatrice and cost their closeness, that was certain. At least until Beatrice began to love another, if she ever loved another. Miranda had become the girl's mother when Beatrice was six, and she knew they both considered themselves mother and daughter as much as any pair born to it. So how could Miranda then plunge a dagger into her beloved girl's heart? Beatrice might say she was not yet in love, but who knew the real depth of those feelings? Even if Bea were fortunate enough to find her affection for Mr. Wolfe shallow and undeveloped and capable of being expunged, it would still take time. And in the meanwhile, the loving relationship between the two would be broken, leaving Beatrice to suffer alone.

It was not even a decision as such. But the pain was real, and the sacrifice was real, and Miranda was not a very skilled liar to begin with.

"It is not 'nothing' to like you as a friend, Mr. Wolfe," she began. "Which I do. But—I have already been married once to someone I was fond of in that way, and that will be quite enough for me."

"You didn't love Ellsworth?"

"I—he was a good man and a good husband, and I was fond of him and grateful to him for all his kindnesses to me."

"You didn't love him." There was a rising note of what could only be described as triumph in his voice, and Miranda began to fear he was going to "push" again. Would she possibly have the strength to withstand him, and, if yes, for how long?

"I didn't love my wife Doria either," he said baldly. "She was my cousin, and the Wolfes offered our family the salvation of money, if I would marry her and take their name. What could I do? I was cornered by circumstances, though I tried for years to make the best of it. But I'm not certain we even reached the comparatively ardent heights of mutual fondness. If she didn't actively dislike me, it was because active dislike requires thinking about a person, and I'm not sure Doria ever thought of me."

"I'm sorry," she murmured, amazed at the confidence he shared and hardly believing him. How could anyone *ignore* a man such as Colin Wolfe? To Miranda's mind he dominated every room, every conversation, by his mere presence.

"Don't be. It's over. But now we can make of our lives what we will, and why should we then not want more? If you like me as a friend, Mrs. Ellsworth, I will take that for the present. Because I believe we share a natural sympathy. I believe you could learn to feel more for me, if you chose to make the attempt. And I don't mean just fondness—I wouldn't settle for something so feeble as your fondness. Because I want all of you, Miranda. All your heart. And all your person, for good measure."

"Stop it," she burst out desperately. "Stop pushing me. Stop bullying me."

It worked. While she could not argue with him, she could beg for mercy, and he could not help but relent.

His enormous shoulders slumping, he hung his head. "I *am* bullying you. As much as the worthless Grimes ever bullied Edmund. You probably wish I would trip over a pile of cricket bats."

In spite of everything, this drew a wavering smile. "I wish no such thing. May you never suffer a single bone of yours to be broken, Mr. Wolfe."

"I thank you," he muttered, just as the sound of footsteps approached in the passage, "if that is all the good you can wish me."

"It is," was her choked, whispered reply. "I'm sorry."

"Then may you, Mrs. Ellsworth, never suffer your heart broken, as you have done mine."

Chapter Twenty

**Lo how I vanysshe, flessh and blood and skyn.
— Chaucer, "The Pardoner's Tale" (c.1386)**

M r. Wolfe disappeared from Miranda's life as if he had been written out of existence. He and Lady Hufton did not call again. Nor was he seen in the High Street when the girls doggedly shopped. Their visits to the circulating library and the booksellers and the draper's did not take them into his path. He was not to be found walking the downs or emerging from a coffee house or cutting through Oram's Arbour. Though Miranda lost a full night of sleep fearing she would see him at the quiristers' concert, she was as much disappointed as relieved when he did not come.

There is just the feast of St. Luke to get through, she fretted for the entirety of the concert as she and Florence sat in the beautiful chapel. Their boys fidgeted beside each other nearer the choir stalls, but

Miranda and Flossie could barely see the edges of William and Peter's gowns and surplices around the bulk of Edmund Wolfe in the pew directly behind them. Would Willie bring Edmund to Hollowgate this time? If he did, she would be obligated to invite Mr. Wolfe and Lady Hufton to join them. But even this predicament was avoided. Willie and Peter came shortly after noon, and the Fairchilds were sent for, but when Miranda timidly asked after Edmund, Willie just shrugged. "He said his aunt is here, and his father insisted he go to Beaumond."

All in all, if Miranda had not continued to hear *of* Mr. Wolfe, she might have begun to think she dreamed him.

Nearly a fortnight had passed before she glimpsed him again. Just as she emerged from the Charles Ellsworths' home in St Thomas Street, his phaeton passed. She recognized his bulk and posture before his face, her hand flying to her throat, but he merely gave a frosty nod without slowing and touched the brim of his hat.

"*La,* Mireille," breathed Jeanne Ellsworth, using her pet name for her sister-in-law and leaning out from the step to look after the vehicle, "who was that, *cet Hercule?*"

"A new neighbor."

"A new married neighbor?"

"A new widowed neighbor. And don't give me that look, Jeanne."

"*Quel regard?* If you think there is any 'look,' that is your own *gêne*, or how do you say it? Your own conscience. But tell me—why does the new widowed neighbor hate you?"

"He doesn't hate me!"

Jeanne merely raised her eyebrows with a look that simultaneously spoke a thousand words and made Miranda want to knock her down.

She knew better than to argue, however. "Well," she said, "off I go."

"*Attends, ma chère,*" Jeanne held up a detaining hand and then tugged her back into the entryway. "You, Mireille, who have always lived at peace with all your neighbors. Why should there now be one who does not hold you in estimation?"

"Who says he does not? I daresay if another neighbor such as Mr. Weeks drove past, his greeting would be no different."

"Then I would say you have angered Mr. Weeks as well," returned Jeanne inexorably. "For that was how he greeted every Ellsworth right after Tyrone and Aggie eloped. Let me guess: this Hercule has asked to marry our Beatrice, and you have refused your blessing."

Miranda choked, to have her sister-in-law's speculation come so near. But Mrs. Charles Ellsworth merely laughed. "*Pauvre niais!* How many possibilities can there be? Either he fights with you over neighborly boundaries and whether *la meute* may cross over Hollowgate lands during the hunt, or it is a love problem. And since it is my nephew Tyrone who manages the estate and handles those sorts of disputes—C.F.Q.D., as my dear husband would say. *Ce qu'il fallait démontrer*, it is love. So why do you disapprove of him for our Beatrice? He is too old?"

"He is certainly much older."

"But not even as much older as our lost William was to you." Jeanne cocked her head, one of her springing, greying curls brushing her cheek. "Is he poor?"

"No."

"Of no reputation?"

"No...others think well of him."

"He has twenty children?"

"Just one. A son the same age as William and Peter."

"Then what can be the problem, Mireille? Why do you refuse your consent?"

"I have not refused my consent, Jeanne. He has not asked for it."

"But he can tell you disapprove. Does Beatrice love him?"

Miranda hesitated. She knew Jeanne well enough that, if she said Yes, poor Beatrice would be subjected to a similar interrogation, for Jeanne adored a good love story. "She...begins to like him. But Jeanne, you must say nothing to her! You know our Beatrice. If you hound her, she will crumble and deny it and never confess it again, even if her affection grows. But—yes—she has told me she begins to like him."

"Ah," sighed Jeanne, eyes aglow. "I would like to meet this Hercule. How will you arrange that?"

"For heaven's sake! I don't know, even if I were willing to. Why don't you and Charles go to the next assembly? Most likely he will be there with his sister. I don't believe he has missed one since he arrived in Hampshire."

Miranda was right, and Colin Wolfe and Lady Hufton did not miss this one either.

"If she is there, will you...ask Mrs. Ellsworth to dance?" Lady Hufton ventured as she sat beside him in the landau. Rain drummed on the leather hood, and she had to raise her voice.

"No," said Colin.

He had told her, tersely, of having offered and been refused, and Lady Hufton had been too cowed by his demeanor to ask questions or give voice to her own indignation. But tonight they would almost certainly see Mrs. Ellsworth again, and to avoid touching on her brother's wound, Lady Hufton would fain know where she stood.

"Shall I...acknowledge her, Colin? Or pretend not to see her?"

He grimaced. "There is no call for rudeness, and it would be impossible in any case, if she shepherds Miss Ellsworth and Miss Wright. We will all behave as if nothing whatever happened, if you please. As it is, I would vouch for it being a dark secret known only to the three of us."

He understood Miranda well, for she had not told a soul and had lectured herself at length to behave in as natural a manner as possible, that her charges never guess at the dreadful awkwardness beneath the surface. It was too bad, however, that the assembly was so reduced in numbers. There was no one to hide behind when Mr. Wolfe and Lady Hufton entered the room in Upper Brook Street, even if Jeanne Ellsworth had not drawn a sharp breath and prodded her. "Hercule!"

Mr. Hogwood, the Upper Brook Street master of ceremonies, had just welcomed Mrs. Charles Ellsworth and thus hastened to say, "Have you met Mr. Wolfe and Lady Hufton yet, madam? Do allow me..."

Miranda's courage and good intentions deserted her. With a murmur to Beatrice about needing to do something-something-something, she slipped away as fast as her feet could carry her to the coffee room. The girls didn't need her with Jeanne there, she told herself. And if she remained, Mr. Wolfe would be forced to ask her for a dance if he asked Jeanne and Beatrice and Emmy.

She could have said she did not intend to dance, of course. She *should* have said that, instead of panicking and running away like an embarrassed schoolgirl. But she had already promised to stand up with her brother-in-law, and the indefatigable Messieurs Dodge and Bracewell had called at Hollowgate to claim their dues, so refusing Mr. Wolfe would have required feigning an ankle sprain at least.

"Mrs. Ellsworth?"

Her heart sank.

"Oh! Good evening, Mr. Dodge."

"What good fortune, to find you by yourself for a moment," he said in his tired way. "You are not often alone, you know."

"Nor am I now," she rejoined quickly. "I merely withdrew for a moment to—fix a hairpin, and now I must return. Mr. Charles Ellsworth will be looking for me for the first dance."

"Please—the musicians aren't finished tuning yet. If you would grant me a word…"

"Mrs. Fairchild and I thought the quiristers' concert such a treat," she said, hoping to forestall his own choice of topic. She took a step toward the ballroom, but he held up a hand in entreaty.

"Mrs. Ellsworth—I thank you for the compliment and was deeply flattered by your attendance—and Mrs. Fairchild's, of course, but it was not the concert I wished to speak with you about. If you would grant me but one minute!"

Trapped, her shoulders sagged, and she pinned a half-smile to her face. "Very well."

He looked behind and before and then laid his palm to his breastbone. "Worthy Mrs. Ellsworth, this can come as no surprise to you that, since I made your acquaintance, I have found it impossible to put you from my mind. Your—"

"Oh, Mr. Dodge," she could not refrain from interrupting. "Please—don't."

"—Your modesty," he bowed, as if it were simply from shyness she urged him to forbear. "As well as the admiration you excite from all and sundry. Even your lingering beauty..."

In truth, her lingering beauty was considerably marred by this reference to it. Because odors lingered. Winter lingered. Unwelcome visitors lingered. Unwelcome suitors lingered, for that matter. But beauty was only said to "linger" when one was amazed to find traces of it still there.

Miranda frowned. "Really, Mr. Dodge. I thank you, but I will stop you there."

"Mrs. Ellsworth! I beg you—I must speak or die! You have captured my heart! I dream of—"

But she was shaking her head with vehemence. She had had enough of men *pushing*. And if she refused to hear the man she loved when he opened his heart to her, she most certainly did not intend to grant the privilege to Mr. Dodge. He might die if he insisted on it, but that was his choice, not hers. Making to move past him, she was astonished to find herself the next second taken by the shoulders.

"Mrs. Ellsworth!" he cried, releasing her the very moment she raised outraged eyes. He wriggled his fingers wildly as if they had acted on their own accord. "Forgive me, but I must know! Will you marry me?"

She stared, still too indignant for courtesy. "No, Mr. Dodge. *No.* I never offered you the least encouragement, and I hope you will take me at my word. We would not suit. At all. But—I thank you for the honor."

"You came to the quiristers' concert," he accused.

"To see my son!"

"Then you refuse me?" He drew himself up with what weary dignity he could muster. "Mrs. Ellsworth, I will not ask again."

Is that a promise? she wanted to ask. Instead she swept away, not even looking back when he called, "Go, then. But you must excuse me from the dance I promised you."

When she returned to the ballroom, her brother-in-law Charles Ellsworth soon found her. "There you are, Miranda. I told Jeanne you must be trying to dodge me."

"Of course not, Charles." His choice of words almost made her giggle. As her husband's younger brother, he must be sixty now, and though he like William had lost his hair, he was still an upright, good-looking man who would do credit to any partner. He too boasted *lingering beauty*. Then she did giggle.

"Are you quite well?" he asked. "You are rather flushed. We might sit through our dance, if you prefer, though then I will be left to gnash my teeth while that 'Hercule' stands up with my wife."

"May we, Charles? I am a little out of sorts. We might—sit where you may best keep an eye on him."

He led her to the chairs nearest the top of the room where the set began to form. Lady Hufton and her archdeacon partner were given the honor of leading the dance, with Mr. Wolfe and Jeanne just below them. Miranda squirmed inwardly to see the latter two, not because she took her brother-in-law's pretended jealousy seriously, but because Jeanne was sure to sound Mr. Wolfe on his feelings toward her Ellsworth relations.

Colin berated himself. He should have been pleased when Mrs. Ellsworth ran away—it saved them the trouble of both conversation and pretense—but he was not. Should she not have remained, to endure the full weight of his coldness? Nor did it mend matters to see that arrant ass Dodge follow her to the coffee room. Colin would stake his ruby ring the man intended to come to the point, and the mere thought made him want to roar. Mrs. Ellsworth would refuse Dodge, of course, but nothing made a man feel more a fool than to think a booby like Dodge followed in his footsteps, as Colin himself had followed in Lyfford's.

While these vexing thoughts chased through his head and Jenny maintained dutiful small talk with Miss Ellsworth and Miss Wright, the older lady beside him plied her fan slowly, observing him. Resenting this, Colin turned his cool gaze upon her—Mrs. Charles Ellsworth, wasn't that her name?—to find she bore it with complete equanimity. Indeed, far from being abashed, she tilted her head with its abundance of pepper-and-salt curls and said in her purring accent, "Monsieur, you drove very fast past my house last week."

"Did I? I suspect I must have been in something of a hurry."

"I am relieved to hear it. Otherwise I might have thought you were in a hurry to get away from my dear sister Mrs. Ellsworth. Which would be very odd because she is so well-beloved in general, you know. Or perhaps you do not know. Because you are new here, *n'est-ce pas?*"

"I am," he answered warily.

"Then I will tell you: she is admired for her good judgment and her kindness. Only see how she agrees to chaperone this Miss Wright."

Colin made an indeterminate sound in his throat, suddenly aware that Miss Ellsworth and Miss Wright and his sister were now listening.

"Miss Ellsworth, may I have the pleasure of standing up with you?" he blurted.

Beatrice blushed and Emmy slumped, neither of which was lost on Jeanne.

"Mr. Dodge has asked for the first and Mr. Bracewell the second," Beatrice murmured.

He gave a mock sigh. "Alas. I am always forestalled by that pair. I assume you too are engaged for the first two, Miss Wright?"

"The first and third," said Emmy eagerly.

Beatrice explained, "Mr. Dodge and Mr. Bracewell never fail to call before an assembly to claim dances from my mama. But she already promised my uncle the first, so they had to settle for second and third. It's all quite complicated."

"So it is. Perhaps, then, you would honor me, Mrs. Charles Ellsworth—?"

He had made better decisions, he thought later. Because Mrs. Charles Ellsworth was pure mischief.

"My niece Beatrice is so pretty, is she not? So fresh and youthful. She is my *youngest* niece, you know."

"Miss Ellsworth is very pleasant to look at and very young."

"Ah, but there are so many pretty flowers in Winchester, *n'est-ce pas*? And you must be so popular, Mr. Wolfe."

"I don't know about that."

"And *si gentil et agréable*, not only to partner the young ladies, but also the older ones like myself."

He smiled at her. "Are you so very old?"

"But of course. In a few years I will be sixty like my beloved husband. I am older by twenty years than dear Miranda—Mrs. William Ellsworth. What would you call her? Young or old or in the middle?"

Despite his best efforts he felt his face heat.

"I suspect Mrs. William Ellsworth is my age or younger," he managed. "Perhaps that would be called 'in the middle.'"

"How gallant you are!" Her lips curling, she studied him from the corner of her dark eyes. "I will tell you a secret of women, Mr. Wolfe. A man may be considered 'in the middle' when a woman is already called 'old.' Therefore, if *ma chère* Mireille is your age, she is unfortunately already 'old.'"

"Nonsense," he said fiercely.

"Oh, dear me, yes," sighed Mrs. Charles Ellsworth, shaking her head with regret. "I am sorry to contradict you. I have wondered if I should tell Mireille to give over curling her hair and instead just cover it with a dowager's cap."

His response to this, being unfit for polite company, was uttered under this breath.

"—Because, I would say, the danger of curling her hair is that it tells the gentlemen she does not yet admit she is an old woman. She does not yet admit no one would marry her, if not for her money."

Jeanne had the delight of seeing the giant Hercule's eyes flash lightning at her. Perhaps she would have done better to nickname him Zeus.

"Her fortune is the least interesting thing about Mrs. William Ellsworth," he bit out.

"Of course, of course. *Il va sans dire, monsieur.* It also goes without saying that Mireille is homely—no! Is that the word I want?—homeish? She is comfortable. Pleasant, like bread and milk. Even the infants and invalids can enjoy her."

"She is indeed comfortable to be in company with," he rejoined through a hard jaw. "Though I would say 'homely' means something altogether different and not flattering. She is the best company. Sympathetic, calm, rational, kind—"

"Yes," interrupted Jeanne with another teeny sigh, "which is why it is too bad her looks are gone."

They armed left, and his limbs might have been carved from marble, he was so stiff. This rigidity did not extend to his lips, though, for he said swiftly enough, "Mrs. Ellsworth is loveliness itself."

"—And therefore," Jeanne mourned, "men in their blindness look only at the daughter—"

"Con*found* the daughter!" This emerged loudly enough for Lady Hufton to start and blink at him, and Colin struggled to master himself, only then noticing that his partner's lips were pressed together not in disapproval but rather in hidden amusement. *The blasted woman has played upon me. Am I that transparent?*

Whatever Mrs. Charles Ellsworth had wanted to learn from him she had learned, for she spoke no more of either her sister-in-law or her niece, and when the dance ended she thanked him prettily. "You need not take me back to my husband, Mr. Wolfe, for he is seated with *chère* Mireille, and perhaps that would be awkward for you. *Au revoir. Merci bien.*"

He had control enough not to glance toward the people indicated, but it was as much as he could manage, and he willingly accepted her permission to disappear and go in search of his next partner.

Chapter Twenty-One

As Mr. Dodge had threatened, he did not appear to claim his dance from Miranda. So when her brother- and sister-in-law sailed away, she was left alone. Serenely, she folded her hands in her lap and observed those lining up for the next set, her gaze sweeping past Mr. Wolfe and Emmy Wright without a hitch, though she swallowed a sigh.

She was proud to have been loved by such a man, if only briefly, for in her opinion he had not his equal in the room.

Would he ever come to return Beatrice's budding feelings? He would never care for Emmy, Miranda was certain, but Beatrice was something else. Beatrice—was more like Miranda herself, if that was what he preferred. More reserved and self-collected, fond of family and the snugness of home.

Looking down she realized she had begun to pick at a thread in the seam of her silk glove, and if she was not careful a hole would open.

If it must be, it must be.

And she would have to bear it, as she had borne other things in life.

Because it was safe to watch her daughter with Mr. Bracewell, she did, remembering with some puzzlement how she had imagined Beatrice's attraction to the handsome curate. Clearly whatever blushes Mr. Bracewell's looks drew from the girl when they first met, she had nevertheless come to prefer the older man. That Beatrice was blushing again now meant nothing, for her aunt Jeanne was circling with her and no doubt whispered something which made her niece self-conscious. Poor Beatrice. Perhaps Miranda should not even have *hinted* at the girl's feelings for Mr. Wolfe, but surely Jeanne would show a little restraint, having been cautioned?

Here Miranda did her sister-in-law an injustice, however, for it was her brother-in-law Charles who inadvertently distressed Beatrice.

"Hey ho, Bea," he rallied her as their respective partners performed a figure eight about them. "How did you come to be so grown up? The next thing we know, you will be announcing your engagement to one of these handsome fellows, I daresay."

"Pooh," she answered. "I will announce nothing of the kind, for I don't intend to marry anytime soon, if ever."

Her uncle's brows rose at the obvious ease with which she declared this, for, in truth, a little bird had told him of their beloved niece's incipient fondness for a certain gentleman. "Ah. Of course I was teasing you and do not expect you to confess anything to your old uncle."

But Beatrice laughed, crossing in front of him for their own figure eight. "Dear uncle, I promise you I will tell you when there is something to tell. Not first, of course—that must be Mama—but second."

When Charles took hands with his wife, he told her, "I have caught you in a mistake, my love, for our little Bea is no more in love with your mythological hero than I am."

"Charles!" she gasped. "You have not teased her about him! Mireille will be angry with me."

"I didn't tease her about him in particular, but she told me with admirable conviction that she had no plans of marriage."

"Well, of course she doesn't have plans! She hardly yet knows she loves him, Mireille says."

"Jeanne, I tell you, if the girl feels anything for anyone, it is too weak and puling an inclination to deserve the name. But doubt me if you dare." He pressed her fingers in his own, his lips twitching in a kiss for her eyes alone. "I know more of love than you do, I daresay."

"Bah!" she returned, with a flutter of her lashes. "*N'écoute jamais ton coeur, mon trésor.*" Never listen to your heart, my darling.

Faced with such a challenge, when the figures brought the dancers back to their beginning positions on the floor, Charles Ellsworth leaned over to his niece and accosted her with, "You must prove me right, dear Beatrice, and your aunt wrong. You must tell her you love no one and nobody, because she lets her fancy run wild."

But Beatrice had had twenty minutes to come to her senses. Twenty minutes in which to remember her professions of admiration for Mr. Wolfe and the reason for them. It had not been difficult to draw conclusions from her uncle's teasing—to understand Uncle Charles could only have the ideas he had because Aunt Jeanne planted them, and that Aunt Jeanne could only have planted them had she been told in her turn. In short, Beatrice understood her mother had shared her supposed secret and that, she herself, by her own thoughtlessness, had deprived it of any weight. Oh, heaven! She must, if she could, repair. Rebuild. Restore.

With an apologetic smile she ignored Mr. Bracewell's arm and took instead her uncle's. In her distress it was no hardship to flush rosily and to whisper, "Shh...please, Uncle Charles. I meant to mislead you so you would stop talking of it where someone might overhear. But I am indeed—quite fond of someone. Not fond enough to—to—mean anything by it, but fond."

"*Tu vois? Je te l'avais dit,*" hissed Jeanne, taking Beatrice's other arm and her husband's to form a tight little circle.

"Yes, you told me," he chuckled. "I was utterly mistaken." He eyed his niece wryly. "To complete your aunt's triumph, I suppose it is her 'Hercule' who is your idol?"

Despite her resolution, Beatrice could not prevent a fleeting scowl. "Idol? *Nonsense!*"

Jeanne gave her husband a playful pinch. "You will land us in hot water. Winning such a heart will already be one of Hercule's most difficult labors—"

A throat cleared behind her, and the trio sprang apart guiltily.

"Miss Ellsworth, this is our dance, I believe?" said Colin. His gaze flicked from one face to the next.

Hardly able to look at the man, Beatrice placed a hand on his arm and allowed him to lead her away, feeling her aunt and uncle's continued scrutiny.

Charles shrugged. "Thank heaven for his nom de guerre, my love, or that might have been an awkward business." He gave her arm a swing. "Since I've already danced with Miranda and you, and Wolfe has Beatrice, shall we have some coffee? You can tell me again how you were right and I was wrong."

But his wife was frowning in thought. "I am not so certain, Charles. Did you see her face when you called him her idol?"

"She didn't like the word."

"She didn't like the *idea*," Jeanne corrected. "There is something very odd happening. Do you know—I think our Beatrice is as heart-whole as you claimed. *You* were right, and Mireille and I were wrong. But the girl wants us to believe she is fond of him. Now, why would that be?"

Her husband whistled along with the music (Jamaica) as they retreated to the window. Mr. Wolfe and Beatrice danced near the bottom of the room and Miranda and Mr. Bracewell near the top.

"Girls her age will have their intrigues," he replied. "Perhaps she and her friend Miss Wright make a game of it. Miss Wright seems definitely star-struck by him. As do a handful of other young ladies. I wonder which of them all he will choose."

"None of them," said Jeanne.

"How can you be so sure? Unless he already fell in love with you during your dance."

"He has no heart to give to any lady, young or old," Jeanne declared, "because he has already lost it—to our Mireille."

"To Miranda? Good gracious! What makes you say that? Something he said to you when you were dancing?"

"I teased him a little about her because—because of the way he looked when she walked away earlier this evening and because of the way he drove past her outside our house the other day. I teased him, Charles, and he showed his temper. A man who is indifferent does not care, much less lose his temper."

"So if Hercule cares for Miranda, and Miranda thinks Beatrice cares for Hercule, but Beatrice does not, it will all come right in the end. That is, Hercule will offer for Miranda, and she will have to make a decision."

"She will refuse him, Charles."

"Because she does not return his feelings?"

"Who can say? But she would refuse him in any case, if she thought it would hurt Beatrice."

They turned to study those in question. By this point Miranda and Mr. Bracewell had progressed down the room, while Beatrice and Mr. Wolfe progressed upward, conveniently bringing the foursome together in the figures. Charles thought his niece appeared uneasy and shy, but Jeanne paid no attention to either Beatrice or Mr. Bracewell.

"Ah," she said, when the pattern was complete, and the two couples moved onward in their opposite directions.

"Yes, my dear?"

"Hercule has already asked and been refused. You saw how they behaved as if they had not even been introduced."

"I didn't, as a matter of fact. But too bad for Wolfe. He seems a decent fellow. And I like him the better for noticing her, when all those young ladies could easily have swelled him with his own importance. I would counsel him to try again in a year. Chances are, Beatrice will be married or have her eye on someone else by then, and Miranda would feel free to look about her."

His wife made no reply. She was looking at Beatrice now, and when she caught the girl's eye, her niece shrank visibly, guiltily.

Mr. Bracewell was Miranda's last partner of the evening. She knew Mr. Wolfe would not ask her—Mr. Wolfe disdained even to look at her—but rather than stand wistfully in waiting, she chose a chair beside old Mrs. Browning, great-aunt to the Miss Browning from Mr. Wolfe's cadre of admirers. A contemporary of Miranda's late father, old Mrs. Browning still remembered and resented how the reverend Mr. Samuel Gregory dismissed her cousin's husband from parish duties for drunkenness, so she took advantage of Miranda's proximity to rehearse in exhaustive detail the long-ago incident: its players, its causes, its misapprehensions, its injustices, its aftermath. After twenty minutes of this Miranda felt tears of self-pity threaten, in spite of herself. Would this be her fate, in time? Would she metamorphose into a Mrs. Browning? Growing older and more unpleasant, no longer participating in life but rather watching, grumbling, ruminating over wrongs done thirty years earlier?

Mrs. Browning's voice faded to a buzz, though Miranda continued to nod and murmur, and it was not until she heard "—that Mr. Wolfe," that she straightened sharply.

"What was that, Mrs. Browning? It is quite noisy in here."

"I said," repeated the old woman crossly, "that Aurelia thinks she can make her cousin jealous by flirting with that Mr. Wolfe, but it's all for naught because Henry only cares about sport and would not notice if she were to ride up and down the High Street dressed as Napoleon. But what do the young people understand? We old people know what's what, don't we, Mrs. Ellsworth? Wisdom comes with the years and the rheumatism, eh? Has your near vision started to go yet? It only gets worse, let me tell you. And—ah!—I declare my lower back pains me something terrible most mornings. It will be the death of me one day. The house will catch fire, and I will be unable to get out of bed, and no one will think of me. Or one morning I won't be able to get up at all. My own grandmother lay in bed for the last five years of her life, mind you—"

"Pardon me," breathed Miranda, scrambling up. "Do pardon me, Mrs. Browning! Ahem! Something—must get air—something in my eye—I mean, throat—"

"Well, which is it?" Mrs. Browning barked. "Your eye or your throat?"

But Miranda had already fled. She had to. Her heart raced and there was no air to breathe beside Mrs. Browning or, indeed, in the entire Upper Brook Street assembly room.

She burst out of the entrance where a few waiting chairmen loitered in hopes of an early summons, but when she turned sharply away from the torchlight they knew better than to approach her. Hurrying away into the shadows, she tried to suppress a silent sob. The air was biting, but Miranda welcomed it because it gave her something else to feel. Pressing her hands to her midsection, she struggled to catch hold of breath and reason.

You are not yet eighty years old, Miranda Ellsworth. Not in years and not in body and not in spirit! Mrs. Browning has been old in spirit—from your first memory of her—always complaining and trying to pull others into her unhappiness. Remember how she was the bane of your father's existence!

Oh, oh—but what if Mrs. Browning had once been kind and gracious and young at heart, until the day she refused the man she loved and became bitter and peevish as a result?

Stop. Stop that. You can't think like that.

Slowly, slowly, Miranda's throat began to loosen, but that presented its own problems because she then found herself gasping, racked by hiccupping sobs which she could not entirely muffle, even when she pressed her gloved hands to her mouth.

Warmth dropped down unexpectedly about her shoulders.

A cloak?

Miranda whirled to find someone beside her in the darkness, an enormous shadow lightened by only the glowing end of a cheroot.

"M-Mr. Wolfe?" she croaked. "What are—what are you doing out here?"

The glowing cheroot tip traced an arc. "Just—blowing a quick cloud." He raised it to his shadowy lips, only to double over the next instant, seized by a fit of racking coughs.

"Good heavens, sir! Are you all right?"

He was such a big man and his spasms so violent that Miranda thought he might cough up a lung while she watched helplessly.

"Beggin' your pardon, sir," interpolated one of the chairmen, stealing closer, "but you didn't inhale the smoke, did you? You mustn't, you know."

Still hacking, Wolfe waved him away, tossing down the offending item to grind under his heel. The two stood in silence another minute, if it could be considered silent when he still suffered sporadic fits and her hiccupping sobs had transmuted to actual hiccups.

"Where—did the cloak come from?" she gasped.

"I don't know—ahem! Ahem! It was the nearest at hand. I—thought you might be cold."

"Do you—always cough so much when you smoke? It can't be—very pleasant."

"I don't know—*ahem!* I've never smoked before."

She gaped at him, so surprised by such an answer that it cured her at once of her hiccups. And then she was laughing. "Never smoked before? Then why on earth did you decide to make this the first occasion?"

He laughed too, which brought on another bout of hacking. But when he mastered it he managed to rasp, "Because I wanted to follow you outside, and I needed an excuse to leave the ballroom. They are probably all in there now discussing my desperate tobacco habit."

He followed her outside? Miranda's heart leaped at the words. Could he possibly have forgiven her? He must have, or he would not have cared or noticed whether she were inside, outside, or on the moon. Oh—in the moment it felt like more than she could have hoped, to have his friendship and goodwill again, if she could never have anything else.

"What—distressed you?" he pursued.

Miranda pressed her lips together, whether to keep from smiling or weeping she could hardly say. "It was—it was foolish. Mrs. Browning—she is an...unhappy woman. Complaining and such."

"So was Mrs. Jerome, but I don't recall you fleeing the Jeromes' sad little hovel."

Another warm little clutch at her heart—he remembered their coinciding visits to the Jeromes!

Miranda sighed. "No. I will tell you all, then, though you will think me vain for it. It was not Mrs. Browning's complaints which upset me. Or not altogether her complaints, though she did draw on a vast and ancient reserve of them. It was that she talked of her aches and pains and kept saying, 'we old people.' '*We* old people,' as if I were her contemporary. 'We old people.'"

"Miranda, you are not old."

But her confession had its own irresistible momentum now, and she did not even register that he had used her Christian name again. "—She asked if my near vision was worsening yet, and all I could think was—am I like her? Would this be my life? Was Mrs. Browning who I would become or was already becoming? Old and unhappy and invisible? 'We old people'—"

"Miranda, you are *not* old."

And then he grasped her by the shoulders and pulled her to his chest so roughly that her head fell back of its own accord. In the shadows, his mouth came down on hers—he had expected to kiss her hair but met with her lips, and he uttered a groan and pressed *harder*. Yielding, Miranda sighed in response, her lips parting so that they shared one kiss, one breath.

"*Miranda,*" he said against her mouth.

For one blissful, timeless spell which might have lasted ten seconds or thirty or so long as forty-five, they were lost to the world. Neither felt the chill; neither heard anything, saw anything. There was only the other. The other's arms, the other's lips, the other's nearness which could not be near enough.

But in one critical respect, Mrs. Browning was absolutely right.

Miranda was not young.

At least, she was not young enough to forget herself for long. Not young enough to set propriety at naught for more than those fleeting moments. Not young enough to scorn the reasons she had refused the man in the first place.

With a gasp, she shoved Mr. Wolfe away (or tried to—he didn't actually go anywhere, but at her unexpected show of resistance he dropped his arms). The cloak he had draped over her shoulders slipped to the ground.

"Oh, dear. Oh, no." At the raggedness of her breath, she thanked God for the shadows they stood in.

"What's the matter, darling?" His hands ran up the length of her silk gloves, but she pulled away, childishly hiding her arms behind her back.

"Don't—you mustn't call me that!"

"Why mustn't I?" His voice was silky, teasing. "Here we find ourselves, in this hopelessly compromising situation. And man of wax that I am, I intend to do the honorable thing and marry you. Kiss me again, Miranda."

"No." She was shaking her head, and she gave him another ineffectual push. "No one has seen us. Nothing needs to be done. We must never do this again."

His low laugh sent a ripple through her. "What can you possibly mean? Are you in the habit of kissing gentlemen like you just kissed me and then telling them it must never happen again?"

"I must go back inside. The girls will wonder what became of me."

"And if you go, *I* will wonder what became of you," he retorted. "Miranda, are you going to marry me or not?"

"I am not, sir." She retrieved the fallen cloak. "I have—as I told you—I have no intention of marrying."

"You persist in saying that to me, after what just happened?"

She couldn't defend herself, but she could nod.

"But you love me!" he insisted. "Tell me you don't love me."

"I—I—" Her panic was returning. She had to lie—she had to tell the blackest lie she had ever told. At the very thought of it, her throat tightened. *Oh, God, help me.* She could tell the truth instead, she thought desperately. But not about loving him—if she spoke that aloud she would be lost.

She would give him another truth. A different one. Because a truth would be better than a lie.

"There—is one who loves you better," she whispered. "And whom I love with my whole heart, and you—perhaps you might come to love—this person—as well."

Without waiting for his response, Miranda did the only thing left to her.

She fled.

Chapter Twenty-Two

I puzzled my brains about this secret,
but could not come at it.
— F. W. Haussner, *Phraseologia Anglo-Germanica*
(1798)

She could only have been referring to one other person, he deduced. Mrs. Ellsworth was responsible for her own daughter and for the dean's granddaughter Miss Wright, but surely it was Miss Ellsworth whom she "loved with all her heart." But if it was, what the deuce did she mean by saying Miss Ellsworth loved him better than she did?

"Miss Ellsworth doesn't care in the slightest whether I be alive or dead," Colin muttered the following day, as he rode Titus over the Beaumond grounds. His horse was not having an easy time of it, for the master was unusually capricious that afternoon, now demanding a charge and a leap, now letting the reins almost drop and slowing to an amble. One moment stiff and upright, the next sagging like an imbalanced load of wineskins.

Miss Beatrice Ellsworth was a pleasant young lady and all that a young lady should be: fair, good-humored, reasonably intelligent, reasonably accomplished, and so forth. Colin would even go so far as to say she was a favorite among what his sister had called the "indistinguishable" crop of fresh-faced, cheerful Winchester maidens, being altogether less silly and clumsily artful than the rest. But as for "coming to love her"—! The thought had not entered his mind, nor was it likely to now simply because the woman he did love suggested it.

Where could Mrs. Ellsworth have come by such an idea? And more importantly, how could she be disabused of it?

He was some ways down the Weeke footpath before Colin arrived at his first conclusion: it hardly mattered where Mrs. Ellsworth got the idea. Whether Miss Ellsworth herself said something, or Miss Wright planted the notion or some other Winchester gossip, Mrs. Ellsworth would have gone at once to her daughter for confirmation. Had Miss Ellsworth then denied it, the matter would have ended there, and Mrs. Ellsworth would not have thrown it at him the night before. Therefore, whoever originated the belief, Miss Ellsworth must have corroborated it.

"But *why*, confound it? If that girl has conceived a *tendre* for me, I'll eat my hat, for I've given her no encouragement, nor has she shown any sign of it. Unless she's as lumpish as Doria, and her feelings never reach the pitch of requiring expression."

Titus' ears flicked backward at the speech, feeling the rigidity in his rider's legs.

But would Miranda renounce him for so faint an inclination on her daughter's part, if there was indeed an inclination?

One thing was clear: Colin must prove the precise extent of Miss Ellsworth's feelings. If they did exist, they must be gently discouraged. And if they did not...

If they did not, their nonexistence must be exposed. When Miranda had dashed away from him the night before, Colin's instinct had been to pursue her. But the cool hand of reason stayed him. She was not the sort of woman to say what she did not mean or to blow hot and cold. If she told him she could not love him because someone stood in the way, well, that someone must be removed.

Fortune soon favored him, and he spied in the distance the very person he sought. Miss Ellsworth, accompanied by Miss Wright, approaching along the same footpath. The giddy Miss Wright spied him as well, to judge by her sudden waving and hallooing.

"Shall we?" Colin murmured to his horse. To Titus's relief, the master sat upright and squeezed his thighs together with a click of his tongue.

"Ladies," he called when he was within earshot. "Dear ladies, what good luck to meet with you." Dismounting, he looped Titus's reins over his forearm and exchanged the usual pleasantries. Both girls were flushed, and while he was used to Miss Wright blushing and bumbling around him, it did disturb him to see Miss Ellsworth's high color. *Did* she care something for him? That would complicate things.

It would have reassured him had he heard their interchange a minute earlier.

Emmy had gasped and clutched Beatrice's arm. "Look there! What luck. It's him. It's Mr. Wolfe." At which announcement Beatrice had inhaled nearly as sharply and replied, "He might not have seen us! Let us duck into the wood here."

Emmy, of course, would not hear of this, and so they had remained, Emmy sighing, "I told my grandmama that I am more in love with him than ever, and she said I had better mind Mrs. Ellsworth and not do anything foolish, or she would send me back to Mama at Meadowsweep. Wouldn't that be dreadful? To miss the Beaumond ball in November! It would be more than I could bear. Don't you begin to love him even a little bit, Beatrice? I wish you would. Then I might have company."

Remembering her failure with her aunt and uncle, Beatrice replied unwillingly, "Perhaps I begin to. Just a little."

"I knew it!" crowed Emmy, bouncing on her toes. "Do you suppose he returns our feelings at all?"

"What do you mean, 'our'? You can't love two people at once," frowned Beatrice, already regretting her lie. "If you do, you're unworthy of either person's affections."

"Nonsense. It simply means you haven't decided yet. Second to Mr. Wolfe, I like Mr. Bracewell, but of course he likes Mrs. Ellsworth."

That was all they had time for before Mr. Wolfe drew within earshot, but it was long enough for Beatrice to feel suddenly very tired of all this foolishness. There was more to come, however.

"As October gives way to November, wild-flowers grow rarer, but see my windfall in coming here upon two of them."

At this most uncharacteristic compliment, Emmy drew a shaky breath, her eyes wide and wondering, but Beatrice could not help pulling a face. Pah! Mr. Wolfe had never before reminded her of Mr. Lyfford, but that was just the sort of fustian the hospital chaplain spoke. As soon as she could manage it, however, Beatrice ducked her gaze and echoed Emmy's murmury giggle.

"Oh, Mr. Wolfe," breathed Emmy, "I did not know you could be so poetical. You have a secret side."

"Indeed? And if I do, may not a gentleman keep secrets as well as a young lady?"

"Secrets!" Emmy collapsed against Beatrice, who shouldered her back up. "What secrets could we possibly be keeping, sir?"

"The usual youthful fodder, I daresay. Secret hatreds and se-cret...loves."

Emmy gave a squeal of mock protest, burying her face again in Beatrice's sleeve, so that it was only the latter who received Mr. Wolfe's penetrating look and arched eyebrow. She nearly collapsed herself, for it was as if the man could see all the way to the back of her brain. But he couldn't, could he?

"It appears I assumed correctly," he said urbanely. "Should I press my luck and try to guess specifics?"

Both girls screamed—Emmy piercingly and Beatrice's more of a yelp.

"Oh, Mr. Wolfe!" cried Emmy. "How—whimsical you are today. We are almost afraid of you."

He smiled, but to Beatrice's eyes it was not a pleasant smile. "Who shall I begin with? You, Miss Wright, or Miss Ellsworth?"

Emmy shrieked again. "You mustn't! You mustn't! Oh, Beatrice, how shall we stop him?"

"I don't suppose it's possible," said Beatrice bleakly. "But I will say the whole point of a secret is that it's *secret*, and not for other people's ears, unless the person whose secret it is chooses to share it."

Emmy scowled at her for being such a wet blanket to the fun, especially when Mr. Wolfe rejoined, "Well said, Miss Ellsworth. I had better hold my tongue in that case."

They proceeded in silence a few yards, Emmy still pinching Beatrice and Beatrice completely at a loss for anything else to talk about. It was Mr. Wolfe who saved them. Running his hand along his horse's neck, he said, "Titus here could tell you all my secrets, if he were the indiscreet sort of horse, but I chose him deliberately for his tactfulness."

"Do you mean to say you talk to your horse, Mr. Wolfe?" asked Emmy.

"How else might I unburden himself? I have no wife, you know, no companion of the bosom."

Neither girl could formulate a reply to this. Had Emmy possessed a few more years of experience, she might have turned such a remark to teasing advantage, but alas. And as for Beatrice, she could not shrink far enough beside her friend. What could Mr. Wolfe mean by saying such things? He had never talked thus to them before.

Colin's mind was hard at work in the meantime, scheming how to get rid of Miss Wright. Not that there would be any point in getting rid of her *here* along the footpath from Weeke, because that would only leave him in a compromising situation with Miss Ellsworth, the last place he wanted to be. But before they reached Hollowgate, something must be done.

Subtly he quickened their pace, changing the subject as well to hurry things along. "I can't say anything to my sister Jenny, you know. She hasn't the time to listen, being so occupied with preparations for the ball at Beaumond. All I hear is soup and 'space enough,' orgeat and allemands, negus and neighbors."

"We can hardly contain our anticipation," Emmy said eagerly. "My grandfather the dean even talks of going, though he and my grandmother have not gone to a ball in ever so long."

"Their presence would be an honor, Miss Wright. And what of your family, Miss Ellsworth? Would a ball at Beaumond be a sufficient lure for all your family members?"

"I expect so."

"Even your aunt and uncle Mr. and Mrs. Charles Ellsworth? I had the pleasure of making their acquaintance yesterday. Mrs. Charles Ellsworth in particular is a very clever woman. Observant, I would say."

Beatrice coughed. *Oh, heavens. What had Aunt Jeanne said to the man?*

"In fact, if I had not my horse to confide in," continued Mr. Wolfe, "I would be inclined to consult her on matters of the heart, for such matters seem very near to hers."

"Yes," agreed Beatrice faintly. "Aunt Jeanne loves to talk about love."

"What a convenient counselor she must be, then," he mused. "As everyone loves, at one time or another, I suppose every Ellsworth must then consult her at one time or another."

"Mm," said Beatrice. Though she could not forbear adding, "Your horse Titus is perhaps better able to keep confidences than Aunt Jeanne, however."

"Indeed?"

But here Beatrice was rescued by them reaching the Cock Lane gate, where a carriage had halted to pay the toll.

"Emmy!" called a voice unexpectedly.

"Grandmama!" Emmy wondered. "Whatever are you doing here?"

"We were coming to fetch you, dear," Mrs. Fellowes answered, "for I have just received a note that your parents will be arriving shortly to see you and stay for supper. Hop in, child, and we may beat them back to the deanery. Mr. Wolfe, I suppose I may ask you to walk Miss Ellsworth the remaining quarter-mile to the Hollowgate drive?"

He bowed, masking his pleasure at this development. With a sigh, Emmy climbed into the chaise beside her grandmother, giving Beatrice and Mr. Wolfe a mournful wave as the groom turned the horses back toward town.

"Shall we, Miss Ellsworth?" said Mr. Wolfe, when the others had gone.

As if she had a choice! He offered his arm, and she tried to take it with a smile. She should try to appear delighted. If she were in love with him—if this were Emmy in her place—Emmy would certainly be delighted. Elated. Emmy would glow with happiness and prance and toss her head like a trained horse.

But Beatrice could not do it. Her heart began to pound and her mouth to go dry and her head to empty. Her grip on his arm tightened, for fear she would crumple to the ground. Mr. Wolfe, on the other hand, looked as calm as Titus, who paced leisurely alongside.

"Miss Wright does not appear to have missed her parents, in her time at the deanery," he said mildly.

"No," admitted Beatrice, unsure whether this was a betrayal of her friend or not. "She likes all the activity of a town."

"To be sure. Which would you choose, Miss Ellsworth, if you did not have the good fortune of living in the bosom of your family with so many amusements ready at hand? Would you rather have the amusements but be separated from your family, or stay with your family and forego the amusements?"

"Forego the amusements," she said at once. "That is, I like dancing, but we dance at home often. And we have music. And Tyrone reads to us. Home is perfect. I—did not particularly want to attend all the things we have been attending, but Mama told Mrs. Fellowes she would chaperone Emmy. Besides which, Mama thinks a girl my age ought to attend such things."

"And you always listen to your mama, do you?"

She looked at him warily, suspecting a trap, but his expression was bland and guileless.

"You are most unusual, Miss Ellsworth. Your mama is right—most young ladies are more like Miss Wright. Eager to experience the world. Eager to find love. Eager to establish their own households."

"Mm."

"Do none of those sound tempting?" He could feel her hand tremble on his sleeve, but he could not yield to mercy. A desperate disease must have a desperate remedy.

"I do not understand why you ask me these things," Beatrice replied slowly.

"Has your mother not told you? These are questions any young lady your age should be prepared to answer."

They reached the arch at the end of the Hollowgate drive, and Beatrice hoped he would mount his horse and ride away, but the inexorable Mr. Wolfe continued to stroll beside her, as if they talked of no more than the weather or the previous night's assembly, and short of dropping his arm and fleeing, she did not know what she could do.

What if someone were to see them? They were not doing anything wrong. Indeed, they were on Hollowgate grounds now, and the dean's wife—a more respectable person could hardly be named in Winchester—had instructed Mr. Wolfe to see her home. Or, at least, to the Hollowgate drive. But if he walked her further, would that be bad?

"In answer, then," she murmured, the words dragged from her, "I would say, just to err on the side of caution, that I must be the unusual creature you call me because I feel no lack at present. I would have everything go on exactly as it is for—I don't know—years and years."

"Is such a thing possible? Only look at the last two years of your life. You lost your father—I am sorry to mention it and cause you pain—and then, in these last few months, you lost your younger brother to school."

"Yes, yes," she conceded quickly. "That is true. But all the more reason why I would prefer the—rest of my circumstances to stay constant."

"Ah," he sighed with regret (or was it mock regret?). "But you have likely heard the proverb, if wishes were thrushes, we might all eat birds."

Her chin rose indignantly. "I don't think this preference of mine is outlandish. We lost my father, yes, but he was older. And William went to school, yes, but we still see him. Nothing more might change for years. We are all in good health, and—and—I need not marry anyone."

He nodded like a sagacious philosopher hearing out a neophyte.

"And—thank you for your company," she hurried on, dropping his arm, "but I will be fine from here."

"What?" He glanced around as if only just realizing where he was. "Well. As I have come this far, I had better continue. Titus and I need not return by the Weeke footpath, you know, when we might cut across the grounds."

Her lips disappearing in a thin line, Beatrice once more took his arm.

After another minute, when she was about to say she hoped it would not rain the night of the Beaumond ball, he reflected, "That's all very well about *you* not marrying yet, Miss Ellsworth, but suppose Mrs. Ellsworth does? I know for a fact that Lyfford at least has tried his chances."

Then Beatrice went alternately red and white, and her voice shook a little. "Yes, and she refused him! Just as she will Mr. Dodge and Mr. Bracewell, if they ask."

"And you think she will continue to refuse for as long as you would like her to, for your comfort?"

They were a hairsbreadth from him asking if she thought Mrs. Ellsworth would refuse *him*. Beatrice released his arm yet again, this time on pretense of detaching a wet leaf from the hem of her pelisse. Oh, heaven—what could she say?

She must make some show of affection for him, however faint. Something which would be just enough to persuade him that such an affection existed. And then she must somehow hint that he should abandon hope of winning her mama, without coming right out and saying that Mrs. Ellsworth would *never* marry him, nor even permit herself to come to care for him, if she thought Beatrice herself wanted him.

These two things. They must, must be done. If only he were not so old and enormous and daunting!

Pretend you are Emmy.

They emerged from the avenue of limes. The house was before them. If she was going to do anything, it must be now.

Beatrice gulped. Then she gathered her hands in fists. "I-I-I think my mama not so s-susceptible to—ahem!—matters of the heart as I am."

"Have you got something in your eye, Miss Ellsworth?" he asked solicitously.

"What? No." So much for fluttering her lashes at him. "That is—I did. A speck of dust. It's gone now."

"You were saying...your heart is more susceptible than Mrs. Ellsworth's?"

"That's right." *Do something* now, *Beatrice Ellsworth!* As if it were no part of her body, she glared at her arm and willed it to rise. She would tap her fingertips on his sleeve, like a trill played upon the pianoforte. Yes. She would play a trill on his arm and then—giggle.

Holding her breath, she reached for him. But luck was not with her, for Titus chose that very moment to whicker and lift his head. Mr. Wolfe then flung up an arm to stroke and soothe his horse, so that instead of Beatrice's hand landing with playful lightness, her fingertips smote him with the force of a traveler shoving down the lid on an overstuffed trunk.

"Ooh!" cried Beatrice.

"Mercy!" exclaimed Mr. Wolfe.

"How—strong you are, Mr. Wolfe!"

"Was that my strength?" he wondered. "Or was that you, falling upon me like a tiger?"

"Tee hee," tittered Beatrice. "Sometimes my—er—impulses can be ungovernable, where—where—where my heart is concerned."

"And apparently also where it is not."

"No—but that's what I meant in this instance, sir," she fumbled to explain. "That my—heart was—concerned."

At the skeptical look he gave her, Beatrice wanted to dive into the shrubbery and hide there till nightfall, but she had gone too far to draw back now. "I mean to say, what a dashing gentleman you are, Mr. Wolfe. Everyone thinks so. I—tell everyone I think so. Too."

One eyebrow rose, reminding Bea uncomfortably of how Bobbins the footman regarded one of the dogs when he caught it chewing a corner of the carpet.

"You've told 'everyone' you think so?" Mr. Wolfe asked.

She tried to say "yes," but no sound emerged, and she had to nod her head violently to jar some words loose. "Y-yes. That is, not *everyone*. But girls will talk, you know. And—and—and girls will talk to their mothers about such things. Or mothers ask about such things and then girls admit to it—them. Tee hee."

"You told your mother about this particular 'thing'?"

Another violent nod. Her brain was beginning to feel like it had been thrown in a bucket and whirled overhead. Nor did it help that his quiet amusement had given place to a wintry chill.

"And what did Mrs. Ellsworth have to say about these...ungovernable impulses of your heart?"

Beatrice dragged the toe of her boot in the gravel. "She said you were older than I was, but she had no other objections. She only said nothing needed to be done in haste."

He was silent a long moment, so long that they reached the loop of the drive before the house, and Beatrice considered simply muttering a good-bye and disappearing within. Mr. Wolfe's fierce look had more in common with a furious parent than a delighted lover, so of course she could never have prepared for what happened next.

Slowly he secured Titus's reins over the saddle's pommel, which puzzled her because, if Mr. Wolfe were going to call at Hollowgate, he would surely have tethered him to the post. *Not* that Beatrice wanted him to call.

All became clear the next instant when he lowered himself to one knee.

"What are you doing?" she gasped.

"When Mrs. Ellsworth told you nothing needed to be done in haste, she did not take into account *my* feelings on the matter."

No. No, no, no, no! Beatrice backed away a step, but his arms were too long and his motion too quick for her. He snatched her hand in a powerful grip.

"Perhaps you are not the only one, Miss Ellsworth, with ungovernable impulses of the heart."

"What is happening? What are you doing, Mr. Wolfe?"

"What does it look like I'm doing? If you're so fond of me, you should be beside yourself with joy."

Beatrice thought she would faint. The bucket with her head in it was whirling faster and faster. How had she got herself in such a rare kettle of fish? She meant it all to be so clean and simple.

"Don't swoon on me, girl," he said through a tight jaw. "Or at least not before you've given me an answer."

"An answer?" she echoed. "But Mr. Wolfe—you don't love me."

"You don't love me either, despite your recent pronouncement, so I fail to see what that has to do with anything."

"I—might come to love you," she insisted. She gave an exploratory tug to see if he would release her hand, but he didn't.

"Then perhaps you'd better come to say Yes."

Faster and faster whirled the bucket with her brain in it. Now she saw dots in the sky. In the sky and everywhere. Mr. Wolfe was squeezing her hand too tightly, and no blood could get to her fingers, so the blood ought to flow back to her head, but it didn't seem to be going there either. Where was the blood going?

Her lips parted. She would tell him—

But instead of telling him anything, she gave a little "ooh" of surprise.

Then she fainted.

Chapter Twenty-Three

Marriage is a very solemn engagement, enough to make
a young creature's heart ache, with the best prospects,
when she thinks seriously of it! -- TO be given up to
a strange man; to be engrafted into a strange family;
to give up her very name, as a mark of her becoming
his absolute and dependent property; to be obliged to
prefer this strange man to father, mother
-- to every body.
— Samuel Richardson, *Clarissa* (1748)

Jeanne Ellsworth flew back into the parlor, still carrying the
basket of sweet chestnuts she and Miranda had gathered, her
sudden halt sending a few of the prickly balls tumbling out.

"It is Mr. Wolfe! Carrying Beatrice!"

Miranda sprang up, hands at her throat, as utter confusion followed. Family members and servants ran hither and yon and everyone talked over each other before Mr. Wolfe shouldered his way in, a limp Beatrice in his arms. Before him and around him everyone naturally gave way, except Miranda, who had not stirred an inch, only her gaze moving from her daughter to Mr. Wolfe's face.

And it was to Miranda that Mr. Wolfe spoke, ignoring the questions buzzing like so many gnats about him. "She is not hurt," he said at once. "She has only fainted. Where shall I put her?"

Her heart retreating from her throat, Miranda sagged in relief. "Oh, thank you, Mr. Wolfe! But—what happened?" she asked as he lowered Beatrice to the sofa she indicated. "Were you there when she fainted? And what became of Emmy?"

He backed away, Scamp giving a fearful yelp when Wolfe's heavy boot narrowly missed his paw. "Yes, I was with her. I was out riding this afternoon and came upon the girls walking. But we met the dean's wife in her carriage at Cock Lane Gate, and she fetched Miss Wright away to see her parents. Mrs. Fellowes—er—asked me to escort Miss Ellsworth home, and—I suspect the walk must have been too much for her."

This was his explanation? Miranda was already seated beside her daughter, taking up Beatrice's hands to remove her gloves while other family members hemmed them in. "Too much for her?" she repeated helplessly. Raising her eyes once more to his remote, unreadable ones, she forced herself to add, "That must be it, I suppose.

Perhaps she has caught a cold, and it weakens her. In any event, Mr. Wolfe, we are glad you were there to assist her."

"I will leave her to your care, then," he said. "I'm afraid my horse is not tied up, and I had better go." Bowing generally to the gathered company, he left them, and they returned their attention to Beatrice. It was only sometime later that Miranda realized Jeanne too had gone.

"What happened?" the girl groaned when her eyes flickered open. "Where am I?"

"Home, dear," her stepmother replied, smothering the urge to pepper her with questions. She was glad when Aggie leaned over the back of the sofa saying, "You fainted, Goosey, and Mr. Wolfe brought you in. Did you crack your head?"

Beatrice touched it tentatively, frowning. "I don't think so. It doesn't hurt, at any rate. I was dizzy." All at once her eyes widened. "Did you say Mr. Wolfe brought me in?"

"Yes. Don't you remember?"

"Of course she doesn't remember," Tyrone put in. "She was unconscious."

"I meant, don't you remember he was with you?" Aggie clarified. "If we send for Mr. Carlisle, he will want to know if she has amnesia."

"I'm perfectly well. I don't need Mr. Carlisle," said Beatrice hastily, trying to sit up. Several hands took her by the shoulders and pushed her back down.

"Then what is the last thing you remember?" Aggie demanded. "Do you remember Mr. Wolfe was with you?"

"Er—yes. Barely."

"Barely? He says he walked with you and Emmy to Cock Lane Gate and then back to Hollowgate with you." Aggie turned on her husband. "See? She does have amnesia. Should we call Mr. Carlisle, Mrs. Ellsworth?"

"I don't need a doctor!" protested Beatrice, trying unsuccessfully again to struggle up. "I do remember everything! I just didn't want to tell you. I fainted because—because—Mr. Wolfe—" With another groan she threw an arm across her eyes.

There was a collective indrawn breath. Miranda shivered.

"Mr. Wolfe...*what*?" asked her brother quietly.

At his tone, Beatrice uncovered her eyes straight away. "Ooh! Nothing like that! That sounded bad. It's just that I—you see—I got short of breath because I was a little nervous because Mr. Wolfe—he...*proposed* to me."

Thankfully no one was looking at Miranda, for she had a feeling she went altogether green.

Mr. Wolfe had proposed to Beatrice? So soon after telling Miranda he loved her?

Who do you have to blame for it, after all? she told herself ruthlessly. *You were the one who hinted at Beatrice's affections. He has always been a man of action.* But why, oh why, did he act so soon? Had his heart changed the moment his eyes were opened? Or did he act to spite her, Miranda? *We are too old for spite.*

At least, she was.

"And what did you say to him?" gasped Aggie.

"I didn't say anything," replied Beatrice. "I fainted."

"Well, that's one way to handle it," Tyrone chuckled.

"I would not have guessed it from his calls here," Aggie wondered, shaking her head. "He seemed pleasant enough, to be sure, but he never singled you out, that I noticed. Imagine. Emmy Wright will be beside herself. What will you say to him, Bea?"

"*Must* I say something?" Beatrice whined.

"Of course you must," interjected Miranda firmly, finding her voice for the first time. "Even if it is just to say you need more time to consider. You may send a note, however. You needn't say it to his face."

The girl turned anguished eyes on her. "I can't do it, Mama. I can't write to him."

"Why not, darling? If you...don't feel ready to give an answer, simply say you would like a week to think about it. Or a fortnight, even."

"I want to say No!"

"Then say it," laughed Aggie. "Only, don't make a poor man wait for a No if you've already decided." She gave her husband a playful jab. "And if you're too afraid to write the note, Bea, I know someone who might prove handy."

Miranda took her daughter's hand and stroked it. She thought later it was one of the hardest things she ever had to do, but she said, "Be careful, dearest. We...spoke before of this. If you refuse Mr. Wolfe outright, it is unlikely he will ask again." Who knew that truth better or feared it more than Miranda herself?

Beatrice shut her eyes. "I know."

"I think he's too old for you," said Aggie. "Don't you, Mrs. Ellsworth? Beatrice is only eighteen, and she likely will receive a dozen proposals before she is through. No need to be over-hasty."

"I would never ask Beatrice to do anything she did not want to do," returned Miranda, "but one must think matters through thoroughly. Aggie, Tyrone—if you would let us have a word in private…"

Reluctant as they were to miss anything, the Tyrone Ellsworths had no alternative but to decamp, though before going Aggie bent to hiss in her sister-in-law's ear, "Don't do it, Bea!"

When the door shut behind them, Beatrice sat up. "I don't want to marry him, Mama."

"I know you did tell me that earlier," Miranda answered, "and I do not press you out of any desire to *force* you. But remember—you are already fond of him, and there is…nothing in his person or character to make your feelings weaken as you know him better. I am sure of it. Good marriages have been made on less than the…respect and incipient esteem you feel."

Beatrice bit her lip, still shaking her head.

"Suppose you were to refuse him," her stepmother continued gently, "and he marries someone else. How would you feel about that?"

"I don't know," choked Beatrice. She rolled over and buried her face in the sofa cushions, her stepmother's searching eyes too much to bear. Should she confess that Mr. Wolfe might marry whomever he pleased, and she would not care a jot, so long as he did not marry an Ellsworth? Possibly, possibly it was safe now.

As her mother rubbed her back to soothe her, Beatrice decided on a compromise. She would tell one truth and one lie, but this second lie would be comparatively harmless. And when the Beaumond ball was past and the danger possibly done with, she would tell all.

Rolling back over, she pushed herself up. "Mama, I think it worth the chance. Refusing Mr. Wolfe, I mean. Because it wouldn't be courteous to hold him in suspense, would it, if it takes me a long time to make up my mind, or to learn to like him better? So I had better refuse. Because—while he is an admirable person—he is not the only admirable person."

Miranda could not help but stare. Such words might be commonplace with any other vacillating young lady in Winchester, but with the steady Beatrice they were astonishing.

The girl's chin lifted. "That is—what I want to say is—Mr. Bracewell too is—worthy of esteem."

Miranda tried to comprehend this. "Do you mean to say you…are fond of Mr. Bracewell…*as well as* Mr. Wolfe?"

"Yes," declared Beatrice boldly, hoping vehemence would serve in place of truth. "As well as, yes. I know Mr. Bracewell doesn't return my feelings, but I begin to like him just the same. So, you see, I couldn't possibly accept Mr. Wolfe when—when I am…torn. So I had better refuse."

Miranda's thoughts raced beneath her calm surface. Whatever Mr. Wolfe's reasons in proposing so suddenly to Beatrice, if the girl refused him, what would he do? Would he ask Miranda again? And if he did, could she possibly accept him now? She couldn't, it seemed. Not without consulting Beatrice first. It was one thing for a young lady to refuse a gentleman and quite another for her then to welcome the same man as a stepfather! But much as Miranda might want to ask Beatrice on the spot, she could hardly do so right then, when her daughter's decision was so new and tentative.

"Perhaps you should sleep upon it," Miranda murmured. "It is a big decision to make so quickly, and you did have a fainting spell."

"But I fainted because it was so distressing, not because I was undecided."

"Still. Tomorrow is soon enough. If he does not hear from you today, he will certainly ask after you tomorrow."

But at this Beatrice's eyes grew round as buttons, and she shook her head. "Please don't make me see him tomorrow, Mama! If I don't change my mind, couldn't *you* receive him and tell him?"

"I?" gasped Miranda, horrorstruck. "No. No, I couldn't. It isn't done, to pass off one's refusals on someone else."

"Then couldn't you take pity on me and write the refusal for me, and send it first thing tomorrow morning? Write it as me, I mean. Or write it, and I will copy it? Please, Mama!"

For fear that renewed distress would bring on another fit, Miranda reluctantly agreed. Rising and moving slowly to the desk, she thought surely she must be the only woman in history who had to write a refusal to the man she loved, for a proposal she had not been offered.

"Monsieur—Mr. Wolfe—a word!"

One foot in the stirrup, Colin looked up to see Mrs. Charles Ellsworth hurrying down the five broad steps of Hollowgate with surprising agility for her age, waving her handkerchief. *What now?*

But he withdrew his boot and, with a pat for the patient Titus, waited to hear what the woman had to say.

"Monsieur, we must thank you again for coming to our *chère* Beatrice's aid," she said, a trifle breathless from her dash, one of the spiky chestnuts bouncing out and landing beside his boot.

He bent deliberately to retrieve it, giving himself an instant to think. The mischievous woman had surely followed him to pump him as she had at the assembly, and he did not doubt she would succeed in learning what she wanted to know. Well, and what of it? Every Ellsworth and possibly all Winchester would hear by nightfall that he had offered for Miss Ellsworth, so it was useless to hide the fact.

Colin restored the chestnut to her basket. "I am only too glad I was nearby."

"Yes. I will not detain you long, Mr. Wolfe. No doubt you think me an interfering woman, but perhaps it will help you to understand if I say that the Ellsworths—all of them—are the only family I have. Like you I came as a stranger to Hampshire, oh, years ago, having left my country to accompany my dear husband. And my adopted family has been a blessing and a joy. They will tell you I am only interested in love, but you see, it is love which makes life full."

He bowed in response. "You have indeed been fortunate in your family."

"And if I am not mistaken, sir, you too would like to be a part of it."

When he did not reply, her pretty mouth curved in a smile. "My husband said to me last night that he likes you the better for noticing the many virtues and charms of our beloved Mireille. *Miranda.* She is so much deserving of happiness. My brother William Ellsworth was a good man, but—how does one say it?—he was much older and did not touch her heart."

Colin was very still, like prey which knew it had been seen by a predator. Then he said, "I had better tell you at once that I have just offered for Miss Ellsworth."

"For Beatrice?" breathed Jeanne. "Why would you do that when it is Mireille you love?"

Had she been anyone else he would have denied it, but Colin knew she had seen through him at the assembly. Moreover, that strange paralysis held him. Though Mrs. Charles Ellsworth would not devour him—she was not cruel—she had laid his heart open where anything and anyone could get at it.

"I...did ask Mrs. Ellsworth...earlier," he said at last. "She said she had no intention of remarrying at present."

Jeanne gave a tiny shrug. "*Tant pis.* Too bad. She cares nothing for you, then, and it is hopeless? Therefore you give up and turn to the daughter?"

His pale eyes grew smoky, opaque. "She cares for me, I swear it. But she will not have me. And—she tells me there is someone she loves who loves me better."

"Beatrice?"

"Who else could it be?"

Jeanne gave a short laugh. "Mr. Wolfe, I pray you will not take this news ill, but I do not believe my dear niece loves you."

"Nor do I. But she must have told her mother so. Where else would Mrs. Ellsworth have got such an idea?"

"Ah. I understand." Absently she swung her basket of chestnuts, frowning at them. "Yes. It must have come from Beatrice. So you ask Beatrice to marry you to prove to her mother that there is nothing there."

"Something like that."

"Yes. It is clever. Risky, but clever. And then you think, when Beatrice refuses you, you will ask Mireille again, and she will give you a different answer."

"That is my hope." When his interlocutor made no response, only continuing to swing her basket absently, he added, "Do you think it will work?"

Jeanne sighed. "A girl may give many reasons for refusing a gentleman."

"What do you mean by that?"

"I mean, Mireille must be persuaded that Beatrice does not love you. At all. *Pas du tout.* And Beatrice must be persuaded that her mother cares for you very much. *De tout son coeur.* Do you understand? They love each other too well to hurt each other. But if

Mireille thinks Beatrice loves you at all, she will never marry you, Mr. Wolfe. And if Beatrice thinks her mother loves you, she would never want to break her heart, no matter if it breaks her own."

"I must get Miranda to confess her love to Beatrice?" He looked aghast. "But I could not even get her to tell *me* she cared!"

Jeanne wagged an admonitory finger. "It need not be in words, monsieur. But you must not go on as you have been. You must not ignore Mireille and pay her no attention in front of others. You must be cunning and trick her into showing affection for you in front of Beatrice. At your ball, you must ask her to dance. You must flirt with her at every opportunity. Mireille is careful and reserved, so you must outwit her."

"It would be a pleasure to do those things, Mrs. Ellsworth, but what if she does not respond? She is not coquettish by nature."

"Listen to the man!" Jeanne appealed to heaven. "You would think every girl in Winchester was not chasing him!"

"Mrs. Ellsworth is not every girl," he muttered. "That's plain as a packsaddle."

She only gave him a playful tap on the breastbone. "You must do your best. I will help you, if I see opportunity. *Je suis sûr que tout s'arrangera*. It will work out. But it may take time. Mireille has spent her life waiting, but I do not know if you understand waiting. Men like to leap at the prize."

He gave a rueful smile, thinking of the long years with Doria, full of fruitless waiting. To give so much of his life to one whom he had not even been able to love in the end...could he not do as much for Miranda?

In any event, he was not sure he had a choice. "Leaping at the prize" had gained him nothing.

"I can wait."

CHAPTER TWENTY-FOUR

'A watched pot is slow to boil,' as Poor Richard says.
— Benjamin Franklin, Report from Paris to Louis XVI
(c.1785)

C olin's plans to act immediately on Mrs. Charles Ellsworth's advice met their first impediment the following morning when the post arrived.

He glanced at Jenny, but she was clucking and muttering over a letter from her husband, leaving him perfect privacy to open the missive.

Hollowgate

24 October 1812

Dear Mr. Wolfe,

Thank you very much for your offer of marriage. I have given it thought, and while you have my utmost respect, and I am very sensible of your kind intentions, I must refuse. I have no desire to marry anyone at the present time.

I hope any disappointment you might feel at this reply will be brief and that the cordial intercourse between our families may continue as if no word had ever been spoken.

Your obedient servant,
Beatrice Ellsworth

Of course he had expected such an answer. He would never have made his offer to begin with, had an acceptance been possible. But he was sorry the fact of the note made a call at Hollowgate that day out of the question. Not only that day. Indeed, it would be awkwardness itself to force his company upon the girl in her own home. He must let the first meeting be one of chance. But when it was accomplished, Colin told himself he would indeed continue as if no word had ever been spoken and begin his assault on Mrs. Ellsworth's reserve.

"Jenny," Colin addressed his sister abruptly, "you will likely hear of it sooner or later, so you should know that I proposed to Miss Ellsworth and was refused."

His sister's mind, having been far away in Kent with her husband's concerns, took some minutes to assimilate this news, and

Colin answered her questions with what patience he could muster. Yes, he meant *Miss* Ellsworth, not Mrs. William Ellsworth. Yes, it had been very sudden. Yes, on the whole he did prefer the mother but thought he would try his chances with the daughter.

"I never heard of such a strategy!" cried Lady Hufton. "Suppose the girl had accepted you!"

"She never would," he said shortly. "If anything, I asked her in order to prove the point."

More marveling and sputtering followed, but at last it was got through, and his despairing sister asked helplessly, "Do you suppose they will still come to the ball, the Ellsworths? What use will all my efforts be if they will not?"

"The ball is still nearly a fortnight away. I think they will. But we must smooth matters before then. In fact, we must smooth matters before Sunday because Edmund will have a holiday."

"Did you write to him? Will he be home for All Saints Day?"

Colin gave a mirthless chuckle. "You act as if the boy would have replied, even if I had. I fear it would exasperate him if we were to order him home again. He may come on his own, but he may not. However, if he goes to Hollowgate with William Ellsworth, I want to make sure we are invited to dinner there."

"How do you propose to see them before then, Colin? You know I will do anything you like."

She was as good as her word. In the week which followed, they made another round of calls wherever Mrs. Ellsworth and her daughter might also call: the deanery, St. Thomas Street at the Charles Ellsworths', Kingsgate Street at the Robert Fairchilds', in the cathedral close at the Simon Kenners', and Canon Street at the Nicholas Carlisles'. Nowhere did they encounter any of the Hollowgate Ellsworths.

"What poor luck," complained Lady Hufton as brother and sister returned from Canon Street up Southgate. "And even worse, I suspect they all know you proposed to Miss Ellsworth and were refused, for Mrs. Fairchild dropped her voice every time she addressed you, as if you were on your deathbed, and Mrs. Kenner kept talking of how there were twice as many pretty young ladies in Winchester as there used to be, and Mrs. Carlisle was unrelentingly jolly. Oh, Colin! At this rate, if Edmund goes to Hollowgate on Sunday, Mrs. Ellsworth might just send him home to Beaumond, and then won't he be cross?"

"Well, Jenny, the good news is, Edmund behaves about the same when he is cross as when he is happy."

When the calls were exhausted, they tried charity. Baskets and flowers were brought to Miss Hambly and even the Jeromes, but the confinement and tedium were for naught. In an effort to ferret out information for her brother, Lady Hufton said cheerfully to old Mrs. Jerome, "I hope you will like Beaumond pork as well as Hollowgate's, for I daresay Mrs. Ellsworth sends a haunch every autumn."

This only brought on a five-minute lamentation about the multitudinous ways decency had fallen off from when the Baldrics lived at Hollowgate, and it was left to young Mrs. Jerome to whisper to them as they departed that, yes, Mrs. Ellsworth had indeed sent very good pork.

The following day brought heavy rain, frustrating Colin's plans to saddle Titus for a long ride as near Hollowgate as he could venture. Nor would Mrs. Ellsworth likely go walking the day after, with the roads so muddy.

Watched pots being slow to boil, Colin stayed at Beaumond on the muddy day to meet with the steward, so naturally it was his sister who finally encountered Mrs. and Miss Ellsworth in town.

"Oh, Colin!" Lady Hufton panted, rushing into his office while still untying her bonnet. "I have come from the circulating library, where I have seen them and talked to them at last, after wandering in and out of every shop in Winchester all morning!"

She had the gratification of seeing her brother immediately shut the register he was consulting so that he might draw up a chair for her by the fire.

"I saw them first, of course, because I have done nothing this week but stare with all my eyes hoping to see them. They entered, and I thought I would fly around to take up a post between them and the door, so that they could not leave again without speaking to me, but it proved unnecessary because Mrs. Ellsworth noticed me. I had a novel in my hand—Ann of Swansea's *Cambrian Pictures*—which I declare I left there because I was so distracted, and now I will have to return for it because I did so want to read it." Here she ran out of breath and Colin showed admirable patience, only imagining in his mind's eye giving his sister a good shake.

"Miss Ellsworth was shy, but Mrs. Ellsworth came forward to greet me," Lady Hufton continued. "It was rather constrained at first. We said the usual things, I suppose, but I was so afraid I would not say the most important part that I burst out with it and asked if they had heard from their William. And Miss Ellsworth spoke up and said, yes, he would come home for the holiday on Sunday. And I said, 'We confess, we have not heard from Edmund.' Then—oh, Colin!—there was this dreadful pause! Miss Ellsworth looked at the floor, and Mrs. Ellsworth was pink, and I daresay I was too. But then Mrs. Ellsworth said, 'If Edmund should happen to come with Willie, we will be certain to send a note to Beaumond because of course you must dine with us.'"

Colin clapped his hands together with a report like a gunshot and went so far as to kiss Lady Hufton's cheek. "Well done, Jenny!"

She flushed with pleasure. "And I said it was a hundred to one, but if William came home with Edmund, of course the Ellsworths must come to Beaumond. Then I wanted to put Miss Ellsworth at her ease, so I asked her a dozen questions about books and such and told her about *Cambrian Pictures,* which they hadn't read, and by the end of it all she smiled at me. I wish you had been there, Colin, but the permission to come was what mattered, and I know, once there, you will manage the rest."

As they had predicted, the note came when they returned from church on All Saints Day. Just a sentence, but Colin's pulse jumped: *"Edmund is here if you would like to join us – M.E."*

"The boy really ought to have told us," Lady Hufton sniffed, but Colin could understand how seeing an aunt for the second time in a fortnight might not have the allure of being at Hollowgate again after longer than a month. Colin was eager to go himself, his

keenness increased by a desire to have done with the entire propos-
ing-to-Miss-Ellsworth sham.

A pale and ineffectual sun alternated with light rain as Downing
drove them to Hollowgate, inclement enough weather that the boys
were not to be seen out of doors. Nor were they in the drawing room
where the footman led them, though many others seemed to be. The
Robert Fairchilds were there again and an older couple he did not
know, along with the Tyrone Ellsworths of course—a great crowd
of witnesses whose presence made the two dogs quite boisterous.

"Welcome, Lady Hufton, Mr. Wolfe," said Mrs. Ellsworth from
across the vast room, one of the scrambling dogs in her arms. "Allow
me to introduce Mr. and Mrs. Hemple. Mr. Hemple is the curate
of our parish church, St. Eadburh's." Scamp wriggled extravagantly
from her grasp, landing on the carpet with a thump and bolting
across the room to do his usual snarling at Colin.

"I can't imagine what you did to him, Mr. Wolfe," mused Mrs.
Tyrone Ellsworth, "that Scamp should object to you so."

"Whatever it was, he did not do it to Pickles," her husband observed, nodding at the latter, who was indecorously chewing his
inner haunch.

"Pickles is stupider, however," Aggie pointed out.

"Pickles *is* stupider," agreed Colin, "for Scamp has discovered the
truth—that I had a dog before whom I loathed."

The strength of his chosen word demanded explanation, which
led to Colin regaling the company with the tale of the dreadful
Ding-Ding. And when he wound up with Ding-Ding's role in Mrs.
Wolfe's death, even Miss Ellsworth said, "How terrible! I see why

you chose to leave the creature in Kent. Scamp, you silly beast, you must pardon Mr. Wolfe."

No sooner did Miss Ellsworth address Colin than the mood of the gathering shifted. It became easier, and Colin realized they had all been holding themselves stiffly, too aware that this was the first meeting between him and Miss Ellsworth. His gaze flicked to Mrs. Ellsworth, still standing beside the pianoforte, and she gave him a tiny smile.

Ah, she did it on purpose. Invited extra people, made a fuss with the dog. She knew it would be awkward. It was like her to think how they might all be made comfortable again with as little delay and fuss as possible.

He returned her smile. "But so much for my sad history. Where are the boys? I assume all three of them are somewhere about, Edmund and William and Peter."

"It seems, after so many weeks at school, the temptations offered by our cook Wilcomb were more alluring than our company," Mrs. Ellsworth laughed. "But she promised to shoo them out presently, after they satisfied their sharpest hunger pangs. I think I hear them coming."

The addition of three boys added to the hubbub, but Colin was grateful that Edmund at least came over to accept his aunt's kiss and bow to his father.

"Dear Edmund," Lady Lufton said, patting his arm. "I do believe you have grown."

As even children chattier in nature find little to say to such observations, Edmund could not be blamed for making no reply at all.

"Were you made to watch out before you came?" Colin asked him.

"Wanted to," said Edmund.

"You wanted to?"

It was William who explained. "Edmund made a bargain with Dockery—he's the biggest fellow in Senior Part. If Mundo made a catch in the first quarter-hour, not only would he be let off the rest of the day, but Peter and I could go too."

"I made a catch," said Edmund.

Such brevity did not satisfy Peter and William, however, and the two boys gave a more detailed account, complete with each doubling parts as bowler and batter and fielders.

"But what of Grimes the prefect, Willsie?" asked Miss Ellsworth. "Are his bones still broken?"

Her younger brother shrugged with boyish indifference. "He's all right. Still following Mundo about."

"He's got bigger," offered Edmund. He held a hand out at the height of the sofa back. "Almost to my shoulder now."

Colin then boldly turned to address the young lady who disdained marrying him. "Did you attend the quiristers' concert, Miss Ellsworth? You might have seen Grimes with your very own eyes."

With equal boldness she replied, "Thank you, sir, but I did not. Mama went with Florence. Did you or Flossie see him, Mama?"

Colin was glad of the excuse to look at Mrs. Ellsworth, but she only glanced up from her embroidery to beam at William. "I don't know. We did see Edmund though, and, just around him, the edges of Willie and Peter."

"Not likely to see Grimes," Edmund said. "He was opposite us. Prefects, you know."

When they were proceeding to the dining room later, Lady Hufton took Colin's arm and whispered, "I vow, I've never heard Edmund say half as many words! Perhaps he would have been a more talkative boy if you and Doria had ever contrived to give him a sibling."

Colin repressed a grimace, but the memory of Doria was losing its bitterness. If not for Doria, he would never have had Edmund; and if not for Edmund, he would never have met Mrs. Ellsworth.

There was no opportunity to speak with her at the dinner, for he was placed between Tyrone Ellsworth and Mrs. Hemple, at the very opposite end of the table from her. But he heard the murmur of her voice when she spoke to the curate, and he frankly looked at her when attending to conversation further down. Mrs. Charles Ellsworth's admonitions rang in his head: he must demonstrate to Mrs. Ellsworth that her daughter did not care for him, and he must demonstrate to the daughter that her mother *did*. But he sensed instinctively that Mrs. Ellsworth would not like him to call down the table to her nor embarrass her with attentions in front of her family. It would be wiser, therefore, to apply his energies toward subtly vexing Miss Beatrice.

The curate's wife must not have known of his proposal to Miss Ellsworth because if she had she would never have probed his marriage prospects as she did, by way of addressing Lady Hufton to her right. "You know my dear friend Mrs. Spence, I suppose, Lady Hufton? Your vicar's wife at St. Anastasius? She tells me she and Mr.

Spence are too old and doddering to dance at your Beaumond ball next Saturday, but they will attend nevertheless to see for themselves the outcome of the *great contest*." This last was delivered in a loud whisper and accompanied by a roll of her eyes in Colin's direction.

Lady Hufton gave an uneasy titter. "Contest? Oh. We will have a room set up for cards, naturally."

"Cards? No, indeed! I meant…" (A lift of the eyebrows and tilt of the head toward Colin.) "*That* contest, where every young lady tries her hand. Was he so popular in Kent?"

Poor Lady Hufton was spared answering by a most unexpected interjection. "Who d'you mean?" asked Edmund from across the table. And either Willie to one side or Peter to the other must have kicked him because he added belatedly, "Ma'am."

"Oh!" The curate's wife flushed to be caught out. "Dear boy. I was not addressing you, but rather your aunt."

Edmund subsided into silence, if so large a boy could be said to subside, but his brow was troubled.

Mrs. Fairchild tactfully revived the conversation, asking Mrs. Tyrone Ellsworth what she planned to wear to the ball, and talk moved on from there. Penitently, Mrs. Hemple asked Colin and Mr. Tyrone Ellsworth questions about the late-autumn plowing and whether they expected the winter to be as harsh as the previous year's, but nobody's heart was in it, and Colin was glad to see the parson and his wife take their leave soon after the gentleman rejoined the ladies in the drawing room. There Tyrone took up his violin, accompanied by his sister Miss Ellsworth on the pianoforte, while Mrs. Ellsworth prepared the tea. There were further surprises in store, however, for his stolid boy soon abandoned his place by the table where William and Peter played at draughts to wander the room, peeking now and then at his father by the fire.

After several minutes of this, Mrs. Ellsworth detained him on one of these lumbering circuits. "Edmund," she said, "would you kindly give your father this cup of tea? You might ask him if he would like more sugar and milk as well."

It was fortunate the boy's rank and education made it unlikely he would ever enter domestic service, for the cup rattled against the saucer the length of the room, some of the beverage slopping over the brim.

"Sir," said Edmund.

Colin took it gingerly, his mind less concerned with the state of the offering than with what might be occupying his son, for Edmund lingered beside him like an overlarge piece of statuary.

"Does it need more milk or sugar?" the boy mumbled.

Colin took a sip. "It is perfect. Just how I like it." Nevertheless, he set it upon the carved stone mantel. How convenient it would be if Mrs. Ellsworth might also get them over this little difficulty! Colin did not doubt she could manage it as well as she did the tea preparation. His gaze stole to where she sat, calm in her work, and he envied the freedom Mrs. Fairchild had to sit down beside her.

It was Edmund who took the bull by the horns, since his few words always had the effect of bluntness. "Are you going to marry again, sir?" he blurted.

Colin straightened sharply. "Why do you ask? Is this because of that busybody of a parson's wife at dinner?"

Edmund gave a nod, frowning. He did not seem inclined to say more, and Colin was left to debate what more should be said. The fact was, he did intend to marry again, as soon as ever he could manage it, so there was nothing to be gained by denial.

"I think it likely I will," he replied at last in a quiet voice. And when his son's features sank even further into grimness, Colin added, "Would it be so bad to have a stepmother?"

No answer. Edmund lifted a hand to the chimney-piece and began to pick at the carved scroll nearest him.

"The—er—the elder Ellsworths—not William, of course—were all raised with a series of stepmothers," Colin resumed, "and they seem a close and happy family." He gestured unobtrusively in the direction of Mrs. Ellsworth and her oldest stepdaughter. "I believe Mrs. Fairchild was already a grown woman before Mrs. Ellsworth became her stepmother, and she seems nearly as fond of her as Miss Ellsworth does, who was much, much younger when her father remarried."

Edmund grunted.

But this was too important a subject for Colin to be satisfied with a grunt.

"Tell me," he urged. "Tell me what you're thinking."

The stone scroll having been thoroughly picked at, Edmund turned next to the cluster of flowers and leaves. "They don't mind because she's Mrs. Ellsworth," he mumbled. He did not meet his father's eyes, but if he had, he would have been confused by the leaping excitement in them. As it was, the invisible barrier which kept all the boy's words dammed up had been breached, and before the dike could be repaired, more tumbled out. "Puncher's father remarried," said Edmund, "and Puncher says his new stepmother hates him, and he has a new little brother, and they only care about that one."

Colin's lips parted, but he said nothing, unwilling to break the spell.

"And—and Metcalf says his stepmother is hardly older than his sister, and everyone thinks they *are* sisters, and *she* likes it, but they're mortified." Leaving off running his finger over the carvings, Edmund began to fiddle with the malachite-and-ormolu clock, shifting its position forward and back on the mantel. He took a deep, shuddering breath, the line of his jaw appearing through his boyishly rounded cheek. "That is, of course you must marry again if you like, sir, but—but I expect it will be an unpleasant business for me."

"I understand," answered Colin after a minute, when it appeared no more confidences were forthcoming. He had the breathless feeling he had witnessed a miracle. "I understand your...concerns. Thank you for telling them to me. I believe I may safely pass my word to you that, if I do remarry, it would be to someone after the...Mrs. Ellsworth style. That is, someone who would care for you and treat you kindly and who would—er—never be mistaken for your sister."

Puncher's and Metcalf's fathers may once have promised something along the same lines, but Colin had never given his son any cause to doubt his word, and it must have sufficed because Edmund nodded once at the clock and then a second time at the sconce over Colin's left shoulder. Then he cleared his throat and lumbered back to the draughts table to join his friends.

Chapter Twenty-Five

You shall not finde me (Daughter) After the slander of most Step-Mothers, Euill-ey'd vnto you.
— Shakespeare, *Cymbeline*, I.i.71 (c.1616)

For courage, Beatrice had chosen her place deliberately by her mother, in the event of Mr. Wolfe approaching or addressing her directly. Which was precisely what he did, when his son Edmund left him.

"If I might trouble you for more, Mrs. Ellsworth...? I'm afraid Edmund will never be hired as a waiter in a coffee house." With a grin, he indicated the spilled tea in his saucer.

"Let me give you a fresh cup," Miranda said, pleased to hear the steadiness of her voice. She sensed Beatrice shrinking beside her and half hoped Mr. Wolfe would take his drink and go, but instead he drew a chair closer to them.

"Something unusual has happened," he said thoughtfully, when he had taken a sip and set his cup down again. "Did you notice Edmund speaking to me? I suppose that's two unusual things: Edmund speaking, and Edmund speaking to *me*."

"I daresay he speaks to you as much as to anyone," Miranda teased. "But I am glad he did so."

Mr. Wolfe swept the room with his gaze, but the boys and musicians were occupied, and the others engaged in conversation as they listened. He edged his chair another inch nearer.

"I had better take full advantage of this moment of privacy to tell you, Miss Ellsworth—I assume your mother is in your confidence?—that had you accepted me, I would now be in a most awkward position."

Beatrice's eyes grew round. She knew she was inexperienced, but surely it was not the custom for a gentleman to discuss his rejection after the fact with the one who rejected him? One look at her mother told her Mrs. Ellsworth was equally startled.

"For it happens," Mr. Wolfe continued, "Edmund was troubled enough by Mrs. Hemple's rather indelicate references at the dinner table to ask me if I planned to marry again. Yes! I see you share my astonishment. It seems a pair of his classmates have had regrettable experiences with stepmothers, and Miss Ellsworth, it grieves me to say that one instance derived from the relative youth of the new stepmother. So, you understand, if you had accepted me, I would have been obliged to make the sorry confession to my son that, indeed, his new stepmother might be mistaken for a sister."

"I—I—am glad you were spared this," choked Beatrice.

"Thank you." His pale eyes gleamed. "How kind of you to say."

"You say 'experiences' in the plural," ventured Miranda, both to relieve Beatrice from embarrassment and to satisfy her own curiosity. "Did Edmund name another regrettable situation?"

Their companion sighed. "Ah, alas, yes. He mentioned the un-fortunately-named Puncher—you recall him? The one whose in-competence when watching out at cricket so enraged the prefect Grimes? It seems poor Puncher's stepmother dislikes and neglects him in favor of her own child, his infant half-brother. But I would never lay such a charge to your account, Miss Ellsworth, even as a possibility, for I do not believe an unkind and neglectful Ellsworth exists."

Beatrice impulsively seized Miranda's hand. "Such a stepmother would be dreadful! Poor Puncher!" She threw Mr. Wolfe a fierce look, forgetting her discomfiture. "You mustn't marry anybody like that, Mr. Wolfe, if you love your son. Because—oh, Mama! It would have killed me if you didn't love me, and you only loved Willsie."

Blushing, Miranda hushed her, trying to turn it to a joke. "What a good thing you were such a loveable child, then." But Beatrice's distress was such that Miranda leaned and kissed her cheek. "Never mind. What nonsense. I'm sure Puncher's stepmother loves him. It is only that babies do require a fearful amount of care and atten-tion." To Mr. Wolfe she added lightly, "You see what a tender heart my Beatrice has."

"I do see that," he replied, "though she disposed of me in a sentence or two. A most tender heart and the winning Ellsworth kindness. Are you absolutely certain you don't want to marry me later, Miss Ellsworth? We could wait until you're a fair deal older—haggard, even, so no one would think you Edmund's sister."

"Sir, I don't want to marry you *at all*," retorted Beatrice, goaded at last by his pricking at her. "Not now, not ever. So please never mention it again, even in jest."

"'A hit, a very palpable hit,'" said Mr. Wolfe with a theatrical clutch at his breast.

But Miranda was staring at her daughter. "Beatrice, dearest! Such vehemence."

"I'm sorry," her daughter groaned, now burying her face against Miranda's shoulder. "I know it's bad manners."

"It's not only that—" Miranda broke off, coloring again. It was just that the girl did not speak as one who had thought herself so recently in love with the man. Had it genuinely been such a passing fancy? Beatrice had never before shown signs of caprice, but perhaps her age or Emmy Wright's influence marked a new stage. Whatever the reason and whatever the depth of her previous feelings, Beatrice now spoke as if Emmy could have Mr. Wolfe and welcome! Moreover, the disdained suitor did not appear the least annoyed by his summary treatment. Had he not cared for Beatrice at all, then? But if he had not, had it indeed been a proposal made from spite?

She turned quizzical eyes upon him, but his bland demeanor revealed nothing. There was no more time for questions in any case, however, for the musical performance ended and applause broke out, Mrs. Fairchild rising from the instrument to say, "Peter, dear, you and Willsie and Edmund had better be going back, I daresay.

Tyrone, can you call for the coach? It's far too dark and cold for the boys to walk back to school."

The dutiful hostess, Miranda herself rose to go through the motions of seeing them off. But she wondered throughout. Her ardent earlier scenes with Mr. Wolfe might have been an invention of her own fancy, for all the signs he gave of remembering them. He and Beatrice did not love each other, it seemed, but neither was there the slightest hint that he intended to renew his claim on Miranda's heart.

When the company was gone, Aggie came and put an arm about her sister-in-law. "That went as well as could be expected, wouldn't you say, Bea? I knew Mr. Wolfe was too much the gentleman to make a fuss or to mope about, pouting."

"On the contrary," said Beatrice. "He seemed determined to tease me about it, so I do not think I broke his heart."

"Well, whatever the case, I rejoice at everyone's good behavior, for now we may all go to the ball and enjoy ourselves. Even Lady Hufton didn't frown at you, Bea, and I feared she would."

"I think," said Tyrone from where he was stretched full-length on the sofa, a book opened on his chest and Pickles circling to find a comfortable position between his ankles, "Lady Hufton's chief end is to do whatever pleases her brother best. May I suggest you emulate her virtuous sisterhood, Bea, and play something lulling? I did slave away with Flossie, sawing and sawing at my fiddle, so that you and he might have your say to each other."

And so contented was Beatrice with her world at that moment that she went directly to the instrument and performed her brother's favorites, one right after the other, only stopping when the nurse brought babies Joan and Margaret in to be kissed good night.

The day of the Beaumond ball dawned frosty and clear, and hearts throughout Winchester gave thanks. Miranda could not prevent her spirits lifting at the thought of hours spent in Mr. Wolfe's company, even if he felt nothing for her on reflection. Surely he would ask her to dance this time, now that they were speaking again. They could be friends, if nothing else.

That is, they could be friends until Mr. Wolfe proposed to another woman. It was unthinkable, unimaginable, that such a man could be refused three times running.

In all the furor over Mr. Wolfe's proposal to Beatrice, Miranda entirely forgot about Mr. Bracewell until he reappeared. The Hollowgate women had been assisting Wilcomb and Clement with bottling the elderberry wine when the footman summoned them to the morning room, and Miranda only had time for an anxious peek at Beatrice as she removed her apron. Was the girl's heart beating faster, to see her would-be sweetheart?

"I am happy to report the roads are dry," he announced after making his bow. "And the glass is high. There will be neither mud nor rain to spoil the evening's festivities."

"Splendid," said Miranda.

Whisking from behind his back a nosegay of asters and daisies and greenery, he held it out to her. "And I hope you will grant me the pleasure of dancing with you, Mrs. Ellsworth," he continued.

"Thank you. Of course." As pretty as the flowers were, it would never do. Laying them on the nearest table, she tried not to look at Beatrice, who had taken up her netting.

It was Aggie who took charge. "I declare, Mr. Bracewell, you make me quite envious with all your invitations to dance. I know my husband and I have not been at many of these occasions this summer and autumn, but we will be at Beaumond tonight, so I really must shamelessly insist on my share of you, if you have dances to spare for me and Beatrice."

Miranda laughed, giving a reproachful, *"Aggie!"* but Mr. Bracewell assured them at once that he was more than willing to partner each of them. At this Beatrice blushed rosily, though whether from delight or from embarrassment at Aggie's forwardness it was impossible to tell.

As Miranda stitched she chided herself for neglecting to think over Beatrice's confessed fondness for the clergyman. Should such feelings be encouraged or discouraged? In Mr. Bracewell's favor, he was young and handsome, well-mannered and a good dancer. But to his detriment, there was no denying he openly pursued Miranda for no other reason than her money, and even if he were to transfer his spurious affections to the more suitable Beatrice, had he not already disqualified himself as unworthy?

He had, in Miranda's estimation. But there again his youth came into play. And however foolish she thought him to sacrifice his future happiness for money, there was no denying it was commonplace enough in their world. Who knew but that, as he grew older and wiser, he might come to regret his current conduct. There was no guarantee of this, however, and she could only hope that, if his thoughts did turn to Beatrice, it would not happen overly soon because Miranda did not think she could give him her honest blessing.

Having come to this conclusion, she hardly thought it advisable to encourage anything between the young people, and she regarded her daughter pensively. Beatrice netted on, her blush persisting. Oh, dear, oh, dear. All these years Miranda had thought she understood her daughter and her daughter's character, but now, when so much was at stake, Beatrice grew mysterious!

A sudden pang of longing for her lost husband struck Miranda. Given how William Ellsworth's thoughts had always been unfailingly rose-colored, Miranda would have appreciated some of his native optimism now. And only see how well his older children's marriages turned out! Suppose she were not equally successful? Suppose, in her lone hands, she could not prevent Beatrice and Willsie from making poor matches, and they were made miserable for life?

Impatient for Mr. Bracewell to be gone, Miranda endured ten more minutes of small talk while she considered hints she might employ to speed him on his way, when he said abruptly, "I suppose your brother has told you of Knolles' sudden stroke of palsy?"

"Dear me, no." Mr. Knolles was the extremely ancient vicar of St. John in the Soke, whom Miranda's brother had been assisting for some years. "But I have not seen Clifford for some weeks. What happened? And is poor Mr. Knolles expected to recover?"

"Who can say? The maid discovered him stricken in bed when she went to build the morning fire," said Mr. Bracewell with that peculiar mixture of solemnity and eagerness common to young clergymen when they heard of a possible vacancy. "The dean holds the advowson, I believe? It would only be natural that he award the living to Mr. Gregory, I suppose, your brother having been so long there."

"I don't know about that," said Miranda honestly. "Clifford speaks of retiring soon himself."

"Ah," Mr. Bracewell said, his hands flexing restlessly. "He has worked hard these many years." Pacing between the window and the fireplace, his eagerness began to overtake his solemnity, despite his best efforts. "Will you—er—be chaperoning Miss Wright at the ball, Mrs. Ellsworth, or will the dean and Mrs. Fellowes be present?"

"They will be present." She could not hide her smile at the transparent workings of his mind. "You may speak to them yourself."

At this he blustered, but his discomposure did at last succeed in driving him from the house.

Countless lanterns illuminated the entrance steps and façade of Beaumond. Taking Greaves's hand to descend from the Ellsworth coach, Miranda marveled at the glitter and finery before her and was grateful she had yielded to her maid's urgings. "If ever there was an occasion for the gold-colored silk with the beads, madam, surely it is this!" Monk insisted. And so it was. Miranda wore the burnished silk with its bugle beads, as well as a matching fillet of the same lustrous cloth about her head, from which curls spilled in abundance.

Her appearance in the entrance hall drew flattering gasps from her family and flooded her cheeks with conscious color, color which returned now as she mounted Beaumond's steps on Tyrone's other arm. There stood Mr. Wolfe beside Lady Hufton just within the double doors, his bulk unmistakable. He too was impeccably dressed, the silver at his temples gleaming in the candlelight. She felt her heart rising to her throat, and her grip tightened on Tyrone till he glanced at her.

Then they were before the host and hostess. Miranda made her curtsey, almost afraid to meet Mr. Wolfe's eyes, for fear her whole heart would be in her own.

His voice was no more than a rumble. "Mrs. Ellsworth. If I might have the honor of your second or third dance? I assume Dodge and Bracewell have planted their colors on the first and second."

"Mr. Bracewell did claim the first," she answered. "But Mr. Dodge—has yielded the field."

Then she did look at him in time to catch the twinkle her reply provoked. "The second it is, then."

Lady Hufton had outdone herself. Beaumond had no ballroom, but the long gallery did service, with potted ferns, chairs, and benches demarcating the larger dancing space from the sitting area, while the musicians occupied the first-floor balcony at the nearer end. From the sitting area on the far side, pairs of flanking doors opened, one set leading to the card room and the other to the largest drawing room, made over for the occasion into a dining room.

When Emmy Wright flew at Beatrice with a squeal, even she stopped to gape at Miranda, saying artlessly, "Why, Mrs. Ellsworth! You're a picture."

"Thank you, dear girl. Where are your grandparents?"

Emmy pointed before accosting her friend. "Bea, did you see Mr. Wolfe?" She rolled her eyes dramatically and clasped her hands to her bosom. "I declare, he has never been handsomer than he is tonight! Tonight I may even begrudge him to *you*."

"Well, you needn't," said Beatrice shortly, "because my affection turned out to be fleeting in nature. You may have all the liking to yourself now."

Emmy's mouth dropped open, and she stamped her foot, notwithstanding her most recent words. "Beatrice Ellsworth, if you aren't the most contrary thing! You had only begun, and now you are already done? But we were going to have such fun! There's no understanding you."

Miranda turned away with a smile. There, at least, she and her dissimilar charge were in perfect agreement.

Her rueful amusement was compounded when Mr. Bracewell appeared at her elbow, a frown marring his admirable brow. "Mrs. Ellsworth, you are...a vision." It was so obvious that he had never before noticed her looks, much less considered them a strong point, that Miranda almost laughed.

"Thank you, Mr. Bracewell. If peerages were awarded for services of the curling tongs, my maid would be worthy of a dukedom."

He could think of no reply to this, but Miranda was more interested in observing Beatrice's response to the man's presence. To her dismay, she noted uneasiness and heightened color. But because Miranda could not encourage her daughter's new tenderness, she must risk Beatrice's ire by doing what she could to thwart it.

"Mr. Bracewell," she began again, "I believe there is enough time before the first dance to greet the dean and his wife, if you care to accompany me."

He leaped at this suggestion, and leaving the girls they sought the Felloweses in the sitting side of the gallery. The dean was enthroned in an armchair, surrounded by clergymen of all ages and stations, and Miranda again felt a surge of amusement. Why, with poor palsied Mr. Knolles struck down and the living of St. John in the Soke hanging in the balance, Dean Fellowes was the belle of the ball, to be courted with as much zeal as Miranda or Mr. Wolfe!

"My dear Miranda," he greeted her, attempting to rise. "How lovely you look. Do my eyes deceive me, or do you grow younger by the day?"

"No, please don't get up, Dean Fellowes," she told him, coming forward to kiss his cheek. "It is a pleasure simply to see you and Mrs. Fellowes outside the cathedral close. I was so very sorry to hear about Mr. Knolles..."

"Indeed, indeed, child," sighed the dean. "I do not imagine he will linger long. It is fortunate that your brother Mr. Gregory has so long assisted there, and has, I daresay, taken on a greater and greater share of the duties. Clifford tells me he can manage for a few months, but that he and Mrs. Gregory intended to spend the spring in London." He gave her the shadow of a wink before adding *sotto voce*, "By God's grace I will find a new rector before then." In a louder voice he said,

"And here is our good friend of St. Martin Winnall, Mr. Bracewell! How goes the rebuilding of the church porch, my friend?"

It was Mr. Bracewell's moment to shine. His chest swelling with nerves and importance, the young curate stepped forth, prepared to describe the repairs in a speech humble, but not too humble, and detailed, but not too detailed. He would link the function of the church porch with the firm foundation of which the Lord spoke; he would connect his role in overseeing construction with Zerubbabel's responsibility for the Second Temple.

But it was not to be.

Before he uttered more than, "I find the work proceeds—" a sweep of strings was heard and a rising buzz from the other side of the gallery.

"The dancing begins!" cried Dean Fellowes. "Have you a partner, Miranda? If I were not old and infirm, I would partner you myself. Make haste, my dear! And come, help me up, Bracewell. I'll not spend the evening hidden by ferns. I will watch the dancers from the top of the room."

CHAPTER TWENTY-SIX

**The Perfection of Virtue is from long
Art and Management, Self-Controul.
— 3rd Earl of Shaftesbury, *Characteristicks of men,
manners, opinions, times* (1711)**

Turning to greet the next group of guests required all Colin's self-command because he would far rather have watched Mrs. Ellsworth and her party continue into the house. She looked...there weren't words for how she looked. Because what words sufficed to describe someone whose quiet sweetness could so flame out into beauty? The gold of her gown and fillet found reflections in the brown of her curling hair and made the soft blue of her eyes shine to advantage. And her low, warm voice sent a thrill through him, even as she made her little joke.

Tonight.

It would be tonight.

He would have her in his arms, his mouth against hers, tonight, if it was the last thing he did. No more beating about the bush, placating the feelings of their respective children, by heaven!

These were the thoughts behind his uniformly amiable countenance as he stood beside his sister to bow and smile and welcome. Each compliment to Beaumond's transformation he directed to Jenny, and Lady Hufton was soon beaming with satisfaction, a satisfaction only increased when the last guest was greeted and Colin placed her hand on his arm to lead her to the long gallery.

When the musicians spied them, they concluded their tuning and hastily began to feed and refresh themselves before their labors began. Lady Hufton bent to one of the violinists. "We will have Upon a Summer's Day, followed by Every Lad His Lass, please." Then she sailed back to her brother, secretly thankful Mrs. Ellsworth was claimed for the first dance, leaving Colin to partner her. Moreover, her rank would place them near the top of the set.

"Colin," she hissed, tugging on his sleeve as he stood, block-like. "This way."

He tore his gaze from Mr. Bracewell and Mrs. Ellsworth, half of a mind to drag Jenny further down the room toward them, but she guessed it and shook her head. "It isn't done! Come—I have already given them the dances *you* chose. What more can you want?"

It might have comforted him to know that Miranda was equally distracted as she took her place across from Mr. Bracewell. A plan was forming in her head. If what Mr. Bracewell truly sought was advancement and enough income to marry on, would it not be better that he be given the living of St. John in the Soke than that he marry her? The living might be as out of his reach as Miranda herself, but if Miranda promised she would speak to the dean about him, might he not be persuaded to abandon his pursuit of her? Getting rid of the man, moreover, would have the double benefit of removing him from Beatrice's orbit.

Meanwhile, the curate's brow knotted, as if being thwarted in the business of describing St. Martin Winnall's battered porch made him all the more determined to have his say elsewhere. Even the sight of his parishioner Miss Paulson lining up with a puffy prebendary—one of the clergymen who had encircled the dean—failed to distract him.

"Mrs. Ellsworth," he began as the musicians plunged into Upon a Summer's Day and the two of them armed left. "We have known each other a few months now."

"So we have."

"And I apologize if I have never told you what a—what a remarkable woman you are."

Miranda shivered with dread. Though this particular dance allowed for only minimal bursts of speech in passing, she would rather not receive even his piecemeal compliments. She must act quickly. At once!

"Thank you," she said, taking his hand and releasing it to weave through the second and third couples in their sextet. "Mr. Bracewell, I have been thinking about St. John in the Soke. Would your duties at St. Martin Winnall permit you to take on more?" (This sentence required a full time through the pattern to be delivered in its entirety.)

Bracewell's eyes lit with eagerness, and he answered her in short bursts when the figures allowed. "Yes. Absolutely yes. I have, in fact, been yearning—for a wider scope."

"Perhaps I might say a word to the dean, then," Miranda told him in the same intermittent style. "I don't know that my opinion will count for much, but I have known him all my life."

If she hoped her words would immediately put their relationship on an unamorous footing, she was disappointed. The fervor in his eyes only deepened. "You would do that for me, Mrs. Ellsworth?"

By this point they had reached the third "verse" of Upon a Summer's Day, in which the partners clasped each other's forearms as they circled, and Miranda found his clasp become suddenly more of a clutch. Shrinking from this intensity, she murmured, "I hope I would do as much for any friend."

Here Mr. Bracewell met his second baffling of the evening, for following the final "chorus" of the dance, in which there were too many separations to allow for coherent conversation, the musicians wound to a premature close. He was not the only dancer with complaining looks, for many a gentleman who had expected twenty minutes with his fair partner must be satisfied with a paltry five.

"Mrs. Ellsworth," said the curate, taking her hand after his bow and leading her from the floor, "thank you for your friendship. I cannot express how precious it is to me. If you are not otherwise engaged, would you be so kind as to take a turn about the room with me? We might even go out upon the terrace to discuss this further."

"I have granted Mr. Wolfe the second dance," she fluttered. But inwardly she knew she must capitulate. Just as with Mr. Lyfford and Mr. Dodge, when a gentleman has been permitted to call and partner one repeatedly, the piper must be paid. Mr. Bracewell was determined to have his say, and if she was ever to be rid of him, he had better say it. Therefore she added with a tight smile, "Would later in the evening serve?"

At once he brightened. "Yes! Perhaps directly after your dance with Mr. Wolfe?"

As graciously as she could, she nodded her agreement, but she could not refrain from a dismissive little wave of her hand when he lingered, gawping. *One more hour, at the utmost,* Miranda promised herself. *And then I will be rid of him. And if I am rid of him, he cannot hang about to worm his way further into Beatrice's affections.* At least if he were thinking about Miranda while he danced with Beatrice, his absence of mind might vex the girl.

There was no more time to devote to Mr. Bracewell, however, for a shadow fell on her, and she looked up with heart fluttering to find Mr. Wolfe.

"Good evening again, Mrs. Ellsworth. I do hope you are Mrs. Ellsworth. She's a dear little creature but has a decided knack for avoiding attention."

"I don't know what you mean, sir," she said, blushing at being called a "dear little creature."

"Ah." One brow arched, and he smiled at her. "You *sound* like Mrs. Ellsworth. It was all this...golden glory which perplexed me." He indicated her *tout ensemble* with his hand. "But if you are indeed she, I told a Mrs. Ellsworth I would dance with her, and I must keep my word."

"What nonsense," Miranda scolded, rosier than ever.

"Not a bit of it," he returned. But then his mouth twitched. "Well, perhaps just a *bit* of a bit of it, but you do look splendid. Beautiful. Now what can I have said? You've turned red as a poppy."

"It is too much," she whispered.

He chuckled. "Is it? How many times in your life have you been told that you are beautiful? Does the novelty begin to pall?"

Miranda hardly knew what to say. For a fact, she had never before in her life been told she was beautiful, and she had never before in her life been spoken to as Mr. Wolfe spoke to her now.

He extended his arm, and she lay a gloved hand lightly on it, thinking he would place her in the line nearest where they stood, but instead he led her down the room—toward where Beatrice and Mr. Bracewell were joining the set!

Without thought, Miranda pulled back. "Oh—not by Mr. Bracewell, if you please."

His expression was all mocking innocence. "It will only be for the beginning and the end of the dance, you know, in the longways set, and I thought you might like to be beside your daughter."

It was too late in any event, and as everyone took hands four, Beatrice and Mr. Bracewell made up their initial foursome. Miranda was able to forget her own embarrassment in concern for Beatrice, who, if her stepmother had gone red as a poppy, managed a respectable vermilion of her own. Poor girl, to be confronted with both objects of her tenderness! One, whom she had so lately rejected, and the other, who had yet to notice her.

"Once more I am graced by your nearness, Mrs. Ellsworth," said the parson with a bow.

Miranda gave a pained smile.

"And by mine," Wolfe said with a bow of his own. "But no matter if I escaped your notice, Bracewell. I expect Mrs. Ellsworth's brilliance eclipsed me."

The clergyman frowned at him. "Sir, Mrs. Ellsworth is too respectable a lady for you to make a jest of her."

"Precisely. Which is why I was entirely sincere. She dazzles this evening, does she not?"

"How was your first dance, Beatrice?" cried Miranda, unable to bear more of this.

"Short," her daughter replied. Her gaze traveled from Mr. Wolfe to her mother and back.

"That *was* a short dance," Mr. Bracewell took it up, frowning again at Mr. Wolfe. "I do not recall an opening dance ever being so brief."

"You were dancing with Mrs. Ellsworth, were you not?" asked Mr. Wolfe mildly. "Time does fly in her company."

"No," insisted the curate. "That is, yes, it does, but it genuinely was a short dance."

Mr. Wolfe bowed again, amiably. "Then let this one make amends. Longways duple minor...would you say twenty or twenty-five couples in each set? It will take a great deal of time to work through the progression. And supposing we were to do it twice through? Upwards of twenty minutes, I calculate."

"But what use will this longer dance be, if I am not dancing with Mrs. Ellsworth!" protested Mr. Bracewell.

Miranda winced at this discourtesy to Beatrice, but the music began, and she hurried to set and cast outward as Mr. Bracewell and Beatrice took hands to move up. When Mr. Wolfe took her own hand to lead her back to their starting position, he did not need to press it for Miranda to feel heat rise to her face. Oh! She could not hide her feelings for twenty minutes of this! Before the end, every couple in their set and everyone who happened to look on would know that she loved him. Worst of all, Beatrice would know!

But fretting about it only made it worse, as did the next step in the pattern. As the first corners, Mr. Wolfe and Beatrice came together in the center and gave a hop (Mr. Wolfe's leap surprisingly graceful for so large a man) and were then joined by Mr. Bracewell and Miranda—an awkward enough conjunction when Mr. Bracewell had been on the edge of quarreling with Mr. Wolfe and when Miranda wished she could avoid all scrutiny. Far from sharing her discomfiture, a smile played on Mr. Wolfe's lips before the four of them turned in place. Then, thank heavens, each couple in the quartet went its own way, Mr. Wolfe and Miranda down the room and Mr. Bracewell and Beatrice up.

Faces blurred; voices faded. Each repetition of the figures brought different partners to them with which to turn and hop and smile and greet, many of them Miranda's own family members, and yet she was aware of only Mr. Wolfe's regard. His smiles. The grasp of his hand. Each grasp so light and yet so unsettling. A breathlessness seizing her which was half fear and half tremulous joy.

Oh, yes indeed. Everyone with eyes would know.

"Are you enjoying yourself?" he asked her when they neared the bottom of the room.

Her throat not cooperating, Miranda gave one nod as she crossed in front of him to circle down past the Fairchilds.

"We might, you know, do this always," his low murmur continued. "You and I, forever and ever."

Making no immediate answer, she was glad not to stumble in her surprise. He *did* want to marry her, then? How confusing it all was! Just at the last assembly they kissed, and then he had proposed to Beatrice, and now he returned to her? Her heart was his, of course. It had been all along. Miranda knew it, though she never said so to him, and though she feared it went without saying.

It took several more times through the figures before she swallowed away the constriction strangling her. Then she waited until they reached the bottom and were waiting out one turn before she blurted, "But what about Beatrice?"

"What *about* Miss Ellsworth?"

"You—proposed to her not a week ago."

"Yes, and the mere idea horrified her to the point of fainting. She doesn't care a straw for me."

Or she did no longer, Miranda now knew, so it was not worth arguing. But—

"But—if you cared enough to propose to her so recently, sir—surely your own feelings were not so...elastic?"

"On this matter it would be more accurate to call my feelings rigid and inflexible," he replied lightly. "For I did not care for Miss Ellsworth that way when I offered for her, and neither do I care for her that way now. How could I, when I have formed an unconquerable preference for another?"

With that his pale eyes met hers and Miranda shivered to her very core.

"You—were fortunate then that she did not accept you," she said, flustered, as they began to travel back up the room. "If you were to go around proposing to other young ladies you didn't care for, you would not find yourself at liberty for long."

"Ah, but I have no intention of proposing to any other young ladies. Nor would I have offered for Miss Ellsworth had I thought there the slightest chance she would welcome it. No. You told me, in so many words, Miranda, that Miss Ellsworth's 'fondness' for me would be an insuperable barrier to you accepting me, and so I went out of my way to prove to you that the barrier was not only superable but was, in truth, nonexistent."

"Still, Beatrice would not like it," she whispered. "It would break up her happy home."

Then he did grip her fingers tightly, though his voice was still faintly teasing. "When Miss Ellsworth falls in love herself, she will break up her happy home with a speed which astonishes you, I daresay."

"She has told me she doesn't want to marry for a long time."

Then his patience ran out. "And so say they all, until the particular person comes along. Look at me, Miran—Mrs. Ellsworth. How much of our lives have we lived for others? Yielded to others? If they love us even a little in return, how long would they begrudge us seizing our own chance of happiness?"

"They would forgive us, of course, eventually," she admitted, wanting so badly to yield that she felt tears rising, "but I might only have this little time left with her, and if—if we—she would have to choose, you understand—between me and the only home she has known—she and Willie both!"

"William is at school eight months of the year!"

"Beatrice, then—" It was all she could do to keep her voice lowered and the anguish from it. "If perhaps we were to wait until she married—"

"And if she never marries?"

"A few years, then," pleaded Miranda. "If we were to wait a few years..."

They were but one couple away again from Beatrice and Mr. Bracewell now, and the ice in Mr. Wolfe's glittering eyes chilled her. "You would have me dangle after you for an indeterminate period of years, then?" he demanded. "A bold assumption of your power, madam."

"No," whispered Miranda, the room blurring slightly. She *must not* give way to tears. "No. I make no assumptions. You are free."

There was no time for more. She faced Beatrice again with a trembling smile and received an equally tentative one in return.

And when the closing notes played and Miranda rose from her curtsey, Mr. Bracewell was instantly beside her, though he addressed Beatrice. "Who is your next partner, Miss Ellsworth? Your mother and I will deliver you to him." This, with a proprietary hand hovering near Miranda's elbow.

"It's my brother Tyrone," mumbled Beatrice. "And you needn't deliver me, for he is coming this way."

"Capital," declared the curate. "Shall we then, Mrs. Ellsworth?" He gestured for her to lead the way from the floor.

His presumption succeeded in vexing her, at least, and she found exasperation a pleasant alternative to distress. Even a trace of humor flickered through her again. *Very well, let us have done with it. If I drove Mr. Wolfe away so easily, surely I can do the same with Mr. Bracewell.*

Heaving a resigned breath, Miranda moved in the direction indicated. She could not help throwing one last glance toward the lover she had alienated, however, only to find he had already turned on his heel and disappeared in the crowd.

Chapter
Twenty-Seven

**Widows are indeed the great
Game of your Fortune-hunters.
— J. Addison, *Spectator,* No. 311 (1712)**

It being early November there were few souls on the terrace apart from them, though Lady Hufton had thoughtfully placed charcoal braziers in various spots beside benches and statuary and potted shrubbery, so that any who spilled out in search of fresh air might be comfortable. Light shone through the several French doors, and one set of them stood ajar, allowing the music and conversation to drift out.

Miranda would have liked Mr. Bracewell to have his say just outside these doors, so she could slip back in the second she uttered her refusal, but naturally he preferred privacy for the baring of his soul. Therefore he led her toward the leftmost edge, beside a statue of Diana, and there he stopped, turning to her with jaw set and fists balled.

"Mrs. Ellsworth, you said to me a half-hour ago that you thought of me as a friend," he began.

"Indeed," she replied. "And so I do."

"And that is why you proposed speaking to the dean about me?"

"Yes."

He drew a step nearer, but Miranda managed to hold her ground, her gloved hand reaching for the goddess's foot to steady herself.

"Are you certain it is nothing more than friendship which inspires you?" he persisted. "Because—if you were not yet aware, there has been something more than friendship inspiring *me* to seek your company these past few months."

Would that "something" be the love of gain? This waspish retort nearly escaped her, but she succeeded in stuffing it down. Instead she released Diana's foot and folded her hands quietly.

"Mr. Bracewell. I have indeed examined my own feelings and will tell you straight away that it is friendship, and only friendship, which impels me."

Undismayed, he pressed on. "Ah. I see. Though I realize it is not the 'done' thing for a lady to express her affection without the gentleman having first expressed his own—"

"Mr. Bracewell," she interrupted, "I cannot speak to whether something is 'done' or 'not done,' but I beg you to believe me when I tell you I have just now expressed all the affection for you which will ever be possible for me to give, and it does not amount to more than my firm friendship."

She could hardly be clearer, and though it was such an unpleasant situation, it filled her with unutterable relief to see her words sink in. Either her insistence or her calm had finally, finally got through to him, and her own shoulders sloped in relief. The last of her trio of unwanted suitors, disposed of. Hurrah!

Thinking he would welcome solitude, she said, "Well then, if you will excuse me, Mr. Bracewell, I will return indoors."

But he moved to block her. "Wait. Mrs. Ellsworth. If you would still hear me—out of courtesy alone. I have more to say which you might find persuasive, being a reasonable woman and not in your first youth. That is—while you may not have feelings beyond friendship for me at present, many successful marriages are built on just such a foundation, and I think you would not ultimately regret the match."

Miranda tried to hide her annoyance. "Thank you, sir, but I would rather not take the chance."

"But with you by my side I would rise in my profession," he insisted.

"Mr. Bracewell," she rejoined, her temper escaping in spite of herself. "While I wish you every good fortune in your profession and, indeed, in your *life*, whether you are to rise beyond your present state is not my responsibility. I intend no discourtesy, but I tell you again that I cannot love you. Ever. And you will never persuade me that to marry without love would make either of us happy, even if you were one day to become bishop of Winchester."

Anger lit his eyes, startling her, it quite transformed his handsome face into something ferocious. "How can you not see it? Why would you refuse even to consider the possibility? No—I will listen to no more of your objections. If you cannot see the good that would come of it, madam, I must *make* you see the good!"

He took another step toward her, and Miranda raised a cautioning hand. "I will stop you there. You must let me pass. There is nothing more to be said on the matter—Mr. Bracewell!" This last broke from her in a cry, for the curate had seized her hand and crushed it to his lips, peppering her palm with fevered kisses.

"Mrs. Ellsworth!" he groaned. "Beauteous Mrs. Ellsworth!"

Some part of her was detached enough to observe, *Beauteous? Why, that's twice in one evening, though I suppose he doesn't mean it like Mr. Wolfe did.* But the rest of her was torn between exasperation and outrage as she struggled to wrench her hand away. Outrage prevailed, however, when his other arm snaked about her waist and his mouth began to travel up her glove along the inside of her arm.

"How dare you, sir! Release me at once!" she commanded through gritted teeth. Struggling in his tightening grasp, she soon found herself crushed to his chest. Desperately Miranda began to stamp her feet, kicking wildly and hissing like a goose in response to the assault.

"Let go of her!" came a screech, and the next instant the ardent curate found himself beset on all sides—his toes hammered by Mrs. Ellsworth's heels, his head rapped sharply with some object, a sprawling weight scaling his back, hands clawing for purchase around his neck. What could he do under this onslaught but give way? And so he did, crashing into the base of the statue and carrying his assailants with him. They fell with screams and a bellowed curse (the latter from Mr. Bracewell), the corner of the plinth striking Miranda's head a blow which sent her to the cold hard pavement seeing stars.

"Mama, are you hurt? *Mama!*" Through her fog Miranda heard Beatrice calling, and then her daughter was hovering above her—above them?—crying, "You vile *snake*! Get away from us!"

"I'm all right," said Miranda. Or she thought she said it. Everything was terribly muddled. She shut her eyes to stop the spinning.

Crack! Smack!

"Miss Ellsworth, please! I beg you to calm yourself," pleaded Mr. Bracewell. Miranda felt something shift which might have been the curate attempting to wriggle his arm out from where it was pinned beneath her.

"How can I be calm—" panted Beatrice, and another crunch was heard "—when I discover you forcing your attentions on my mother?" Miranda cracked an eyelid to see her dear daughter actually administering little blows to the man's head with her closed fan, eliciting from him one pained "Ooh!" after another.

With one arm raised to ward off Beatrice's attack, Mr. Bracewell twisted and writhed, the dizzy Miranda trying to shrink away, as eager to free him as he was to be freed. And then, to their mutual surprise, his trapped arm whisked away, attached as it was to the rest of his person, which was one instant rolling on the terrace and the next upright and being shaken like a rat in a terrier's jaws.

"What can be the meaning of this?" came another familiar voice, this one belonging to Mr. Wolfe, though Miranda had never before heard it so hard and humorless. With an effort she raised her head, in time to see him grasping the collar of Mr. Bracewell's coat, handling him so roughly that the man slipped and staggered.

"This does not concern you," protested the curate, with as much dignity as he could muster under the circumstances. Twisting and jerking, he tried to pry loose his captor's hand, only to have Mr. Wolfe release him so suddenly that he staggered. Steadying himself, he straightened his clothing. "I'm afraid Miss Ellsworth caught Mrs. Ellsworth and me in a—compromising embrace—and took umbrage at it."

Even in her lightheadedness and distress Miranda felt a pang for poor Beatrice. To find the nascent object of her affections with his arms about her own mother! "Beatrice," she uttered, pulling herself to a sitting position.

Her daughter, who had begun to sputter at Mr. Bracewell's speech, crouched beside her at once, a gentle arm at her back. "Don't move too quickly, Mama. *Are* you all right? Let me help you up."

"Beatrice," Miranda said again. "I was not embracing him."

"I know that," her daughter assured her. "I saw what happened. How he grabbed at you."

Miranda was relieved to find the world relatively fixed, though she took hold of the statue's foot again for good measure.

"It was *not* a compromising embrace, Mr. Wolfe," protested Beatrice earnestly. "You must not listen to him because an embrace takes two participants, does it not, and Mama was not participating! She was trying to get away from him."

"You, miss, should not spend your time spying upon your elders," snapped Mr. Bracewell, "and interfering in what does not concern you. You have only succeeded in drawing attention to what was a private moment."

Indeed, Miranda noted with horror that, not only had the music stopped, but faces were turned toward the series of French doors.

"They can't see anything," Mr. Wolfe said swiftly, following her gaze. "It's darker out here. They would have to press their faces to the glass or come out—which they will any second because the musicians are taking their first interval, it sounds like." He turned on the curate then. "I assume you have made your offer and been refused, Bracewell, so if you don't want to be tossed from the house by me and my footmen, I would encourage you to go."

"What business is this of yours?" Mr. Bracewell retorted. "If Miss Ellsworth interfered, at least she did so on behalf of her mother."

"And I do so on behalf of my guests," Mr. Wolfe said coolly. "While I am host, no one under my roof will be harassed. The only person who can grant you clemency is Mrs. Ellsworth herself. Mrs. Ellsworth, if you would prefer Bracewell to stay, it is in your power."

Of course Miranda wished Mr. Bracewell in the Antipodes, but she reached for Beatrice's hand. "Dearest—"

"Never mind me, Mama," her daughter interjected at once. "There is nothing—there is *no reason* he should not go. In fact, if my own preferences were consulted—"

"*Your* preferences have nothing to do with it," Mr. Bracewell rounded on her, but Mr. Wolfe gave a sigh of mocking regret. "I'm afraid, Bracewell, that Miss Ellsworth's preferences are the pole-star by which *Mrs.* Ellsworth guides her bark."

Beatrice looked from Mr. Wolfe to her mother again, and then she resumed quietly, "I would ask that Mr. Bracewell go, Mama. At once."

"Your wish is our command," answered Mr. Wolfe wryly. With a bow to the ladies, he raised an eyebrow at the curate and indicated the terrace steps with a tilt of his head. "We need not return within. There's no need to proclaim it from the house-top that you're going." The frustrated Mr. Bracewell threw one last scowl at Miranda before he too bowed and preceded Mr. Wolfe down the steps into the shadowed grounds.

"Oh, Mama," wailed Beatrice, throwing herself at her stepmother. "That was horrible! *He* is horrible! I saw him take you out here, and I was so uneasy that I told Tyrone halfway through the dance I wanted to go find you. He let me go, and thank heavens our sextet was all family, so they forgave us breaking things up. And then to come out here and see—and see—oh!"

Miranda soothed and hushed her, rocking her in her arms. "It's all right, dear. I am sorry you had to see that. I know how you...how you felt about him."

"But you don't!" cried Beatrice, hiding her burning face against Miranda's neck. "You haven't any idea how I feel about him."

"Of course I do. I know because you told me you...cared for him, dear. At least a little bit, and therefore I am sorry for his actions."

"But you don't know," Beatrice said again, sadly. She raised her head. "Because I *lied*. I told you I was fond of him, but I wasn't. I mean, I thought he was handsome—everyone thinks so—but it wasn't anything more than that."

The nonplussed Miranda took two tries before she could say, "I can't tell you how that relieves me, dearest. But why should you have thought it necessary to tell me such a thing, if it were not true?"

"It was a diversion, Mama," the girl confessed, hiding her face again. "I—wanted to mislead you. It was wicked of me, I daresay, but I will tell you all now."

Miranda's heart began to thump, as did Beatrice's, and they clung to each other.

"When Mr. Wolfe proposed to me," the girl whispered, "I—didn't care a bit for him. He knew it, and I knew it, but I think—I think he only asked me because he wanted to force me to admit it. But I was too ashamed to tell you so—because I had misled you—so that was why I pretended I had begun to like Mr. Bracewell instead."

"But...why did you want to mislead me, Beatrice?"

Another muffled wail. "Because—because—I guessed Mr. Wolfe was in love with you, and I didn't want him to marry you!" Beatrice felt her mother sway under this news, and she tightened her hold. "I thought my lie wouldn't matter because *you* didn't care for him, Mama, or I didn't think you did. Truly! I even asked my sisters if they thought you cared for him, and they said no. But I was afraid you might begin to, if he chased you, because so many of the girls find him irresistible. I had to do something to prevent it, see? I didn't mind if *he* was disappointed, you understand, because I thought he would just choose someone else. But he didn't, and—and—when I began to pay close attention—when I began to admit what was really there in front of my eyes, instead of denying it or only seeing what I wanted to see—I knew that you..."

Miranda swallowed. Well, she had confessed as much to herself. Anyone looking would have known as surely as Beatrice did that Miranda had given her heart to Mr. Wolfe. Still, it was mortifying to hear it said aloud.

"And Aunt Jeanne—" Beatrice continued to sniff, "—when she and Uncle Charles reached Mr. Bracewell and me—when you were dancing with Mr. Wolfe—Aunt Jeanne whispered to me, 'Only see how radiant your mama is.' But she didn't need to point it out because I had already seen for myself the moment he took your hand. You were scarlet as a sunset, Mama."

"Shhhh..." Miranda pulled her behind the Diana statue.

"You want to marry him, don't you, Mama?" insisted her daughter. "And if he asked me so quickly, just to expose my deceit, I'll warrant he has asked you as well. Has he?"

"Yes," Miranda conceded reluctantly. "He has."

"And you refused him."

Miranda sighed. "I refused him."

"Oh, Mama!" Beatrice moaned. "Can you forgive me? I really, truly, honestly did think you didn't care! Until tonight—or maybe until I fainted and began to think very hard about things! Please say you believe me and can forgive me."

"Shhh...dearest." Miranda kissed the top of her head, even as a lump formed in her throat. "I believe you, and I can forgive you. When you refused him yourself, and I began to understand you—no longer—cared for him, I thought perhaps, in a few years, if his feelings for me persisted..." Feeling Beatrice's tears dampening her neck, she set her gently away and gave a deprecating shrug. "He won't, of course. You said yourself how popular he is. He doesn't need money or care about titles, so he may marry anyone he pleases, and he will easily find someone younger and prettier."

"Then he'll be a fool," declared Beatrice, stamping her foot, "and I won't think much of his judgment. There is nobody better than you, Mama. It is all my fault you could not say yes to him when he asked. You must say yes now, because if your heart breaks and it is my fault, I couldn't bear it!"

The swiftness with which Beatrice demolished the barriers between Miranda and her heart's desire alarmed Miranda. Instead of feeling triumph, she felt fear. She was afraid to imagine being allowed to have what she wanted. She was afraid of hope.

Hugging her arms about her, Miranda began to pace. "Even if I marched straight over to him and said, bold as brass, that I would marry him after all," she said slowly, "and even if he said, very well, then, he would still have me, there would be difficulties. Complications. Things you would not like. Where would you live, dearest, if I went to live at Beaumond?"

"I would want to go with you," said Beatrice, but her eyes filled again. "If he would let me. I would miss Hollowgate, of course—but—I could walk over every single day, if I liked." She could say no more, emotion overcoming her—overcoming them both—but Miranda heard enough and took her daughter to her once more.

"Dearest, sweetest girl."

It was some minutes before they could calm themselves and make repairs to their appearance, but at last it was done, and Miranda had only to wonder then how, precisely, one went about asking a man who had been twice refused whether he would like to press his suit again.

Chapter Twenty-Eight

When ladies crave to be encounter'd with.
You may not, my lord, despise her gentle suit.
— Shakespeare, *Henry VI, Part I,* **II.ii.805 (1591)**

Colin no sooner dispatched Mr. Bracewell with a mental boot to the backside, to find his way back to town however he might, than he found his sister beside him.

"Colin, where have you been? The musicians finally abandoned hope of you reappearing and started up again. I can't tell you how many young ladies have asked me if I'd seen you. I suppose, since you got your dance with Mrs. Ellsworth you have forgotten your duties to everyone else."

"There, there. Here I am," was his unsatisfactory reply as he followed her back up the steps. "Tell the musicians to keep the next several ones brief. Under ten minutes apiece, or even five, if they can manage it. It doesn't matter if we finish the progression. Line 'em up and I'll knock 'em down."

They were indeed lined up, after a fashion, Emmy Wright fairly pushing past Miss Paulson to cross Colin's path and affecting surprise when he bowed to her and asked her to dance. The vivacious girl chattered about all manner of things as they stepped through the figures, but he could not match her attention for attention, his eye and his mind being drawn repeatedly to the terrace doors. They should reappear soon, should they not? What was Miss Ellsworth saying to her mother? When Colin had seen the girl leave the floor and throw the rest of her set into confusion, he had been standing idly beside old Mrs. Browning, listening to the woman complain about the conduct of young girls in the present day. He almost deserted her mid-sentence. But at least his abandonment of her at that juncture would provide her a roundabout satisfaction, Colin told himself, for then she might take umbrage at him as well.

Some elements of the scene which met him on the terrace were expected but others surprised. He expected to discover Bracewell proposing to Mrs. Ellsworth—surely the man had lured her out there to no other end—but he had not expected to find Miss Beatrice Ellsworth clinging to the man's back, attempting, it appeared, to climb him as a cat would a tree trunk. Nor had Colin expected such a neat and respectable young miss to be beating the curate about the head with her closed fan, but there it was.

"—Mr. Wolfe?" asked his partner.

He glanced at Miss Wright and shook the clouds from his head.

"Did you hear me?"

"You must pardon me, Miss Wright. At my age, and in such a setting, I confess it can be difficult for me to catch everything said to me."

"Oh!" said Miss Wright, her own gaze flicking to the silver at his temples. She raised her voice. "Somehow I have never thought of you as old."

"Thank you. But I assure you, every day it is an increasing struggle to mask my decrepitude. I welcome occasions such as these, however, because the dancing and movement help my rheumatism."

"Rheumatism?" she echoed faintly.

"A wretched affliction," he sighed. "Some mornings it is all I can do to hang upon my valet and hobble about. Cold weather is an especial trial."

Such a revelation, specious though it was, succeeded in silencing her. The dance ended, he trotted her back to her grandmother, and then bowed over the hand of Miss Terwilliger.

He would have to remember to tip the musicians generously for their diligence in following commands, for his turn with Miss Terwilliger was likewise satisfyingly truncated, though he noted with alarm her improvement at flirtation. In response, he was obliged to drop hints regarding his imminent lameness and senility

Miss Simpkins he treated to details of his chronic cough. Then, just as he was disposing of her to take up Miss Banks, he glimpsed the return of the Ellsworth ladies, restored to neatness, Miss Ellsworth hovering at her mother's side.

The elbow Colin had been extending to Miss Banks jabbed her in the midriff because she had come closer without him noticing.

"Do pardon me," he said hastily, as she exhaled in a sharp huff. "I find, as I grow older, that my eyesight is not what it used to be."

His eyesight improved, however, when he saw Mrs. Ellsworth safely ensconced in one of the chairs along the wall beside Mrs. Fellowes, and he returned his attention to his partner.

"Oh, Mr. Wolfe," Miss Banks giggled as he led her up the room, "Must we lead? I shrink from being so prominent."

"You must forgive me, then," replied Colin. "I find, at my age, it helps me at the commencement of the dance to hear the musicians clearly." It also helped him to catch the violist's eye so that he might pinch his thumb and forefinger together with hardly a space between. Flustered, the poor musician leaned to the others. *The man wanted this one to be even shorter?* At this rate they would have played their entire repertoire before supper, and then what would they do?

Miss Banks was followed by Miss Browning, who, when she mentioned looking forward to the supper and asked if Lady Hufton chose the dishes, was told by Colin, "She did indeed, and I hope you enjoy it. As for me, I will have to eat lightly, lest the rich foods aggravate my gout." The young lady's dismay could not be disguised, as her very large, very bald, very cross uncle suffered terribly from the ailment.

The last to be dealt with was Miss Paulson. She had been so awkward with him since her unauthorized visit to Beaumond that Colin wondered if it was still necessary to repel her, but when he asked her opinion of the ball she had been so kind to suggest, following up her response with additional questions, his courtesy kindled a disconcerting light in her eyes.

Better safe than sorry, then.

In this spirit, within the remaining minutes of their abbreviated turn about the room, he proceeded to tell the same anecdote twice and to call her by his sister's name.

"Dear me—please pardon me, Miss Paulson," he said after this last *faux pas.* "Lady Hufton is much on my mind. She will likely have to return to Kent soon, to aid my other sisters in the care of our parents."

"Are they unwell?" asked Miss Paulson uncertainly.

He blinked. "Who?"

"Your parents."

"Oh! My parents. Perfectly well. That is, they are the most cheerful invalids you will ever meet, despite having been bedridden for the last decade. It took us all by surprise because their health seemed so robust until they reached—well—until they reached my age. And then it was a rapid and steady decline for both. But on good days they can feed themselves—not a minor feat, you understand, given how few teeth they have left."

When the closing notes sounded, Colin brought Miss Paulson back to her mama and favored his sister with the smug expression of a man who had seen to every particular. His time was now his own.

Miranda saw him approaching, of course. He was impossible to miss. And she was grateful to be seated, lest she crumple to the ground for the second time in an hour. She had a terrible, cowardly urge to run away. The dean's wife vanished as if melted into thin air, and if Mrs. Fellowes said a word in parting, Miranda couldn't take it in, much less make a fitting reply.

"He is coming, Mama," whispered Beatrice, sounding as fearful as Miranda felt. "Shall I go away?"

"I don't know." But when Beatrice made to rise, Miranda said, "No—on second thought—" and the girl subsided once more in her chair.

"Mrs. Ellsworth. Miss Ellsworth." He executed his unusually graceful bow. "I hope you are recovered from the...excitement on the terrace." When neither mustered a reply, he gestured at the chair Mrs. Fellowes had vacated. "May I?"

Once that was accomplished, a silence fell. If it could be called silent when the musicians played Hole in the Wall and feet skipped along the floorboards and people talked.

"What—became of Mr. Bracewell?" ventured Miranda when she could bear it no longer.

"Who can say for certain? With any luck, footpads have fallen upon him on the path from Weeke."

Her mouth twitched. But then, in spite of herself, a chuckle escaped.

"Your suitors have all been sent on their way," he continued. "Lyfford, Dodge, Bracewell. And the same can be said for any and all young ladies who demonstrated interest in me, including Miss Ellsworth beside you, if she will forgive me for mentioning it yet again."

Miranda inhaled sharply. "Sent on their way? But—how?"

"As you pointed out, Mrs. Ellsworth, it would be dangerous to dispose of them as I did Miss Ellsworth (if you will pardon me yet once more, Miss Ellsworth). That is, I could not propose to each of them, but I did have just enough time to plant a seed of trepidation in each young heart." Shortly he summarized the catalogue of woes he had shared with Winchester's most eligible young misses, until Beatrice looked horrified, and Miranda's mirth could no longer be contained.

"You didn't, sir!" she gasped. "Gout? Rheumatism? Bedridden, toothless parents?"

Clicking his tongue with mock reproach he answered, "For shame, Mrs. Ellsworth, making light of such things. Death and debility come for us all, but perhaps the sooner for wicked people like you."

His teasing only made Miranda laugh harder, and it felt so wonderful to laugh. It drove back her fear and panic.

"Truly, you had better stop," he said then, in a different voice, "or I will be forced to take you in my arms this very moment and kiss you until you haven't any breath."

That did succeed in checking her. A ribbon of panic returned to wind about her midsection, and she gazed at him with all her eyes.

"Oh!" breathed Beatrice, embarrassed in turn. She sat forward in her chair, preparing to rise again, but Mr. Wolfe lifted a lazy hand

"No, Miss Ellsworth, you had better hear this. Because I have learned, in an inseparable family like yours, I will never win your mother's hand if she thinks it would hurt you. Therefore my proposal is as much to you as to her."

Though his words were addressed to Beatrice, his gaze never left her mother. "I tell you I love your mother with my whole heart, which I think you will understand, loving her so dearly yourself. And I would give anything—*do* anything—to make her mine. If she tells me I must wait, I will wait. If she tells me she will go nowhere without you or William or any other Ellsworth she cares to name, I will welcome all or one or none to Beaumond. If she tells me she will never accept me unless *you* can give your blessing, I will abide by it, though you may find my ceaseless attempts to persuade you a trial. This is the whole truth. Therefore, what answer will you give for the both of you, Beatrice?"

The girl took an uneven breath and cast another glance at her mother, whose eyes, though they remained fixed on Mr. Wolfe, now glistened with tears. Then Beatrice said hoarsely, "In that case, Mr. Wolfe, I had better say—I say—*we* say, *yes*." It emerged hardly louder than a squeak, and she clutched her mother's hand so tightly no blood reached their fingertips.

Then Miranda's tears did spill over, though she laughed again and kissed her daughter because she could not kiss her intended. "Thank you, dearest, you have made me the happiest of women."

"And I, the happiest of men," rejoined Mr. Wolfe, "though I may not kiss either of you, nor sing or shout or jump or overturn tables as I would like to do in the moment." He had to satisfy his feelings by clapping his hands heartily twice or thrice, but it sufficed. "Still," he said, "I hope I may, with the permission of you both, make an announcement at the supper?"

Though her daughter made no reply, Miranda raised Beatrice's hands to her lips and kissed them. "We would like that, sir."

"'Sir,' indeed! You will sir me no sirs, Miranda. In fact, you had better dance with me now because I trust you will at least permit me to take your hand and to arm right and left in recognition of our pact?"

"I will, sir—Mr. Wolfe, that is," she answered with a pretty blush. "But we will have to wait a while, for the present dance has just begun."

"Oh, I'll see to that," he said with a grin. "I must say, the trouble and expense of hosting a private ball is more than made up for by the convenience of ordering the musicians about. Did you not wonder why our dance was the longest of the evening? Only to be outdone by this next, if I have anything to say in the matter. Shall we make it the supper dance?"

He was off in a flash, leaving Miranda to dab away her remaining tears and to kiss Beatrice once more. "You are certain about this, Bea?" she asked wistfully.

"Even if I weren't, I could hardly take back my permission now," Beatrice chuckled. "But yes, I am certain. If he loved you any less, he would not be worthy of you, Mama. And I suppose removing to Beaumond will be a good intermediate step for me. I could never marry or go away altogether, you understand, if I could not adjust myself to living a half mile from Hollowgate."

"It will be no worse than going to school at Mrs. Turcotte's," Miranda reassured her. "You did not want to attend school at first, but then you came to be used to it. In the same way, if you miss Hollowgate too much, Tyrone and Aggie will not mind if you call on them constantly. I might do so myself, for it would be a shame not to see the babies every day."

Beatrice's eyes widened, even as the music came to its premature close. "But Mama! *Will* it be Tyrone and Aggie at Hollowgate? Or would it be Flossie and Robert? Or both? And what will Willie say, to hear he will have a new home and a new brother?"

"I—don't know," replied Miranda. "I suppose it will all have to be sorted out."

"Or what if Tyrone and Aggie remove as well," Beatrice persisted, "and they decide they would like to live at Beaumond? Do you think Mr. Wolfe would let us reconstruct our present household there, only with him and his Edmund included? Or would Mr. Weeks not renew Mr. Wolfe's lease next year, so that Tyrone and Aggie could have the place? Would *we* then have to find a *third* home?"

"Gracious," Miranda said, giving a playful pinch to her daughter's arm. "It is a good thing Mr. Wolfe has given us *carte blanche* because we will plainly try his patience to the utmost." But there was no more time for Beatrice to fidget herself (or her mother), for Mr. Wolfe had his way and the supper dance was announced. Charles Ellsworth appeared to claim his niece's hand, leaving Miranda to float away with Mr. Wolfe, her feet and heart equally weightless.

"When last we danced, sir," she addressed him teasingly, "you made me understand that you resented any deference paid to Beatrice's feelings. Almost as much as you resented being asked to wait. How then did you change your mind so quickly?"

He could not answer her until he had circled with a prebendary's wife on his corner, but then he murmured, "That's easy enough. I saw the two of you grappling with Bracewell on the terrace and knew my grumbles and plaints were 'much cry but little wool.' If I wasn't willing to have you on whatever terms you set, someone else would, and I was plenty willing to have you, Miranda, abuse the liberty though you might."

At his choice of words she gave his sleeve a flick. "I daresay you will be happy enough when it is your own concerns I take into account."

"I don't doubt it." Linking arms for the turn, he bent toward her. "The other half of my revelation on the terrace was that you and Beatrice were taking on Bracewell *together*. That everything which drew me to you—or nearly everything—was part and parcel of your place in your family. How much you loved them and how much they loved you."

Miranda's throat tightened. He could not have said anything which pleased her more, and it showed on her face.

"If my son Edmund and I play our cards well," he continued more lightly, "with any luck, we might be enfolded into the Ellsworths."

"You will," Miranda declared. "Of course you will."

When he took her hand for the promenade, he raised it halfway to his lips before he remembered himself. "Because of my own history, the notion of 'family' has not always had pleasant associations for me, but I trust our union will redeem it. In the interim, however, I wonder if you might grant me one indulgence tonight, as a reward for my sweetness of temper and as a deposit on future goodness."

Even before he named it, she guessed it from the smoke of his gaze, and a shiver ran through her.

"When we reach the top of the set," he said softly, "instead of working our way back down the room, let us abandon our fellow dancers and pay our own visit to the terrace."

"Scandalous," Miranda whispered.

"Nonsense. A mere nine minutes' wonder," he returned. "For no sooner will everyone be seated for supper than I will share our good news."

CHAPTER TWENTY-NINE

Let not this long-awaited joy forsake me.
— Wm. Taylor translation of Goethe, *Iphigenia in*
***Tauris*, III.65 (1793)**

If it had been chilly when she emerged with Mr. Bracewell, it was positively frosty now, but Miranda hardly had a moment to register the temperature before she was swept into the shadows and crushed to her intended's very large, very warm chest.

"Where are your lips, my golden darling?" There was no mistaking his own, for they were everywhere he could reach, and Miranda felt her fillet slipping its pins and her curls tumbling down at the attack. The only defense she could afford her hair was to intercept his mouth with her own and return the compliment, which she did, whole-heartedly and gladly.

"My entirely beloved Miranda," he murmured against her neck when they were obliged to catch their breath. "So calm and reserved on the outside, but within she is my fiery, glorious, sweet, passionate wife!"

"Soon-to-be wife," she breathed, her head falling back. "Oh, Colin, I have never been loved before. Not like this."

"And I have never loved before. Not like this. We have much, much time to make up for—years and years—but the rest of our lives to do it in."

"Yes, my dearest. But I feel almost frightened to be this happy! Do you think we *will* be happy?" There was only one possible answer to this question, but when she could free her mouth again she said, "Wait a moment, Colin—wait. I must tell you, Beatrice is already anxious over who will live where and when—"

"And I have told you," he said, arms tightening about her, "that I am content to live with whomever, wherever, so long as you are one of the party. If we have the banns read this Sunday, we may be married by month's end. Unless the boys would like to be home for the wedding, in which case we could possibly delay until the middle of December and take our wedding journey when they return to school..."

"Either date would be too soon!" she objected. "I do not know if it could be done. My situation is so complicated, I'm afraid. You see, my interest in Hollowgate is a life estate, meaning—"

His hold did not loosen a jot, and she felt his shrug. "And isn't your son-in-law the family lawyer? Let Fairchild sort it out. It must be no later than the middle of December, Miranda, or I might go up in flames with the Christmas pudding."

Laughing again, she yielded and gave her promise, just as the music within began to wind down.

"Already?" he complained. "I told them to make this one twenty minutes, at least!"

"We have been kissing an indecently long time," Miranda pointed out, pushing him away to twist her hair up and pin her fillet in place again. "And they probably thought, since you were nowhere in sight, they might skip to the end with impunity. Go in, go in, sir—it will never do to have us reappear together."

Still he hesitated, regarding her as if she might vanish if he turned his back. "I could not have imagined this, Miranda, when I first saw you in Parchment Street, but I should have. It was a hot, dry day, but you wore blue and looked like peace itself, though I was so rude to you."

She shook her head, reaching to caress his arm again. "Indeed, Colin, I can hardly credit it now, that we should have such joy and blessing showered on us after so long."

Countering such doubt required further proofs naturally, but when these were duly given, she smiled up at him. "And only see, Colin—perhaps I will get Beaumond after all, snatching it right from under your nose!"

He tapped the tip of hers. "It's hardly snatching it from under my nose if my nose will still be there after the snatching is done. But I see what you mean. You will win in the end. It paid to take your time."

"But we mustn't take our time now," she urged, giving him another push. "If that was the supper dance ending, they will make their way to the tables, and you aren't there to host with Lady Hufton!"

Chuckling, he bestowed a last kiss on her cheek. "Don't be long."

She had intended to follow as soon as she put herself in order and felt her pulse slow, but that was easier said than done, and she found herself drifting to the terrace railing to lean her elbows on it.

"I am going to be married again," Miranda whispered to the world. To the moon and the stars and the terrace and the Diana and the rolling Beaumond grounds.

It had been a near thing. She had put her fate in the hands of her family—of her daughter in particular. She, a widow of eight and thirty, still so intent on pleasing others and keeping the peace! It had been a gamble and might have ended in costing her the only man she ever loved.

And yet...was that even true?

Colin had said it was this very commitment to her family, maddening though it had been for him, which drew him. Ah, could she be any more fortunate, than to be loved by such a man?

Who knew what Florence and Robert would decide about Hollowgate, or Tyrone and Aggie, for that matter. No doubt there would be chopping and changing, swapping and shuffling. Everything Beatrice hated most. But Beatrice was willing to undergo it, for love of her. And somehow the dashing and decided Mr. Wolfe was willing to undergo it as well, for love of her. Miranda did not know how it could be, but somehow it was.

Dear, dear Mr. Wolfe! He would fit in very well indeed.

With a trembling smile, she smoothed her gloves and gave her hair a final pat.

Then she turned toward the French doors to rejoin her family.

The adventures of the Ellsworth Assortment continue with Beatrice's story in *A Capital Arrangement.*

THE HAPGOODS OF BRAMLEIGH

The Naturalist
A Very Plain Young Man
School for Love
Matchless Margaret
The Purloined Portrait
A Fickle Fortune

THE ELLSWORTH ASSORTMENT

Tempted by Folly
The Belle of Winchester
Minta in Spite of Herself
A Scholarly Pursuit
Miranda at Heart
A Capital Arrangement

PRIDE AND PRESTON LIN

www.christinadudley.com